The BLACK SHEEP and the PRINCESS

The BLACK SHEEP and the PRINCESS

DONNA KAUFFMAN

BRAVA

KENSINGTON PUBLISHING CORP.

BRAVA BOOKS are published by

Kensington Publishing Corp.
850 Third Avenue
New York, NY 10022

ISBN-13: 978-0-7394-8754-9

Printed in the United States of America

Mom, you were the key.
I couldn't have done this without you.

Chapter 1

Donovan MacLeod ducked as the compressed-air tank shot like a cannonball over his head and slammed into the shelves lining the cinderblock wall behind him. The impact reverberated through the cavernous warehouse.

Mac scooted over next to his partner, pressing his back against the overturned desk as he pulled his gun from his ankle holster. "Could be worse."

"Oh?"

"He could have a grenade launcher."

Rafe glared at him. "You said the place was secure, Mr. Motion Detectors Don't Lie."

"Shh. They don't."

There was a humming noise; then something began plinking into the cinderblock, spraying clumps of gray debris everywhere.

Rafe hunched down farther. "So, those are what, pretend bullets? And all those crates of antiques, including the urn with Mr. Fortenberry's ashes, must have just gotten up and walked out on their own. Because if the sensors didn't go off, no one could possibly have gotten in here to steal them, right? All ten of them. Which means Frank couldn't possibly be in here shooting at us."

"So cranky." Mac propped his semiautomatic on his knee as he shifted closer to one end of the heavy oak desk. Thank

God for old office furniture. They didn't make stuff out of real wood anymore. It was all compressed crap these days. Compressed crap wasn't worth shit for stopping bullets. "He has to get through us to get out of here. I say we make that a bit more difficult for him."

There was a pause in the shooting. Reloading.

"On three," Mac said, not needing to glance over his shoulder to know that Rafe had shifted down to the other end.

"One . . . two—"

"Three" was interrupted by a tremendous explosion that rocked both Mac and Rafe back a good five feet and would have sent them farther still if the metal shelving hadn't abruptly stopped their trajectory. A thick haze of dust and grit instantly filled the air, forcing them to shield their eyes and yank the fronts of their shirts over their mouths to keep from gagging.

As the dust began to filter through the air and sift to the floor, Mac motioned to Rafe and pointed across the empty space. There was now a very large hole in the opposite wall of the previously secure riverfront warehouse. A hole easily big enough to drive a tank through. Frank DiMateo was a big guy, but he wasn't Humvee big.

"Damn," Mac murmured. "I didn't think he had that in him."

"Son of a bitchin' bitch." Rafe was already on his feet, brushing the cinderblock debris and dust from his tailored black leather jacket, alternately coughing and swearing. "Asshole actually tried to blow me up."

"Us," Mac corrected, standing up now, too, albeit a bit more slowly. Cop knees. Unlike his partner, Mac was completely unconcerned about his appearance and did little more than rub his hand over his face to keep the grit from getting in his eyes. "Asshole tried to blow us up. I believe there are two of us here trying not to get ourselves killed."

"Yeah, but only one of us thought the place was secure."

"Hey, I checked the place last night and everything was

functioning properly. I don't know how the sensors were tampered with, but I can easily find out. Frank is too damn stupid to override the system, which means he had help."

"You think Shanahan would risk getting personally involved?"

"An art collector? No. But he sure as hell has the funds to send someone who would. I just can't figure out how they even knew we were here. We should have been in and out with the urn before they had a clue anything was up."

"Gee, maybe their sensors worked," Rafe deadpanned.

"Very funny. But even if they suspected they were being cased and moved the stuff early, why hang around? Seems like a stupid risk to take. Why go to the trouble of messing up their warehouse and inviting an official investigation unless—" Mac broke off and stared at his partner as comprehension dawned on both of them at the same time. "Shit!"

"*Run!*" they both yelled simultaneously.

Rafe grabbed Mac by the arm, and they lit out across the empty warehouse floor at a dead run, leaving behind Frank's makeshift office and whatever trail of evidence might still be there as they headed for daylight. It never ceased to amaze Mac what a good punch of adrenaline could do for a bum knee. He ran like a track star, with the far more agile Rafe only a half step ahead of him. They made it maybe ten yards through the gaping hole in the wall before both of them were bodily launched across the remainder of the cracked-cement parking lot when the rest of the warehouse went up in a second explosion.

Fortunately a cargo-sized dumpster stopped their abrupt exodus before they both went flipping into the Hudson River.

It took a minute or two before his head stopped ringing from the impact. He groaned and rolled over. "We need to be right on his ass," Mac croaked out, lying half on his side, legs sprawled, one elbow jammed under the dumpster. "You go get the car."

"I'm missing a shoe," was Rafe's only response. "It was Italian."

"Well, then, that does it. We certainly can't be chasing bad guys, hopping around on one designer loafer."

Rafe ignored the jibe, as he pretty much always did. It was true he took a fair amount of care with his appearance and an unfair amount of grief for it. It was just, when contrasted with Mac's Fashion-by-Goodwill sensibility, well, it made for good ribbing material.

"You know, when we tracked Frank as the go-between, he was just a paid schmuck too stupid to know the trouble he was involved in. I didn't like the guy, but as long as we got Doris Fortenberry her urn back, it was live and let live as far as I was concerned." Rafe swore again and went digging for his shoe. "Now, it's personal."

Mac dislodged his arm and righted himself, leaning back against the dumpster, hoping he'd get most of his hearing back at some point. He flexed his jaw and tried to make his ears pop. "You know, I thought when we started working for Finn, our lives would improve and we'd deal with a better class of people."

"We do," Rafe reminded him, still digging. "These days our clients actually deserve our help."

"Yeah, yeah." Mac gave up trying to pop his ears and re-signed himself to feeling as if he was living underwater for the time being. As a police detective he'd spent most of his days tracking down scum who preyed on other scum. And those were just the cases he actually made progress on. Sure, there were the redeeming cases, too: A child saved, a teenager kept off the streets, a mom able to bury her child with some peace of mind, knowing the killer was behind bars, unable to hurt anyone else's kids. He'd taken redemption where he'd found it.

Now, however, he got to choose his own clients, and all of them deserved justice. With the extended resources of Trinity behind him, he could make sure they always got it, too. One way, or the other. He usually liked it when getting the job done included the "other" part. Today? Not so much.

"Of course, that's what I thought when I took that job with Hightower, too," Mac said.

Rafe snorted as he dug through the debris and trash that had collected under the dumpster. "I told you working high-end security systems for a tight-ass white-collar agency wasn't for you. We're not white-collar guys, Mac. Never were, wouldn't want to be." Grimacing, he straightened with his missing shoe in hand. It was covered in . . . something. "We just dress better than our blue-collar compadres." He brushed off the dumpster scum with a piece of crumpled newspaper, then glanced down at his partner. "Some of us, anyway."

"Very amusing." Mac winced as he rolled to his knees and pushed to a stand. "At least when I worked for Hightower and NYPD, no one tried to blow me up. In fact, never once did I get shot across a parking lot like a cannonball." He made a cursory effort at brushing the soot and grime off his pants, then gave up with a shrug. "Toss a coin. Heads gets to chase down Frank and beat his sorry ass until he tells us where the hell the crates went, and tails gets to call Doris Fortenberry."

But Rafe wasn't answering him. He'd smoothed open the newspaper he'd been cleaning his shoe with and was reading something.

Mac turned his head, trying again to pop his ears, then paused. "Shit. I hear sirens. We gotta roll." He looked at Rafe, who was still engrossed. "Come on, you can find out how the two-headed alien baby survived being raised by wolves later."

Rafe continued to read, ignoring him. Finally Mac reached out and snatched the paper from him.

"Hey!" Rafe protested, trying to grab it back. "Wait, don't—"

"They start putting nude photos in the *Times* now or what?" Mac joked, flipping the paper over.

"Mac, it's not—" Rafe broke off when the smile on Mac's face died a swift death. He sighed and shoved his shoe back on.

Mac wasn't paying him any attention. Actually, he'd forgotten his partner was even there. Or, for that matter, that the two of them were standing on an old shipping pier in the Red Hook District of Brooklyn, having just narrowly escaped death.

He'd taken one look at her picture, and the words "Camp Winnimocca" in the caption beneath, and been instantly transported to another time, another place, where he'd also narrowly escaped death, albeit a far more protracted one. Otherwise known as his childhood.

"Hard to believe Big Lou finally kicked the bucket," Rafe said, in a lame attempt to lighten the sudden shift in mood.

Mac absently thought that if Louisa Sutherland, the severely elegant owner of the elite retreat for children of the very wealthy, had ever heard them call her that, she'd probably come back from the grave just to kick their sorry asses. At the moment, he'd welcome the chance to kick back.

He skimmed the headline again: SUTHERLAND HEIRESS GIVES UP FORTUNE TO INHERIT FAMILY LAKE PROPERTY.

"This makes no sense," he muttered, mostly to himself, as he reread the article. "Why would Kate do something so stupid for a place she hated?"

"We were teenagers the last time we saw either her or Shelby," Rafe needlessly reminded him. "Who knows what's gone on since then. I'm surprised we never heard about Louisa dying, though. She really climbed the social register over the years."

Mac wasn't. Unless it was case related, he didn't read the society columns, much less follow the *Town and Country* set of Washington or New York. Hell, he'd been surprised when the Sutherlands' secretary had tracked down Donny Mac's long-lost son a decade ago to tell him his father had died. Mac had been on the force in those days and not impossible to find, even though he hadn't spoken to his father since the day he'd left home.

He wouldn't have thought they'd go to the trouble to locate the camp handyman's next-of-kin. Though by the time
they had, his father was already in the ground, courtesy of
the state. Mac had handled the requisite legal and financial
details, such as they were, over the phone, and paid someone
else to handle whatever was left. He'd never gone back. He
had no regrets. Then, or now.

Rafe and Finn figured into the only memories from his past
that he'd bothered to keep alive. If not for those ten weeks
spent with them every summer, Frank probably wouldn't have
had the opportunity to try and blow him to smithereens today
because he'd have long since been dead.

"Yeah," he said, his voice sounding gruff even to his own
ears. Stupid to get emotional over something that had nothing to do with his life anymore, and hadn't since the day he'd
turned eighteen. Doubly stupid to let Kate Sutherland still
have any effect on him at all.

"Hard to believe she would swap her entire inheritance
with Shelby's for a place she'd barely stepped foot in back
then," Rafe said, cleaning the rest of the muck off his shoe.
"Hell, you'd think they'd be in a race to see who could sell it
to the highest bidder and split the profits."

"Says here Kate plans to turn it into a therapy facility for
disabled kids," Mac read, still not quite believing his eyes.

"No shit? Well, I don't know. I guess people can change,
but you'll pardon me if I don't see Katherine Sutherland as
benefactor to the needy and underprivileged, any more than
her mother was. Hell, your father was as close to charity as
the woman ever came, and she worked his ass into the ground."

Only because Rafe had been there, and only because he'd
suffered as much, if not more, at the hands of his own past,
was he comfortable speaking so frankly. But Mac wasn't
thinking about his father, or Louisa, or any of that.

He was too busy staring at the picture and thinking about
Kate. Even though they'd been teenagers when they'd last
laid eyes on Louisa Sutherland's only daughter, and almost

two decades had since past, Rafe was probably right in his assessment about people changing. But then Rafe had never had much patience for Kate, the unflappable, unapproachable, and most certainly unattainable sleek, blond princess of their youth. Mac had pretended the same indifference, but the truth was he'd spent many a fevered night dreaming about her . . . and hating himself for it. She represented everything he both envied and abhorred. But that didn't stop him from sporting an almost constant, raging hard-on every time she swung through camp. The grainy black-and-white newspaper photo proved that the ensuing years had done little to diminish her impact on him.

"Did you see that part about the developers sniffing around? What do you want to bet this is all some kind of scam to pull one over on some investment group or something? I wouldn't put it past either one of them."

Mac's attention caught on the last line. *Despite several episodes of vandalism and rumors of an attempted buyout by resort developers, Ms. Sutherland hopes to open her camp as scheduled next spring.*

"Maybe Shelby," Mac said. Kate's stepbrother had always been a creepy little weasel. Mac doubted any amount of time would have ground that out of him. "Kate might have been a little stuck up, but I doubt—"

"A little?" Rafe let out a harsh laugh, then stopped abruptly and tilted his head.

Sirens were closing in.

"Your colleagues are about to show up and we're standing here in broad daylight with our thumbs up our collective asses. Let's get the hell out of here."

Rafe tried to take the paper away from him again, but Mac stuffed it in his pocket and took off along the edge of decaying pier, Rafe right beside him, both of them moving swiftly toward the abandoned sugar refinery where they'd stashed their car from sight.

Mac knew he should let the whole thing go, but his mind

was already working, analyzing. It was the cop in him, or so he told himself. But something about that story didn't add up. As much as he hated to admit it, Rafe might be right; it might all be some scam, a way to get out of paying estate taxes or something. He wouldn't put it past Shelby. And yet, his detective instincts said otherwise. And what was that part about the vandalism? Where did that come into play?

Rafe reached the car first and jumped in behind the wheel. Mac was still shutting the passenger door as they swung around the back side of the lot and edged out into traffic, two blocks away from the scene of what was now a crime.

"Wonder what Finn will think of this latest twist."

Mac realized Rafe was talking about the Fortenberry case, not the sudden reappearance of Kate Sutherland. "Finn will think we should figure out where the hell Frank is hiding, pin the bomb-happy asshole to the nearest wall, get Mr. Fortenberry's ashes back, then get the hell out of here and back to Virginia."

Rafe maneuvered through traffic heading toward the interstate. As the silence stretched out, he finally said, "It's that last part that's bugging you, isn't it?"

Mac pretended not to understand. "Going back to Virginia? Or getting our hands on an urn full of dead guy? Because I've grown to like Virginia. And dead guys don't bug me much. It's the ones who are still alive and shooting at me I have a problem with."

Another few minutes passed; then Rafe sighed and said, "You know, I can handle the rest of this cluster. Finn should be done with the Thomason deal, so he'll find someone to help me or come up himself. He'd be the first one to tell you to go check this out. Why don't you just—"

"Why don't you just mind your own goddamn business, okay?" Mac kept his gaze firmly forward. Rafe knew him far too well. Which, most of the time, was a good thing, since it had saved his ass on more than one occasion. At the moment, however, he'd be more than happy to toss his best friend right into the Hudson if it meant shutting him up about Win-nimocca, Kate Sutherland, and anything having to do with their collective past.

Rafe drove on in silence, letting Mac stew.

"No one asked for our help," he finally bit out. "And I doubt it would be welcome."

"Probably not," Rafe said, far too agreeably. "But you and I both know you won't be worth a damn until you at least dig some on this. No one says you have to see her."

Mac cast a quick glance at his partner and caught the slight lift at the corner of his mouth. Son of a bitch. He'd probably known all along what effect Kate really had on him. Of course, Rafe had been the first one to explain what they were looking at when Mac had discovered his father's stash of *Penthouse* magazines, too. They couldn't have been much older than nine at the time.

After another long, tension-building silence, Mac swore under his breath. "It would have to be as part of Trinity. To-tally professional. A case just like any other we decide to take on. Or not at all."

Rafe said nothing, just stared ahead as they rolled along with the traffic on Grand Central Parkway. "Whatever works." He cut across two lanes and took the expressway heading to-ward JFK.

"Where do you think—?" Mac snapped his mouth shut and shifted his gaze out the side window. "Turn around," he said flatly, in a tone that used to make even the most desper-ate, hopped-up scumbag take note. "I need time to prepare for this. Let's go round up Frank first, finish this job."

"No," Rafe said, just as flatly. "Every minute you take right now will be time spent talking yourself out of doing what you know you have to do."

"I don't have to do shit. This is not my problem."

Rafe swung into the airport entrance. "I know it's not. Trust me, if it were up to me, I'd steer far clear of the whole Sutherland clan."

"Peachy. Then we're on the same page."

"Except it's not up to me. This one is yours. I'll square everything with Finn. We'll get you whatever you need." He pulled to a stop at the entrance to the car rental counters. "Check in with me later and I'll bring you up to speed on this mess."

Mac looked at his partner, fully intending to tell him where he could take his *Father Knows Best* attitude and stick it, but was caught off guard by the real regret he saw in his partner's eyes.

"I really am sorry—" Rafe began, but was immediately shut down.

Mac raised a hand. "Don't. Being an asshole worked better."

Rafe grinned. "Suits me. Tell Katherine hello from the remaining two-thirds of the Unholy Trinity." He popped the locks on the doors. "And get some new clothes, man. You smell bad."

Mac said nothing, just got out of the car and trudged into the rental agency without so much as a toothbrush to his name. The irony didn't escape him.

You ain't never gonna escape your roots, boy, no matter how far you run from 'em. Cain't escape your genes, neither. You'll see.

His father's wheezing cackle rang in Mac's ears.

"Looks like you were right about some things after all, Pops."

Chapter 2

Going into the city had been a complete waste of two of Kate's most precious commodities: money and time. She'd suspected Shelby wasn't going to make probating the will easy for either of them, and he hadn't. Why should he change spots now? He'd spent a lifetime making things as difficult as humanly possible for her. But even she hadn't seen this latest stunt coming. Everything had been finally decided upon, and well in Shelby's favor, to boot. All he had to do was sign the damn papers.

She took the last couple of mountain curves a little more tightly than might have been perfectly safe. The wheels of her secondhand Toyota pickup squealed in protest, but she didn't ease up on the peddle. She'd been here as a permanent resident for only a little over a month now, but she already knew the roads through this range of the Catskills so well she could drive them blindfolded.

Which was a good thing considering she was blinded with fury at the moment. She'd left Manhattan behind two hours ago, and she still wished she could strangle Shelby with her bare hands.

If such things were possible in the afterlife, she had no doubt her mother was off somewhere enjoying the havoc she'd wrought when she'd changed her will what had turned out to be the final time. Louisa Slavine Hamilton Pepperdine

Sutherland Graham had loved nothing more than wielding the collective assets of her deceased or departed husbands over the heads of her only daughter and stepson. Most especially her last husband, given how their divorce had provided Louisa the most to work with. And by then she'd had plenty of practice and knew exactly what to do with it, too.

She'd tortured Shelby the most, probably because he cared the most. Hell, Kate wasn't even a real Sutherland. She was a Pepperdine. But she'd only been four when her mother had remarried and had her daughter's name legally changed in order to let the world assume George Sutherland had adopted her, which he most definitely had not. Though, to be fair, he'd been more of a father to her than her own, whom she didn't even remember, seeing as how he'd died when she was two.

George had lasted until just after her eleventh birthday when his heart had quite literally given out. After marrying and divorcing quite young her first go around, her mother had developed a penchant for older men. Much older. As with Kate's natural father, Louisa hadn't spent long in mourning for the dear departed George. The only real surprise had been that it had taken her seven years to land husband number four. Although Trenton Graham had been her biggest fish by far, so perhaps worth the wait. Even though the union had been short-lived, a tumultuous four years that she often said felt like fourteen, her divorce settlement alone had insured her continued residence amongst the highest of high society. Her transformation finally complete.

And although Kate had never gotten along with her sole stepsibling, by rights, the pile of assets her mother had accrued upon her death should have gone to Shelby. No matter whether the slimy little toad had actually deserved any of it or not, he was the one who had stuck by Louisa's side, year in, year out, husband in, husband out. He was the one who'd endured working for her all those years, helping to grow her fortune, doing whatever was asked of him, taking her abuse with a smile and a nod, waiting for the day it would all pay off.

Kate, her only natural child, hadn't done any of those things. So no one had been more shocked than Kate when Louisa's lawyer had calmly recited the contents of the will stating Shelby was to inherit Winnimocca—which had belonged to his father and was, at the time, the single greatest asset he'd brought to his union with Louisa—and only Winnimocca. Leaving Kate to inherit everything else.

Although, to be fair, perhaps Shelby had been even more shocked. If the instantaneous blanching of every bit of color from his already florid complexion and the white-knuckled grip he'd had on his Hermes briefcase were any indication. She'd been half afraid he'd go into full coronary occlusion right then and there.

The final irony was, she'd wanted the only thing Shelby had gotten. She'd wanted Winnimocca. Kate turned onto the long drive that led into the camp grounds. Well, maybe it wasn't so ironic. Just before her death, Kate had ended her long estrangement with her family to ask about leasing Winnimocca. So, with that bit of information at hand, Louisa could use her last will and testament to deprive both of her children their hearts' desire in one fell swoop.

A small smile curved Kate's lips. *Well, Mother*, she thought, *you can't control things now*. Before they'd even left the probate lawyers' office, Kate had proposed a deal to essentially swap her inheritance with Shelby's, giving them both what they wanted. Perhaps it had been an emotional and not entirely rational decision on her part, but, of course, Shelby had jumped at her offer.

Her expression grew more determined as she passed the cheerfully painted sign announcing the new Winnimocca Youth Camp. She'd officially moved in thirty-seven days ago. Shelby hadn't said a word about it, which she'd taken as a good sign, as their arbitration had headed into the final stages. The sign had been the first thing she'd changed. More as a statement to herself, one of hope and optimism, than to the world at large, but it was only a matter of time. If everything went as planned, next year at this time, the whole world would know. And Winnimocca Youth Camp would be open for business.

She tightened her grip on the wheel as she thought about her endless wait that morning, and the formality that had never happened. She didn't know what stupid game Shelby was playing, but he was going to find out, and find out quite swiftly, that she wasn't going to be jerked around. She and her mother might not have had a loving relationship by any definition, but he was going to learn that there was, in fact, a bit of Louisa Slavine, secretary from the Bronx, in the daughter. Kate had already put a call in to her attorney to see what leverage she had in bartering her inheritance back from Shelby. He wasn't the only one who could jerk the marionette strings.

Her determined smile slipped a little when she saw the neon orange spray paint streaking across the trunks of several red spruce and old-growth hemlocks that crowded the steep camp terrain down to the lake. Not again. Hadn't she suffered enough setbacks for one foul day?

Apparently not.

GO HOME, RICH BITCH!

Same as before. If she hadn't been so emotionally drained, she would have laughed. Rich bitch. If only. On a heavy sigh, she continued past the fresh graffiti, driving through the entrance, past the defunct guard building and equally defunct electric gate, on past the central lodge that housed the kitchens, dining rooms, and staging areas. Or would once the roof and the flooring were replaced. And the porch. She looked away, keeping her eyes focused straight ahead. So much work to do. None of which she could officially start until the paperwork was signed.

Normally she was a determined optimist, but her spirit had suffered a bit too much of a beating today. She'd go home, call Sheriff Gilby about the graffiti—again—and try to figure out what Shelby's latest ploy was all about. But first she was going to indulge in a long, steamy bath. The truck's heater left a lot to be desired, and though April had finally arrived, spring was taking a bit longer to officially show up this year. The breezy days still carried a bite in the higher elevations, and the evenings were downright chilly. Her toes were already numb. She made a mental note to check her firewood before going to bed. She'd have to stack the stove carefully tonight. It felt like it might get close to freezing. Praying for an early summer, she swung into her spot in front of the camp director's cabin. Or what she'd decided was going to be the camp director's cabin.

Her cabin.

A little of the smile returned as she climbed out of the cab and rubbed at the ache that had settled in her lower back. There would be no opening of the champagne she'd reserved for her own private celebration, but that didn't mean she couldn't have a glass of wine. Yes, a glass of chilled White Zinfandel and a long bath were in her immediate future. She deserved that much.

Tomorrow she'd tackle Shelby, the as yet unresponsive sheriff, and . . . whatever else she could handle.

She climbed the five steps up to the screened-in side porch, balancing her purse and briefcase as she bumped the door open with her hip and simultaneously kicked off her low-heeled pumps. To think she used to collect shoes like some people collected earrings. *To think you actually enjoyed wearing them,* she thought, letting out a heartfelt groan of relief as she flexed the soles of her feet and wriggled her toes into the stiff pile of the doormat just inside the porch door. She couldn't wait until it was warm enough for flip-flops.

"Bagel?" she called out, summoning the one male in her life she could always count on. "Where are you, buddy? Mommy's home and she could use a slobbery hug." She was surprised he hadn't been waiting for her at the door, tail thumping, whining with the excitement at the sight of her. You couldn't beat a dog for giving a great welcome home. "Did you get into something? Listen, whatever you chewed up, threw up, or peed on, today you get a pass. Come on out."

She let everything slide from her hands onto the small wooden bench that was currently doubling as a side table by the front door. She'd worry about all that later. Right now, the only decision she had to make was red wine or the chilled white. She'd found a stash of both along with a few bottles of champagne in the wine cellar of the main lodge while doing her initial walk-through assessment and brought a couple of each to her cabin. She'd put the champagne in the fridge before leaving, thinking she'd celebrate closing the deal with a little private toast. Now the white would have to do. "Might just drink the whole damn bottle, too. So there."

"I have some spare beer, if you're interested."

She let out a little scream of shock and spun around, heart lodged in her throat as she searched the far shadows at the opposite end of the wraparound porch. The light had dimmed quickly in the falling twilight. "Who's there?" she demanded, wishing like hell she had her truck keys in her hand. Not much of a weapon, but they'd have been better than nothing. They were still in the ignition, where she always left them. Though she'd been debating changing that policy with the recent vandalism. But they'd never locked things up around camp, and old habits died hard.

She tried not to think about that dying part.

She was debating just making a run for the truck and driving straight down to Gilby's office, when the disembodied voice stepped from the shadows . . . and she froze to the spot, unable to move or breathe. No. Her mind spun wildly, trying to make some sense of it all. It couldn't be.

"Hello, Kate."

But it was. Eighteen years melted away in a blink of an eye. Though he'd been only seventeen the last time she'd laid eyes on him, she'd know those eyes anywhere. That chin.

And that voice. That slow, lazy, sexy-as-hell voice.

"Donovan?"

There was a pause; then he said, "It's been a long time. My condolences on your mother's passing."

She accepted the platitude with a jerky nod of her chin, but her mind went immediately to the graffiti that had started popping up shortly after her arrival. But that made no sense. As far as she knew, Donovan had left the day he'd turned eighteen and hadn't even returned for his father's funeral. Did he think with Louisa gone he had some right to the place? She knew there had been some talk in the papers about her wild deal with Shelby, but certainly he didn't think—"Is—is that why you're here? Because she died this past December. The funeral was a long—"

He shook his head. "I didn't come to pay my respects, though you have them."

"Then . . . why?"

He took a scant step forward, and she was suddenly painfully aware of her appearance, which was ridiculous, but true nevertheless. He'd always had that effect on her. And it had always been ridiculous. Growing up, he'd been Donovan MacLeod, son of drunken Donny Mac, the camp handyman. Hardly a member of her peer group. Most times when their paths had crossed, he'd been in little more than ragged cutoffs, with callused hands and hair in desperate need of a cut. While she'd been clad to the nines in the latest styles, her hair and makeup nothing less than perfect, as she'd intended when she'd made certain he'd see her.

Her cheeks heated now as they always had when he looked at her with those silver-gray eyes of his, somehow always managing to make her feel like the discombobulated one. This time he probably could make a case for it. She resisted the urge to push her hair behind her ears, smooth the rumpled suit jacket she'd forgotten to take off when she'd stormed out of Shelby's attorney's office.

"I read about you—your camp, I mean—in the paper."

It was the slight hesitation in his voice that snagged her attention, dragging it from past to present. He'd always been laconic, with a bit of a cocky edge. Or maybe the challenging edge to his tone had been exclusively for her. Regardless, she didn't think she'd ever heard him sound anything less than certain. Of course, though it shamed her to say that she could probably still recall every single second of every encounter they'd ever had, they hadn't exactly shared long conversations together. Most of what she knew about him had come from obsessive observation and listening to the other girls' comments.

He'd been the living embodiment of every one of her fevered, youthful dreams. The proverbial black sheep, the bad boy every good girl would die to have look at her, hold her, touch her . . . take her.

Kate had fantasized about all that and more. In fact, it was the only reason she'd bothered to come anywhere near the lake property every summer. Shelby had always been around, and he'd been just enough of a creep even then that she'd done almost anything to steer clear of him. But the lure of seeing Donovan, dark shaggy hair, rippling belly muscles, piercing gray eyes, working around camp, even if just for a weekend, had been too strong to ignore.

Now, at thirty-four, and thinking herself quite past the age of feverish sexual fantasies, it was a shock to discover just how wrong she actually was.

"You—you read about my camp? Where?" she stuttered, feeling like a complete fool for being so off balance. If he knew the direction of her thoughts, he'd likely laugh himself sick. Though why it mattered what he thought, she had no idea. Old habits, indeed.

"There was a mention in the *Times*."

"Oh." Probably another snide little column about the idiotic heiress who'd given up her fortune, she thought with an inward sigh. What did people think, that when someone died, they just gave their inheriting family member a check for their bulk net worth? "So, uh, what made you come all the way up here? You're still in the city, right? A . . . detective or something?"

She knew exactly what he was because she'd been the one who'd forced her mother into tracking him down when Donny Mac had his heart attack. It was one of the last times Kate had had contact with her mother, until right before her death. But he didn't have to know any of that. "And I'm sorry, too. About your father. I know it's been a very long time since . . . since it happened. But, still, I regret my mother didn't get word to you in time, back then. It was—"

"Water under a very old bridge." He appeared relaxed on the surface, but when he'd stepped closer, she could feel the tension emanating from him. It was costing him, the casual nonchalance.

"Some would say the same about you being here," she said, feeling the same tension coiling inside of her. "Why did you come back, Donovan?"

"Mac," he said, sounding irritated all of a sudden. "Just— it's Mac."

"Okay. Mac. Were you in the area on some other business? Why are you camped out on my porch?"

"I read about the problems you were having. In the article."

That caught her badly off guard. No way could he have known about what happened earlier today. Unless—but no, how on earth could he be part of that? That was all Shelby being typical Shelby.

"With the vandalism, the developers leaning on you," he went on when she didn't immediately respond. "I thought I might be able to help."

She frowned. "You came back here, after all these years, because you read in some article that someone was vandalizing the old camp property? Isn't that taking your oath to protect and defend a little far? We're a bit out of your jurisdiction, Detective."

"I'm no longer with the department. I'm in the private sector now." He rocked back a little on his heels. It was only then she noticed Bagel, sitting quietly by his feet.

Traitor, she thought. So much for dependable males of any species.

Donovan—Mac—followed her gaze downward. "Quite the watchdog you got for yourself."

Kate had to fight to keep from reflexively calling the dog to her side, only half sure he'd listen. She didn't need to look more the fool in front of Donov—Mac—than she already did. "That's Bagel."

He cocked one eyebrow. "You named your dog after breakfast food?"

"He's part basset, part beagle. It's just a combination of— never mind." Her cheeks flushed a little, but she'd be damned if she'd apologize for her choice in canine companionship, much less the name she'd christened him with. "And he's not a watchdog, he's—"

"No kidding." He leaned down and scratched Bagel behind his ears, earning an enthusiastic thumping of tail and a near orgasmic whimper of pleasure. This didn't come as a surprise to Kate, who would have likely whimpered in near orgasmic pleasure if he'd touched her, too.

She struggled to rally her wayward thoughts and blatant physical reaction. *Like you ever could before.* "I still don't understand why you drove all the way up here. Surely not because of some silly article. Were you here on other business?" And did it have anything to do with her camp?

He straightened and looked at her intently again, in that way he had of making her feel as though she was the only one in the universe. His universe. It was both disconcerting . . . and quite a turn-on.

She really needed to find a way to turn it back off again.

"I've done a little research," he said, not directly answering her question. "You might want to reconsider the guard dog option. You're being looked at pretty closely. Or your property is."

Kate couldn't keep up with the barrage of information her tired brain was being asked to process. First him showing up, now him standing there telling her he knew all about her business. It was all simply too much. Eighteen years had passed, yet here Donovan MacLeod stood, in the still rippling flesh, still making her heart pound. Her camp was under siege. She was under siege. By too many memories and too much responsibility. And, to be perfectly honest, more than a passing ripple of fear. She hadn't really let herself think about it too much, focusing on Shelby as the source of her problems. Once she had him dealt with, then she'd force Sheriff Gilby to stop brushing off her concerns and figure out who was playing stupid games on her property.

"I appreciate the concern, but that still doesn't explain why you just popped up out of nowhere to stick your nose in my business." She wanted—no, needed—him to go away. She desperately needed to sort out her thoughts, and she couldn't do that with him standing less than five feet away, pinning her with that intent gaze of his. Maybe it was better not to confront him so directly. After all, she really didn't know him or what he was capable of, then or now. "Listen," she went on, trying to sound conciliatory, "I don't mean to sound ungrateful, really, I don't. It's just . . . it's been a very long day, and I'm not really prepared to deal with this"—*or you*—"at the moment."

Given her continued, rather visceral reaction to him, even after all these years, perhaps she'd never be ready to deal with him. She'd been so focused on launching her mission here, it had been quite a while since she'd enjoyed the company of . . . well, anyone, much less a member of the opposite sex. Bagel had pretty much been it in terms of companionship. But even she knew that excuse didn't cover the extent of her reaction. It was as if all the intervening years meant nothing. Everything had changed . . . and yet nothing had changed. The last time she'd felt this pull toward him, she'd been a girl. Almost two full decades had passed, and she was a woman now . . .

and yet the pull was only that much stronger. The kind of pull only an adult truly understood and appreciated.

"Why don't you leave me the number where you're staying, and maybe we can work something out to talk at a later time, if that's okay." She was still staring at him, drinking in all she could, while she could. Pathetic, perhaps, but it only cemented her decision to get him out of there as quickly as possible. "I appreciate the offer of help. I just . . . You caught me off guard." Understatement of the century. He'd caught her hormones off guard, too. Every tingling, oversensitized, and apparently vastly sensory-deprived one of them. "And unfortunately I'm not prepared to discuss any of this tonight."

If he'd been anyone else, she'd have extended her hand for a polite shake, but she was half afraid she didn't have polite in her where he was concerned. And touching him, letting him have any direct contact with her flesh . . . even all these years later . . . no. As badly as she'd wanted him to, she'd never let him touch her then. It would be the height of stupidity to think she could handle it any better now.

"I couldn't find any contact information for the camp, and I didn't have any direct information on contacting you," he said by way of explanation. "Your mother's attorney wouldn't give that out."

Her eyes widened. "You spoke to Donald?"

He nodded. "I didn't know where else to start. You're in trouble here, Kate. Trust me, no one wanted it to be otherwise more than me. I didn't want to come back here. I never wanted to come back here. But . . . helping people is what I do. And I thought I could help you. I know I can."

It just wasn't adding up. No one just dropped everything to race off and play Good Samaritan for someone they hadn't seen in eighteen years. There was only one explanation she could think of that made any sense, though she didn't pretend to understand it. Yet. "Shelby put you up to this, didn't he? Well, I don't know what his game is, or yours, but you can tell him his ploy won't work. We had a deal and, one way

or the other, I'm holding him to it. Good night, Mr. MacLeod."
She slapped her thigh. "Come, Bagel."

Not waiting to see if her fickle dog complied, she went to
storm past Mac into the cabin, but he shifted slightly, causing
her to stop short and almost lose her balance rather than
allow herself to come into even the most incidental contact
with him.

"What on God's green earth would make you think I'd
ever so much as lift a finger for Shelby Sutherland?"

Even if she hadn't heard the banked fury in his tone, she
was close enough now that there was no mistaking the same
emotion in his eyes. "A lot of years have passed," she managed, suddenly feeling a whole lot more than indignation. He
was far too close. "People change."

"Not that much."

She realized she was shaking, but there was nothing she
could do about it. "Then why help me? You wouldn't give
me the time of day eighteen years ago. Why go to all this
trouble now? Have you changed?"

"I thought maybe you had. I guess I was wrong."

"Donovan—Mac," she corrected quickly, automatically,
when his eyes flared, "I don't know what's going on here, or
why you're really standing on my porch." She broke off, was
forced to swallow, her throat suddenly gone dry and tight.
He really was standing far too close. "But I'm going to have
to ask you to leave now. We—we'll talk later, sort this out.
No more accusations, I'm just—it's been a long day."

He said nothing, simply held her gaze. Only there was
nothing really simple about it. She had no idea if he was even
affected by her now, so many years later. Maybe she'd just
dreamed that all those smoldering looks he'd sent her way all
those summers ago had meant something. Had meant he was
as intrigued by her as she'd been by him. For all the opposite
reasons. She'd wanted, badly, to walk on the wrong side of
the tracks. For a while anyway. With him. She'd thought
maybe he'd wanted to get a taste of her life, too. Get a taste

of her. But she'd been young and most definitely foolish where he was concerned.

It appeared that with age didn't necessarily come sensibility.

Then he was lifting his hand, and she knew, with absolute clarity, that the one thing she'd ached for, yearned for, fantasized about, all those hot summers ago, was finally about to happen . . . eighteen years too late. Donovan MacLeod was finally going to put his hands on her. And she wasn't going to be able to let him.

"Good night, Mac." She stared steadily back at him, or as steadily as she could manage, willing him to step back and allow her entrance to her own damn cabin.

He didn't so much as budge. "It's good seeing you again, Kate. I didn't think it would be." For the first time, amusement filtered into those eyes of his, and his mouth curved ever so slightly into a ghost of the cocky smile of his youth.

Her legs felt a little loose and wobbly. And her pulse jackrabbited ahead with an abandon she couldn't control. Dammit, but she wanted him to touch her. Foolish and stupid. He was right. She hadn't changed at all. "Thanks." She fought a sudden urge to smile. "I think." It would be dangerous to let her guard down with him. Even for a split second. While she couldn't really imagine him working with Shelby—there had never been any love lost between the two—his sudden appearance on the same day Shelby had pulled a no-show was too much of a coincidence to dismiss it out of hand.

"I'm sorry I startled you," he said. "I didn't know how else to get in touch."

"You could have left a note."

There was that little quirk again, at the corners of his mouth. Better not to look at his mouth. God, she was looking at his mouth.

"I could have done a lot of things."

Was it her imagination still running wild, or had there been something suggestive in that? She dragged her gaze from his firmly chiseled lips—age had only improved every rugged inch of him—to his eyes. Eyes that had seen too much, more than she'd ever likely know. All that mattered was they probably saw way too much in hers.

"You, uh—" She had to clear her throat. "You staying in town? Maybe we'll grab a bite at Deenie's, talk all this out."

"Deenie's place is still there, huh?"

She frowned a little. "I thought you said you'd done some research."

"On you," he answered directly, apparently having no idea how badly he was unsettling her. Or maybe he did, and just enjoyed it. Lord knew he always had in the past. "I could give a damn about the town."

"Well, the town has a lot to do with things. Or might. I don't know." She sucked in a breath and tried a tight smile. "Tomorrow, then?"

"Tomorrow."

She glanced at the cabin door, wanting badly to be on the other side of it, with something, anything, between them. She needed to regroup. She needed wine. A lot of wine. "Good night."

Still, he didn't shift away, didn't let her past. But he made no move closer. For the longest moment, he simply held her gaze, trapped it in his own, and kept it there while he studied and probed. He never dropped his gaze below her own, and yet she felt thoroughly . . . frisked. She wanted to fold her arms over her chest, hide her reaction to him. She didn't dare move a muscle.

"I can help you," he said quietly. "You'd be wise to let me."

"Tomorrow," she said firmly, if somewhat breathlessly. "We'll talk about it tomorrow."

"Good night, Kate."

It wasn't until he shifted back, putting some semblance of space between them, that she let out the breath she'd been holding. She reached past him for the door, determined to end this little tête-à-tête right now. Before she did something even more reckless than letting him get that close to her. Like inviting him in for a glass of wine.

"Good night." She opened the door, forcing herself to do it calmly, naturally, when what she wanted to do was dart inside, slam the door shut, and bolt it into place. *Like that would keep him out if he really wanted in.* She shivered in renewed awareness. She didn't want Donovan MacLeod back in her life, much less her cabin.

She held the door open for Bagel and flushed when Donovan had to shoo the dog in after her. She could feel him standing behind her, staring at her from the shadows. She made the mistake of glancing back. "Tomorrow."

He surprised her by grinning. Broadly. With every ounce of black sheep bad boy he still had in him. Which, as it turned out, was quite substantial. "Tomorrow it is. See you then, Kate."

"Yeah," she said faintly as she watched him step off the porch and disappear into the darkness. "See you then."

It wasn't until much later, when she was wrapped in more layers than the night chill warranted, third glass of wine in hand, that it occurred to her that he'd never told her where he was staying.

And that she'd never heard a car engine start up after he'd disappeared into the night. Nor had there been one parked anywhere around her cabin or the on road in.

She shivered a little, imagining him still out there, somewhere on the camp property. Watching her, maybe?

The shiver wasn't one of fear . . . It was one of anticipation.

Donovan MacLeod was back in town.

And Kate Sutherland still wanted him.

Chapter 3

Mac paused next to the stand of pine trees and studied the brush of needles scattered around the base of the trunks. Someone had been through here, and recently judging by the way the needles had been disturbed. There were no clear footprints, unless you knew what to look for. He knew.

He stepped behind the trees and positioned himself in the same place, facing the same direction that the intruder had—the other intruder, he amended. He hadn't exactly been invited here, either. At least Kate knew he was on the premises. Perhaps not at that very second, but he doubted she knew anything about the other one. Question was, what did the other intruder know about Kate? Anyone who would go to this much trouble, this far out in the middle of nowhere, had one of two motives. They were either after Kate, or something Kate owned.

Or maybe both.

He looked through the trees, along the same sight line as the person who'd stood there before him. From this spot, he could see her cabin, including both sides of the wraparound screened-in porch. He also had a clear line into the cab of her pickup truck. Someone was definitely spying on her.

He crouched down slightly, but the bows of the tree were closer together there, and his sight line was immediately obstructed. He straightened. A man, then. Or an inordinately tall woman. But his gut told him it was a man. In his experience, women ambushed, and they generally preferred trapping their quarry in as public a place as they could manage. Men hunted. And the fewer people around to contest the hunt, the better.

He looked over his shoulder and noted the direct path of cover from where he stood, straight through a short stand of woods, to where several yet-to-be remodeled camp cabins still stood. Beyond them, he knew it was only a short hike through another dense stand of trees, then a quick scramble up a rocky slide to where the main road wrapped around the top of the mountain before dipping down the other side toward town.

He could track it, and would, but he'd seen enough for now. He'd checked the property boundaries on this side of the lake yesterday before parking himself on Kate's porch with her trusty sidekick. Bagel. Honestly, it was no wonder the dog had defected to his side.

He'd noted the graffiti on several stands of trees and on one of the service sheds, but this was the first evidence of someone actually watching the cabin itself. It was harder to tell if anything had been vandalized in the cabins as most of them were empty and had just been left to suffer the elements for over a decade with no apparent maintenance.

He didn't know why Louisa had shut the place down, or why she'd left it to simply rot rather than sell the property off while it was still in decent shape. That was on his growing list of things to check out. Just as soon as he decided how to handle Kate.

He looked back at her cabin. The curtains were old, the color long since bleached out from the sun. The screens needed patching in a dozen places, something she'd need to do before the mosquitoes hatched for the season. The steps to the porch sagged in the middle where the cinderblock propping them up had sunk into the ground. The roof needed new shingles. The stovepipe chimney worked, though. A wispy curl of smoke wafted from the top and drifted slowly upward through the trees.

His stomach growled, and he could already feel the back of his neck tightening up. The result of sleeping in a cramped rental car with no supplies. He'd kill for a cup of coffee and a better-fitting pair of boots. The ones he'd been wearing when he left the city the day before yesterday smelled like that harbor dumpster. Unfortunately, the little general store he'd stopped in on the drive up hadn't exactly sported a huge variety of men's clothing. He could have gone on ahead to Ralston, the town closest to the camp, but it had been hard enough just coming here.

He shuttered any thoughts of the past away, just as he'd done from the moment he'd crossed the county line. He was here to do a job. Kate Sutherland was just another client. Even if she didn't know that yet. Rubbing a hand along the back of his neck, he turned away from the cabin and began tracing the trail of evidence back through the woods, past two of the cabins, doing whatever it took to keep his thoughts focused exclusively on the situation here. Trying like hell not to care about how pathetic and rundown the place had gotten. Like it mattered. He hadn't given Winnimocca a single thought since he'd peeled out of here on the old FXS Low Rider he'd spent two long summers rebuilding.

And yet, the swiftness with which he moved through the trees and up the side of the mountain belied his own past there. He'd been gone half his own lifetime, yet easily traversed the grounds as if he still did it every day. It shouldn't have surprised him, shouldn't have bothered him. It was just a place. But as he dug his way up the last rise to the side of the main road, he admitted to himself that it did.

He pulled out the new slim satellite phone Finn had gotten for them each to carry and made some notes, used the camera function to snap a few more shots, then added a few more things to the list of equipment he was going to need Finn to ship up to him. The property was expansive and mostly wooded, which would make it a bitch to secure. It wasn't going to be easy, and it wasn't going to be cheap, but it could be done. Fortunately for Trinity, money was never the issue.

What he really wanted to do, though, was dig a little more, find out who the hell was watching her, track those fuckers down, and make the whole problem go away without installing so much as a single surveillance camera. That would also take care of having to talk to Kate again. He wasn't sure which was the more daunting task, and didn't want to know.

Whoever was bothering her wasn't putting much muscle behind it. Yet. They were using grade school scare tactics designed to discourage rather than harm. Zap Kate's will by hitting her in the checkbook, forcing her to spend money cleaning up the vandalized property, and slowing down the progress on restoration work.

If they knew Kate, they'd know this wasn't going to work. He paused, then chuckled ruefully. Like he knew Kate, or knew what the hell had really motivated her to take on this camp. He'd done some digging on her, too, had to if he was going to understand his client's needs. Which was mostly a bunch of bullshit, even if true in any other case. Kate wasn't any other case, and he'd probably be better off admitting that to himself right now. The ten minutes he'd spent with her on her porch last night should have made that blisteringly clear.

At fifteen, hell, seventeen, he'd lusted for her in every possible way a boy could lust for a girl. She'd kept him so jacked up he didn't know if he was coming or going. Though he'd spent an inordinate amount of time coming on those few times each summer she'd swing through camp. Not once had she ever actually been present, however. No, he'd jerk off, or head down to Benny's and pick up someone willing. Someone more suitable for him. Someone who wasn't Kate Sutherland. But someone he'd pretended was Kate as he'd pounded himself relentlessly into her.

He'd taken Kate every which way a man could take a woman. And he'd never once so much as laid a finger on her. Back then he'd prided himself on his control, on not letting her push him into doing anything rash. Anything that would ever actually give her the chance to outright reject or humiliate him. Like it was some big fucking contest. Only he was the only one playing.

Last night, standing on her porch, a grown man who had moved far, far past his angry, rebellious youth, and even farther from any fantasies he'd held for one long-ago unattainable princess . . . he'd been so razor hard for wanting her he could have cut diamonds. It had taken every last ounce of restraint not to touch her. Not to push, poke, prod, or do whatever it took to see exactly where the boundaries might lie between them now.

He knew she'd watched him when they were teenagers. Knew he could have taken her. Just as he knew she'd never have asked him to, much less begged, as he'd fantasized about. God only knew what she'd have accused him of if he ever had.

But they were adults now. And he didn't know if he wanted her as a way to settle some past score that had existed only in his frustrated, confused mind . . . or if he wanted her because she was still the finest damn thing he'd ever laid eyes on.

She hadn't looked like the adult version of the unattainable, rich princess teenager last night. Cool, poised, and decked to the hilt in designer everything. She'd looked tired, worried, rumpled. He'd heard the strain in her voice . . . and wanted her so badly it made his teeth ache. Just thinking about the way she'd said his name, his given name, which he hadn't heard in years, made his body twitch to life all over again.

He jammed the phone back in his pocket. Time to hike to his car and make the trek down into town, contact Finn, set up the shipment, then buy whatever real supplies he could to settle in here for the duration. After that, he planned on heading back up here and camping out, literally, on her doorstep, until she heard him out and agreed to his help. Then he'd move into whichever cabin was in the best shape and get to work.

He had it all planned out.

If he could just figure out a way to do all that and not want to take her up against the nearest wall, he might actually survive this.

He started hiking back down the paved road toward the camp entrance. On second thought, maybe he owed her a thank-you. The more distracted he was by fighting his constant hard-on, the less time he spent having to fight the avalanche of childhood memories that threatened to bury him every time he let his guard down for half a second.

The sound of an engine slowed his steps. A moment later Kate rounded the bend in her little pickup. He made a mental note to look that up, too. He could understand the need for a truck over a sports car, but this one was not only undersized for the task, but had seen far better days. From his look around the camp, it also seemed to be the only vehicle she had on premises. He recalled her first car had been a gleaming midnight blue Porsche 911 that he'd wanted to get his hands on almost as badly as he wanted his hands on her. The Kate Sutherland he knew was not a pickup truck kind of woman, and definitely not a used-vehicle-of-any-kind type.

Which did absolutely nothing to explain why his pulse kicked up a notch and his body tightened in immediate response when she braked to a stop next to him and rolled down the window. Her mouth was pinched at the corners. Clearly she was not happy to see him. Perversely, that made him want to smile.

"Car break down?" she asked.

He debated on whether to get into it here, or wait until he had more of an advantage. Any advantage would be nice. So far, Kate had unknowingly robbed him of it, and quite easily, too. "No," he said, opting for blunt honesty. After all, it had gotten him pretty far in the world. "I was doing a perimeter check on the property."

Her eyes widened and her throat worked, but when she spoke, her tone gave no indication of how she felt about his unwanted incursion. Still the cool princess. Even with her trademark shoulder-length blond hair pulled back in a loose ponytail, not so much as a dab of makeup enhancing her smooth as silk skin, and sporting a faded blue sweater, she was every inch the debutante.

He curled his fingers inward and propped his fists on his hips. It was that or reach for her, see if he could muss up that too perfect control a little to match the rest of her look.

"A perimeter check," she repeated. "Funny, I don't remember hiring you on as a security guard."

"Yet," he responded, giving in to the grin that threatened out of nowhere. She frustrated him to the extreme in ways he didn't begin to try and understand. She sure as hell couldn't know. So why the almost giddy response his body had to even a hint of banter, he hadn't a frigging clue. He should have stayed in the damn city with Rafe. Chasing scum like Frank DiMateo, even getting shot at and blown up, was preferable to dealing with this inner turmoil shit. He'd spent the last eighteen years doing whatever he had to, to escape exactly that. He'd gotten pretty good at it, too. And yet, here he was. Right back where he'd started.

"You've got some guests," he told her. "Uninvited, as far as I can tell. Unless you're into playing some kind of kinky hide-and-go-seek that involves orange Day-Glo spray paint."

"It's just graffiti," she said, but her casual tone was belied by a quick swallow and the way her hands flexed on the steering wheel. "A pain in the ass, but harmless, I think."

"A pain, yes. Harmless, I'm not so sure. But I wasn't talking about the graffiti, or not only the graffiti."

She tensed further, and he could see her wage her own internal battle. He had no idea where she was off to this early in the morning, but it was clear she hadn't intended to deal with him, much less the news he was bringing her. For a moment, he felt bad about ruining her morning, which he was clearly doing. A night's sleep hadn't erased any of the strain on her porcelain-fine features. But she'd have other mornings, better ones, if she'd listen to him now.

"There's more," he told her, deciding there was no point in sugarcoating anything. If he wanted her to enlist his help, laying it out as bluntly as possible was probably best. The sooner he could get her to understand the potential depth of her situation, the sooner she'd agree to let him fix the problem. And the sooner he could get the hell out of there. "Where are you headed?"

"Ralston. Errands."

"At seven-fifteen in the morning?"

She simply stared at him, and for a second, dropped her guard. She was tired. But, if he wasn't mistaken, she was also more than a little unsettled. Either by what was going on at the camp, or by something else entirely, he had no idea. He didn't know Kate or what was going on in her personal life. A salient point he should make a personal note of.

"I was headed there myself. Let me ride along and I'll fill you in on what I know so far. And what my recommendations are."

She looked as if she was about to argue, but in the end, she jerked her chin to the other door. "Get in, then."

He found himself smiling again. "Please, no need to thank me, my pleasure." Like hell it was. Pleasure was going to have absolutely nothing to do with this little adventure. No matter if his rapidly responding body parts were telling him otherwise.

"I didn't ask for your help," she reminded him flatly when he rounded the other side.

He had to work the handle a few times, but finally wrenched the door open. "That's the beauty of this arrangement. You don't have to ask."

"Exactly. You're here because—well, because I don't know why exactly—but you don't have to be, so don't expect me to fall all over myself in gratitude."

"Yet," he said as he climbed in. His knees protested a little as he crammed them into the too small cab. "What, couldn't afford a real truck?"

She peeled out, spewing gravel behind her and making him grab for the door handle and his seat belt at the same time. "I'll be more than glad to drop you at your car."

He shot her a sideways glance, surprised to see the flash of real anger, not just irritation. He doubted she was all that angry with him. He hadn't been around long enough yet for that. *Give it time*, he thought. "What's got under your skin this morning?" he asked. "Besides me."

"None of your concern." She glanced at him, then shifted her gaze firmly back to the winding mountain road. "Why are you here, Donovan? Just tell me."

"Mac," he reminded her, shifting a little in his seat as the fit of his jeans got that much more uncomfortable. Dammit. "Just Mac. And I told you. I saw the write-up in the paper, saw you needed some help." He lifted a shoulder in what he hoped came off as a nonchalant shrug. "I happen to be in the helping people line of business these days. Or you can just consider it assistance from an old friend."

She snorted at that, then looked almost surprised at her own outburst. "We were hardly friends," she said, shifting uncomfortably, possibly feeling his steady regard.

He didn't look away. Couldn't, actually. The morning light was far more revealing than the porch light had been last night. Much to the detriment of his physical comfort, but it also got his mind to working, too. And not strictly on the business end of things. Not a good sign, but perhaps if he just indulged himself now, he could get it out of his system and find a way to take her out of his past and put her squarely into the present. As his client. Not some teenage sexual fantasy come true.

"No, I guess we weren't. Sentimental reasons, then. I grew up here, after all. Is it so strange to want to give back?"

She looked at him again, clearly suspicious. "You couldn't be bothered to come home after your father was buried, and please forgive me if I'm being completely insensitive, but you don't strike me as the sentimental type. Especially where Winnimocca is concerned. Not that I blame you."

Mac decided to drop all pretense. "You're right about that. I'd just as soon never step foot back on this property. A lot of memories are tied up here, most of them bad."

"Then my question stands. Why did you come back? And don't tell me it's about some stupid newspaper article. There has to be more to it than that."

"It's the God's honest truth that if not for that article, I wouldn't be here. But, actually, it was Rafe who spotted it."

"Rafael Santiago? You're still in touch with him?"

"I work with him. Finn Dalton, too. Rafe ordered me to come up here and fix the situation you're in. Finn backed him up." He raised his hand. "Scout's honor."

He saw the corner of her mouth quirk slightly. "Like any of you were ever scouts. Finn, maybe." She paused for a split second. "No, I don't see him playing by anyone else's rules either."

Mac smiled and settled back in his seat a little. She was talking to him, and, for the moment, not threatening to leave him on the side of the road. It was a start. "True. But my word is still good. Always has been. There have been times when that's all I had, so I don't give it lightly."

She didn't say anything to that, concentrating on the road instead, probably choosing her next words. Or figuring out how she could ditch him in town. "So you're saying the Unholy Trinity has this sudden vested interest in saving a rotting old camp for sentimental reasons, or because of some little newspaper write-up."

"Hardly little. It was the *New York Times*. And the headline was something about an heiress giving up her inheritance to take control of family lake property in order to open up a camp for disabled kids. Is that true?"

"Which part? That I swapped my inheritance with Shelby? Or that I'm planning on a camp for kids? And why is it I think both of those things surprise the hell out of you?"

"They both do, frankly. Although, perhaps you're doing well enough on your own not to need Louisa's money."

"Does it look like I'm rolling in it, Donovan?" She briefly lifted a hand. "Mac."

"I have no idea what game you might be playing at. With Shelby involved and an inheritance worth a lot of zeros, now vandalism, and rumors of developers being involved—"

Kate braked and abruptly pulled over. "Get out."

"I'm not judging, Kate. I'm just calling it like I see it. Do you want me to sugarcoat it?"

"I want you to get out. And stay off camp property. My property." She wasn't looking at him, and her tone was flat and hard. But he saw the tremor in her jaw, the vein standing out in stark relief along the side of her neck, and the white knuckles gripping the steering wheel.

"Someone isn't just spraying unhappy little messages on trees, Kate. Someone has been watching you," he said without preamble. "You may not like me or what I have to say, or believe why I'm here, but that's beside the point. The point is I have the resources to help get you out of whatever it is you've gotten yourself into."

Her cheeks drained of color, and she swallowed hard.

"You may not even know what you're up against," he said, a tad less stridently. "So stop looking the gift horse you have in the mouth and let me help you."

Her chest rose and fell more quickly.

"Look at me."

Her throat worked.

"Kate."

She swung her gaze to his, and there was no mistaking the

fatigue, wariness, and the healthy dose of fear he saw there. "What?"

"To be perfectly honest, I haven't the faintest freaking clue why I'm here. Maybe it's some sort of whack karmic justice, or God having a really big laugh at my expense. All I know is that I felt—we all felt—like it was the right thing to do." Now it was his turn to look away. Because he still wasn't being completely truthful with her. "And maybe it's because once I saw your picture, it stirred up a bunch of stuff I thought I was long done with. Stuff that not even my father dying stirred up."

He felt her gaze flicker to his and looked up in time to catch it, hold it.

"Meaning what?" she asked.

"Meaning we have unfinished business, you and me."

"We don't have any business. We never did."

"I know." His grin was slow, but it kept on growing until he saw the color steal back into her cheeks. "That's the unfinished part."

Chapter 4

Kate didn't know whether to laugh, cry, or throw up. Her stomach was in knots, her emotions were all over the map . . . and her body was responding to Donovan's grin as though she were still seventeen and prowling the campgrounds trying to sneak a glimpse of him with his shirt off.

"The only business I'm interested in is getting my camp up and running."

"What's the holdup on starting the renovations? How long have you been up here?"

"A month. I'm still assessing what needs to be done and organizing the labor I'll need." Although that had also proved to be a more difficult challenge than she'd anticipated.

"And?"

"And what? It's not something that gets done overnight. My target opening date is next spring. I'm in good shape."

"Tell me about the developers. Did the papers have that right? Is there interest from them on the property?"

"I—I wouldn't know. Exactly."

He frowned. "What do you mean, exactly?"

"Shelby and I still have some details to work out. He's—still the legal owner of the property. Any dealings with developers would have been through him." Something she'd thought long and hard about after Donovan had left last night. Could they be any part of the reason why he hadn't shown up? She knew about the articles; her attorney had mentioned them to her during their last talk, that word had gotten out about the wacky heiress to Louisa Graham's fortune giving it all away. She hadn't read them or paid any real attention to what he'd been saying about them. She didn't get the *Times* up here in Ralston. And her focus was on getting started on the renovations, not on what Manhattan society thought of her business dealings. But maybe she should have paid closer attention. The developer angle had been news to her.

"What do you know about Timberline?"

"Is that the development company? I've never heard of them."

"The news story made it sound like—"

"I don't care what they made it sound like. I haven't heard of them. If it wasn't for my lawyer—and you—I wouldn't even know my inheritance situation was news."

"They didn't interview you for the article?"

She shook her head.

That quieted him for a moment.

The silence didn't soothe her rapidly fraying nerves. "Is there a problem? What in the world did it say? I thought it was just some piece ridiculing me for giving up Louisa's fortune."

She felt his gaze on her.

"I wouldn't have come up here if that had been the case. It specifically mentioned the vandalism and the developers. If you didn't tell them about that, who did? Shelby?"

Her mind was spinning again. "I—I don't know. I suppose it would have to have been." Except her stepbrother didn't know about the vandalism. Not through her anyway. And she seriously doubted he was keeping close tabs on the property itself. It had sat vacant now for almost a decade, and clearly no one had been paying any attention to it up to this point.

But then he hadn't mentioned the developers to her either.

Had he suddenly developed a renewed interest in his initial inheritance?

"What steps have you taken regarding the graffiti and any other damage?"

"What did the article say about the development deal, specifically?" she asked at the same time.

Mac answered first. "Not much, other than an attempted buyout had been made. And that there had been reports of vandalism on the property. Did you report that to the sheriff's office?"

"Yes." For all the good it had done. Gilby had assured her it was nothing but some local delinquents. Except Ralston, the nearest town to Winnimocca, was still almost an hour away. She had no "locals." She'd gotten up this morning and called his office, only to be brushed off again. So she'd decided to head down and park herself in front of Gilby himself until he agreed to send someone out again to look at the new damage.

"Did you file a report?"

"For what it was worth, yes."

"What's been done?"

She debated telling him. She still didn't know why he was really here. But a trip to see Gilby would give him the same information. "They sent someone out, but he essentially patted me on the shoulder and told me not to worry my pretty little head about it, that it was just some kids having a laugh at my expense. He said if I actually saw anybody and could give a description, or saw a vehicle on the property that I could get plate information off of, he'd be happy to follow up on that. Otherwise, it was a matter for me to take up with my insurance company."

"But he didn't happen to mention that anyone else's property was being vandalized in the area." Mac made it a statement.

She shook her head. "No. And I sort of thought 'Go Home, Rich Bitch' was pretty personal, but they didn't seem to share my concern."

"Is the sheriff aware of the particulars in terms of ownership of the property?"

She glanced over at him, her wariness returning. "I don't know why he would. Through me filing the report, he knows I've come back to rebuild here and open a camp. But I've also been making calls to some of the construction businesses in Ralston, trying to line up estimates." Not that she'd been all that successful on that front either. She'd chalked it up to the old-fashioned mentality of most of the guys she'd talked to, who didn't want to deal with a woman. They'd find out she was more determined than they were narrow-minded. She figured as soon as she hired one crew, and they realized she was serious and could pay them, the rest would come calling. "Ralston is a small town, word travels, so I'm sure it's no secret around the whole county that I'm here and planning to reopen the camp. I assume they all believe I'm the owner, and I let them believe that. It's merely a formality anyway."

"When does it become official?"

She faltered. "I—I'm not sure."

There was a brief pause; then he asked, "Where were you yesterday?" When she looked at him warily, he lifted his shoulders. "You were wearing a nice suit when I saw you last night, carrying a briefcase. I don't imagine there's much need for that in Ralston."

"I was in the city for meetings pertaining to the property. But . . . it's not finalized yet."

She waited for him to poke and prod further, but he switched tactics. "I'm just trying to follow the same path the reporter did who put the article together. So far, their sources would—or could—include Shelby and the sheriff."

"Or possibly anyone in Ralston. For all I know the vandalism is common knowledge."

"Is the *Sentinel* still up and running?" Donovan was referring to the paper that was based in Ralston, but pretty much served everyone on this side of the county.

"Yes. I used it when I started compiling names and businesses to call."

"Did they run a story on the vandalism?"

"No. I mean, not that I know of. No one contacted me. It might have been mentioned in the little sheriff's crime column, but other than that—why do you ask? What difference would that make?"

"I don't know yet. But, at least back when I lived here, it was big news if someone ran the only light in town. You'd think this would have been at least filler on the local interest page if nothing else."

She shrugged, though if his goal was to further unnerve her, he was doing a good job. "Winnimocca isn't all that close to town. Maybe it never came up."

"And after telling the sheriff about your plans to open a camp for disabled kids, no one came out here to do a little local feature story either?"

"No, but honestly, Donov—Mac, I didn't really assume they would. I haven't even begun repairs yet. Maybe they're waiting until there's more of a story. Who knows?" She didn't tell him that her other mission this morning, after seeing Gilby, was to pay a visit to the head of the Ralston Chamber of Commerce. Her intent there was to talk up the camp a little, see if she could get his support by bringing to his attention the future business the camp might provide to Ralston, in exchange for him talking it up a little with the local merchants, most notably anyone having anything to do with construction.

"Is there anyone else?"

Lost in her thoughts, she didn't follow the question. "Anyone else what?"

"Anyone else who might be talking. Do you have any partners, silent or otherwise? Anyone helping you in any way or otherwise involved with you?"

She knew he was talking business. He sounded just like the detective he used to be, and she was definitely starting to feel interrogated. And yet she didn't dare so much as glance at him. On the off chance there was anything personal behind the question. "No. Just me. I—I have connections with people I hope to hire as instructors and counselors, but in terms of ownership and management, it's just me."

He fell silent again, and maybe it was her own mounting tension over the increasingly negative situation she was finding herself in that made the air between them seem to crackle. But, at least from her perspective, the awareness and tension were operating on another level as well. She did risk a quick sideways glance at him then; she couldn't help it. His profile was solemn, his jaw hard and set. His gaze was fixed on some point out the front windshield. And she had no clue what was going through his mind. Chances were he really was here on something of a lark, to help her out. Chances were, he didn't want or desire anything else from her other than a job well done and maybe a polite thank-you.

She settled more deeply into the sprung cushion seat and tried to tell herself all the reasons why being disappointed with that probable reality was a really dangerous way to feel.

"What are you planning to do during the off season?" he asked rather abruptly.

"What off season? Spring is here. Perfect time to get work done. By winter all the exterior work should be done, leaving only the inside refurbishing for the colder months."

"I meant what are your plans during the off season of the camp. Louisa wintered in Manhattan or whatever island beckoned." She felt his gaze shift to her. "Where do you plan to hibernate?"

She wanted to ask him what that had to do with the vandalism and possible developer intrusion, but didn't. Maybe his mind was following the same personal track hers was. Only what difference it made, she had no idea. "Are you—is your people-helper business based in the city?" she asked in return.

"No. Virginia. We have Finn's father's old place. It's the base of operations for Trinity."

She happened to know that "old place" was a majestic sea of acreage in the old-wealth section of Virginia horse country. "Trinity? As in—" She glanced at him in time to see his lips curve.

"Yes," he admitted, "as in Unholy Trinity."

"I can't believe you guys stuck together all these years."

Mac didn't respond to that; instead, he shifted the focus back to her. "So, where do you live? I mean, normally."

"I live in that cabin back at camp." She knew what he was getting after, but she wanted to let him hang himself on his own narrow-minded preconceptions of her. It wouldn't be the first time.

"Okay," he said with the same exaggerated patience. "And this winter?"

"I'll still be living in the cabin. It is my sole residence now."

"Where were you before moving up here?"

"Not that it has anything to do with the situation at hand, but before moving here I lived in university-funded housing just off campus from where I was teaching."

"You're a teacher?"

She did look at him then. "I'm opening up a camp to help disabled kids learn new methods to help them cope with their limitations. What did you think I did?"

"I—I don't know. I hadn't really thought about it."

She liked that little momentary catch in his voice. She doubted he was often caught off guard. Unreasonably cheered by having the upper hand, even if it was likely short-lived, she took advantage. "I'm not my mother, Donovan," she said, purposely using his given name. And maybe he'd just have to get used to it. He simply wasn't Mac to her. "I'm not here to play camp owner to the offspring of the wealthy as a way to springboard myself into the realms of high society. This will be a working camp dedicated to helping those who need it, whether they can afford it or not. I am already working with several nonprofits and other charitable foundations in hopes of raising money to fund scholarships or something similar for kids who can't otherwise attend. And I won't be handing off the day-to-day management to someone else. I will be running this place from the ground up. It is my dream to see this camp realized, and I'll do whatever it takes to make it a reality."

He didn't say anything at first, then, finally, "I'm sorry."

"For?" she said archly, still revved up from her little speech and not quite ready to abdicate her temporary throne.

"It's been a long time. We really don't know each other. I shouldn't have made assumptions."

It wasn't the best apology she'd ever gotten, or even the most heartfelt, but coming from him, it was more than she'd expected.

She shifted her attention back to the road. "As for winter, I don't plan for this to be a summer-only camp, though that will be when we'll do the most work. Spring and fall will be heavily utilized and, if I can make it happen, I'm hoping to use the winter months as a teachers retreat where instructors can come and study and learn more about the alternative methods I plan to implement here."

"An impressive agenda." He paused for a moment, then said, "Not that it's any of my business, but—"

She barked out a laugh. "Not that it's stopped you so far."

They both smiled a little. "True," he said. "But what I was going to ask doesn't really pertain to the case; it's personal. I'm just curious." So, she was just a case. She'd felt as though a lot of what was transpiring between them was personal.

Being all business would certainly be smarter. Only she wasn't feeling all that smart at the moment. "What are you curious about?"

"Why you gave up the fortune Louisa left you for a run-down camp. You could have helped a lot of kids with that money, opened up a camp anywhere."

She smiled. "Oh, that."

"Well, it's a valid question."

"It is, and, trust me, you're not the first to ask it." She laughed wearily. "My attorney was the first to ask me; only his language was a little more direct." She steered the truck around a particularly tight curve and tried to decide how best to explain. Not that she had to. But for whatever reason, his opinion seemed to matter, at the moment anyway. He'd already found out she wasn't the spoiled society girl he seemed to think she'd become. If she could dismantle a few other misconceptions, that was fine by her, too.

"Initially, it was a knee-jerk reaction to the disbursement of her assets. Both Shelby and I were shocked. Though, once that wore off, we both agreed that it was quintessential Louisa to pull something like that. One of the few things we ever agreed on." She sighed a little. "Anyway, long story short, I'd been estranged from my mother for a very long time, since my college years. Shelby, on the other hand, had stood by her and helped her invest her money and build her empire. By rights it was his."

"So why dump the camp on him? Was it more to punish him, then?"

"No, she got us both. Shelby's father, George, was Louisa's third husband, and Winnimocca was his when they married, so, by rights, it passed to Shelby. I was Louisa's only biological and legal child, as she'd never adopted Shelby and went on to remarry after his father's death. So, along that line of thinking, I was heiress to her personal throne, so to speak. Only neither of us wanted what we got. I blurted out that we should swap, both because it was the right thing to do, and, admittedly, because it thwarted my mother's final exertion of control over us."

"But then you, or your attorney, came to your senses . . ."

She smiled. "Well, yes and no. The emotional part of my reaction passed, but the rational part was still there." She glanced at him. "Inheriting that kind of estate is a lot more complicated than people understand. It's not like I won the lottery and someone was just going to hand me some huge check. Her money was all tied up in a variety of business investments, all kinds of things. Just randomly liquidating things in order to get an influx of cash to use to buy and fund a camp wasn't all that simple, and would put a lot of people out of work. And that's just the part that could be sold off. A lot of it was tied up in all kinds of partnerships and the like. Like I said, really complicated."

"Actually, I do understand that a little. More than you might think." He waved a hand. "But go on."

She was going to ask him to elaborate, but decided to circle back to it when she was done. "I had no desire to step in and run or dismantle her empire."

"Empire?"

"She was married to Trenton Graham—"

"I know. They mentioned it in the article. But they divorced."

"Well, that particular divorce settlement pole-vaulted her the rest of the way into the stratosphere of society and wealth, and she'd apparently learned more than a thing or two about empire building while married to the king of empire building. More importantly, though, so did Shelby. He'd helped her build it, and was more than ready to tackle the whole thing. I was more than ready to let him. I just wanted my camp—his camp. Which he had no interest in and neither had Louisa. It wasn't on their radar. They couldn't have cared less about the property."

"Still, he had to know—"

"Let me finish. I'm not a complete idiot. I might not have

agreed with my mother's methods, personally or in business, and I wasn't around while she amassed most of what she'd left behind, but I wasn't going to walk away from everything either. It took a while, but Shelby and I hammered out an agreement that resulted in me getting the deed to the Winni-mocca property, along with a cash settlement that will enable me to cover taxes, reconstruction, and some seed money to launch the place. If I can't make a go of it from there . . ." She shrugged. "Then I lose. Ultimately, I'm responsible for my success or failure. So I took the launch, but beyond that, it's up to me. And, even with all the headaches and Shelby challenges and now whatever the heck is going on with the vandalism and maybe the people in town . . . I still wouldn't have it any other way."

"I can see your point."

She laughed again. "Good, because a lot of people thought I was nuts. I guess I just want to be in control of my destiny, not following my mother's. I'll take the helping hand, whether she intended it or not, but nothing more. That's Shelby's domain and he's welcome to it." *Or will be,* she thought, if she could figure out why he hadn't shown up to sign the papers. "So, now it's my turn. You said you had personal experience with inheritance; only I didn't think Donny Mac—"

"Not my father, Finn's. I don't know how much you knew of their relationship, but it sounds like the mirror image of yours and Louisa's. Only in Finn's father's case, he was rather unscrupulous about how he went about amassing his fortune."

"Whereas my mother just married hers," she said with a smile. It was odd, talking to him like this, about things that she'd been so sensitive about before. It wasn't like that with him. His pragmatism made it easier, she supposed. And his own past.

"Well, to each his own, but Finn had personal reasons why taking on his father's empire—also a surprise inheritance—

was untenable to him. He didn't want it, at first, but, as you say, it's not as easy as just saying no thanks. It was his whether he wanted it or not, and there was no Shelby in the wings. Like your mother's situation, the inheritance was complicated. It took quite a long time, years in fact, but he did dismantle the empire, piece by piece, doing his best not to screw over the little people, but it happened on occasion. Even just putting the more unscrupulous ones out of business, there was no way to protect everyone, and there were innocent bystanders, so to speak. But the bigger plan was to use the money to help the very same people whose backs Harrison Dalton spent a lifetime stepping on in order to move up in the world."

"So, some karmic justice, then. I can appreciate that."

He smiled. "You know, I'm beginning to think you can."

She shot him a smile. "Beginning to?"

He lifted a shoulder. "I'm still getting to know you."

She shouldn't have been warmed by his easy tone, the hint of a friendly smile on his lips. His apparent interest in getting to know her, case or no case. What she did know was that leaning on him, even a little bit, would be dangerous. She'd spent most of her adult life learning how to lean only on herself. Just because things were looking a little tricky didn't mean she had to drape herself over the first shoulder that presented itself. "I'm surprised you didn't already know more about all of it, what with all your skulking around."

"I only had a day to dig. I hadn't gotten around to that yet. I was too busy trying to figure out how dangerous this person is who's getting his jollies from vandalizing your property." There was a long pause; then he added, "And I don't skulk. I track."

She tried mightily to ignore his dry tone. He'd been a bad boy charmer in his youth, all moody and temperamental with the male campers, but never without a smile for anything in pink camp shorts or a tennis skirt. She'd been as susceptible as the next girl. Though he'd never once aimed that grin at her. For someone who'd passed the thirty-year mark a few years ago, she shouldn't feel all giddy because Donovan MacLeod had finally aimed that heart-stopping grin at her.

"I do admire what you're doing, Kate. Or trying to do. It's a lot of work. Refurbishing the buildings for year-round use alone is quite an undertaking."

"Trust me, I'm fully aware of the monumental task in front of me. I just want to settle whatever it is that needs settling, and get on with it. I mean, what's the big deal about me taking on this old, unwanted property anyway?"

"Maybe it's not as unwanted as you think it is."

She sighed and tried not to think about that. What she wanted to believe was that there was some simple explanation for why Shelby was a no-show yesterday, and that they'd set another day and time, sign the papers, then she'd show the people of Ralston what a woman was capable of when her mind was set, and everything else would fall into place. "Maybe, maybe not. I'll know more when I talk to Shelby. So, are we all done with the interrogation, Detective?"

He smiled at her dry tone. "I'm not interrogating. I'm researching, just trying to fill in as many of the blanks as possible. When will you be able to get started on the renovation work and construction? Do you have everything lined up?" He shifted slightly in his seat, which wasn't easy considering his tall, broad-shouldered frame was all but crammed into the cab of her truck. A tall, broad-shouldered frame she was having an increasingly difficult time ignoring. It didn't help any that she could feel his gaze pinned on her.

"That's actually part of my agenda in town this morning. I'm going to see Sheriff Gilby about the latest graffiti hit-and-run; then I have an appointment with the head of the chamber of commerce to try and get a little goodwill established."

"You say that like you expect resistance."

"Oh, I didn't expect it, but I'm getting it all the same."

"Why? You're bringing work in the short term and a customer base in the long run. They should be lining up to help you out. What's the reaction been?"

"I'm not sure I understand it entirely, but I think it's just old-fashioned resistance to working with or for a woman. I can't actually hire anyone yet, until Shelby and I settle things, but—"

"And you don't think that might be related to the vandalism?"

"I don't know. I hadn't put those two things together. The town isn't exactly right down the road from the camp."

"Well, if the townsfolk aren't happy to see you, and someone is spray painting 'go home' on your trees, you might want to." He shifted back. "Something's not adding up here, Kate."

She wanted to believe he'd spent too much time on the streets of New York City and, therefore, had just jumped to the worst case scenario out of habit, but when he put it that way, it was hard to deny he might have a point. "It's not like anyone has been hostile, or said a negative word. I'm just having a hard time finding my niche in town. I haven't been here all that long. I figure once I actually hire someone, anyone, and they see I'm serious, they'll be a little more excited about the possibility of getting some work from me. I chalked it up to them not wanting to commit labor and supplies to a job they don't fully trust is happening yet, possibly turning down other work in the meantime."

"And you might be right. But have you thought about the possibility that it might be more than old-fashioned prejudice at work here? Maybe they've gotten wind of the developer interest."

She shrugged, suddenly feeling very inept and not liking it one bit. "I don't know. I mean, I didn't know about it, so I'm not sure it's common knowledge, but then I don't spend a lot of time in town. I've only been down a few times, for supplies and to gather information on the local construction busi-

nesses and the like. I haven't exactly been a presence there."
Yet.

She wasn't sure what direction his thoughts were taking,
but hers were going in a number of disturbing directions all
by themselves. As much as she didn't want to believe it, it
looked as if there was a possibility she was caught up in
something a little more serious than she thought. She'd been
so focused on getting things done with Shelby, she'd never
taken the time to connect everything together. She'd just
wanted to get her name in print as owner of the place, then
figure out the rest.

"This isn't your problem, you know," she told him at
length.

"I'm not going away, if that's where you're going with this.
One way or the other, I'm here for the duration."

Her eyes widened. "The duration of what?"

"The duration of however long it takes to resolve the
problems you're facing. At the very least, until you get your
name on those papers and we make sure you're not under
any kind of serious threat from whoever is vandalizing the
place. We should look into the developer end of things, too."

"What could they possibly have to do with vandalizing my
property?"

Mac shrugged. "They want something bad enough and
can't get it through proper channels . . ."

"I think you're being paranoid."

"And I think you should find out exactly what Shelby is up
to, too. What contact he's had with them. I'm telling you, it
all probably factors in."

"And you know this because . . . ?"

"Because my instincts tell me so. And they're rarely
wrong. I wouldn't be sitting here in this truck if I didn't listen
to them."

He was so intent, so serious, so certain. It was unnerving,
both his mere presence and his focus on what, by rights, was
none of his business. She'd be lying if she said there wasn't a

tiny part of her that was grateful for his timely intrusion. But it was that timely part that still had her concerned. Maybe she was the paranoid one. "Exactly what kind of business is it that you three run anyway?"

Which should have been the first question out of her mouth when the other two names came up. They'd been known as the Unholy Trinity with good reason from the first summer they'd united at camp. If there was trouble brewing, the trail had inevitably led back to one of the three, or, as was more often the case, all three combined.

Kate hadn't spent much time out there each summer, but between her brief jaunts and listening to her mother complain about, well, everything, it was no secret that the three of them hadn't done much to make camp life run smoothly. Each of them was so different, but still a black sheep of sorts in his own way. Donovan was the bastard kid of the camp handyman, Donny Mac, who'd spent a fair share of time in the Ralston drunk tank, when he wasn't beating up on his only son. Rafe was an inner city kid whose mom worked several jobs, one as a maid for some Wall Street shark who made himself feel better by sending her kid to rich kids' camp every summer. He'd been a fish out of water with an attitude the size of the Empire State Building. He'd bonded with Donovan immediately.

Finn was the unexpected addition to the trio. Every bit as wealthy as his camp counterparts, if not more so, he should have fit right in at Camp Winnimocca. He was the stereotypical golden boy, from his blond, bronzed good looks to his big fat trust fund. By all rights, he should have been camp leader. Except Finn had been rebelling against his father, his own wealth, and his defacto place in the world, pretty much, it seemed, since birth. He'd intentionally aligned himself with the camp outcasts and all but dared anyone to challenge his choice in friends. In fact, he had challenged them, and their preconceived notions, all the time.

Kate had secretly admired, even coveted, his rebellious nature. But it wasn't Finn's gleaming perfection that had caught her eye, or fueled her midnight fantasies. The source of every single one of those had been Donovan.

"So if Finn spent years tearing down his father's empire while you were chasing bad guys and Rafe was doing God knows what, when did you start this joint venture?"

"About eighteen months ago. Once Finn had everything set and control over his own destiny, so to speak, he brought us in."

Doing what, exactly?"

There was a pause. Then he said, "Helping people."

She glanced at him. "In what capacity, exactly?"

"In whatever capacity they need us. I'm all for justice and the American way; it's part of why I became a cop. I'm proof positive you can make anything out of yourself if you want it badly enough. This is the land of opportunity. Only, some folks don't always get a fair shake. Either because they can't help themselves, or because the system fails them, which it often does. Having been on the inside of it, it's an under-staffed, underpaid, overworked system, which, frankly, works far better than it should given the circumstances it op-erates under. I credit that to the human spirit of those in-volved. But there are insurmountable obstacles, both within and without. We . . . overcome those obstacles for people who otherwise can't do so on their own."

"And how do they pay you for these . . . services you pro-vide them?"

"They don't."

"Finn ended up with that much?"

Donovan smiled. "Let's just say it was more than enough seed money to start a global chain of your camps. In our case, we rather enjoy spending all of Harrison's ill-gotten gains helping people. And Finn's smart about money. He knows how to make money with money. Without stepping on any-one to do it."

She glanced at him. "So, I'm one of your charity cases, then?

Although I suppose the irony of you having to rescue me is somewhat satisfying, I'm still having a hard time with—"

"It's not charity," he said, cutting her off abruptly. "We fix things that need fixing. Things that shouldn't have gone wrong in the first place. People benefit, yes, but they're far from charity cases. They're victims in need of a little extra help. When the system doesn't work, or simply can't work, we do. All three of us spent a lot of time trying to work it from the other side. Now we work it from our side."

She sat back a little, surprised by the vehemence of his response. "Okay. So it's a noble endeavor. I still don't see where I rate your assistance. Even you admit you still thought I was living the high life, perhaps just dabbling in this little camp venture. Surely there are other, far more pressing cases out there."

"There always are. More than we can do anything about. But we're not a charity. We don't advertise. We're not Make-A-Wish. And it's definitely not about being noble. If anything, it's a purely selfish endeavor."

"You help people out of jams and don't charge them. How is that selfish?"

"We pick and choose who we help. Our reasons are our own. Sometimes because it's the right thing to do, and sometimes because it feels good to stick it to someone who needs to be stuck." He tensed his shoulders, then flattened them out, as if purposefully trying to control his temper. And she was reminded then of the angry, recalcitrant youth he'd once been. She'd be wise to remember that side of him was still there, too, no matter how deeply buried or tamed into submission.

"We're fortunate to have the resources to indulge our little endeavor. And yes, it feels good—no, great—to be able to make good things happen, to set things right. But it's not like we're performing miracles here. We're just making sure the good guys win every once in a while." He grinned suddenly, and her entire body went on red-hot alert.

Yeah, she'd be real wise to remember all the sides to Dono-van MacLeod were still there.

"I just wouldn't necessarily say we always use good guy methods, is all."

She slowed down as she rounded one of the last curves be-fore the road bottomed out in the valley, heading across and into Ralston. "Exactly what kind of methods are you talking about?"

"Let's just say we basically go by the all's-well-that-ends-well motto. How we get there is the fun part. And nobody's business but ours."

She was almost sorry she'd asked. The three of them had taken mischievous behavior to new highs—and lows—back in the camp days. She couldn't even imagine what that meant as adults . . . with endless funds at their disposal. "So," she said at length, "if I'm not a charity case, then I'm what, some sort of joke to you guys?" She held up her hand. "I mean, you had no use for me or 'my kind' when you were young, and I'm not getting that your opinion of the privileged or wealthy has changed all that much. So this must have been quite amusing to you guys, helping out the poor little rich girl."

"There is nothing remotely amusing about this job for me. Coming back here . . . well, I think I've made my opinion clear on that. I was honest when I said I really don't know why I took this on. I just knew—we all did—that it was something we needed to do. Does it really have to be any more complicated than that?"

"No. But you'll have to forgive me for being at least a lit-tle suspicious. After all, there's no denying I am having a few problems getting the camp up and running. And then you bounce in from out of nowhere, riding to my rescue for no ap-parent gain, when, if you'd asked me up until that moment, I'd have said you'd probably enjoy knowing I was in trouble."

"Who else could I be here helping? Shelby? Hardly. If it

will make you feel any better, check with Finn or Rafe and talk to them. I'll call right now."

"On what? Cell service is highly unreliable."

He slipped out a slender black and silver phone from his jacket pocket. "Satellite phone. Finn's latest toy."

"Awesome," she said dryly, even as she had to restrain herself from asking to see it. Just because she didn't live the high life any longer, and hadn't for longer than she could remember, didn't mean her head couldn't be turned by the occasional bright, shiny object. Which was the very last thing she'd admit to Donovan, all things considered. "But it wouldn't matter. Like I could trust them any more than I can trust you."

His eyes widened at that. "When have I ever done anything untrustworthy?"

"You couldn't stand the sight of me when we were young. You hated me and everything I represented. It was clear on your face every time I stepped foot on camp property. Of course, their having money didn't keep you from charming the pants—literally—off of every other girl in camp, but—" She broke off when he started laughing. "What's so damn funny?"

"You were jealous."

"I was not! Why in the hell would I be jealous of—" She stopped abruptly, but it was far too late.

His smile died. Well, not completely. What remained was rueful and, if she wasn't mistaken, a bit disappointed. "Why would you be jealous of the attentions of the son of the local drunk? Yeah, I don't know the answer to that either. As to why I didn't favor you with my apparently much wanted attentions way back when, I'll be frank and honest with you. Something, by the way, I have always been and will always be, with you and everyone else."

She didn't say anything. She was too busy feeling exactly like the rich society bitch he'd always thought her to be. She slowed down to a stop in front of the train tracks that crossed the main road before entering town. Just her luck the lights were flashing and the bars were lowered.

Mac shifted his weight and turned toward her more fully this time, his shoulders filling up way too much of the rapidly shrinking space between them. She felt his hot gaze on her and was completely helpless not to turn and gaze directly back. Her skin prickled in awareness, her nipples tightened to two painful little points, and no amount of squeezing was going to stop the ache building between her thighs. She wanted to damn him for that, but she suspected the problem—as it had always been—was hers and hers alone.

So his next words stunned the hell out of her.

"I've wanted to put my hands on you from the very moment I first laid eyes on you. So badly I could taste it. I spent an inordinate amount of my summer months thinking about you, wondering when you'd show up, wondering if I'd make it through the torture once again without acting on it."

She had no idea how to respond to that. "I—I thought you couldn't stand me. The way you looked at me—"

"Could have melted the polar ice cap. You saw what you wanted to see."

"What I saw was you smiling at every girl but me. With me, you were always scowling. Why?"

"I learned very early not to want things I couldn't get for myself. So I never let myself want anything I couldn't have. Except you."

That shocked her silent. When she finally found her voice again, it was tight, and a bit raspy due to her throat having gone completely dry. "Why—why did you think you couldn't—"

He laughed rather harshly. "Oh, come on, you just admitted it yourself when you questioned why someone like you would be jealous of the attention someone like me would pay to other girls."

"I didn't say that. Not exactly," she added, knowing she'd

done exactly that. "I wasn't speaking from my own perspective, just the expectations of our surroundings and, for that matter, of you."

"Cop-out."

Her cheeks burned. Mostly because he was right. "We were from opposite sides of the tracks. That was a fact I couldn't change. Nor could I change that I was the owner's daughter. Or that I led a privileged life that you did not. But that's exactly what I'm getting at. What did or didn't happen between us was more a product of our respective backgrounds, and the surroundings we found ourselves in, than a reflection of what we might have really wanted." Too late, she realized what she'd admitted.

If she'd thought his gaze intense a moment ago, she'd had no idea of the intensity of which he was capable. Perhaps it was the close confines, the air between them growing more damp and humid as their body heat changed the temperature inside the cab of the truck. Or maybe it was simply Donovan.

"What did you really want, Kate?"

She looked at him for a long time, knowing she should shut this conversation down right then and there. Instead, she told him the truth. "I wanted you." She leaned back, wishing she could put more distance between them. "There, ego satisfied now?"

He smiled, but it didn't diminish one whit the heat in his gaze. "This isn't about ego. I know you watched me. I know I might have talked my way into your fancy French panties."

Her mouth dropped open. "How do you know what underwear I wore?"

He laughed then. "I flat out state I could have gotten into your pants anytime I wanted, and you're indignant because I know what you were wearing under those prim little designer slacks?"

Her face burned again, and she folded her arms across her chest. He was overwhelming every part of her, physically and emotionally. It was too much all at once. She wasn't prepared to handle this—or him. She should have never let him climb in her truck. Hell, she should have never let him on her property in the first place, not that he'd asked permission.

Thankfully, she could still do something about that.

Before she could open her mouth, though, Donovan reached over and fingered a loose tendril of hair that had escaped from the soft ponytail she'd put her hair in that morning.

She should swat his hand away, yet she discovered she was absolutely incapable of doing so. In fact, it took considerable will not to turn her head slightly so her cheek would brush the backs of his fingers. Honestly, she had to get him the hell out of this truck. And out of her life.

"I knew you wanted me, Kate. I might not have smiled at you, but I thought you understood the feeling was mutual," he said, his voice an octave lower and more than a shade rougher. "With the other girls, it didn't matter if they rejected me. Or if they went running back to their rich boyfriends after tasting what I had to offer. I knew I wasn't anything more than a cheap thrill, but that didn't bother me. In fact, it sort of amused me, to know I could have them, make them come back looking for more."

She swallowed hard when he let his blunt fingertips slide down the length of the strand of hair, then let it go. She held her breath, wondering if he was going to touch her skin, touch . . . anything he wanted to.

"But you," he said, his voice so quiet now, so deep, it vibrated the air in the close confines of the truck. "I couldn't stand the thought of you looking at me like that. Thinking of me like that. With you it was different."

"Why?" she managed on a choked whisper.

"You mattered." He shook his head, that rueful smile flickering across his still handsome as sin features. "One of the mysteries of the universe, I guess. But I knew it when I laid eyes on you. And no one was more surprised than I was to discover that when I looked at you again, in that newspaper article, after all these years, all I've seen, all I've done . . . something in my gut twisted up like I was seventeen all over again." He brushed the tips of his fingers over her lips, making her breath catch in her throat. "You always had that effect on me, Kate. I guess time and distance, and a lot of growing up, didn't change that."

"Is—is that why you came back, then? You had some wild reaction to a picture of me, so . . . you came back as some sort of personal test?"

His gaze dropped to her mouth, and it was all she could do not to wet her lips.

"Maybe that's part of it. I don't know. I do know one thing, though." He pressed his fingers beneath her chin, tilted her head slightly. And she did absolutely nothing to stop him. "I no longer seem to have any restraint around you. Or maybe it's just I see no reason to any longer. I'm not the insecure teenager I was back then, desperate for approval, terrified of rejection."

"You were hardly that," she murmured, surprised she could form words at all.

"I was exactly that, with those who mattered. It was a very short list. But you were on it."

He leaned closer. She swallowed hard.

"Donovan—"

"Kick me out of the truck now, Kate."

"I—"

"On second thought, don't. Not yet." He tipped her chin up farther and leaned closer. "At least not until I give you a better reason to."

Chapter 5

Even as he took her mouth with his, Mac knew it was the wrong thing to do. And he didn't give a flat damn. He was finally getting a taste of Kate Sutherland. And from the moment his lips brushed hers, he knew it was going to be worth the wait.

No seventeen-year-old could have appreciated a mouth that sweet, or understood the complexity of that one tiny breath caught at the back of her throat. At thirty-five, every nuance registered.

If he'd planned this, he would have crushed his mouth to hers, overwhelmed them both right off, so neither would have a moment to think or react until it was too late, the deed finally done and out of the way, no longer taunting him with its inevitability. Then he might have had a fighting chance at focusing on the job at hand . . . and not the hands he wanted to put all over her.

But then there was that little hitch in her breath. And those incredibly soft lips beneath his. And just like that, the image of the always perfect princess, so cool, so collected, her superiority over him ordained from birth by the number of zeros in her stepfather's bank account alone . . . all of it gone, vanished. In its place burned the image of how she'd been last night. Suit rumpled, feet bare, mascara smudged. She'd been weary, stressed, her guard definitely down. What little cool she'd managed to collect had come from sheer willpower.

That one little hitch . . . and he'd immediately found himself gentling his kiss, soothing rather than inflaming, caretaking rather than conquering. She tasted so damn sweet. She didn't feel perfect, or poised, or like much of a princess. She felt fragile, and vulnerable, and damn if he didn't want to save her.

He kissed the corners of her lips before taking her mouth once again. He was unhurried in his exploration, reveling in the moment, knowing it could end at any time with no guarantee of a repeat performance. No matter how many years went by in between. He kissed her with a gentleness he didn't typically express, and carefully avoided examining any further why that particular side of him had surfaced now of all times. The fragility he'd sensed was probably temporary at best, no matter what his jacked-up libido wanted him to believe. But he quickly discovered kissing her like this wasn't just soothing her; it was soothing something deep inside himself, too.

When she sighed into his mouth, urging him on with a little moan deep in her throat, the part of him that was still a rock-hard teenager wanted to leap on that, leap on her, take her racing to the edge with him. But the man he'd become found a different kind of contentment skimming his fingertips over her cheeks, sliding them into the long, sleek strands of her hair, loosening her soft ponytail so he could feel that silken wave cascade over the backs of his hands, all the while taking in her breath with his own.

She was no longer some deeply closeted ghost from his childhood who needed vanquishing. She was a flesh-and-blood woman, who, in all truth, was a stranger to him. A woman whose plight should matter to him only in the strictest professional sense. She shouldn't otherwise matter to him at all.

And because he was very much afraid she still did, he

broke their kiss and tipped her head back just enough so he could look into her eyes. He forced a smile and a casual tone. The haze of desire still clouding her blue eyes didn't make it any easier. "Well. That should have complicated everything."

"It didn't?" She cleared her throat a little.

He shook his head. "Simplified a lot of things, actually."

"Such as?" she asked, her gaze dipping from his eyes to his mouth, then back again.

His body twitched hard at that telltale slip. He had to fight not to follow its lead, and it took a lot more effort than he liked to admit. "Such as I finally realized why I came here."

"Oh?" Her tone darkened slightly.

"I guess in some part of my admittedly murky subconscious, I thought I could finally prove—to you, to myself, to who the hell knows—that you needed me."

She stiffened slightly and tried to pull away.

"Not like that," he said quickly, not letting her go. "We both already agreed I could have pushed that particular boundary a long time ago."

Her quick retreat behind cool blue eyes triggered that thing in him it had in the past. He found himself grinning in the face of her aloofness, as cocky as he'd ever been and completely unrepentant. She'd been right in there with him on that kiss. He'd be damned if he'd let her pretend otherwise. "Well, maybe it was a little about slaking that pent-up lust of youth."

To her credit, a hint of a smile briefly curved her lips, but the light didn't reach as far as her eyes. "Glad I could help you out with that."

He sighed inwardly, feeling a bit callow for baiting her. There was a lingering ghost or two between them, and he'd be wise to remember that. "But what I meant was, I wanted to prove that you could depend on me." His casual smile became a tad harder to maintain. "Donny Mac's worthless son rides to the rescue of the golden princess of Lake Winnimocca or some such foolish bullshit like that."

There was a flash of something across her face that tipped dangerously toward pity, but then she was rolling her eyes, her tone when she spoke, dust dry, and he wondered if he'd misread her. Wouldn't be the first time, it seemed.

"I'm no princess," she assured him, "golden or otherwise."

"I know," he said, quite serious now. "That's what I just found out."

Her brows furrowed slightly. "What do you mean?"

"I mean that I realized why I thought I had to come back, and at the same time realized that I was wrong. I don't have anything left to prove, to you or to me."

"Good for you."

She sounded almost a little miffed with him, although for the life of him he couldn't have said why. "I also know that you're not whatever I might have built you up to be in my idiot teenager mind all those years ago. In fact, I don't know what or who you are. You're a complete stranger to me."

"I always have been."

"Exactly my point. I don't know the real you, Kate. Not then, not now. Any more than you know the real me."

She tilted her head. "All that from a kiss, huh?"

He shouldn't touch her again, should have, in fact, moved back to his side of the truck. Instead, he slid his hands back into her hair, surprised that she let him, and brushed the pads of his thumbs across the soft center of her bottom lip. And heard that tiny catch. It did in whatever control he'd built back up. "Yeah," he said, his voice not as strong as he'd have liked. "All that." He was leaning back in for another taste of her before he even realized his intent.

She immediately shifted back, enough so that his mouth didn't brush hers, but not enough to completely dislodge his fingers from her hair. "You didn't ask why I let you kiss me," she said, a little unsteadily.

"Okay. Why did you?" he said, sitting back.

There was no playful air in her tone now. She was as serious and sincere as he'd been. He appreciated that more than she could know.

"Maybe for me it was simply about slaking the lust of youth, sorting out a few old ghosts from my past."

It shouldn't have bothered him, despite the fact that he'd teased her by saying the same. Only she wasn't teasing, and her cool assessment of what, for him, had been something of a moment of reckoning didn't sit well. "Fair enough."

"So," she said, not quite meeting his eyes, "now that you've gotten things figured out, does that mean you're leaving?"

She'd tried to ask it casually, as if his answer mattered little to her, but he'd been staring at her too intently to miss the telltale way her throat worked, the way her gaze darted to his mouth again. Huh. Not so cool and collected after all.

"Afraid not," he said, cocky grin resurfacing, as he totally disregarded every single reason why he should have taken her easy out, driven straight back to the car rental counter at JFK, and booked the first flight home. He could still fix her problem, but he didn't need to personally be here to do it. Finn would pitch a fit, but, if he wanted to, he could hire someone to come up here and dig into the situation, install whatever equipment might be necessary to provide surveillance and security for the property, figure out exactly what was going on, then report back. Someone who would get to work rather than spend his time wondering when he might taste Kate's incredibly soft lips again. . . .

He was rewarded for his complete stupidity by getting to watch her pupils dilate a little in response. And not in fear. His body charged right back into the fray with complete and utter abandon.

"Why?" she asked. "Why stay? I can handle my own problems. Like you said, you always have too many pressing cases to handle as it is."

"I won't pretend to know anything about who you are

now, or what you're about, but the one thing I do know is that you're in trouble. The kind of trouble I can help you with."

She bristled. "Then it is still about me needing you."

"Not like that. I think the past is finally where it belongs. But the fact still remains that you need help. And I am here. And I have the resources and time to help you out. All you have to do is let me. No strings, no games."

"Donovan—"

"Mac," he said automatically, despite how hearing that name on her lips moved him in ways he didn't really want to explore. Certainly not now, after declaring he was only here to help. He curled his fingers inward to keep from reaching for her again. It couldn't matter that he was diamond hard and she was right there within reach. If he really was here to simply help her out, as he claimed, then continuing anything else with her was definitely out of bounds.

Of course, he and his partners had started Trinity for the sole purpose of having the freedom to operate outside a lot of the boundaries that hamstrung most other organizations. He'd never been one to stay inside the lines much anyway.

"You'd be a fool to turn down the offer." And he'd be a fool to expect anything more to come of this without paying a price for it later. "I may not know much about the real you, but I don't think you're a fool."

She let out a short laugh at that. "You'd be surprised. I'm not feeling all that smart here lately." She looked at him, studying his face, as if trying to find something there to help her make a decision. "Of all the times for you to show up."

He couldn't help but see the faint shadows beneath her eyes, the strain tightening the skin at the corners of her mouth. She wasn't smiling, but something had softened in her voice all the same. His own smile came more naturally now. "You say that like it's a bad thing. I'm a good guy to have in your corner."

"That may be true these days, but don't forget, even though we didn't get to know each other personally back then, I still happen to know a great deal about your youthful exploits."

"Hey, reformed black sheep are some of the best guys around."

"That kiss just now didn't seem all that reformed to me."

He couldn't help it, he grinned. "Yeah, well . . . some things don't need reforming."

She rolled her eyes, but at least she was smiling now.

He should have kept it light. Her walls were lowering, she was less guarded, and they were talking more easily now than they had since he'd first arrived. But when he opened his mouth, what came out was something completely serious. "I wasn't always in the right place, doing the right thing. Often times far from it. I won't apologize for that now, but I won't make excuses for it either. My less-than-picture-perfect youth wasn't laudable, but it is what shaped me into the man I am today."

She regarded him with a half-amused smile, but also with eyes that suddenly looked way older than her years. It didn't fit with someone who had led such a privileged life, but maybe it did with the teacher who wanted to help disabled children lead an easier life. And his curiosity about her intensified.

"So what does that unreformed kiss say about the man you've become?" she asked.

"That I'm secure enough now to go after what I want."

"Or too impatient to wait."

He barked out a laugh. "I waited eighteen years!" He shook his head then, looked down at the hands curled into fists in his lap. They were callused and scarred, and had saved him more often than they'd gotten him into trouble. "One thing I have learned is that life is short. And tenuous at best. I used to think that with all I had to face just to get through the day growing up, nothing else could touch me. If

I survived that part of my life, I was invincible. Then I spent a few years on the streets of New York and learned and saw a hundred different ways what no one should ever have to know or see, which is just how frail and destructible we all really are. No matter who we are." He glanced over at her. "So, yeah, I can be a little impatient at times. I don't wait for things to come my way if I can do something about going out and getting them. Why waste precious time?"

"Do you always get what you go after?"

He held her gaze for a few long seconds. His smile, when it came, was slow, steady, and direct. "Most of the time."

Her lips twitched, and the corners of her eyes crinkled a little. "Still cocky."

"Only when I know I can back it up."

She didn't stifle her smile. "Something tells me you always think you can back it up."

"So, it was worth waiting for, then?"

She laughed, and the sound of it, all soft and natural, filled the truck cab with warmth. She shook her head a little, as if to say he was incorrigible, then resolutely shifted in her seat, revved the engine a little.

The bars were up, the lights no longer flashing. He hadn't even heard the train go by. No one had honked, and a quick check showed no one was waiting behind them.

"I'm going to refuse to answer that on the grounds that it might get me—"

He looked back at her. "Seduced?"

She had just started to pull forward, but braked suddenly and hard, forcing him to brace himself on the dashboard.

She shot him a look, and he couldn't tell if she was amused or annoyed. Probably a little of both. Something he was thinking they'd both likely have to get used to if they were going to be spending any amount of time in each other's company.

She braced her hands on the wheel and squared her shoulders. "Okay," she said firmly, but not harshly. "If you're staying, free help or not, there are going to be some ground rules."

"We have rules?"

She looked at him. "We have rules."

"I suck at following rules."

"Tell me something I don't know." Then a troubled look crossed her face. "That's not why you left the force, is it? Was it not by your choice?"

"Don't worry, it was by my choice," he said. "Ask Rafe, or Finn, if you don't believe me."

"Again, that's like asking Mo and Larry to back up Curly."

"Very funny. And how come I get to be Curly?"

"Men," she muttered, maybe a little impatiently.

"Call my old precinct, then. I made detective before I turned twenty-five. I was even decorated a few times." Though he'd never once mentioned that to anyone else. What was it about Kate that tweaked at those still twitchy, vulnerable parts of him anyway?

"But ultimately, I guess it was the rules that sent me to the private sector. I have a lot more . . . flexibility now."

She shot him a sideways glance. "Working with Rafe and Finn and a bottomless bankroll? Oh, I just bet you do. You know, maybe I should rethink this whole thing. More legal trouble I don't need."

Legal trouble? So, maybe there was more going on with Shelby and their little deal than she'd alluded to. He wisely kept the question to himself. For now. But he added it to the list of things to look into once they reached Ralston. "You forget, I didn't ask your permission to stay here."

"If you plan on staying on my property, you're going to need it. I may seem like a foolish, naïve woman, but I assure you, I can take care of myself. Have been for years. If you step foot onto my property again without it, you can continue this conversation up close and personal with the business end of my shotgun."

He grinned at that. Kate Sutherland, all feisty and loaded for bear. He rather liked it. "I might just do that."

"Fine."

"Fine," he said quite agreeably, which only made her scowl deepen. "You know, maybe you should consider doing some target practice, though."

She shot him a look. "Why, do you think I'll need it?"

"Not for me. I was just thinking that if the person getting his kicks out of plastering the place with Day-Glo paint knew you were armed and dangerous, he might think twice about messing with you."

"You really don't think I have a gun, do you?"

"Do you?"

She pulled ahead, banging the truck over the tracks a little more heavily than necessary. "You're still insufferable. That much hasn't changed."

He didn't laugh outright, but it cost him. "Just trying to help," he said, ever-so-conversationally. "Coming from someone with some experience being on the business end of a firearm, for the gun threat to work, the person being threatened has to actually believe they're in danger of being shot."

"Who said I wouldn't pull the trigger?" The look she gave him was surprisingly . . . homicidal.

Hunh. He leaned back in his seat and adjusted his seat belt a bit tighter as she continued to take the road leading into town a tad too fast.

"Okay. What are they?"

"What are what?"

"The rules."

She shot him another quick glare. "Dare I even bother?"

"Please dare. I mean do," he added, unable to keep from smiling. She was cute when she scowled. He was smart enough to keep that opinion to himself, however. He'd remained bullet-hole-free all these years for a good reason.

She stewed for another couple seconds, then finally blurted out, "Here's the deal. You're right, it would be unwise of me not to take you up on your offer of help. I'll tell you what you need to know, but I'll expect to be totally involved in, and approve of, any steps you take."

He waved his hand. "Boring rule. Next."

She lifted one eyebrow.

"We'll talk it through," he said, attempting to sound as if he were capitulating, which he doubted she was buying. Good thing, too. Because, while he didn't mind keeping her in the loop, if he thought something was going to keep her and the camp safe, he was doing it whether she okayed it or not.

"Rule number two. Hands off."

Now he lifted an eyebrow. "Except—"

"No exceptions."

"There are always exceptions."

She slowed down slightly and stared at him.

"Okay, okay," he said, lifting his hands. "Eyes on the road."

"Promise?"

"Hands off," he responded.

"Promise," she reiterated.

"You trust my word, but not me?"

"Promise."

He sighed. "I can't."

She started to say something, then stopped as his answer apparently sunk in.

"Road," he said casually.

She swerved back into her lane, swearing under her breath. "What do you mean you can't? You mean you won't."

"No, I mean I can't. I don't lie, Kate. And since I can't guarantee I'm never going to put my hands on you again, I'm not going to promise you that I won't. I can promise I'd try, but why bother? We both know I won't try all that hard if I don't want to. Either we will get tangled up again or we won't; it's as simple and as complicated as that. You can't go making rules about it."

"Sure you can. You might be impulsive and impatient, but

even as a teenager you had self-control. At least where I was concerned anyway."

She sounded almost . . . put out by that. He hid his smile this time. He wanted to get the rest of the way into town in one piece. "That was then. I've tasted you now."

He glanced over in time to see her swallow hard and notice how her knuckles grew even whiter, which was saying something considering she already had a death grip on the steering wheel. What she didn't do was argue with him. He relaxed. Just a little. "I can make you one promise, though."

"I'm dying to hear it," she said, not bothering to temper her sarcasm.

"I won't do anything you don't want me to."

The truck pulled a little to the right when she convulsively loosened her hold on the wheel, and she said something under her breath that sounded a lot like "sweet Jesus," which he doubted had anything to do with keeping the truck in the right lane. But he wouldn't swear to it.

He took greater stock in the blush that stained her previously pale skin. "You know, you look better with a little color in your cheeks. I don't think you're getting enough sleep. Or something. So, what are the other rules?"

"Oh, shut up. I don't know why I bothered."

"See? Just what I said." He grinned. "I'm growing on you, aren't I?"

"Getting under my skin is more like it," she muttered.

"As long as I'm getting somewhere."

"Donovan, I swear, if you—what?" she said when she glimpsed something in his expression.

He didn't think he'd been that obvious. "Mac."

"What? Oh. Right. What difference does it make? It's not like you don't know who I'm talking to."

She slowed as they came around the final bend into town. They had maybe a few minutes left at best. He debated on getting into it, or just letting it go. But, if they were talking about things getting under her skin, she had no idea how hearing her say his birth name got under his.

She shrugged. "You've always been Donovan to me. At least, that's how I've always thought of you, not that we talked or anything."

The only other woman who'd ever called him that was his mother. Not that he remembered much about her, other than the stories that had followed her right out of Winnimocca. But he knew from those stories that she'd always called his dad by his full name, had been the only one in the county to do so. She thought it sounded romantic and exotic. Of course, she'd been all of sixteen at the time. A year later she'd bestowed that name on her first and only son.

She'd taken off before his fifth birthday with some biker named Binky. Apparently not as interested in romantic names by then. Or no longer caring. Word got back that she'd killed herself driving drunk a few years later. No one knew what happened to Binky. It had been the general consensus that it was a good thing she'd never had any more kids.

Mac met Rafe and Finn the following summer. By then he'd heard about all he cared to about his dead mother. Rafe and Finn didn't care about any of that, though. Or that his father had a worse reputation than she did. He didn't remember when, exactly, he'd started insisting on everyone calling him Mac. But thinking back, it had been sometime right around then.

"I could try," she said in response, then shot him a dry smile. "But I can't make any promises."

"Touché," he said, gladly shaking off the memories. "I'd appreciate the attempt."

"Same goes with my hands-off rule."

"You sure know how to hit a guy where it counts."

"Not really," she said, more seriously than he was comfortable with.

He wasn't sure, but he didn't think she was talking about him. And it surprised him how much he wanted to know to whom she was referring. The curiosity wasn't entirely professional either. Or even mostly. Up until today, he'd have thought he was hardened pretty much clear through. One taste of Kate Sutherland had blown that illusion to smithereens.

"I'm sorry it bothers you, though," she added. "I'll do my best."

He waited for her to dig a little, prod him about why it bothered him so much. As it was, he'd already made a bigger deal out of it than he should have. It was habit mostly, and he wouldn't have corrected her at all, but . . . maybe being back here again, with her, past memories getting all roiled up, had made him more sensitive to it.

Or, it could be that it didn't bother him as much as he wanted it to, and that, maybe, he even liked it. A little. From her, anyway. Which perversely bothered him even more.

To her credit, and his relief, she let it go. He owed her for that. And because he always liked to pay his debts sooner rather than later, he vowed to do his best to stick to Kate's Rules of Conduct. Even if it killed him.

He slid his gaze over to her and watched how she handled the wheel, how her long legs stretched out over the worn-out vinyl seat. How her jeans fit over those long legs of hers . . . and he remembered why he hated playing by the rules. He sighed and resolved himself to the fact that most of his showers in the near future were likely to be short, and very, very cold.

They pulled into town just then, and his thoughts were mercifully dragged away from Kate . . . and plunged headlong right into his past. Even though he'd been somewhat prepared for it after seeing the camp, he still felt as if he'd entered a time warp. For all it was the nearest town of any size to Winnimocca, it was barely a blip on the map itself.

Almost two decades had passed, but the only difference Mac saw was that Wylie's Hardware was now a cluttered junk shop, and whoever owned the Gas 'Em Up had replaced the rusted Camel cigarette sign promising a fresh menthol flavor with a new Diet Dr. Pepper sign promising the same great taste with fewer calories.

There might be more cracks in the sidewalks, and the roads were pitted with a few more potholes, buildings were a little dingier looking, and there were a few more stores boarded up, but, for the most part, it was the same Ralston he'd rolled into one night at age fifteen, fake ID in hand, to buy his first six-pack. Becker's Pool Hall was still there, where he'd gotten drunk in public for the first time. They drove past the parking lot of the Kwikee Mart, where he'd gotten into his first fight that had involved knives as well as fists. Still didn't have any damn lighting to speak of, he thought, absently rubbing his fingertips over the four-inch scar on this thigh.

And Weaver's Pharmacy, which still stood right across the street from the bank where he'd opened his first account, had the honor of being the first place he'd ever bought a condom. And a pregnancy test. Ralston Cinema. First place he'd ever made out at the movies. Third row, balcony. Last place, too, come to think of it. He needed to get out more. Sheriff's office. His gaze lingered there, almost as a test. Didn't look any different now than it had when he'd shown up Sunday mornings to pick up his father. The cruiser parked out front was newer, but that was about it.

"You okay?"

He jerked his gaze to Kate's. So caught up, he'd forgotten she was even there. Watching him, seeing God knew what cross his face. He wasn't used to anyone watching him. Usually, he did all the observing. He didn't much like the reversal of roles. "Fine. I have a few things to take care of. Why don't you go see the chamber of commerce guy, and I'll meet you back here in about an hour. We'll go see the sheriff together."

He didn't wait for her to respond. They'd gotten as up close and personal as he was willing to get. He pushed open the door and uncurled himself from the cab, wincing a little as his knees protested the sudden movement after being cramped up for so long. He heard her opening her door as he walked away, no immediate destination in mind other than to get away from her, and those blue eyes of hers that saw too much. Knew too much. About him, about his past, about the memories he was presently grappling with.

He stalked off down Tower Street, knowing he had to get a grip and get it fast. He should be sticking beside her, involving himself in the meeting with the chamber of commerce guy, watching the townspeople interact with her, testing his instincts about what he thought might be going on here. Not to mention, walking off like this would only give her time to regroup and rally her defenses back into place. Making his job that much more difficult.

But he kept walking.

At the moment, that was a risk he'd have to take. As soon as he'd gotten his bearings back and was certain he was emotionally bulletproof, he'd find her. After all, how much trouble could she get herself into inside one hour?

Chapter 6

Kate watched Donovan stalk off, her heart aching a bit more than it should. He was a grown man. It had been his decision to come back here, not hers. Still . . . Maybe he didn't think he was being obvious, that she'd think the reason he was suddenly being all business was on account of her hands-off rule. But she'd seen emotions flicker across that handsome face of his that had nothing to do with the kisses they'd shared, or the fact that he was disappointed he wouldn't be getting any more of them. Or of anything else, for that matter.

She shivered a little, thinking about how he'd tasted, how he'd kissed her as though he knew her, as though he'd been kissing her for decades. No. She firmly shook her head. No more of those. One little make-out session was already one session too many. But she found herself watching Donovan's retreat, nonetheless.

She shouldn't feel sorry for him. He'd hate it if he knew she'd felt an ounce of pity, even for a second. He was right—they were both products of their upbringing, but mostly as a measure of their ability to overcome some pretty serious obstacles. Hers might not have been so obvious, but his . . . his had been out there for all the world to see. And judge. Which had made his obstacles that much bigger. Donny Mac hadn't made any attempt to hide his contempt over being saddled with Marlene's "brat kid" as he'd often called his only son. Conveniently forgetting he'd been involved in the business end of creating his son, too. Then, in addition to dealing with an alcoholic father and a less than stable home life, Mac had spent Memorial Day through Labor Day each and every summer surrounded by an immediate peer group who happened to not only be from the better side of the tracks, but so far beyond the MacLeod's as to be in a different stratosphere.

Louisa had kept Donny Mac in her employ only because, despite his drinking and occasional brushups with the local law, he had magic hands when it came to any kind of machinery. He could fix anything, keep anything running, and though not always the most dependable person, he had saved the day on more than one occasion.

Donovan had inherited that gift, but it didn't earn him any respect from the campers. To them, he was just the scruffy son of the drunk handyman. A fact they took great pleasure in torturing him with all summer long, as far back as she could remember. Humiliating him—or trying to—had been one of their favorite sports. Even the counselors, who most often came from outlying counties, were from more improved circumstances than his, and tended to look the other way when their young charges indulged in their smug torment.

Donovan had always more than held his own, his hands being good for more than fixing engines as it turned out. Even so, it hadn't been right. But Kate had known better than to interfere directly. She'd tried to talk to her mother about it on several occasions, but Louisa felt she'd already done her civic duty in providing a job for Donny Mac in the first place. "Giving him a hand up in the world," she'd say, as if her benevolence was strictly charitable and she gained nothing from their arrangement. When the truth was that Louisa Sutherland saw life as an endless business proposition, and ran her own—and her children's when she could—accordingly. Louisa already had what she wanted from Donny Mac and flatly refused to involve herself further. She'd allowed him to park his tiny, beat-up trailer behind the mechanic's building on the far side of the maintenance lot, and she'd said nothing about him having his son work for him at a far younger age than was acceptable. It wasn't her place to step in between parent and child, she'd say. Kate knew better than to argue further.

Instead, she'd watched from a distance as Donovan had handled the ribbing, the catcalls, the demands that he step and fetch, all with a seething grace. He'd never looked bowed, or beaten, which she was certain had been a big part of why they never left him alone. It irritated them that someone so obviously beneath them in every measurable standard managed to somehow maintain his dignity and integrity, no matter how boldly they tried to rob him of it.

Worse by far was the fact that all the girls at camp wanted him almost desperately. And though he seemed rather nonchalant about it, Kate suspected he'd taken enormous pleasure in claiming what they saw as theirs. *And claim them he had*, she thought with a sigh. The girls all talked about him, lusted after him, drooled over him . . . and found many a reason to wander down the dusty road to the maintenance sheds after dark.

Except for Kate. Who, by virtue of being the camp owner's daughter, was an outsider in her own way at Winnimocca. Her family bank account might have slowly grown to rival those of the camp attendees, and, in fact, exceed a few. But no matter how high scale the camp, or the fact that it was one of many things Louisa owned, at Winnimocca, Kate was the innkeeper's daughter. She smiled, thinking of the resentment Donovan had felt toward her privileged lifestyle.

And yet, ironically, she'd rarely felt the pampered princess he'd thought her to be. Okay . . . pampered, maybe. Her life was a far stretch from his in that regard. But princess? Hardly. There was room for only one royal in their little dysfunctional family, and it was Louisa who'd worn that crown.

She and Shelby had been mere pawns, used to an advantage, set against each other when deemed necessary. Now that crown had been passed to Shelby.

Who's become an even bigger royal pain, she thought with a grimace. Impossible as that seemed. Her thoughts came full circle back to her reason for coming to town today. She got out of the truck, eyes still on Donovan—Mac's—retreating form. So different, the two of them, but more alike than he'd ever want to admit.

Yes, as a teenager, she'd known she had a privileged lifestyle. She was surrounded by everything a girl could ever want. Except the one thing money couldn't buy: love she didn't have to earn. George, her stepfather, had come closer than anyone, but left their lives too soon to help her during the more trying adolescent years. Louisa's affection had always come with conditions. Ever-changing conditions.

Shelby played her game and played it quite well. Not Kate. From the day she'd become a legal adult, she had refused to join in any further, and had instantly become the black sheep for her indifference. She'd been cut off and put out. It wasn't until she'd made the move to contact her mother's attorney to set up the meeting about the camp property that she'd learned her mother was even ill. Shelby, of course, hadn't bothered to tell her. Not that they'd kept in any kind of regular contact, either, but still. They were the only family each other had.

Wasn't it odd, she thought, as she watched Donovan turn the corner up Brevard, that of all the people she'd known growing up, he'd been the one person her romantic teenage heart had always imagined would understand her plight. She remembered thinking that if she could only explain to him that they had more in common than he realized, he'd stop looking at her like he did, with that disconcerting combination of lust and disdain . . . and look at her the way she wanted him to.

Which was a whole lot like he had back in the cab of her truck. Right before he'd kissed her senseless.

It was her only excuse for letting him . . . for kissing him back. Or so she told herself. She looked at the now empty street corner and wondered if he'd stick to her rules.

Wondered if she really wanted him to.

Resolutely, she turned away and headed the opposite direction down Tower. She had business to take care of, which didn't involve Donovan "Mac" MacLeod, no matter that he thought he should know all about her business. She wasn't going to turn down help if it meant getting the camp up and running, but if there was going to be a camp to get up and running, then she had to figure out how to get the town to back her endeavor with more enthusiasm. Any enthusiasm, really.

She thought about the connection Donovan had made between the vandalism and the townspeople being apathetic to her business propositions. Was the developer involved in some way? And how did that tie into Shelby's no-show yesterday, if at all?

She smiled ruefully now, remembering the highly detailed fantasies she'd had of how she and Donovan would share their tales of woe, become star-crossed lovers, with a unique bond that no one else understood but them, joined forever to face down the taunts and torments of the outside world, so strong in their union that no one could defeat them.

Typical foolish teenage fantasy.

So that did little to explain why she was having a hard time shaking the feeling that he'd finally ridden to her rescue after all. It had just taken a little longer than she'd imagined.

Shoving shaky hands into her pockets, she congratulated herself on being strong enough, mature enough, to rise above her foolish weakness where he was concerned. She'd laid down the law, and he'd listened. Now all she had to do was uphold her own rules.

"No sweat." Uncurling her hands and smoothing them on her pants, she slowed as she reached her destination. She had to shove Donovan from her mind and focus on her reason for coming into town.

She'd planned on seeing Gilby first, but decided it was for the best to accept Mac's help in that particular case. While she'd like to think she didn't need rescuing at this point in her life, she hadn't gotten anywhere with Gilby the last time. Perhaps having someone with Donovan's police background by her side would change that. She was kind of hoping he'd know what to say to motivate Gilby to take a stronger interest in looking into her vandalism problem.

A bell jingled when she pushed open the door to the Ralston Chamber of Commerce. Hopefully Stan wouldn't mind her showing up a bit earlier than planned. The office was a cramped space squeezed between the town's only barber and beauty shop. The faint smell of permanent wave solution and coffee lingered in the air. She tried not to wrinkle her nose, but it wasn't easy.

She was ostensibly meeting with Stan to garner his support and pick his brain over ideas and ways to promote her camp in both Ralston and the rest of the county. Her real mission, however, was to make sure he knew how serious she was about getting the camp up and running, and maybe gain a little insight about why the townspeople were being so standoffish. Donovan's ideas about the vandalism and the supposed developer deal being connected had to be factored in now, too. She wasn't sure she believed there was a bigger conspiracy to this whole thing, but until she talked to Shelby, she'd have to at least take it into consideration.

The reception area was tiny. There was a Formica-topped desk, the surface of which was mostly consumed by an old computer monitor and keyboard. What little space was left over held a bank of two phones and a card file. On the paneled wall behind the desk was a rather grand plaque, bearing a shiny gold plate announcing the offices of the Ralston Chamber of Commerce, founded in 1927, and proudly delivering over 75 years of dedicated service to the community.

There was no one, dedicated or not, seated at the desk, so Kate stepped around it to the only two doors leading from the room. One was propped open, revealing a coat and stor-age closet, so she knocked on the closed one. "Stan?" she called out, and tapped again. "It's Kate Sutherland. I'm early. Hope that's okay."

She stepped back and waited, but no one came out. She checked her watch. She'd called him before leaving for the city yesterday to confirm their meeting, and the secretary—or whoever had answered the phone, a woman anyway—had told her they were in by eight and to drop by anytime. She'd confirmed for nine o'clock, which wasn't for another forty-five minutes, but that didn't explain why they'd left the place unlocked and empty. "So much for dedicated community service," she murmured.

She stepped back and glanced in the coat closet. It was still early enough in the spring to warrant at least a jacket most mornings. There was only a handful of empty hangars, and one lone umbrella, propped just inside the door, along with several cartons of printer paper and a bulk package of paper towels shoved in the opposite end.

Where the hell was everybody? Not that the streets of Ralston were ever a beehive of activity, but, come to think of it, she hadn't seen a single soul on her way into town. Of course, it was after eight on a weekday morning. Everybody was likely busy doing whatever it was they got paid to do.

She turned and saw the wall behind her sported two framed prints of what looked like early paintings of the town. But the predominant feature was a giant cork board, filled to bursting with flyers, business cards, anything and everything any business or businessperson in town might want to advertise. Including . . . she leaned closer . . . yep, that's what the postcard said all right.

Mounted deer head for sale. Nice eight-point. Will look good over your fireplace!

Then she smiled when she saw the name scribbled next to the phone numbers on the fringe of handy tear-off tags:

Edna. Somehow she doubted the deer head was Edna's, but around here, you could never be too sure.

She skimmed the other cards, half expecting to see another one from Edna listing a recliner, television, and remote, but no such luck. What she also didn't see was any kind of cohesive promotion for the town businesses. No brochures or print-shop-produced flyers.

She turned back around and leaned over the desk. There was no scheduling book that she saw, and when she inadvertently jiggled the monitor, it shifted out of sleep mode to show a half-played hand of solitaire. She looked at the plaque again and wondered what their definition of "service" was.

If it wasn't for the fact that she needed to pump Stan for information, she'd head back to her truck and wait for Donovan. She hadn't expected miracles, but she had hoped for more than this. Given the looks of the place, she'd probably learn more about the comings and goings of everybody in Ralston sitting next door at the beauty shop, getting her nails done.

She glanced down at her hands. If she still had any, that was.

She debated on leaving a note, but decided she'd try again after visiting Sheriff Gilby. Just as she turned to leave, the bell jingled, and a stooped, gray-haired gentleman stepped through the doorway. He smiled, no look of recognition on his face. No surprise. She hadn't exactly spent a lot of time in Ralston as yet. But that would change. Whether they liked it or not. "Hello," she said brightly, extending her hand. "You must be Stan. I'm Kate. Kate Sutherland."

He regarded her steadily, his expression unreadable. He took her hand in a gentle grip and, after what could barely be called a handshake, let her hand drop. Perhaps he was just one of those men who thought all women were fragile. He was of that generation. In fact, he looked old enough to have been here during all seventy-five years of that so-called dedicated service.

"I'm not Stan," he corrected. "Bob Varnick. Stan's down at Deenie's, having a cup of coffee. Must have forgot you were coming."

Kate nodded, smiled, but privately thought something was off about this little "accidental" meeting. "You and Stan run the office here together?" It was a probing question, since, as he was dressed in overalls, a heavy flannel jacket, and a gimme cap, she seriously doubted it.

"Uh, no, no, in fact, we don't. I—I just stopped by to . . ." He drifted momentarily until spying the tack board behind Kate's head. "Just stopping in like I always do, catch up on what's going on."

"There isn't anyone else here, it seems. I don't know where the receptionist is either."

He nodded toward the board behind her. "Just checking out the board. Stan never locks up. Whole town uses the bulletin board. You'd be surprised what you can piece together from the flotsam that gets posted up there."

Since she'd just been deducing the demise of Edna somebody's marriage, she could hardly call him on that comment. Still, something didn't seem right. "I bet."

"New in town, aren't you? Don't recall seeing you here." He said it matter-of-factly, as though he wasn't exactly interested, or all that happy about spying a newcomer.

Or maybe Donovan's conspiracy theories were just making her paranoid. Of course, she hadn't exactly been feeling the love of the locals even before he'd shown up, but maybe she was seeing shadows where there weren't any. And yet, she couldn't shake the feeling that good ol' Bob here had been sent 'round to check her out. Or something. So far he'd been polite, but just barely, given the set expression on his face.

"Not exactly new here," she answered him. "I used to come up here during the summer while I was growing up. My mother, Louisa, once owned Camp Winnimocca, south of here, on the lake. She passed on, and I've taken over the property. I'm planning on reopening it as a camp for challenged kids. Maybe you've heard something about it."

"Can't say that I have."

It was hard to read the guy, but there wasn't a flicker of recognition. Nor did he seem particularly interested in what she had to say. Still, how could he be older than dirt and not know who Louisa Sutherland was? It wasn't as if people retired and moved to Ralston.

"Well, I think I'll drop by Deenie's and grab a coffee with Stan," she said, with as much sunny cheer as she could inflect, mostly just to annoy the old guy. "Thanks for the heads-up. Appreciate it."

If she wasn't mistaken, Bob didn't look too keen on that idea, but he merely nodded.

Yeah, the townsfolk just loved her. Didn't know who she was, my ass. She took a step toward the door, then turned back. "You wouldn't happen to know of any local contractors looking for work, would you? I'm going to be starting a large-scale renovation and reconstruction shortly, and I'm looking to get bids. I want to support my community, so I'm hoping to hire locally."

She watched him closely, but he was pretty good at the inscrutable thing.

"Might want to post something on the board here. See what you get."

Not a rousing endorsement, nor did he look particularly excited about the opportunity she was proposing. Could mean nothing, he could just be the town grouch, but it wasn't exactly reassuring. "Thanks. I'll do that." She gave him her friendliest smile. "Pleasure to meet you, Bob. I'd appreciate you passing the word, if you wouldn't mind."

He didn't say anything, but touched the bill of his hat, more out of habit, it seemed, than anything. His expression hadn't so much as flickered since he walked in.

"Thanks," she said, trying hard not to let the dry sarcasm she was feeling color her tone. She let herself out of the office, more bemused than anything. Some small towns had strange personalities. Maybe Ralston just wasn't all that friendly to strangers. She'd never felt that way when she'd been younger, but she hadn't really paid all that much attention back then. Nor had she spent much time in town.

There were a few people on the street now, and the sun was making a more concerted effort to poke out from behind the morning clouds. The town didn't look much cheerier, even in the sunlight, and she caught herself wondering how she was going to handle living here full-time. Other than driving a few hours south to New York City, Ralston or a few others just like it would be it in terms of meeting all of her needs. Material and social.

Thank God, then, she'd learned some time ago to live without many of them. Her thoughts immediately went right back to the kiss with Donovan. Just the memory made her body come alive, and she privately cursed him for reminding her that some things were easier to live without than others.

She pushed the door open to Deenie's and was surprised to find it pretty busy, almost half of the two dozen or so assorted tables and booths were occupied by at least one person. Many sipping coffee and reading the morning paper, some in private discussions of various volumes. One thing she didn't see was cell phones and PDAs. Ralston wasn't exactly on the cutting edge of technology, and neither were most of its residents. Simple people, for the most part, leading relatively uncomplicated lives. Maybe that was why they were so resistant to her. Maybe they were just resistant to change.

People glanced up when the bell jingled, but no one seemed to pay her any specific kind of attention before returning to what they were doing. Maybe she was reading more into things than really existed. It could be just as elemental as she'd thought, that she was an outsider whom the locals hadn't come to trust yet. Looking around Deenie's, it was almost impossible to believe in secret developer plans and private conspiracies to keep her camp from becoming a reality. Which didn't explain the vandalism. Or where Shelby had gone off to yesterday. But maybe they were just as easily explained. Maybe Donovan was just jaded and cynical from spending too many years on the streets of New York dealing with real criminals.

She ran a quick scan and tried to guess which customer was Stan. Then she heard a throaty laugh that drew her attention to a booth in the far corner. There sat a man in slacks and tie, no jacket, sleeves rolled up, silvering hair neatly combed to one side. He was cradling a mug of coffee in two hands and paying rapt attention to the short, amazingly buxom brunette seated across from him as she told an animated story punctuated by that laugh. *Well*, Kate thought, trying not to smirk, *that explains where the receptionist was.*

Kate waved the approaching waitress off and wove her way through the tables, back to their corner booth. As she drew closer, she noted that given the direction of Stan's gaze, his attention was more closely fixed on how the woman's animated hand motions made her wonder boobs bounce around than whatever it was she was saying. The woman seemed oblivious, her own coffee untouched as she continued on, clearly enjoying being the center of his attention.

A quick glance at Stan's left hand showed a solid gold band. Hmm, no matching sparkler flashing about on the waving hand of the secretary. *Imagine that.* Stan looked up first when she closed in on their booth. It took the secretary a moment or two longer.

"And so I was saying to Hank, 'Hank, you just can't up and leave Lorinda like that. What will her family say?'" She defied gravity and leaned farther across the table. "And you know her family holds their purse strings tighter than— what?" She glanced up then when she realized she no longer had Stan's exclusive attention. "Oh. Hello. Who are you?"

"Hello," Kate replied, taking the woman's open and not particularly friendly once-over in stride, along with the easy dismissal once she determined Kate was no competition in the bounce department. Maybe she was more aware of what her draw was where Stan was concerned than Kate had given her credit for.

She turned her attention to Stan and stuck out her hand. "Stan Harris? I'm Kate Sutherland. I believe we have an appointment this morning?"

Stan could have been a great used car salesman from the way his guarded expression changed instantly to one of sincere contrition. "Do we?" He released his hold on his coffee mug long enough to give her hand one quick, businesslike shake, his grin never wavering, his gaze easily fixed on hers. "I'm terribly sorry. Apparently we got our dates or the time mixed up." He glanced at his receptionist with no censure, nor did she look remotely abashed. "This is Diane," he said, "my secretary. I guess we'll have to add scheduling to the list of business to be discussed this morning." His accompanying laugh was as fake as Diane's inch-long nails.

Diane didn't offer her aggressively manicured hand to Kate. Having already sized Kate up and decided there was no contest, she merely nodded, then picked up her mug for a sip.

"Well," Kate said, all forced smile and equally fake enthusiasm, "I do hate to interrupt your business meeting." She tried not to put undue emphasis on those last two words, but it was mighty taxing. "But if it wouldn't be too much of an imposition, I'd really appreciate a few moments of your time."

Stan nodded easily, then glanced at his secretary, who continued sipping her coffee, until Stan cleared his throat. "Diane, we can continue our discussion back in the office. Would you mind terribly giving Ms. Sutherland and I a few moments? I so appreciate it. You're a peach."

Diane just stared at him, as if being dismissed for Kate simply would not compute, but when Stan's perma-grin began to fade ever so slightly, she quickly regrouped and beamed an I'm-your-best-gal smile right back at him. "Why, of course. I have those—"

Solitaire games to finish, Kate thought, not entirely kindly.

"—reports to file," she finished brightly, proud of herself for coming up with the cover.

"Thank you, hon," Stan said, already dismissing her before she'd even finished grabbing her hot pink, faux alligator purse and sliding from the booth, apparently unfazed by the somewhat patronizing endearment. He was already motioning the waitress over. "Can I get you some coffee?"

Kate shifted aside to let a now huffy Diane past, then slid into the booth behind her. She smiled at the waitress. "Regular please, with cream?"

The waitress hustled off. Stan didn't watch Diane's stalking retreat. Instead he picked up his mug again. "What was it you wanted to see me about, Ms. Sutherland?"

"Kate, please." She paused while the waitress set her mug down and used the moment to size Stan up. He was tall, with a slender build, and a few decades younger than his cohort back at the office. She figured mid-fifties. Compared to the other locals in the diner, who were mostly in work trousers, boots, and flannel, he appeared every inch the small-town successful businessman, along the lines of a banker or town councilman. His tie was neatly knotted, if a bit out of date, and his shirt pressed, though not tailored. His hair was freshly barbered, his face smoothly shaved, and his gray eyes clear and sharp on hers. Her guess was Stan didn't miss much. And despite Diane's overt lack of sophistication, she imagined his secretary didn't miss much either.

She knew damn well they hadn't forgotten her appointment.

She took a tentative sip, was surprised by the rich taste, and took another for fortification. "So, I wanted to talk to you about my camp."

Stan lifted a hand. "Right, right. I seem to remember hearing something about that. The old Winnimocca place, is it?"

Kate smiled, but she was thinking, *Why are you lying about knowing exactly who I am?* Damn Mac for making her so paranoid. "Yes. That's the place."

"Did I hear right, that you're trying to start up some center for, for crippled kids out at the old rich—" He broke off,
and the slightest of flushes reached his cheeks as he quickly
regrouped. "Your mother, I believe, once ran a summer program on the lake property, is that right?"

Kate nodded, allowing the faux pas to slide. *Rich kids'
camp.* She'd wondered what he might think of her, what
judgments he might make, based on her family background.
To that end, she purposely hadn't dressed up for the occasion, wanting to present herself as she truly was, a hard-
working woman trying to single-handedly resurrect a once
thriving campground. "The program I am hoping—planning
on—instituting is for children who face a number of different
physical and mental challenges."

"Commendable, Ms. Sutherland."

"Kate," she reminded him, then took another sip. "I'm not
trying to be commendable, Mr. Harris—"

"Stan," he offered perfunctorily.

"Stan," she repeated. "I've been working in that field since
graduating, and when my mother passed on and left the
property to us, I thought it was the perfect use for it."

Stan's gaze dropped to her hand cradling the mug, then
quickly back to her face. "Us?" he repeated. "So, you're operating this place with your husband?"

Kate tried not to look insulted. So. Married made a difference. Married meant there was a man involved, which meant
maybe this was actually a serious business proposition and
not some silly dream operation run by a brainless, no-head-
for-business woman. Somehow she managed to keep that
opinion to herself. "No," she answered directly. "Just as my
mother did before me, I'll be running the place myself." She
wasn't sure the reminder would make so much as a dent in
the thought process of someone who'd probably been narrow-
minded since birth, but it couldn't hurt to try. She didn't
linger on it, however, as he'd given her the perfect opening to

probe a little, and she'd be damned if she'd pass it up. "By 'us' I meant my stepbrother, Shelby. Have you two met?"

She lifted her coffee mug, her eyes trained steadily on his face over the rim as she took a slow sip. She'd caught him off guard with that last part. His attention made a telling dip, just for a moment, but long enough to signal that he wasn't being completely honest. "Can't say as I recall. So is he a silent partner in your little endeavor, or . . . ?"

"No. We're just finishing up the details of the will, is all. And he had a hand in running it with my mother when he was younger, so his advice has been invaluable to me." She kept her tone light, but never took her eyes off of him. Nope. Something definitely wasn't right here. Stan wasn't meeting her gaze as easily now. "You know how probates can go," she said dismissively, as casually as possible. "Anyway, we're close to breaking ground on some very extensive renovation work, and so I thought it was a good time to talk to you about getting the word out about my camp. I am definitely planning on involving as many of the local businesses as I can, both in skilled labor as well as printing shops, media outlets, the newspaper, that sort of thing."

"Miss Sutherland—Kate—I'm afraid I'm not a placement office. You're more than welcome to post whatever notices you'd like on our community service board. And I'm sure Jim at the *Sentinel* would be happy to talk to you about taking out a more detailed paid ad, which might reach those who don't come into town as often. We might be a bit backwoods here, unlike the city life you're more accustomed to, but I assure you word travels quite fast. I'm certain you won't have any problem alerting the community to your needs."

Kate noted a couple of things in his little speech that got her attention. One, for a man who purportedly didn't know much about her, he knew she was from New York City. And she also noted he didn't say she wouldn't have a problem hiring people, just that they'd get the word about her intentions. Interesting.

She was sorely tempted to just come out and ask him what was going on, what he had against her and her camp. Or just straight out ask him what he might know about Timberline, for that matter, see what kind of reaction that got. But her mind was spinning a little too fast to sort everything out on the spur, and she didn't want to make a wrong move and tip him off to what she was thinking. Not until she'd had a chance to think it through, anyway. She hated that her first thought had actually been not until she had a chance to talk it over with Donovan.

One day and she was already coming to depend on him. And at a time when she really couldn't afford to depend on anyone but herself.

Apparently taking her silence to mean he'd regained the upper hand, Stan tried his used car salesman smile again. "As far as promoting the camp itself, don't take offense, but I don't know how much help Ralston can be for you. We don't have too many crippled kids around that I know of."

Kate ground her teeth to keep her smile even. "Challenged," she mildly corrected. "And I know Ralston isn't big in size, but I always thought small towns were big in heart." He wasn't the only one with a snakeoil pitch. "Ralston does serve the needs of a large county, many of whom do drive in a distance to do business here. I wasn't thinking to have any big campaign or anything. I was merely hoping to maybe use your network of small businesses here to get the word out. Word of mouth is oftentimes the best method of promotion in a case like this. You never know who knows somebody with a child who might be in need of the kind of services I'll be providing."

Stan listened to her spiel with dwindling interest. "As I said, you can feel free to post anything you'd like on the community service board in the office. Anyone who has an interest will be sure to contact you." He smiled and tried to look abashed. "I know it doesn't sound like much, and probably not what you're used to, given your background, Ms. Sutherland, but we are a small town, and it suits our needs." He signaled for the check. "I wish I could do more to help."

Kate barely kept her temper in check. Ignorant, smarmy ass. He not only knew exactly who she was and what she hoped to do, but he was going to do absolutely nothing to help her. She wouldn't be half surprised if he actively planned to campaign against her. Not that she had a shred of proof, it was just instinct. Hers or Donovan's at this point, she wasn't sure and didn't much care. She needed to get out of the diner before she said something she would regret later. She had to think of her camp first, last, and foremost.

She felt the beginnings of a tension headache spring to life. She slid out of the booth as Stan did the same. "Thank you for the coffee and your time."

His unctuous smile reappeared as he held out his hand. "My pleasure, Ms.—Kate." He gave her hand a quick shake, once again the friendly town councilman. "You stop by the office anytime and post whatever flyer or postcard you want to put up."

"Appreciated," she said, and somehow found a smile. She wondered if Stan thought she was some rich bitch socialite, dabbling in her little charitable endeavor. Her mother had not been the most compassionate person, and she'd probably made one or two enemies in the small town. Louisa Sutherland, to put it bluntly, was a snob. And so were her clients. Whenever possible, she'd avoided using the town's admittedly limited resources. Only the best would do. And the best was certainly not going to be found in Ralston.

But something told her this had to do with more than the possibility of her mother's lingering reputation. The camp had been closed down for almost a decade, and she'd abdicated a lion's share of the day-to-day management long before that. And while the town might not have fully prospered from the camp, it hadn't been hurt any by it either. And here she was, wanting to help their economy yet again, and it was all the chamber of commerce head could do to give her five seconds of his time. Business was business. Money talked louder than old reputations.

It just didn't add up.

"What do you know of Timberline Industries?" she blurted out, immediately kicking herself for her momentary lapse. But, dammit, she wanted to shake him up a little, let him know he wasn't dealing with some brainless twit.

His gaze narrowed for a fraction of a second, and Kate suddenly wondered if she'd just done something a bit more brainless than she'd intended. But it was too late now.

"Not sure I recognize the name," he said, recovering so smoothly it was as if his momentary lapse in keeping his guard up hadn't even happened. "Why do you ask?"

"Oh, no reason, really. Shelby had made some comment about them—" She stopped, smiled apologetically, and waved off the rest of the sentence. "Never mind."

"Fine, then. I must be getting back." He paused beside the table as she slid out and stepped past him. "And, uh, my condolences on the passing of your mother."

Stan couldn't usher her out of Deenie's fast enough. Kate wasn't sure how awkward it was going to be when they reached the sidewalk and he realized they were headed in the same direction, as she had to pass back by the chamber office on her way back to her truck. "Thank you," she told him as he opened the door for her. Mercifully, someone back in the diner called him over to their table.

"Sorry," he said, his smile not remotely sincere at this point.

"Not a problem. Thank you for your time."

"A pleasure, Ms. Sutherland." Which it clearly hadn't been. For either of them.

The door closed behind her, and Kate stepped onto the sidewalk and let out a long sigh. "Well, that went just peachy," she muttered.

"Didn't look like it." Donovan pushed away from the bus stop sign he was leaning against and fell into step beside her.

Chapter 7

"I thought we were meeting back at the truck."

He thought she seemed a little flustered. "I was headed that way and saw you through the window. Thought I'd wait."

She tucked her hand in the crook of his arm and tugged him gently, but firmly down the block.

"What's going on?" Mac asked, letting her tug him along.

"I don't know," she said. "That's the problem. But until I do, if you're going to help me, maybe it's better that the whole town doesn't see me with you. In fact—" She dropped his arm and stopped. "Why don't you go around the block that way and I'll—"

"Graffiti all over your camp doesn't faze you, but a cup of coffee with Stan Harris and you're spooked. What happened in there?"

"Do you know Stan? Why didn't you tell me that? What can you tell me about him?" She started walking again.

Mac had to step fast to catch up to her. "So Stan did spook you. What the hell did he say?"

She reached the truck and all but flung herself into the driver's seat. "Hurry up before anyone else comes along. I should have thought this through better."

"Which part?" he asked, climbing in the passenger side, barely closing the door before she was already backing out of the space. "The part where you storm into town or the part where you storm back out of it?"

"Very funny. Did you want to help me or not?"

She wasn't looking at him; she was negotiating her way through the only intersection they had to cover and boot-legging it out of town.

"You might want to be careful there, Leadfoot. I know Sheriff Gilby is on the far side of retirement, but I'm guessing that's just made him more ornery. He loves nothing more than a good speed trap."

"What do you know about Stan? And you know Gilby?" She slowed momentarily and shot him a wary look of suspicion that he definitely didn't like.

"I don't think I like what you're implying. In fact, I know damn well I don't."

"Just answer me. You knew I was coming into town to see Stan, yet you didn't say anything about knowing him."

"I don't know him. Not personally. But I know his family. And I just told you, Gilby has been on the force here since I was a teenager. I can assure you, I sincerely wish he didn't happen to be sheriff, as it would probably be easier to get the information we need from someone who hadn't personally arrested me for being drunk in public when I was seventeen. But he was just a beat cop in those days. I doubt he remembers me."

Kate fell silent and kept her gaze on the road. He wasn't sure where her thoughts were, but they didn't seem to be on him any longer. It wasn't much of a bonus.

He let her have a minute, then calmly asked, "What did Stan say?"

"It's more what he didn't say." She paused a moment, then asked, "What do you know about his family? He's probably a good twenty years older than we are, so—"

"So, I know his dad was vice president at the bank when I left. Wouldn't be surprised if he was president now."

"Wouldn't he be retired? He'd have to be well into his seventies."

Mac shook his head. "Jim Harris is just the type to work until he drops dead rather than let anyone else take over. The only reason I know anything about Stan is I remember there being a bit of a to-do when he came back to town."

"Came back? From where?"

"Stan went to college, which was rare enough from this place, then stayed in the city for a while. But he came back with big plans of running for the county seat, and using that as a springboard to a state political office. His daddy couldn't have been prouder and let everyone know it."

"And?"

Mac shrugged. "I don't know. I'm guessing given the position he currently holds, that that was as far as he made it. You'd think he'd have gotten the hell back out by now."

"Why do you say that?"

"I passed by his office on the way to Deenie's. Not exactly burning up the place with his fancy degree, is he?"

"So that's the only measure of success? Having a degree and using it in some ostentatious way?"

"You know better than that."

"I thought I did."

He didn't like that she was so quick to judge him harshly. "Given my background, I'd hardly be a snob about degrees and such."

"Did you go to college?"

"No. I bounced around the city for a bit, doing odd jobs, mostly working as a mechanic. Ended up at the police academy."

"How did that happen?"

Mac shifted in his seat. He'd never been comfortable talking about himself, and now was definitely no different. "I grew up with a lot of injustice, and I guess I decided I could make a bigger difference in the world than just turning wrenches like my old man. And I wasn't dismissing Stan for being what he is. It just seemed a waste, given his education and his aspirations. I'd think you'd understand. You're using yours, after all."

She cut him a sharp glance. "What do you know about my degree?"

He smiled unapologetically. "Everything I could dig up on-line in the twenty minutes I had."

"On-line? Where can you get on-line in Ralston?"

"Library." He didn't bother to tell her he could access the Internet from his sat phone, too. He glanced at the road. They were headed out of town, but in the opposite direction. "Where are we going?"

"The mall."

"Mall?" he said, mentally adjusting his plans. He should have asked her what her plans were sooner. "How far a hike is that going to be?"

"About ten minutes. They built one out by the interstate exit a few years ago. Bagel needs some food, and they have a pet store there." She glanced at him again. "You could pick up a few things if you need to."

He looked down at himself. "What, my sartorial choices not meeting with your social standards?"

She didn't take offense to his teasing, which he took as a positive sign. She'd calmed down and gotten herself back on track quickly, which was good to note. Not that it had been an entirely bad thing to see her so disturbed back there. It was past time that she took things a bit more seriously. And if he couldn't shake her up, then he was just glad someone had.

"I really don't have time for a shopping spree," he said. "We didn't talk to Gilby yet, and—"

"Gilby will have to wait." She kept driving, but looked at him and shook her head a little. He even caught a hint of a smile, which relieved him a little. And that wasn't entirely a good thing. He needed to take the situation seriously, too. They couldn't both afford to be distracted.

Then she swallowed something that sounded like a snicker. It wasn't a sound he'd have associated with the Kate he thought he knew. It sounded good on the Kate she actually was.

Yeah, he was definitely getting distracted. Thirty minutes apart hadn't been near enough time for him to get his bearings back. "What's wrong with what I have on?"

"Nothing, really. I just never figured you for a Taz type."

He glanced down at the cartoon character stitched above the pocket of his black T-shirt. "Taz and I have a lot in common. I refuse to take full responsibility, though. The little general store I stopped in on my way up was rather limiting in their selection of menswear."

"You stopped on your way up here to go clothes shopping?"

"Well, it was that or live in the same jeans and T-shirt for who knows how long. And trust me, the ones I had on when I left were not something I could wear for any length of time."

Her smile faded. "What happened to your luggage?"

"Nothing. I didn't happen to have any on me when Rafe dumped me curbside at JFK."

"JFK?"

"We were in the city on a job. Rafe needed the vehicle we had, so I had to get another car to get up here. JFK has rentals. Plus, when I bring it back, I can just hop a flight home."

"So . . . coming here really was Rafe's idea?"

"Let's just say he didn't give me any time to talk myself back out of it."

She stared at the road again, letting the silence grow, then abruptly said, "What else do you know about Stan? Do you really think his father runs the bank now?"

Back to business. He knew he'd be wise to follow her lead. "Tell me what went on this morning. For that matter, now's a good time for you to give me a rundown of the whole story."

"You know pretty much everything. You probably know more than I do, for that matter. You've been cruising the Internet, and, I imagine, talking to your cohorts back in Virginia. Why don't you tell me what you already know?"

He smiled, liking how she always met him head-on. "You know, if we ever expand the business, take on more cohorts, you'd probably fit right in."

"I'll keep it in mind," she said dryly. "So what dirt did you dig up on me?"

"Just that your mother apparently stunned everyone by leaving you, the estranged daughter, everything, while favored son Shelby just got the camp property."

"Nothing new there. Go on."

"What caused the estrangement? You said before you hadn't talked to her since leaving for college."

"She wanted Shelby and me to jump to her bidding, and only one of us was willing to play that game. Shelby's always had his eye on the prize, that being the Sutherland-Graham fortune. He was more than willing to sell his soul for it. When I turned eighteen, I wanted to lead my life on my own terms. That didn't sit too well with her, so she cut me off."

Mac hadn't had a lot of time and had barely skimmed the surface of information on Louisa and her dysfunctional family. Kate had briefly mentioned the estrangement earlier, but he didn't know about the financial reversal. "That must have been tough on you."

"I was heading off to college at the time. My mother had certain ideas about where I would go and what I would study. I had other ideas. But I had a few partial scholarship offers, so I chose a small in-state school and worked off the rest of my tuition. It wasn't easy, but it was very likely the best thing that ever happened to me. I became fully independent, it got Shelby off my back, and my mother finally had nothing left to hold over me." She glanced at him, then right back to the road. "Even rich families aren't necessarily happy ones."

Thinking of his partner, Finn, Mac already knew that to be true. "Money doesn't buy everything, no, but it would have gone a long way toward getting your camp up and running. So, tell me more about this deal you and Shelby struck with the trade. Just how much of a cash settlement did you work out? Seems like no matter how you look at it, Shelby is coming out a giant winner here. If you were willing to settle for so little, what was there to hammer out? I'm surprised he didn't sign the deed over to you that day and write you a check."

"It wasn't just the amount on the bottom net worth line. It was about what was right. And, to Shelby, what was right was inheriting the Sutherland-Graham fortune, lock, stock, and barrel."

"So, what, he's doing you a favor by letting you have the campground and a little spending money?"

"You . . . well, you knew Shelby, at least somewhat, back then. He was around camp all the time in the summer, watching over Louisa's interests."

Mac remembered Shelby as being a rat-faced little weasel who'd go running to Louisa the moment he thought he knew something that could get someone else in trouble.

"Nothing much has changed. He felt that since I had abdicated my position in the family, it was, by default, all his. And, to some degree, I can understand his viewpoint. He might not have wanted the camp per se, or even given a thought to the property itself in years; it was the point of the thing. It was his father's, and now it was his, and I wanted it."

"And you had Louisa's entire empire, which he wanted. Come on."

"And he could have kept me and the will in probate for the rest of my natural life, too, and would have, over something essentially that stupid. But that's Shelby, and also something I couldn't afford. But I know how to handle Shelby, and that's to make him think he's getting the better of me, while making him think it's also his idea to be the benevolent dictator. He learned well at my mother's knee, but so did I."

"And?"

"And so we spent an inordinate amount of time hammering out all the details, but far less time than we would have otherwise. We recently came to a final agreement, which is that I get the campground, as well as a few of the stocks, specifically ones that had been in my mother's name prior to her marriage to George Sutherland, when she'd been married to my biological father. That was enough, or will be, to secure a loan from the bank to finance the rehab and reconstruction of the property and get the camp started. It's more than I'd hoped for when I contacted them again to look into leasing the property in the first place. And it's all I feel comfortable taking, to be perfectly honest with you."

She'd inherited millions in assets and was going to rely on a bank loan to finance her camp? "I still say you should have held on to a hell of lot more than that."

"I did what was right for me."

Mac didn't say anything to that, knowing she had a point. "So, she knew you were interested in leasing the property before she died?"

Kate nodded. "I'd approached her with a lease agreement proposal before she died. Well, I approached her attorney. She took ill before we could set anything up."

"But she knew you wanted it."

She nodded. "If I had any doubts, the inheritance sort of cemented those."

"Which begs the question of why you'd go back and willingly tie yourself to her in any way again. Why give her that hold over you again after so many years? If she knew you really wanted it, wouldn't she have taken advantage of that? Obviously she would have, seeing what she did with her will."

"I'm sure she would have, but I felt I could handle it now, as an adult. And I guess a part of me thought maybe we'd all grown up enough that it was time to make some inroads into at least being civil with one another. I'd long since come to accept my family situation, but that doesn't mean I was content with it. The lake property was perfect for what I wanted to do. I didn't have the kind of resources I needed to lease any other property. It seemed like a good olive branch and a wise business decision."

"And if you hadn't made contact, would Shelby have notified you of her illness?"

"Hard to say, but I'm guessing I'd have likely read about it in the papers, same as you. Or from a family attorney when the will was slated to be read."

Ouch. She was speaking matter-of-factly, much the same way he did when talking about his past. Which he made a point never to do. And for her this was far more recent. He knew firsthand that it was likely costing her more than she was letting on. Who'd have thought he'd have so much in common with Kate Sutherland after all?

"I'm sorry."

"Thanks," she said, sounding a little surprised by his sentiment, but then, so was he. "Like I said, though, I made peace with my less than lovely circumstances with my family a long time ago. Does that suck in a lot of ways? Yes. But you know better than anyone that family life can suck for a lot of people. I have no room to complain, and I have a lot to be thankful for. I have a career that I'm very passionate about, and the drive to make a particular dream of mine come true. All I needed was the resources, and although that didn't happen quite the way I expected, it looks like it will come to pass. My mother is gone, and this won't bring Shelby and I any closer, but I realize now that nothing will ever do that. At least I tried, and I have whatever peace of mind there is to be gained out of knowing he has what he wanted so badly. All in all, not much to complain about from where I sit."

"Except someone still doesn't want you to have your camp. We're just not sure who."

She didn't say anything for a few seconds, then finally let out a reluctant sigh. "No. It's not all going according to plan. Not exactly. I need to talk to Shelby. I'm sure there's a simple explanation for things with him. Then we'll talk to Gilby and see what we can get from him. I guess I just have a hard time buying into any deep conspiracy theory here. I know there are a lot of things going on simultaneously that make it appear to be fishy, but you know, there could be simple explanations for all of it."

"There could," he agreed.

She glanced at him, eyebrow raised, but he merely said, "You were in the city yesterday. Why not talk to Shelby then?"

"We were supposed to. We had an appointment to finalize the paperwork, transferring the inheritances. He didn't show."

"And you don't find that a little suspicious?"

She slowed and turned into the vast parking lot of the shopping mall. "Not really. Shelby is a major pain in the ass about almost everything. For all I know, it conflicted with his biweekly spa treatment. You never know with him. But until I talk to him myself, I'm not going to jump to any nefarious assumptions."

"Were there any hang-ups with the contract?"

"Oh, there were dozens. It's taken us months to hammer this out, with almost constant communication, but we're both satisfied with the result. In fact, up until yesterday, I'd have said the rest was a mere formality. I mean, he knows I've moved in up here and that I'm doing the preliminary work on starting the restoration. If he had any real beef with the settlement, he'd have never let me take physical hold of the property."

"You've already taken out the loan, then?"

She shook her head. "No, I won't have the stock collateral

until the papers are signed. What little I've done so far, mostly to make my cabin habitable, has come from my own pocket."

"Do you think Shelby will pick up where your mother left off, in terms of trying to leverage you even after the agreement is signed? You're giving him a lot of power."

"I don't see why he'd care what I do once he has what he wants. Yes, it was his father's, but he was personally involved with it only because it positioned him at Louisa's right elbow. He has no use for it now. Honestly, I think the only thing he really hates is that he has to trade it away to me, rather than sell it to me. But that's Shelby for you. As long as I end up with the camp and a way to get it up and running, frankly, I don't much care about the rest."

"So why isn't he signing off? Something tells me that a guy like Shelby is going to make sure his schedule is clear when it comes to securing his multimillion-dollar inheritance. No call, nothing?"

She shook her head. "I haven't tried yet today. I was still pretty upset when I got home last night, and then—"

"I show up." He smiled.

She managed a smile in return. "I know I've been dealing with some problems at the camp. I—I hadn't really connected it to Shelby, or anything else really, because there was no reason to."

"But?"

She lifted a shoulder. "Now I don't know. I feel like I'm being paranoid, but—" She broke off, didn't continue.

"But what? Trust your instincts."

"Well, the stuff going on at camp . . . now you've got me wondering if maybe there's something more going on with that and the reluctance of the townspeople to help me. It seems so ridiculous to me. I mean, they don't even know me and, if anything, when the camp was up and running before, it helped Ralston economically. So all I can figure is that there is something pending out there that could help them even more. What else would make them so resentful?"

"You mean the rumored resort development deal?"

"Do you know anything else about that?"

"Not yet." He paused, then said, "I know you're taking in a lot here, but I really want you to think about the possibility that Shelby not signing yesterday might be tied up with that, too."

She sighed wearily, but she didn't argue. "I tried to push Stan in that direction a little this morning."

Mac sat up a little straighter. "And? What did you say?"

"I asked him if he'd spoken to Shelby, and he had no idea what I was talking about. But I'm telling you, the whole conversation was weird. I kept thinking it was because you planted those seeds in my mind and I was just imagining things, but I really think something is going on with the townsfolk. Or some of them anyway."

"Why? What did he say?"

"It was more what he didn't say. He just sort of spouted the party line and pretended to be helpful and interested, but the entire time I couldn't shake the feeling he was lying to me. About what, I don't know. Or hiding something. I had to go track him down; he wasn't even in the office to meet me. He acted like he knew nothing about me, and I know that's not true." She shrugged. "It's just not adding up, but I can't give you anything specific."

"Never ignore gut instincts. They might not be dead accurate, but they're usually grounded in something." Sort of like his instincts about Kate being someone special. He'd gotten all hung up on the superficial stuff way back when and let it dull those burgeoning instincts. Now? Now he was just all hung up. "Something's going on, and my money is on there being a better than average chance that Stan, possibly his father, Timberline, and Shelby could all be a part of it."

He popped his seat belt off, opened the door and climbed out.

"Wait! You're going to just drop that little bomb on me, then go off shopping?"

He bent back down and looked into the cab. "No. I'm dropping that little bomb, and you're coming shopping with me." He smiled. "It was your idea."

She stared at him, shoulders set, jaw momentarily mutinous, then relented and popped her seat belt buckle. "Fine. But you start picking out cartoon clothing and I'm not holding back my opinions."

He closed the door and looked at her over the cab roof as she got out. "I wouldn't have it any other way."

She made a noise that clearly stated she found him completely insufferable. He could be, so there was no point attempting to change her mind. But before the day was over, she'd also find out he was doggedly determined about getting the job done.

"We need to do more research on Timberline, and I need to get a hold of Shelby, so I don't want to take too long here," she said, setting off across the parking lot with long, determined strides. "I still have to get in Gilby's face, too, about the most recent round of graffiti, but I'm thinking now maybe that should wait until we know more. I don't know if we should snoop around town any more at this point. We need to find a way to dig a little, but discreetly. Maybe I could head back into the city and—"

Mac just smiled and pulled his satellite phone from the clip on his belt. He punched a number in, waited a second, then said, "Things are getting interesting. I'm going to need to update that list a little."

Finn just hummed his little I-told-you-so hum.

Mac knew he deserved nothing less. "I'll have a shipping address for you by tonight, but in the meantime, I need a few more reports run." He reeled off some of the same names Kate had just mentioned. "Anything you can find connecting them together wins you the bonus prize."

"Do I get to pick?" Finn shot back. "Because I was doing

some research today on another little project and stumbled across this unbelievably sweet little deal on a new toy we really need to have. It'll make some of our current jobs much easier and allow us to expand our—"

Mac grinned as he clicked the phone off cutting his partner off mid-drool. Finn definitely used his vast asset base to do good deeds, but that didn't mean he didn't enjoy an interesting perk or two. Or three. They were always business-related investments, but only Finn could find a way to turn something like, oh, say, buying a small island into a business investment. God only knew what he was eyeballing now. Lately he'd gotten rather . . . creative.

Mac looked at a worried Kate and thought, if Finn could dig up some information that would help him take away the fear in those baby blues of hers, he'd personally see to it that Finn had whatever toy he wanted.

He shot Kate a wide smile meant to reassure and distract. Not necessarily in that order. "Discreet enough for you?" He crooked an elbow and held it out to her. "Come on, let's spend some more of Finn's money."

"Mac—"

He brightened at her automatic use of his nickname. "See? You're already getting with the program." He took her hand and tucked it through his arm, clamping down a little so she couldn't pull it back. He tugged her a few steps across the parking lot before she gave up and fell into step beside him. "Trust me, Kate," he said, more serious than he'd intended. "You're not fighting this alone. Whatever we dig up, you've got Trinity behind you all the way."

She shook her head. "I still can't believe you used that as your company name."

"Hey, at least we left the 'unholy' part off the letterhead."

He got a wry smile for that. "Something tells me your clients figure out that part all on their own. Probably within five seconds of meeting any one of the three of you." She tried to tug her hand free.

He kept it easily pinned to his side. "True. But no complaints so far."

"I bet."

He grinned. "We get the job done."

She shot him a sideways glance, lips quirking slightly. "Like I said . . ." She tugged harder this time, and he let her hand go.

"How did I suddenly get to be the bad guy again?"

"Bad boy is more like it," she said as she walked in front of him.

He took her elbow and gently swung her back around to face him. "I thought we cleared this up back in the truck."

"We did. You're an unrepentant womanizer, and you have a strong work ethic, so I bargained your integrity against your libido, and won. Now you're already reneging on the deal."

"How?" he asked, honestly perplexed. "I'm playing by the rules. Your rules."

She sent a pointed look to where his hands were bracing both of her elbows.

"That's different," he said immediately. When she just looked at him, he smiled, but lifted his hands away, palms up. "Fine. But, for future reference, if I'm going to put my hands on you in a rule-breaking way, I'm not going to waste time with your elbows, okay?"

Her skin pinked and her eyes darkened, and Mac was reminded why he shouldn't play with her particular brand of fire. She only had to stand there and stare him down and he was suddenly in trouble. "All I was trying to say was that unlike your mother and Shelby and who knows who else in your life, there are no strings attached to my help." He grinned. "I'm your proverbial fairy godmother."

A laugh snorted out of her, catching them both off guard.

"Fairy godfather?" he amended.

She laughed outright. "Stop."

And he thought, *I could so fall for you*. Which shouldn't

have come as such a complete shock to him. But it was a fact that a whole lot more than his hormones were getting engaged here.

He struck off across the parking lot. "Come on, we'll get Bagel his fancy-schmancy doggie food—although you do realize you're unmanning the poor guy. Just give him regular old dog chow—then you can help me pick out some mountain man stuff. After that, I need to find a place to rent a post office box. I'll buy you lunch and we'll go over everything, set up a game plan you can live with. We should have something from Finn by then. I'll even drive home—back to camp."

Home. It wasn't a word that sprang to his lips, even casually. Maybe especially then.

"We'll see," was all she said, and matched his long-legged stride across the lot.

Chapter 8

"You shop like a man."

Kate walked around to the driver's side of the truck. "I'm going to take that as a compliment."

Donovan followed her around and reached past her for the door handle. "Take a break, General Patton. I'll drive."

She beat him to the door handle and shot him a look, debating the relative merits of fighting that particular battle. She was bone tired, still a little freaked out despite his attempts to lighten things up during their little impromptu shopping spree, and she'd just spent a mind-numbing forty-five minutes in a noisy mall speed shopping with Neanderthal Man so she could get them out of there and back to the more important business of finding out what the hell was going on.

She lifted her hand from the handle. "Fine." She dropped her key ring into the waiting palm of his hand, ignoring his look of surprise.

He tossed his shopping bags in the back and quickly climbed in as she walked around to the other side and got in.

"I asked at the information desk while you were trying on that God-awful green and black plaid shirt, and they said there're no postal box rental places anywhere around here. I'm not even sure they knew what I was talking about. But I'm fairly certain they're right. Most folks here wouldn't have the need of a separate box. Why can't you just use the Winnimocca address?"

"Security. Don't worry, I've got another idea." He pulled out on the main road and continued heading in the opposite direction of the camp.

"Shouldn't we start heading back? Did you check to see if Finn called?"

"Yes, dear. Five minutes ago when we left the mall, right around the last time you asked." He didn't turn the truck around.

"And to think I was nice and let you drive. Where are we going?"

"You're beat, I'm starved, and we could use a little refueling. So could your truck from the look of the gauge."

"It's broken. I go by the mile counter." She leaned over to get a look, instantly regretting the move when she got a whiff of, well, Donovan. He smelled all woodsy and good and—she looked at him. "What?"

"You sniffed me."

"I did not." She straightened back to her side of the truck and tried not to look mortified.

"Cologne Girl ambushed me going into Melton's department store." He glanced at her, gray eyes twinkling. "Do you like it?"

She turned her attention resolutely forward. Couldn't incriminate herself—or worse, encourage him further—if she kept her mouth shut.

He drove for another minute, then shot a grin her way that she couldn't miss even in her peripheral vision. Donovan had the kind of smile you felt.

"That good, huh? Maybe I should go back and—"

Her hand shot out when he changed lanes and looked as if he were going to pull a U-turn. "No. Food is the only thing I want to be sniffing right now."

He let her keep her dignity. For three seconds. "Liar."

She ignored him and his tangible grin. "How long do you think it will take Finn to get back to you? And what, exactly, are you having sent up here? Why not just ship it directly to the camp? Who'd know?"

"We just paraded ourselves all over Ralston. Word will spread that you're not living alone out at the camp."

"Does anyone know you're back? Has anyone recognized you?"

He shook his head. "No, and I didn't recognize anyone either, but it won't take long to figure out."

"Does it really matter?"

He shrugged. "Don't know yet. But it might not be bad for them to realize you're not fending for yourself out there. And if they figure out it's me keeping you company, that might actually work in our favor."

"Why is that?"

"Who'd ever suspect drunk Donny Mac's son had amounted to anything?"

Kate massaged her temples, but the beginnings of a tension headache persisted. "I really want to believe you're wrong about all of this. I want to believe that I'll get a hold of Shelby. He'll sign the papers. I can start hiring work crews and they'll see I mean business. And who knows, maybe just having the laborers around will deter whoever is spray painting messages all over the property. Problems solved."

That was the plan she should be preparing for. All this wild speculation about developers wanting to take over her property and the townsfolk wanting her out, or Shelby maybe working some kind of side deal intending to screw her over, was pure fantasy. He was selfish, greedy, and petulant, but she didn't want to believe he'd go this far.

"I'm not going to tell you that's an impossible scenario. I don't know enough yet. But highly improbable? I'm afraid so."

"So you think Shelby is somehow linked to the townsfolk, the developers, and the graffiti? Why would he risk losing the entire Sutherland inheritance?" When Donovan didn't say anything, she folded her arms. "What?"

He glanced at her, then back to the road. "I didn't say anything."

"If you know something else, just say it."

"I don't. But it's not a bad thing to talk out alternatives. You never know what correlation we might draw, or put together some other lead we might have missed. Speculation isn't a bad thing. Even if it's wrong."

She wanted to be mad at him, even though she realized it was just an excuse to focus her feelings of helplessness on something tangible. Or someone. Instead, she took a deep breath and let it out slowly, forcing herself to relax back against the seat. Getting worked up wasn't going to help matters any. Besides, she'd already gotten worked up quite enough for one morning, thank you. Her gaze slid sideways across the seat, to where Donovan's hand rested on the gear shift. His jean-clad legs just beyond in the same line of sight.

His hands were broad, flat, with wide, scarred fingers. And there was nothing scrawny about those thighs of his either. She swallowed another urge to sigh; only this time she was afraid it would sound more wistful than weary. He'd put his hands on her, his mouth on her . . . Her heart kicked up just thinking about what had happened in this very cab on the way here. Yes, she was tired, and scared and worried about getting her dream realized . . . but that wasn't the reason her pulse was racing and her palms grew damp.

No, the reason for that was driving her old pickup like he'd been born to it . . . and driving her to distraction while he was at it.

The truck bounced hard as he turned off the main road onto a dirt and gravel route. "Where in the heck—?"

He held up his hand. "Trust me."

"I'm already getting tired of that one. Just tell me. I'm not feeble-minded or fragile."

He glanced at her. "Never said you were."

"So, then . . . ?"

"I need to pin down an alternate delivery address."

"Out here?"

"Hope so." They bumped and bounced over the rutted road, making her grab the dash and the armrest to keep from cracking her head against the roof. She already knew better than to ask him anything else. She'd find out soon enough anyway.

A few teeth-jarring minutes later, he pulled off into an overgrown field. A weather-beaten barn held court amongst the shoulder-high weeds.

He parked and got out. She sighed and followed him. "I don't think this thing has a mailing address."

"Nope." He stopped and stared at the barn, hands on his hips. "Makes one hell of a nice mailbox, though. Can't beat the price either."

He started walking toward it, beating aside the grass as he went. "Watch out for snakes."

"If you're expecting me to leap and squeal, you're going to be sorely disappointed. You might have wanted to change out of those running shoes, though. Snake teeth'll go right through that open mesh weave. Perfectly nice, brand-new boots back in the truck."

The grass and weeds were so tall they kept the sun from penetrating all the way down, and the ground beneath their feet was more muck and mire than packed dirt.

"I'll manage."

"Men."

He chuckled, and she found herself smiling.

They walked the circumference of the weather-beaten building, which was surprisingly solid. No boards missing, the roof still mostly intact. "We're probably on private property, you know."

"Oh, I know we are."

He had driven right to this place, so he obviously knew more about it. "Who owns it?"

"Growing up, it was old George Stanfield's place. Probably his daughter, Deirdre's, now, or his grandkids'. Doesn't much matter. I'm only going to need it for about thirty minutes. An hour tops."

She stopped in front of the double doors and watched him throw his muscle behind lifting the iron lever that shifted the bar out of the handles. *Impressive*, she couldn't help but think, when the thing slowly ground and squealed its way out of the rusted-over tracks.

Once he got the bar free, they both pushed at the wooden doors and trundled them open enough to let the sunlight in before stepping into the cool, gloomy interior. The barn rose two stories at the center with parallel lofts framing either end. Both appeared empty from where she stood, as did the barn floor itself. It smelled dank and musty; the packed dirt floor was concrete hard. Mac walked to the matching set of double doors at the opposite end, then turned back and surveyed the barn as a whole.

"This'll do." He unclipped his phone, but apparently couldn't get a signal, or something, and put it back. He slid another gizmo out of his jacket pocket, along with what looked like a slender PDA. He walked the perimeter, tapping in notes, then took some kind of reading from the gizmo, noted that down, then looked up at her and smiled. "I need to walk around a bit outside."

She followed him back out, but stayed by the open doors as he walked out farther into the grass field, tapping in other notes, taking more readings.

"What are you measuring?"

"Not measuring now. Getting coordinates."

"For?"

He turned, smiled. "Landing pad."

"Landing p—" She broke off, shook her head. "Why do I ask questions I might not want the answers to?" *Landing pad*. Not landing strip. Or drop zone. That could mean only one thing.

He swatted his way back through the tall grass. He was less than ten yards away when she said, "Helicoptor?" At his nod, she asked, "What on earth do you need delivered that badly?"

He didn't even blink. "It's not the urgency, though this kind of is. You do have a deadline you're operating under. It's more a matter of getting what I need, when I need, how I need, without anyone else needing to know I have it."

"And you think having a helicopter land in the middle of a field just outside of town isn't going to raise one or two eyebrows?"

"First of all, we're far enough outside of town to be on the backside of the range separating us from Ralston. If we use the right approach pattern"—he patted his PDA—"which we will, no one will see us come in or go out. In case you haven't noticed, not a lot of traffic or established residences on this side of the mountain." She glanced up as he pointed to the rise behind her, which she noticed was mostly all sheer rock wall. Nary a chimney or building marred the vista for as far as she could see.

"I picked this place for elevation—most farmland is in the valley. This is tucked away, high up, easy access. In and out."

"I'm building a camp for challenged kids. I don't think it requires planning like we're evacuating refugees out of Cambodia."

"A plan is a plan, regardless of the objective."

She just stared at him. *Who is this man?* He'd said, in the truck this morning, after kissing her, that he really didn't know who she was. Clearly she didn't know who he was either. The teenager she'd known could have dismantled and reassembled any engine blindfolded, and was reputedly just as good with his hands in other arenas. But that was where his skill set had begun and ended as far as she knew. The man standing before her now, plotting helicopter coordinates as easily as if he were jotting down directions to the corner store . . . she had no idea who that guy was. Or what he was truly capable of.

"What?" he asked, looking up from tapping on his Black-Berry screen and catching her watching him.

"Just wondering," she said, not bothering to pretend she hadn't been staring. "How did you go from rural boy to city cop to—" She made a half gesture toward his PDA.

"I seem to have a knack for it."

There was an understatement, she was sure. "For what, exactly? I know you had a way with mechanical things when you were younger, but—"

He flashed her a grin. "Clever hands, you mean?"

It was silly to flush, when she'd just gotten done thinking the same exact thing. But when all she could do was think about him putting those clever hands all over her, it was kind of hard not to.

"Turns out my mechanically inclined brain isn't limited to trouble-shooting engine problems. Seems it also does a pretty good job when applied to various kinds of technology," he answered seriously enough, though the grin lingered. "It didn't hurt that my years as a detective fine-tuned my problem-solving skills." He half shrugged. "In my current field, it's a useful combination."

"In your current field," she repeated. "Good Samaritan techno security whiz."

He sketched a short bow. "I'm just a simple fairy godfather, at your service."

Her lips quirked. "You really need to stop saying that."

"Don't worry," he said, "I'm secure enough in my manhood to handle the moniker." He looked back at his PDA and started tapping again. "God knows I've been called worse in my lifetime." He scanned the field, the sky, then, distracted once again by the mission at hand, stepped back into the barn, still tapping on his PDA screen.

She stared openly now, trying to keep up with the information overload that was Donovan MacLeod, her mind spinning . . . her body clamoring. Not a wise combination. Not if she was going to be spending any appreciable alone time with him. Which, apparently, she was, seeing as they'd spent most of the day already all but joined at the hip.

She stepped into the barn behind him, and the question came out before she realized she'd thought it. "Where are you sleeping?"

He looked up, obviously surprised. "Excuse me?"

"Sleeping," she repeated, brazening it out, knowing he'd tease her. Knowing it wouldn't make that whole clamoring thing any easier to handle. But if she was going to get any peace tonight, she had to know where his body was going to be located in relationship to hers. "Back at camp, last night, where did you sleep?"

"In my rental. It was too late when I got up there to scope out any of the cabins. If you don't mind, I'll move my stuff into the first one down the hill from yours. It looks to be in decent shape, and the proximity would be a wise security measure."

"The electricity isn't hooked up and no bathroom facilities yet."

"Not a problem on the electricity. The running water, though . . ."

And instantly visions of him in her shower clouded her already fogged brain. The fog grew even thicker as she wasn't exactly picturing him alone in there. She was staring again, and worse, imagining what he looked like beneath that Taz T-shirt and those beat-up jeans. She'd seen him shirtless more often than not as a teenager. It had been the fuel for more fevered dreams than she could count. Something told her those youthful fantasies wouldn't come close to the images her very adult subconscious mind could conjure up now.

"You, uh, you can always use—" She paused to clear her throat. "We'll work something out."

His lips quirked a little, as if he knew exactly the direction her thoughts had taken her, but, mercifully, he didn't tease her. "Thanks, I appreciate that."

When he didn't return his attention to his PDA, she folded

her arms, tucking her hands against her body, and shifting her feet as if trying to get warm. Truth was, she wasn't remotely cold. Quite the opposite actually. "Are we all done here?"

"Just about." He held her gaze for another too long moment, then made one last sweeping turn, tapping in a few more things, before tucking the PDA away again. "I think we're all set." She turned to go, but he stepped in front of her. "You okay?"

"Yeah, yeah, fine, I'm fine," she said, the words coming too fast. How was she to tell him it wasn't the situation at the camp or the possible problem with Shelby that had her on edge, but her purported "fairy godfather" who was making her crazy? "I just want to get on the road, get somewhere where you can call in and see if Finn has any information for us. Start figuring out what the hell is going on, then maybe I can figure out what Shelby is up to and if I'm going to be able to get him to keep his end of the agreement, or if I'm going to even have the camp I dreamed of, much less get it open in time, and—"

"Whoa, whoa." He took her by the elbows and shook them a little, loosening them away from her body. "We'll get it all figured out. You weren't this spooked before I came along, I know that, but it's not a bad thing that you are now. Only fools don't get scared or nervous in tough situations. Keeps you sharp and alert."

She forced herself to lift her gaze to his. *The only thing that scares me and makes me nervous right now is you.* Though she appreciated the way he'd immediately stepped in and grounded her. How could he be such a calming influence in one way, and total chaos to her system in every other way?

"Yesterday I was worried about a little graffiti and Shelby being a no-show. Yesterday I was thinking I had some teenagers with too much time on their hands playing pranks and an inconsiderate stepbrother who was bogging down the paperwork process because he was probably off doing something self-centered and didn't care if he strung me along a little longer." She took a small breath, tried to square her shoulders and stand straighter, mostly because what she really wanted to do was curl against his nice, broad chest and allow herself a moment, just a moment, of someone else sharing her burden and comforting her and making her believe everything was going to be okay. It was a moment she couldn't afford to take. "Today, I have an entire town involved in what might be some kind of scam to undermine my efforts to build a camp, a stepbrother who very well might be involved in the whole thing. And a man who I haven't seen in eighteen years is plotting coordinates so he can land a helicopter in a cornfield to drop off supersecret spy supplies to put up God knows what kind of surveillance for my little youth camp." She tried for a casual, unaffected-by-all-this smile and likely missed by a mile. "So yeah, spooked is only the beginning of what I am."

Mac held her gaze for far too long. Long enough to make her rethink the relative merits of her hands-off rule. He was a danger to her equilibrium every time she got within five feet of him, but she didn't look away. Just when she was giving in to the need to lean closer—to see if he might drop his chin, lower his head, slide his hands up her arms and cup the back of her neck so he could tilt her mouth up to his, taste her again—he dropped his hands away completely, though he didn't step back.

"That's how things like this happen," he said calmly.

At first she thought by "this" he meant the crazy, out-of-control chemistry popping and sizzling between them, but then he went on, and she felt her cheeks color.

"You'll be going along in life, thinking you've got it all figured out, doing what has to be done, then something happens to change all that, to throw it off. There isn't usually a warning. Maybe lots of little ones in retrospect, but there's always a day when things irrevocably change, when you sit up and realize that it's not going to be just another day. That something's not right, and needs a closer look. You just hope that day comes soon enough so you can make a difference in your favor."

"And has it?" she asked, still struggling to put his words in the context of the vandalizing issues and Shelby's possible involvement in . . . whatever the hell was really going on. It was hard to think of anything except that the single biggest change in her life at the moment was the sudden presence of him in it.

He lifted a hand, as if he was going to caress her cheek, and she held her breath, but didn't move away. He checked the motion at the last second, let his hand fall back by his side. She had to work at not letting her shoulders slump in disappointment. It was her own stupid rule, after all.

"I hope so," he said, quite seriously.

Not the ringing affirmation she was looking for.

Alarm began to creep back in, replacing the zing of pheromones and heightened awareness. He was just being honest, and she'd always be better served by that than false bravado. "Me, too. Thank you," she said.

"For?"

"Showing up. And for knowing how to map helicopter coordinates." Her lips trembled a bit more with this smile. "I guess I need the help after all. I'm—I'm glad you're here."

She didn't get the cocky smile she anticipated. Instead, his expression grew even more serious. "We'll get to the bottom of what's going on, that I can promise you. As for what we can do about it when we find out, that remains to be seen. Sounds like there are legal issues involved, and I won't lie, that complicates things."

"Even for guys with supersecret helicopters at their disposal?"

"Not all rules are made to be broken."

"Can I get that in writing?"

A hint of a smile ghosted the corners of his mouth. "I wish

I could promise you a slam dunk. I can't. But we'll do everything we can, and that's usually a lot more than most."

She shivered, though it had nothing to do with the cool, damp interior of the barn. "'We' isn't a word I've had much experience with."

His lips curved fully then, and in his smile was all the reassurance she found she needed. "You'll get used to it. I'm not going anywhere until we've done all we can do."

There was the tiniest pang, then, at the realization that he'd be leaving again, which was ridiculous as she'd barely gotten used to the idea of him being here in the first place. Which made what she did next that much more foolish. "I am regretting one thing," she blurted, her gaze dropping from his eyes, to his mouth, then forcibly back up to his eyes again. If the way his pupils slowly expanded was any indication, he hadn't missed the slip. But then she'd bank that he rarely missed anything.

"What would that be?" he asked, his voice a shade rougher.

"Rashly made rules of conduct."

His throat worked, and her pulse shot up. "In my experience, self-preservation is always a smart move," he said, but his own gaze dropped to her mouth, all but feasted there for a long moment, if the hungry look in his eyes was any gauge to what he was thinking, then slowly moved back up to hers.

She stood all but quivering before him, realizing she'd put herself in yet another dangerous predicament, but the potential outcome of this one didn't give her a tension headache; it made her muscles tighten in the sweet ache of anticipation. It was an entirely different, rather delicious sort of tension. "Yeah. I've gotten pretty good at that." *Until you showed up*.

"Funny how, before, I wouldn't have guessed you'd have ever had to. Worry about self-preservation, I mean."

"With a mother like Louisa and family like Shelby?"

"True. I guess I wasn't thinking about family members."

"What, then? You know I haven't been living in the lap of luxury all these years, cushioned from the big bad world by some kind of trust fund."

"I was speaking of the seventeen-year-old me. Back then I thought it would be the most wonderful thing in the world to be able to just hop in that little sports car of yours and take off for points unknown."

"As I recall, you had a Harley, or some kind of bike. Why didn't you just hop on and leave?"

"As soon as I got the thing running, and hit legal age, I did. But I only got as far as New York City." He smiled. "Not all of us can hop a jet in addition to a sports car."

"I wasn't a jet-setter, even before Louisa cut me off."

"I know. But you could have been. In other words, you had options that I didn't." He didn't say it with any animosity or jealousy; it was simply fact. She supposed he had a point.

She cocked her head. "What option would you have exercised if money, or the lack thereof, hadn't been an obstacle?"

"I'm more curious to know why you didn't. Exercise those options, I mean. Seems you could have done a world of good with all that Sutherland backing."

"If you're talking about before my mother's death, then the answer is she simply never would have let me control things. Even though I would have had a trust fund and other family income to rely on, the deal would have been that Louisa called all the shots."

"She was a philanthropist, as I recall. Wouldn't she have supported your interest in helping the underprivileged or handicapped?"

"Oh, she loved cutting checks. As long as the *New York Times* got wind of her latest donation. She wouldn't have minded me following in those footsteps. But to actually get in and work at fixing it with my own two hands?" She shook her head. "Too common. She'd worked way too hard to distance herself from the common folk for me to become one of them."

"Was that what caused the final rift between you two?"

"No, we'd been butting heads all along. I never fit in the mold she'd created for me since the day she'd changed my last name from Pepperdine to Sutherland so the world would think I was one of them."

"Why not take back your real last name?"

She shrugged. "Doesn't feel any more mine than this one. And I didn't need the symbolism." She smiled. "Suddenly having zero dollars in my bank account and all my credit cards cut off was symbolism enough for me. It wasn't like my name was opening any doors. No one knew who my mother was if I didn't tell them."

He nodded, smiled a little. "So, when did you start working with kids?" He paused, then cocked his head. "Do you have any? Of your own, I mean?"

He looked so alarmed by the idea, she had to laugh. "No, don't worry, I haven't stashed any away somewhere."

"No, it wasn't that. I just—I guess it keeps hitting me how little I really know of you."

"I figured that would be the first thing you'd Google."

"What, your personal history?" He shook his head. "I was trying to dig up information on the camp and the town."

"Nary a search on my background then?"

He shook his head. "Only the education. And not because I didn't want to know. But I figured I had you here for that. If I wanted to know something about you, I could just ask. I focused on looking for the stuff I didn't have any other way of finding out about."

Made sense. When had he become the practical, level-headed one? "So . . . do you?"

"Do I what?"

"Want to know anything? Anything else, anyway?"

His grin was slow, confident, and downright devastating

to her already engaged libido. What was she thinking, taunting him like that?

"Oh, I want to know it all. But it's going to have to wait. We need to get out of here." He stepped back, putting more distance between them.

Distance she found she didn't like all that much. For a few minutes there, she'd calmed down, relaxed a little. She wondered if he'd purposely driven the conversation that way just for that reason. It made her want to lower her guard with him. Made her want to believe that engaging him in a little harmless flirtation was simply an exercise in taking her mind off her troubles. Except he was trouble. And there was nothing harmless about him. "Do you think Finn has more information by now?"

"Probably. Come on." He led the way out of the barn.

"Do we need to close these back up?" she asked, motioning to the doors.

He shook his head. "Later. After the mailman comes."

She looked from the barn to the field, to the skyline beyond, and tried to imagine a sleek little helicopter swooping in like some kind of stealth bird. Somehow her life had turned into an action adventure flick when she wasn't looking. And the leading man was Donovan MacLeod.

He led the way through the tall grass and bent stalks back toward the truck. "I'll drive."

She didn't bother to argue. She'd be lying if she said she couldn't use a little time to get her thoughts in order. Not to mention getting her physical reaction to him under control. "Okay," she said, opening the door.

He folded his arms on the roof of the little truck and stared at her until she felt it and glanced over at him. "What? Sometimes I don't argue."

"Good to know. But I was just going to say, don't be so put out that I didn't do extensive research on you." He winked. "I like to do my Googling up close and personal. Besides, I like a woman of mystery."

"There's nothing remotely mysterious about me," she said, trying to quell the images of what being personally Googled by a man like Donovan would feel like. Probably pretty damn good. Whatever it entailed. "And I wasn't put out," she added, sounding exactly that. But he was already in the cab.

Rather than prolong the discussion, she climbed in, buckled up, and turned her thoughts back to the camp, and her little talk with Stan in town earlier. As it turned out, that was a surefire way to kill her little libidinal buzz. "I have a bad feeling about all this," she said, not realizing she'd spoken out loud until Donovan responded.

"I'm glad you said it first. Come on," he said, putting the truck in gear and pressing on the gas. "Let's go see what we can do about changing that."

There was that word again. "We." She liked it. Too damn much.

Better not get too used to it. Donovan wasn't going to stick around this time any more than he had when he turned eighteen. Some things didn't change.

She let her gaze slide across the seat and secretly watched the play of muscles along his thigh and forearm as he shifted gears and floored the gas when he hit the paved road.

The scary part was how badly she already wanted him.

Chapter 9

Mac had long since paced a permanent track into the packed dirt outside the barn. He hadn't wanted Kate to come back with him. He'd wanted to handle the delivery without her interference or questions. In fact, he'd been ready to insist she stay behind at the cabin. But the information he'd gotten from Finn had surprised him. He'd encountered a few roadblocks in his attempts to connect Timberline to Shelby or Stan or anyone else in Ralston. That there were any obstacles at all was a red flag in and of itself.

So he'd decided to keep her with him. Now the damn helicopter was late, and even with the sat phone, he was having a devil of a time getting a consistent signal out here. He couldn't make contact with Finn to find out where the damn chopper was, and it took only a glance at the horizon and the rapid descent of the sun to tell him things were going to get a lot trickier if it didn't show up soon. They'd specifically chosen a late landing, but this was cutting it close.

"Is there a problem?" Kate had noted him tapping on his PDA. Again.

He flipped the case shut and stuffed it in his pocket. "Other than my partner making me crazy, no."

She leaned back against the barn, looking for all the world as if she stood around in the middle of nowhere waiting for helicopter deliveries all the time. "I know I keep saying this,

but I still can't believe the three of you are working together."
She smiled. "I think it's kind of cool, actually. Poetic justice,
of sorts."

"You have no idea," Mac muttered, looking at the sky
once again.

"How do you like Virginia?"

He turned his attention back to her. She'd changed her
clothes since this morning. Her hair was back in a ponytail,
and her face was still free of makeup. She wore loose jeans
and an old college sweatshirt. In deference to the chilly spring
evening, she'd donned a canvas jacket that smelled surprisingly like musty stables. Nothing remotely sexy about any of
it. And yet he had a hard time keeping his eyes off of her.

"I like it okay. Pretty, rural, peaceful. Can't say the neigh-
bors like us too much." He smiled a little. "We don't exactly
fit in with the horse set."

Kate laughed shortly. "Even Finn? He's one of theirs."

"He's been a black sheep for way too long to be considered one of theirs. It was old news that he and his father didn't
see eye-to-eye. The locals weren't too happy to hear he di-
vested himself of all of his daddy's companies either."

"Do they know what kind of business you're running out
there?"

Mac shrugged. "We don't exactly advertise. And we don't
exactly care what they think."

"How do you choose who you help?"

"We just keep our ears and eyes open. You don't have to
look very far these days to find people who need a hand up."

She regarded him silently for a few moments, and he expected she would have a lot more questions than he might
have answers for, but instead, she surprised him by saying, "I
guess it's one of those situations where, if you advertised,
people would come climbing out of the woodwork, hitting
you up for God knows what."

"Exactly. Our feeling is anyone we help is one less person
in need than before. We can't help them all, but some is bet-

ter than none." He glanced back at Kate. "You never did tell me how you got started working with kids, much less disabled kids."

"My first roommate in college had cerebral palsy. Although, if you met her, it was hard to think of her as disabled. She was the most empowered woman I'd ever met. I was in awe of her."

"Was?"

Kate nodded. "Marti passed away my senior year. She'd made it much farther than many facing the same challenge do, and she was really strong about it as the end neared. It was the rest of us who completely fell apart."

"I'm sorry."

"Thank you. I was, too. I had already decided I wanted to focus my studies on early childhood development." She paused, then shrugged. "Not sure why, but it had always called to me. Maybe to help me understand the very abnormal one I had, who knows." She waved her hand at him. "And don't say it. I know I led a privileged life growing up, but I would have traded the money and private schools for regular parents who actually sat down to dinner with me more often than on holidays and special occasions."

"I wasn't going to say a word. We come at the situation from opposite sides of the tracks, but neither of us had the optimal childhood."

"I'm not comparing my situation to yours. I know you suffered in a far more—"

"It's okay. You don't have to make excuses. It's not a comparative thing in that way."

She cocked her head and just looked at him.

"What?" he said, letting out a semi-self-conscious laugh. "I mean it."

"I know you do. Thank you." She smiled a little. "You have hidden depths, Donovan MacLeod."

"Aw shucks, thanks, ma'am," he said dryly.

"That wasn't a veiled insult. It's like you said, we don't really know each other." She pushed away from the barn wall. "I'm just saying that I'm liking what I'm finding out."

Mac's palms began to sweat as she took a step closer, her expression unreadable. He had no idea what her intentions were, and the sound of chopper blades cutting through the early evening air ended any chance he had of finding out. *Probably just as well,* he thought, wishing he believed it. Instead, he silently cursed the pilot. They were already behind schedule; another five minutes wouldn't have killed him, would it?

But before he did something he'd probably regret, Kate mercifully turned her attention to the slowly descending whirly bird.

"Shield your eyes. It's going to kick up dust," he cautioned her, then went to the back of the truck for the dolly they'd brought with them from the camp. When he turned back, it was with more than a little surprise that he noticed the shiny black helicopter presently putting its props down in the middle of the field wasn't Trinity's.

He immediately ran back to the barn, took Kate's arm, and tugged her inside the barn. "Stay here!"

Keeping the back of his shoulder against the edge of the barn door, he palmed his clutch piece from his ankle strap.

"Why do I—what the hell is that? Why do you have a gun?"

He waved her silent. "Stay back in the shadows and don't so much as blink unless I call for you."

"What's wrong?" she demanded. "At least tell me that much."

"That's not our chopper."

"But—how could it be anyone else's? Who else would show up out of the blue like—"

Mac didn't hear whatever came next. He'd just spied the very blond, very shaggy head of the pilot and was swearing quite colorfully as he stepped out of the barn.

Blue eyes widened as the pilot noted the gun. "Fine greeting."

Mac tucked his piece back in the bootstrap. "I should shoot you right between the eyes." He motioned to the bird. "That's the new toy? You work fast."

"I tried to tell you about it, but you hung up on me." Finn shrugged, looking far more Peter Pan than the legal eagle he'd once been. "Sorry I'm a little late, but I wanted to give her a spin before I decided on whether to invest, and this seemed like the perfect opportunity. I couldn't radio ahead. I was sort of tied up on something else."

Mac didn't bother asking what. Or who. Between the three of them, they each pretty much always had something going on. Unless they needed to pair up, they didn't waste a lot of time explaining things. "Rafe get things rounded up in the city?"

Finn nodded. "Nailed down Frank this morning, recovered Fortenberry's ashes from our black market collector a few hours ago." He grinned. "Another satisfied customer and a collector who won't be . . . collecting anything else for a little while." He rubbed his hands together. "On to new adventures."

Mac had to smile. For all Finn liked to play, the way he viewed it, the work they did was play of sorts. Everything he did was about Trinity and helping people out. Right down to his choice of toys. "New case lined up?"

Finn nodded. "I think I just took one on that might be a real test of my ability to—" He broke off and looked over Mac's shoulder. "Well, I'll be damned. She's even more beautiful than I remember. And reality beats the hell out of anything I dug up on the Internet." He grinned at Mac. "No nudie pics, nothing. I did my best."

"I just bet you did." Mac turned as Kate walked up. "So much for staying in the barn until I called. You know, when I tell you—"

"What to do, I have to listen," she finished for him. "And I will, when the situation warrants. But I do have two eyes." She turned a bright smile on Finn. "And though it's been a very long time, even I recognized this guy." She extended her hand. "It's great to see you again, Finn."

"That goes double for me." He took her hand in both of his and raised the back to his lips where he pressed a quick kiss, earning a glare from Mac, and a surprisingly girlish giggle from Kate.

Mac cleared his throat. "You get everything on the list? And that report on—"

Finn smacked Mac on the shoulder, never taking his eyes from Kate. "Always business with this guy," he said to her.

"Me?" Mac said. "Me? Whose idea was the new toy as yet another business investment?"

Finn just grinned. "But it's pretty sweet, even you have to admit. You're just jealous because you never learned to fly the damn things with me and Rafe."

"They aren't safe," Mac grumbled, not making eye contact with a suddenly very interested Kate.

"Not real fond of heights, our boy here," Finn explained. "Almost puked the first time I took him up."

"That was more a commentary on your flight skills than the mode of transportation." Or the fact that he'd been pretty damn sure he was going to get tossed out the open door every other second. Sans parachute. "You're a menace on the roads and in the sky."

Finn was unapologetic. "I like fast things." He grinned at Kate.

And Mac had to fight to keep from reacting. Finn was clearly baiting him, but Kate didn't know that. She certainly didn't need to know it was working. "Listen, Speed Racer, did you bring my stash of goodies or what?"

"When do I not deliver as promised?" He was still looking at Kate, who—was she blushing?

"Well, when I asked for a full report on Timberline and their Ralston connection, you came up empty-handed."

Finn reached inside his flight jacket and pulled out a manila envelope, smacked it against Mac's chest, then stepped forward, effectively putting himself between Mac and Kate. "So, tell me, how has life been treating you, Kate?"

Mac scowled, but managed to stay put as Finn and Kate wandered off toward the barn. "I hate it when he does that," he muttered, then flipped open the envelope. If Kate's head was turned by pretty, blond flyboys, then she could have him. Of course, Finn Dalton was a hell of a lot more than a pretty flyboy. And Kate knew it. "Damn it to hell." He purposely turned his back on the two of them and slid out the envelope's contents. The rapidly fading light made it hard to read the fine print of the report, and, given the heft of it, it was probably better to hold off and read it when he could process the information.

At the moment, he was more interested in hitting something. Preferably his partner's too pretty face.

Which, of course, was ridiculous. He loved Finn like a brother, and they all three knew better than to let the occasional—okay, maybe more than occasional where Rafe was concerned—woman come between them. But this was Kate. And Finn had to know how confused and roiled up he was about all this. He glanced back without meaning to. Their heads were bent close, and he could hear Kate's laughter float through the chilly evening air.

He watched Finn's body language. He was engaging her, but he was keeping just enough distance between them to keep it impersonal. The three of them rode each other pretty hard whenever possible, and boundaries got pushed all the time, but when it came down to it, they'd never purposely do anything to get in the way of the other. So, more than likely, Finn was just distracting her a little from the tension and gravity of the situation she was in, while giving Mac a chance to look over the report without her looking over his shoulder.

Still, he didn't have to look like he was having so much damn fun doing it.

Mac slid the report back out, but it took a second longer before he looked away from the two of them. It shouldn't bug him. Not just because Finn was relatively harmless in this particular case, but because . . . Mac had no business feeling anything remotely close to the proprietary feelings he was experiencing at the moment. He forced his attention back to the papers in his hand and began reading the lengthy report.

His scowl deepened as he slowly flipped through the papers. Finn had come through after all. He finally slid the papers back in the envelope, folded it in half and jammed it inside his jacket, then grabbed the hand truck. He already knew he was going to need more than the basic surveillance equipment he'd asked for. They still had no definitive proof—yet—but the prickling warning along the back of his neck was enough proof for Mac.

He flipped open the cargo box behind the pilot's seat and grinned. Finn was one step ahead of him. He quickly went through the gear and made a few mental notes on other things he needed to track down, but for the most part, Finn had anticipated his needs. Mac would have to let him live now, he supposed. He tossed a glance back in their direction. As long as he kept his paws off Kate, anyway.

Satisfied for now, he closed the lid and latched it, then dragged the trunk out and onto the dolly. After that came several long, black canvas duffel bags, which he deposited on the ground, along with two generators. They looked rather small, but he knew they were powerful enough to get the job done. Last, but not least, a small cooler. Mac popped the top and grinned. "All is forgiven," he said, resisting the urge to grab a cold one. Later. He glanced back at Kate, who wasn't smiling anymore, and sighed.

Much later.

Finn and Kate walked over to help stow the gear in the back of Kate's pickup.

"Let me know what else you need, okay?" Finn said, clapping a hand on Mac's shoulder. "Call it in and I'll get someone to leave it in your mailbox there," he said, nodding toward the barn. "Looks like I'll be heading out in the next day or two."

"Maybe it's time to get some extra help in the front office."

"I know, I know. We keep saying that, but it's not like we can just put anyone—" Finn glanced at Kate, who wasn't pretending not to listen, and cut himself off with a quick smile. "Always shoptalk with us, huh? We really need to get a life."

Finn gave a pointed glance toward Kate, then back to Mac. Mac ignored it. Or pretended to. "What's not to love about the one we have?"

"True, true. Okay, I gotta roll. Keep Winnimocca safe," he instructed Mac. "And keep him out of trouble, will ya?" he said to Kate. "Tall order, I know, but somehow I think if anyone can pull it off, you can."

Kate just laughed.

"Go enjoy your new toy," Mac told him, shooing him off. "Tell Rafe I said congratulations and sorry I couldn't be there to help with the roundup. I'd have enjoyed having another . . . conversation with Mr. DiMateo."

"Oh, I think they talked it all out," Finn said with a gleam in his eye. "At length."

Mac smiled then. "Good to hear. Stay safe and keep that thing in one piece," he added, nodding to the helicopter. "Gotta protect our . . . assets."

"Your concern for my well-being is touching," he said dryly. "You do the same."

"Always."

Both Mac and Kate bent low and backed up as Finn started the powerful blades spinning. Less than a minute later, he was slowly hovering upward, then swiftly dipped to the right and took off into the encroaching night like a sleek, black bat out of hell.

"Must be nice," Kate remarked calmly.

"Hey, you could have had a raft of them if you'd kept Louisa's money."

She smiled sweetly at him. "I'd rather have a run-down camp and yards of mosquito netting, thanks."

Mac thought about the reports in his jacket, and the dimming smile on her face earlier. "Did Finn talk to you about what he dug up?"

Surprisingly, she shook her head. "I asked, but he said it was better for the two of us to go over everything, that he gave it all to you."

"He did."

"Have you read it?"

"Skimmed. What were you two talking about, then?" He realized as soon as the question was out how it sounded, but he didn't care enough to correct the impression. Mostly because it was pretty much right on target. What was it about her, anyway?

Her mouth curved in a hint of a smile, but she didn't rib him. "About how he's been, about Rafe. How the three of you got started in the saving-the-world business."

"And?" He doubted she'd been frowning earlier because of anything Finn had to say about Trinity. Not only because their business was going quite well, but Finn could charm the wings off a fly without even trying.

She tilted her head slightly, as if to question what he meant, but answered him instead of playing dumb. He really liked that about her. "He asked after Louisa, and about the camp. Told me to listen to my instincts." Her expression tightened a bit, as if she were internally bracing herself. "It's Shelby, isn't it? I mean, that's what my gut is telling me. He's somehow behind or involved in . . . whatever the hell is going on. Do you know what's going on? Exactly, I mean."

"He dug up some interesting info, but it's still at the connect-the-dots stage, and we need more dots to get the whole pattern nailed down. But more information is power, so we're heading in the right direction." He motioned for her to get in the truck.

She started to, then stopped. "Wait."

"What?"

She looked back to the barn. "What was all the measuring of the interior of the barn before? I thought you were having some kind of massive shipment of stuff or something." She motioned to the contents in the back of her truck. "Hardly worth barn storage."

"No. But you never know when you might need to hide a helicopter."

"Oh, well—oh." She paused. "Do we . . . need to hide a helicopter? Yet?"

He shook his head. "Not yet." He slapped the top of the truck. "Come on, get in. It's getting late, and we have a lot to talk about. I'll drive."

Not only didn't she argue, but she remained uncharacteristically silent until they'd driven back through Ralston and were well into the mountains on their way back to the camp. He could have launched into the information Finn had brought, but, to be honest, he was in no hurry to put that look of fear and worry on her face again.

Not that she looked particularly happy or relaxed at the moment. His attention kept sliding over to her as he switched on his high beams and began the climb up yet another mountain. Though only dimly lit by the dashboard lighting, he could still see how she was twisting her fingers, yet otherwise sitting perfectly still. Too still, like someone deeply lost in their thoughts.

He wondered what she was thinking about. Shelby, most likely. But he'd be lying if he didn't admit to also wondering if he was plaguing her thoughts like she was his. Thoughts that had nothing to do with Winnimocca and everything to do with her little comment about rules made in haste. His mind spun back to that moment at the barn, just before Finn flew in, when she'd made that comment about liking what she was learning about him. On someone else it might have been flirty and provocative, but she'd said it rather straight forwardly, more as a measure of respect.

Which had done nothing to explain why his entire body had begun to tighten when she'd taken that single step forward. Probably it had meant nothing, and she'd just been about to pace back and forth.

And yet he couldn't get his mind to let it alone. That moment when he'd looked into her eyes and wondered if she was as affected by their forced togetherness as he was. And he wasn't sure he'd be so chivalrous and self-controlled the next time. If there was a next time. He pictured Finn's smiling face as he'd chatted Kate up, and her responding giggle. And knew damn well he wanted there to be a next time, and was doubly glad Finn was going to be many miles away when it happened.

"You can tell me," she said suddenly. "I have to know the truth."

Still thinking about the two of them, back in her cabin tonight, while he tried to give her the full report and not think about her bed in the next room . . . he wanted to tell her he didn't have a clue what the truth was at the moment. Other than he wanted her.

"We're almost back. Let's go over all of it then."

"Shelby's involved." She made it a statement, not a question. "Just tell me that much. You didn't exactly answer me before."

He didn't pull any punches with her. "There has been rumored contact between him and Timberline, but nothing we can substantiate yet. Meaning no paper trail to prove it."

"And?"

He turned the truck into the private drive leading up to the campgrounds. "And, I think we should go scrounge up something to eat, then go over the rest of Finn's report in detail."

She surprised him by flashing a brief dry smile. "Because after what I hear, I'm not likely to have an appetite?"

No, he thought, *because if I stuff myself with food, maybe it will kill the craving I'm developing for you.* "One step at a time."

She looked as if she were going to debate the issue, or push him for more, but instead, settled more deeply into her seat and shifted her gaze out the window. "You know," she said, her tone pensive, "I tried to keep myself from caring too much. About whether or not I got to use this property."

"Why did you?" he asked. "I thought you only wanted it because it might be available at the right price."

She half shrugged. "It was my only shot, financially. And, the more I thought about the property itself, the more perfect I knew it would be. Part of our program focuses on working with animals and kids together, horses mostly, as well as water therapy. Winnimocca has the stables, the lake. And I know my family wasn't the best, or even much of a family, really, but this property is ours and has been for a long time. That might not have meant anything before, but maybe it will now."

She sat up a little straighter, warming to her topic, despite the fear and concern. "When I came up with the idea for the camp . . . well, to be fair, it was Marti's idea way back when, but for her it was a pipe dream. For me, once that seed was planted, I could hardly think of anything else. It was because of Marti that I'd gotten involved in studying alternative therapies for kids with disabilities who didn't always respond to conventional methods. The property was here, it was in the family, it wasn't being used . . . and it was perfect for what we needed."

"Pretty remote location."

She smiled. "Camps aren't supposed to be centered in thriving metropolises."

"I know, but in the case of your campers' limitations, wouldn't it be easier if—"

"If they had easier access? Trust me, they've conquered bigger challenges. But the remoteness serves several purposes. Not only does it give the kids the experience of being away from home and the enjoyment of a traditional camplike setting, but they oftentimes need the peace and quiet in order to maintain. Lots of noise, traffic, the intensity of hustle and bustle would overwhelm them. I wanted a place where the stimulation, when it came, was controlled. Constructive rather than destructive."

"So they all stay alone here? No parents?"

She shook her head. "No, parents often stay in situations like this. Depends on the child, the challenges, the camp's directives. It'll be on a case by case basis, but the programs are designed to help both."

He glanced at her before turning up the final stretch of the drive. There was a vibrancy about her now, as she spoke of her dream, her passion, that he hadn't seen in her since his arrival. It gave more than color to her cheeks; it lit her from within. And she'd been pretty powerful stuff before.

He drove past the other cabins, turning right at the fork, away from the lane leading down to the service entrance, without even flashing to his own past and the multitude of memories just seeing that posted sign would normally evoke. He was too immersed in the present to do much more than notice it.

"You're obviously not going to run this program alone. Do you have the staff set up?"

"I've got a few solid confirmations. Once actual progress is being made on renovations, I'll have a little more leverage with a few other teachers I'd like to hire. I have most of it outlined, the people, the programs, the animals we'll need, the scheduling. It's something I've been working toward for a very long time, and I've been fortunate enough to have the help of my former department head at the university as well. I couldn't have gotten this far without Marti pushing me initially, or my chair's support at the end run."

He started to ask her one of the other two dozen questions on the tip of his tongue. Her enthusiasm for the subject was contagious, and he found himself sincerely interested in hearing more about the program, in ways that had nothing to do with the case at hand. Instead, he pulled into the space in front of her cabin and killed the engine. "Sounds like you have it all thought out." He popped open his door and climbed out, needing to get away from her, just for a moment, to break the spell, regroup. But instead, he stopped, turned. "I guess I should have asked sooner, but did we need to stop in town for dinner fixings?"

She climbed out and shook her hair free of the ponytail that had been threatening to fall apart all evening. It was done artlessly, with no apparent awareness of how damn sexy the action was. "Nah, I can throw together something," she said, massaging her scalp and groaning a little.

A sentiment he could easily second at the moment. "I don't mind helping." *With dinner, untangling all that hair of yours* . . .

She grinned. "Good, then you can bring the beer."

"How did you—" He flashed on Finn, heads bent close, her laughter. "Right. Glad to share." And he was. In fact, he was quite willing to share a hell of lot more than his beer with her. He tugged the cooler out of the back of the truck, but left the rest of the equipment there.

"Should we stow that somewhere?"

"I'll get it later. I'm going to stow it in my cabin anyway. There is some assembly required," he added with a smile. He noticed her instinctive glance . . . and it wasn't in the direction of the unoccupied cabins down the hill. She'd instinctively glanced at her own. His body revved up quite nicely to that unconscious suggestion. He fought to quell the reaction. They had a long night ahead of them. And at some point, he had to get back on task. The case had to come first.

Whether or not either of them were going to come later remained to be seen.

He sighed a little as he hefted the cooler and hiked the

steps up to her front porch. And to think he'd once loved this job.

At the moment, he was thinking there might actually be a point to having a life outside of work. Novel concept for a guy like him.

She held the door open for him, and he had to angle himself carefully to keep from brushing up against her, but was trapped as Bagel plastered himself all around his ankles with loving adoration. Cruel, really. Worse was the whiff of her fragrance. And the killer was that it wasn't some fancy perfume. It was the fresh scent of soap and shampoo. Who'd have thought the wafting scent of citrus could give a guy a raging hard-on?

He was so in trouble here.

"Why don't you review the report in full while I cook something up?" She smiled as she stepped into the cabin behind him, then squatted down to rub Bagel's quivering belly. "We can eat while I badger you with a million questions and generally make you crazy."

You have no idea, he thought. *No idea at all.*

Chapter 10

Kate had thought he'd dominated her screened-in porch last night—had it been only last night? His presence was so much bigger than life it felt as though he'd been in it far longer than that. But now that he was standing in her small kitchen, she realized she had sorely underestimated just how big a presence he truly was.

"You cook?" he asked.

"Very funny." She reached into the jar on the little shelf beside the door and tossed Bagel a piece of rawhide.

Donovan walked across the main room of the four-room cabin—the other rooms being her bedroom, her office, and the bathroom—to the open kitchen area and pulled out a chair to the small, two-seat dinette set she'd scrounged at a flea market. "Actually, I wasn't being a smart-ass," he said. "I don't assume a woman can cook just because she's a woman."

"You're so not going to save your behind trying to sound gender enlightened."

"I am gender enlightened," he said, sounding all offended, but there was that twinkle in his eye again.

"Be honest, you assumed I couldn't cook because I grew up with one on staff."

"That, too, but really—" He ducked easily when she

flipped one of the two throw pillows from the couch in his general direction as she passed by. "Careful, you could take an eye out."

"With a pillow?"

He bent down and snagged it from the floor by his feet. "You never know."

She opened the refrigerator door and hid her smile. Her entire dream might be falling apart . . . and here she was, grinning like a fool over a little banter with an attractive man. So what if it had been a while? Okay, a long while. And so what if it was her teenage crush, returned to her life in all his infinite grown-up glory? A little professionalism at the moment would go a long way.

Then there came the scrape of the chair against the hardwood floor, and before she could close the door and move, he was behind her, peering over her shoulder at the meager contents of her refrigerator.

"So, I'm guessing it's PB and J and water," he said, his breath warm on the side of her neck. "Got any chips to go with that?"

His close proximity was making it really difficult to concentrate on what he was saying. Her body was getting the message loud and clear, but it had nothing to do with making dinner. She snatched a bag of ready-made salad from the crisper drawer and a bottle of salad dressing from the rack in the door. "Amateur."

She straightened and deftly moved to one side and away from him so she could open the freezer. She slid a small bag of flash-frozen chicken breasts out and tossed the bag directly at his chest, which had the added bonus of making him straighten and move back a few steps.

He looked down at the bag now clutched to his chest. "They're frozen."

She slipped past him and went to the stove. "They have this new invention; it's called an oven."

He scanned the short countertop wedged between the fridge and the stove. "No microwave? Not even a toaster oven? What kind of heiress are you?"

She tucked the salad and dressing into one hand and snatched the chicken from his hand as she moved past him once again to the small chopping-block island that officially divided the space between kitchen proper and dining area. In her mind it did, anyway. "The poor, starving kind who learned one hundred and one ways to cook entire meals in a dormitory microwave and never wants to see another one as long as she lives." She flashed him a smile and batted her eyelashes. "Or until she has someone else to do the cooking for her. Whichever comes first."

"Ah ha," he said, coming to stand next to her. "I knew your inner rich girl was in there somewhere."

"Very funny." And couldn't he stand somewhere else? She tried not to fidget. "I wasn't talking about the kind that I'd have to put on salary, wiseass. Here." She stepped back and waved him to take her place. "Since you seem bent on getting in my way, you can toss the salad." She opened an overhead cupboard and pulled out a serving bowl, two little bowls, and a box of croutons. "Don't put those on yet. It'll take a few minutes to heat up the chicken."

"Heat?"

"Already grilled and flash frozen. Don't worry, they'll heat up quickly. Give me time and I'll make some garlic bread to go with it."

He stepped around her to the serving bowl and surprisingly put together the salad with an ease that belied his bachelor-at-large status. "No tomatoes?"

She shuddered. "Not unless forced under penalty of death."

"Does that mean this is a no-spaghetti zone?"

She slid two thin chicken breasts out and popped them on a tray and into the oven in one smooth move. "Why?" she asked him as she turned to face him, arms folded. "You planning on dining here often?"

He finished mixing the bowl of salad. "Maybe."

Before she could come up with a retort, and she was certainly going to, he slid by her and put the croutons and dressing on the table.

"Silverware? Dishes?"

"You can set a table?" she asked with feigned surprise.

"Very funny. Although I admit I lived off of paper plates for almost a year after we all moved in together."

Kate's hands stopped in midreach for the fridge door. She looked over her shoulder at him. "You three . . . live together, too?"

"Not in sin or anything. It's legal, I swear."

Her lips twitched. "The Unholy Trinity, all under one roof. And the world is still standing."

"It's a pretty big roof." He stacked silverware on top of the dishes, grabbed a few napkins, and moved over to the table. "And I thought I mentioned it, but we're saving the world." He sent her a sideways look that was anything but innocent. "One downtrodden heiress at a time."

She tried not to be swayed by his devilish charms, really she did. "I'm not downtrodden." She moved around the table in the opposite direction from him—no need testing her sway ability by putting herself in actual contact range—and pulled out a chopping block. She kept her back to him, all the better to not be caught up in those quicksilver eyes of his, and started buttering a few bread slices and sprinkling them with garlic and parmesan cheese she rescued from her meager spice cupboard. "I'm just a little financially challenged at the moment, that's all." She wished that had come out sounding a bit more confidant. "I find it rather ironic that, of the two of us, I'm not the one living the high life in some fancy Virginia mansion. And you give me grief."

Donovan came to stand beside her, holding the bowl of tossed salad greens. She put the knife down. She knew her limits. Bracing herself, she looked at him. Up close like this, almost as close as they'd been in the cab of her truck when he'd kissed her, it was impossible not to get caught up in his intensity. He didn't even have to try. How he worked that laconic smile with those laser beam eyes of his, she had no idea. But anybody fooled by his easygoing demeanor was just that, a fool.

"Tell me something," he said, holding her gaze with a direct look.

Anything, she thought. *I'm an open book for you*. To hell with logic and reasoning. A girl got this lucky only a few times in an entire lifetime. If that.

"Does Shelby value what you do?"

She blinked. What the hell did Shelby have to do with Donovan seducing her? "What?"

"This camp. When you told Louisa—and I assume Shelby knew then, too, what you wanted to do with it—what was his reaction?"

She took the bowl from his hands, still nonplussed. Although she was feeling steadily more foolish for the ridiculous path her mind had been taking for the past twenty minutes. Who was she kidding? Since she'd found him on her porch yesterday, it was all she could do to not think about how badly she wanted him. "What difference does it make?"

"I'm trying to piece this whole thing together and fit Shelby into it more concretely. We need proof for that, so I need a trail to follow."

"I thought you were going to secure the property from vandals."

"I am, but that's not all of it. We have enough to start, but I need to find the thing that ties it all together."

"You mean Shelby and Timberline?"

"And Ralston. And the vandalism. I'm not saying it's for certain every element is tied in, but we have to consider it."

"Okay, but one thing I can't figure is, why would Shelby or a big developer resort to such petty tactics as graffiti? Especially when Shelby holds all of the cards at the moment. He has what I want. And I'm willing to give him everything to get it. If he doesn't want me here, all he has to do is not sign the papers."

"Which is precisely what he did yesterday."

"I know . . . but—" She carried the bowl to the table and set it down with a mindless thump. "None of this makes sense. But what do Shelby's feelings about my camp have to do with anything? He doesn't care what I do with it, as long as I give him the money. At least, that's what I thought was the case."

"Exactly. Wine?"

"Huh?"

He gestured to her meager kitchen. "Happen to have a bottle of wine? I have beer, but it's not really the thing for chicken salad."

Mixing Donovan and alcohol struck her as being even more supremely stupid than she'd already been acting thus far. Which, apparently, was saying something. "There is an open bottle of white in the fridge." She watched him open the door and bend down to look inside. Her gaze followed the action—and hung somewhere around the back pockets of his jeans. Yeah. She'd have water.

He pulled two glasses from the rack, and she said nothing as he poured both. No reason to make a scene about it. "So," she started, sliding the bread onto the top rack in the oven and forking the chicken over. "Why don't we start at the beginning of Finn's report and go from there. Maybe it will spark some thread of logic for me." She could be all business. Really, she could. She pulled her own chair out and sat down before he could move around behind her and took a sip of her wine. "Chicken will take a little bit. Can I look at it while we wait?"

Mac took a sip of wine. "Wouldn't make much sense to you, but sure. We can go over it together."

"Why don't you hit the highlights for me." She didn't say anything when she noticed him slip a crouton under the table to Bagel. It should have been annoying, and instead, it was a little endearing. Which was ridiculous. So he was a soft touch? What difference did that make?

"Okay," he said, spearing a fat baby carrot from the salad bowl and neatly popping the whole thing in his mouth. White teeth flashed, his jaw flexed, as he made short work of it.

Her mouth watered. And it had nothing to do with her meal. "What does Finn think the connection is between Shelby and the vandalism? I get him possibly talking to the developers, but the rest is a bit of a stretch for me. Did he offer any theories? What's his opinion?"

"*Our* opinion is that Shelby's quite possibly involved all the way up to his impeccable credit rating. Finn's research was just following my hunch."

"Okay, okay, don't get your ego in a twist. So Shelby is talking to the developers, but couldn't that be innocent? You said there was no paper trail, so nothing has been proposed or signed that you can find."

"Yet."

"What if they were just making an offer to the current owner? And, on record, that would be Shelby at the moment. He could have just said no, end of story. Perfectly legit. Is there anything showing any dealings between Shelby and any Ralston business? Or"—she brightened—"between Ralston and Timberline? Maybe it's not Shelby at all. Maybe it's just the town and the developer. What about Stan's father and the bank? Would the developers need financing of any sort or is that done privately through investors?"

"I'm not sure on that part yet. Most of it, as you pointed out in the case of Shelby and Timberline having any preliminary discussions, is circumstantial until we get documentation of a deal in the works."

"Meaning we really don't know anything, then." She huffed out a sigh and leaned back in her chair. "This whole thing is just supposition."

"There are too many players with questionable motives in

potential contact here. It's plausible and probable. That's enough to pursue it."

"Okay, okay." She took another sip of her wine, then shoved her chair back and rescued the bread slices from the oven. She slid them into a small basket and put them on the table, then went ahead and took the chicken out and poked at it. Thawed and warm, if not exactly hot. It would have to do. "So, let's focus on Timberline. What do we know, for sure, about their interest in this area, and I don't just mean Winnimocca. There has to be some proof they're looking here, feasibility studies, something." She started slicing up the thin cutlets.

"We do know they've done that much, and you're right, not just the Winnimocca area, a larger range, but they are focusing their attentions in this area and appear quite serious about it."

She turned and slid the chicken pieces into the salad bowl. "Toss," she instructed him as she dumped the cutting board and knife in the sink. She rinsed her hands and wiped them off with the dishtowel tucked by the stove, then pulled out her chair again, wine back in hand. The hell with water. "Do you have anything showing them looking at any other areas? Just how serious are they about developing here?"

"Quite. All their attention seems focused here. In the area anyway."

"Still, as you say, circumstantial. Contacting Shelby can still fall within normal parameters."

"But the graffiti does not."

"Maybe the folks in Ralston think I'm keeping Timberline from building here, so they're trying to scare me off."

Donovan tossed the chicken in the salad, then scooped some into his bowl. "Could be."

"And Shelby has nothing to do with it."

"Too many things happening at the same time make me nervous. As I said, until I have proof otherwise, nothing gets discredited."

"So, exactly what kind of system are you setting up here? I mean, I'm assuming we're targeting the vandalism and trespassing? But that's just a deterrent. How will that help us prove the rest?"

"I'm going to wire the place, and hopefully we'll do more than deter them. We'll catch them in the act."

Her eyes widened. She assumed he meant caught on tape, or whatever. Not actually caught. Then she remembered how easily and naturally he'd drawn a weapon earlier and wasn't all that sure what he meant. "How much work is involved, setting this up, I mean? They've struck all over the property, and it's a big chunk of land covering some pretty inaccessible areas. Just seems like a lot to go through to catch a simple intruder in the act."

"Nothing is simple about this. But don't worry about the system or the difficulty. It's nothing I haven't done before. Besides, it will be handy for keeping an eye on the place later on, when the camp is up and running. You can even advertise the fact that it's electronically monitored, if that helps as a draw. But, for now, I don't plan on announcing the fact."

Her eyes widened slightly. "So, you're not just planning to use the equipment to simply deter the vandal or vandals; you really plan on catching one? Physically, or just digitally? I mean, all we need is proof to get Gilby involved, right, and a digital image of someone trespassing—"

"Well, actually putting our hands on someone directly involved would provide a handy trail to follow, don't you think?"

She sat back in her chair, absorbing this latest round. "Yeah. I guess it would." She folded her arms across her chest and rubbed absently up and down her biceps. If she let herself, she could get completely freaked out here. So she worked hard to focus on the facts, to try and separate herself from the emotional part. From the fear. She didn't ask what his plans were to include the local law enforcement . . . or not. She didn't think she really needed to hear that answer at the moment. "What kind of resort does Timberline want to build here? What's the scope of it? It's too hilly for golf, so what's the attraction—lake recreation? Will it be more intimate and personal, with guests in cabins like our old camp, or is there some huge, central lodge or hotel planned?"

"I don't know. They've done a number of different kinds in the past, of varying scope and focus. We're digging for blueprints. The fact that nothing is on file with the zoning commission or any county official is a bit suspicious, but maybe premature, too. It's also possible there might be something going on under the table, some kind of deal the developer is working on with the county to perhaps overlook certain codes or zoning regulations."

Kate leaned forward, resolutely picking up her fork. "Maybe this is Shelby," she murmured. "Maybe he's trying to snare them into some kind of partnership deal and cut me out. I don't know how he'd pull that off, but I wouldn't put it past him."

"It's something to consider."

Her shoulders slumped a little bit. She really didn't want to believe that was true, but she knew Shelby too well to automatically dismiss it.

Mac waved his fork, motioning her to eat. "Let's have dinner. Then I promise you we'll go over it all, piece by piece."

She put her fork down again and leaned forward. "For you, this is just another one of your charity cases. For me, it's my whole life. So you'll have to pardon me if I'm a little too tense to eat." She shoved back her chair. "I'm going to take Bagel out for a little run."

"He runs?"

She gave Donovan a quelling look. "He's been cooped up in here all day. He's restless. He needs to get out, get some fresh air."

Mac looked down at Bagel, who was sprawled at his feet. "How can you tell?"

"I just can." She slapped her thigh. "Come on, Bagel. Outside?"

The dog's eyes were pinned to Mac's knees, which was as far up as he could see given his position, but exactly the entry spot of any future treats that might be snuck to him.

"Come on, Bagel. Let's go." She walked to the screen door. "Kate—"

She lifted a hand to stall him. "I've been cooped up, too, okay? With you. And I'm restless. You finish eating. We'll talk it out when I get back. I do want to read over Finn's report myself, draw my own conclusions, see if anything triggers something I might think of that you wouldn't know about. Business when I get back, okay? Then I'm going to want to know what's in those gear bags he delivered and what your plan is to install security. Tomorrow, first thing, I'm calling my lawyer and finding out what I need to do to cover my ass in case Shelby is trying to pull a fast one. And if anyone is going to handle Shelby, it's going to be me, so you might as well get used to including me in every part of this."

"Kate—"

"Don't 'Kate' me. I'm dead serious. And you'll soon find out that I can be just as stubborn and bull-headed as you are."

Donovan held her gaze for what felt like an eternity, and she thought he was going to argue, or give her a hard time for her outburst, or make a joke of it, try to disarm her with his charm. But instead, he nodded and stuck his fork in another chunk of lettuce. "Okay. Just stay close."

That's it? she perversely wanted to demand. *You're just going to let me deliver ultimatums and storm out of here?* God, she really did need some air. And the return of some semblance of rational thought would be a welcome change, too. She looked down at her still-sprawled dog, but he had eyes only for Mac's knees. Traitor.

She grabbed her jacket off the peg by the door and banged the porch door open and walked out before she could change her mind. She just needed to get away from him for a little

while so she could clear her head of all the pheromones that
were having a party there and get herself back on track. She
crossed the porch and headed down the stairs. The air had
grown decidedly cooler, and she shoved her hands in her
pockets before striking out on the path that looped around
the main cabins.

She walked this loop often, to stretch her legs and to continue to mentally flesh out the work schedule, visualize how
everything was going to be this time next year. Normally the
walk soothed and invigorated her. Her camp was going to
happen. It thrilled her to no end, anticipating seeing the realization of her dream happening before her very eyes.

This evening none of that anticipation and euphoria was
there. Her shoulders were tense, her hands in tightly balled
fists inside her pockets. Someone was trying to keep her
dream from coming true, dammit. Whether it was Shelby,
someone in Ralston, or just overzealous developers, she didn't
know. And, to a degree, it didn't matter. Except, if it was
Shelby, it did matter. Even all these years later, knowing
they'd never been close and never would be, she still wanted
to believe he wouldn't stoop so low as to screw over family
like this. Even estranged family.

The moon was rising, but clouds had come in over the past
hour, and so it was hidden more often than not. She knew the
path well, and her eyes quickly adjusted to the dark. The central area to the west of her cabin held the main lodge buildings. Her mother had always wanted to tear them down and
put up a single grand lodge, but her stepfather had felt strongly
that a camp, even one for the insanely wealthy, was supposed
to look like a camp, not a hotel. So the buildings were refur-
bished, and new stone walls had been laid, additions put on,
grander landscaping designed, but camp was still camp. Beyond the central quad was a wider circular path on which the
main cabins were located. About fifty yards apart, they were
staggered back into the woods, with varying short walkways

leading to their front porches. Another long path bisected the circle, which led in one direction down to the lake, and in the other, back to the maintenance and service road.

The lake also had a number of more secluded cabins nestled along the banks. Oftentimes the girls would be bunked down there and the boys would be quartered closer to the lodge area.

She didn't head down that way. The stands of trees on either side of the lake path were denser and blocked most of what little moonlight she had. Plus, the lake cabins were in the worst shape and would be the last thing she renovated. Sometimes just seeing them was too stark a reminder of just how much work was in front of her. She didn't need that tonight.

Her students would be housed in the central camp area anyway, so there was no rush. Her hope was that as the camp got established, she'd refurbish the lakeside cabins to house members of her full-time staff.

She sighed, not as quick to smile as she played out her well-developed dream in her mind. She shivered a little instead, and pulled her hands from her pockets so she could wrap her arms around herself and tuck her hands in close to her sides. She looked at the sky, which was growing more heavily clouded by the minute as the stars continued to vanish. She'd been so preoccupied by Donovan since he'd barged into her life, she hadn't followed her normal routine. She hadn't looked at the weather report today, much less the local news.

She trudged on around the circular path, slowing down when she came to the offshoot that led to the stables, paddocks, and the outdoor arena. Both the buildings and the paddocks were in almost complete shambles and needed a total overhaul. Those were high on her list, right up there with the lodge buildings and the first wave of cabin refurbs.

There were no horses yet, but there would be. The methods of therapy she wanted to offer involved using animals as a way to connect with some of the more severely challenged children. She'd witnessed the miracle of that magical connection on many occasions and had become involved in developing a course of study that focused on the benefits of using animals in such therapy.

But while it was becoming a more acceptable adjunct, it was nowhere near the level of acceptance or implementation Kate required in order to get her complete regimen fully integrated into an actual practice or university. The only way to do that was to run her own place, funded by her own money, backed by her own blood, sweat, and tears. She stopped at the crossroads of the trail and looked down the path toward the lake, then ahead to where the stables and corral were situated. She made a slow turn, not caring that it was too dark to see the actual layout of the camp beyond what was right in front of her. She could see it all clearly in her mind's eye. "And I'll be damned if you're going to ruin this, Shelby. Just take my money and give me my damn camp already."

Her stomach tightened, her gut telling her what her heart didn't want to hear. There was a reason he hadn't shown up yesterday. And first thing tomorrow, she was going to do whatever it took to hunt him down and drag the truth out of him. As far as she was concerned, that was the most direct way to take matters into her own hands and solve her problems.

Or, at least define what her problems really were.

She turned down the path toward the lake, without really knowing why. She just knew she wasn't ready to return to her cabin yet. Maybe if she stayed out here long enough, he'd head out to whatever cabin he intended to claim and bunk down for the night. Wasn't it enough that he'd invaded her life unannounced? If she was lucky, he'd leave the report behind so she could look it over alone.

The moon peeked out from behind the clouds just as she rounded the bend in the path that opened up to a view of the lake. The wind had picked up a little, and white sparks of light danced across the rippling surface. Before too long the days would get warmer, and mist would rise from the water when the temperature dropped at night. Fireflies would twinkle along the shore, and the owls would accompany them from their nocturnal perches. She carefully picked her way to the edge of the lake and walked down to the one dock she knew was still in decent shape. Tucking her arms more tightly around her, she made her way to the end, then sat down cross-legged, staring across the water.

Think, Kate. Should she just confront Shelby with what she suspected? Demand answers? Deliver an ultimatum? She tucked her chin and closed her eyes. Why couldn't this just move on as planned? She really didn't want this to be happening. Yesterday, when she'd left the lawyers' offices, she'd been pissed, but not particularly unnerved. Now? Now Donovan was here. Drawing conclusions she didn't want to hear. Making predictions. And she was seeing monsters in the shadows where before there were only minor nuisances.

"What the hell are you doing?"

She startled badly. Good thing she'd been seated or she might have ended up in the freezing cold waters of the lake. Hand pressed to pounding heart, she shifted around, only to see Mac at the other end of the dock. Naturally, the clouds chose that precise moment to part, bathing him in an otherworldly glow. He stood feet braced, hands planted on his hips, his hair a wild halo, his face in shadows. She didn't need to see his expression to know it wasn't charming or sunny.

"I'm solving the problems of the world," she said with exaggerated calm as she willed her rapidly beating heart to slow down. "What are you doing?"

"Wondering where the hell you went and losing a year or so off my life when I walked the base camp path and you weren't on it."

She smiled, which was totally incongruous with the fact that she was getting yelled at. As it turned out, he was pretty cute when he was mad. "You do know I've managed to live out here for a whole month without your help."

"It's a wonder."

Said through such a tightly clenched jaw, she thought, increasingly bemused. She pulled her knees up to her chest and looped her arms around them. "I see you brought your trusty sidekick with you for protection."

Donovan glanced down to where Bagel sat, winsomely, at his feet. "He was worried, too."

"Then he should have come with me." *Or you should have.*

That last thought took her by surprise. She'd left the cabin precisely to get away from him for a bit. So why was she sitting here, more happy than annoyed that he'd tracked her down?

"You ready to head back?"

"Not really. I came down here to sort some things out."

"You don't have all the facts yet."

"That's partly what I'm sorting out. I needed to get out here, clear my head, think things through."

"Which things specifically?" He stepped onto the dock, then paused to signal Bagel to stay. With a little whine, the dog dropped his chin, then sighed and flopped fully down on the ground, chin on his paws.

"How do you do that? He never stays for me."

"You're harder to resist than I am."

Her eyes widened briefly at that. "He wasn't exactly in any hurry to follow me out here."

"Are you kidding? He's been pawing at the door for the past twenty minutes."

She considered that, then said, "So you tracked me down to make my dog feel better?"

He walked closer, until she had to tilt her head back to look up at him. "No, I tracked you down because someone out there doesn't wish you well."

She willed her heart to stay steady. "So they've spray

painted a few words. I'm still not completely convinced I'm in the immediate danger you think I am. Nor am I convinced there is some nefarious scheme going on." She leaned back so she could see his face. "I know you want to keep all the options open, and fine, but can you at least admit to me that it's possible you're seeing problems where none exist? I mean, I have problems, yes, but Shelby will do what is best for him, and what's best for him is to take all my money. I'll get the sheriff to come out and patrol things here, or I'll get a bigger dog." She glanced at Bagel. "Sorry, sport. No insult intended." She looked back to Donovan, but said nothing more.

"So those are the conclusions you've drawn, sitting out here?" He crouched down on his haunches, bringing his face closer to eye level. In the moonlight and dark shadows, his eyes gleamed an almost otherworldly pearl gray. "I didn't just have my partner fly a load of state-of-the-art surveillance equipment out here on a hunch."

"Did I miss something, then? You know for a fact that this isn't just a string of bad luck on my part, but a concerted effort to whip my property and my camp out from underneath me? That this isn't just you seeing monsters and villains where there aren't any?"

"Even you have better instincts than that."

"So now I'm sticking my head in the sand, is that it?"

He stood and reached his hand down. "Come on."

She stayed put. "I don't take kindly to orders."

"Not an order, a request. Come read the thing for yourself, then ask me anything you want explained. Then you can decide where best to focus your energy."

Energy. It emanated off of him in waves without him even trying. His speaking voice was low, calm, smooth. Only the tic in his jaw, the gleam in his eyes, would give away his agitation with her at the moment.

"You wouldn't let me read it earlier. Why now?"

"I didn't earlier because it would be better explained by me. Now, it appears the only way you're going to take this situation seriously is by seeing it with your own eyes." He reached his hand down again. "It's not like I need this job, Kate. I'm here because I think you need me to be here. But read the report and tell me what you think. I can be out of here by morning."

It wasn't until he threatened to leave that she realized how badly she wanted him to stay. Maybe she really did want to hide her head in the sand and pretend nothing was going on; maybe she needed to hear him like he was just now to jolt her into action.

Or maybe she just didn't want him to leave because she wasn't done figuring out what she wanted to do about him yet.

She could have rolled to a stand on her own, but something made her deliberately take his offer. She reached her hand up to his. The contact was every bit as electric as she'd known it would be. His palm was wide and warm, his grip steady and strong as he tugged her easily to her feet. But rather than let her go as she'd expected, he kept tugging, until she stumbled a step closer and came up flush against his body. His free arm was instantly around back, steadying her, keeping her tucked up against him.

"I'm not playing games," he told her, the intensity of his gaze impossible to look away from at such close range. "You're in trouble here, Kate. Don't wander that far off alone like that again."

She was in trouble, all right. Deep, heart-thumping trouble. She opened her mouth to speak, but nothing came out. It had been a very long time since there was anyone in her life who cared where she was, or what she did. Much less if she was safe or okay. She'd be lying if she said she didn't like the feeling of being looked after, for the moment anyway. "I can take care of myself." Her voice wobbled dangerously. He didn't have to know it was more because of him than some unseen enemy.

"I'd like to believe that. More than you know."

"What's that supposed to mean?"

"It means—" He broke off, his gaze making its own tell-tale slip down to her mouth, then back up again. "I don't usually worry that much about other people."

"You don't need to worry about me."

"I may not need to, but I do. Just do me a favor and follow my rules while I'm here."

"Like you're following mine?"

Rather than set her loose, his arm flexed against her back, drawing her even closer, making her gasp as she came up against the full, hard length of him. Harder in some places than others. "You get out of arm's reach, you get into trouble. Seems like the obvious solution is to keep you close."

She tried to smile, tried to find some way to make light of a situation that was rapidly becoming anything but. "That's certainly a new approach, I'll give you that."

He pulled her hand up to his chest, pressed it there before letting it go so he could slide his fingers beneath the hair at her nape and tug her mouth closer to his. And she didn't do a damn thing to stop him. "You made me crazy eighteen years ago, and you're making me crazy now. I have no defense."

"You managed to resist back then," she said, her voice barely more than a whisper against her suddenly constricted throat.

"You have no idea how hard it was for me to stay away from you back then. Now? I'm finding it even harder to remember why I did."

"Convenient excuse."

"No excuses. Just the facts." He brushed a strand of hair off her forehead, and when he spoke, his tone was gentler, completely undoing her.

"Just . . . stick close. Okay?"

"And if I don't?"

"I'll have to find a way to make you want to."

Chapter 11

She tasted like the heat of a sunny day, not the chill of an early spring night. And when she softened rather than stiffened beneath his hands and mouth, he gave up any pretense of trying to control himself where she was concerned.

The past, the present, were so tangled up in his head and in his heart, he didn't even try to convince himself that he knew the difference anymore. He wanted to think he was well past that part of his life. Clearly, he was not. Because no woman of such recent acquaintance would have him this tied up. For that matter, no woman would, regardless of how long he'd known her.

Except, apparently, Kate Sutherland.

"You're supposed to be stopping me," he murmured against her lips.

She slid her arms around his neck and tugged him closer. "Now, why would I want to do that?"

His body soared to life. Like it needed encouragement. "You had rules." He kissed his way along the soft line of her jaw.

She sighed and relaxed more fully into him, tipping her chin to allow him access to that tender spot beneath her ear. "My rules were hasty and very shortsighted."

He kissed the spot where her pulse throbbed, eliciting the tiniest of moans. It was enough to make him hard to the point of pain. And he wanted desperately to hear her do that again. "How so?"

"Life is challenging enough these days." She gasped when he nipped at her earlobe.

"Mm hmm."

"I just—" She broke off on a short moan when he slid his fingers into her hair and massaged her scalp a little as he tilted her head so he could reach that spot where her neck curved into her shoulder. "That," she managed.

"That what?" he murmured, wishing like hell she didn't have a jacket on. Or anything on, for that matter.

She turned her head and surprised him by dropping her own set of fast, hot kisses against his neck, ending with a nip of his earlobe that had his body twitching hard and maybe a groan of his own in the back of his throat.

"That," she said, her voice soft and husky. "There should be more of that in life. Why did I think I should deny myself that?"

"I have no idea." He turned her mouth to his and took it hard and fast.

She didn't miss a heartbeat. She ran her fingertips up the back of his neck and dug them into his hair, holding him where she wanted him, which was with his mouth against hers, lips parting, tongues dueling.

He started to push her jacket down her arms, then remembered where they were standing. Not that she was stopping him. The very idea that she wouldn't stop him—at all—surged through him until standing still became a challenge. "This is crazy, you know that," he said, his breaths coming more rapidly as they tore at each other. "You are—" He was unable to finish the thought as she elicited a long groan of satisfaction from him when she raked her nails down his back and tugged his belt loops so he bumped more tightly against her.

"Tired of waiting, tired of always doing what I'm supposed to do," she said, her voice rough with need, with want, punctuated by the hot press of her lips along the side of his jaw and down the very same line of his neck as he'd explored with her. So damn sensitive, every place she touched, tasted, nibbled. He thought he'd simply explode. Madness, indeed.

She shivered, and he wrapped his arms around her. "Inside," he said, unable to manage more than a single word.

She nodded, but didn't make a single move toward leaving the dock. Instead, she turned her mouth back to his. Only this time, as their lips met, they slowed down, gentled the onslaught, which perversely jacked him up that much higher and harder. She teased, he taunted, they slipped their tongues more sinuously along the other, tasting, touching. Soft moans filled the rapidly cooling night air. His, hers, he wasn't keeping track. He was drowning, and he didn't want to be saved. Reality would rear its ugly head soon enough. It always did. He wasn't going to hurry it along any faster than necessary.

She shivered again, and he wasn't entirely sure it was in pleasure. He wanted her almost savagely at that moment. To throw her down on the dock, strip her naked, and take her like a howling wolf. So he had no idea where the tenderness came from that sprang up within him. He nuzzled the side of her chin, then tipped it up until she opened her eyes and looked at him. "Come on, it's getting cold out here."

"We're outside?"

He saw the twitch at the corner of her mouth, even as the heat in her eyes screamed "Take me!" And he slipped further under her spell for bringing humor into what was already a tantalizing mix.

"Yeah. But not for long." He bent down, intending to scoop her up, but she sidestepped him with surprising agility.

"I can walk just fine."

He almost commented that that made one of them. The fit of his jeans was strained to the point of threatening to emasculate him if he stepped the wrong way. "But why walk when you don't have to?"

She was suddenly once again in his arms, face tilted up to

his, and the moon chose that moment to slip from behind the clouds and illuminate the smile on her face as she looked into his eyes. "Don't go all Neanderthal on me here."

"I like being the guy. Sue me."

"I like being the girl, but that doesn't mean I can't walk."

"I rather like that girl part myself." He bumped hips with her, pulse spiking again when her eyes went darker.

"I'm just not—" She had to stop, clear her throat.

He liked that part, too. A lot. Happy to know he was far from the only one so deeply affected here. Thrilled, in fact. It was a lot easier to lose your mind when the person you were losing it over went merrily along on the same trip.

"I'm not exactly the dainty, scoop-me-up type. I've seen you wince when you straighten your legs after being cramped in my truck. I thought it might kill the mood a little if you picked me up and blew out both knees in the process."

"Boy, I'm feeling all manly now."

She smiled. "I kid because I care." Then she did the darndest thing. She lifted up on her toes and kissed the end of his nose.

He just didn't know quite what to make of that. Or the fact that he kind of liked it. Liked the idea that anyone would ever associate bestowing such a tender gesture on him.

"What?" she asked, her smile fading.

"Nothing, it's just—" He paused, grinned, shook his head. "You kissed me on the nose."

"I know."

"No one has ever done that before."

Rather than looking chagrined, or worse, embarrassed, she tipped right up on her toes and did it again. "Well, they should. It's a very cute one."

"Guy noses aren't cute."

"Yours is. Now, are we going to stand out here debating your general cuteness or lack thereof? Or are we going to head back to my nice, warm cabin and—" She stopped then, her cheeks finally flushing.

He couldn't help it. A gentleman would have covered for her, allowed her to save face. But then, no one had ever accused him of being one of those. "And?" He threw in a Snidely Whiplash eyebrow wiggle for effect, which made her laugh and swat him on the chest.

"And, I'll race you there, Mr. Knees of Steel. Then you'll find out." Using her edge of surprise, she slipped right from his arms and darted around him, dancing easily down the dock and onto terra firma. Bagel, whom he'd completely forgotten was even there, leapt up—or as much as he was able—barked twice, and took off on a lumbering lope after her.

"Now, wait a minute," he said out loud. To no one apparently. "What just happened here?"

"Better hurry up," came her voice, from up the path. "Last one back gets to walk Bagel in the morning!"

He took off at a dead run. Not because he didn't want to walk the damn dog. But because "in the morning" had all kinds of promise written on it. He'd ice his knees later.

Much later, if he was lucky.

"You shouldn't be running through the woods in the dark," he called out.

"It's not dark. I can see," came her voice, floating back at him from somewhere ahead. "And stop with the lame excuses. Cheater."

He smiled at that, so busy focusing on her, he didn't even notice the ease with which he fell right back into the routines of the past. He'd run these paths often when he was little. Hard to remember what he'd been in such a damn hurry about back then, but as kids, it seemed they were always running.

When he got older, he used the run the paths in the wee hours when his father would come home drunk. It served the dual purpose of getting him out of his father's immediate reach and working out his anger at the same time.

He caught up to her as she was rounding the back side of the main lodge building. He looped his arm through one of hers and used their momentum to swing her neatly off the path and up against the lodge wall. He followed, pinning her there, breathless and laughing.

Her eyes danced in the moonlight. "Took you long enough."

He had no choice but to kiss her.

Her laughter quickly subsided into a series of soft gasps as she let him take her. He was beyond thinking about what was smart, and what was supremely stupid. He wanted her. He'd always wanted her. And, right that very moment, she wanted him back. That was all that mattered.

He pushed her up higher, and she took the unspoken cue, wrapping those gloriously long legs of hers around his hips. He wasn't sure whose groan of appreciation was loudest when he finally settled his weight between her legs. Her thighs tightened against his hips, and he moved against her until he thought they'd both go mad.

"Cabin?" she managed.

"Not sure I can walk that far," he said. Or that he'd ever get his jeans off. At this rate, she might have to cut them off. It was a sacrifice he was willing to make.

A long whining sound cut through the night. Mac looked down to find a very forlorn Bagel sitting at his feet, looking confused. "We're scaring the children."

Kate tightened her hold on his neck and looked down over his shoulder. "Bagel, it's okay."

The dog thumped his stub of a tail and shifted closer, until he was all but glued to Mac's ankle. He looked up worshipfully and whined again.

"You're not exactly helping me out here, buddy."

Kate turned Mac's chin back to her. "You're doing just fine," she said, pulling him down to kiss her once again. "Bagel needs to learn to share. It's all part of growing up."

Mac was feeling intensely grown-up at the moment. He hitched Kate up higher on his hips, making her gasp and him groan in frustration. "Hold on."

"But—"

"Just hold on."

He moved away from the wall, making her cling to his neck and hook her ankles behind his back. "You really shouldn't—I can wal—"

"You can do a lot of things—I'm well aware of that—but right now you can hold on." He wrapped his arms around her back, keeping her molded to him, then kissed her until he was staggering slightly as he closed the remaining distance to her cabin stairs.

"Yeah, I—I can hold on," she said, then slid her fingers into his hair and kissed him again.

He banged them both up the porch stairs and slapped through the screen door, pausing long enough to push her up against the wall next to the front door and indulge in another long kiss. Bagel started barking, and they both said, "Bagel, hush," at the same time, then laughed.

Kate slapped her hand around behind her until she found the doorknob and twisted the door open. Then they both half fell, half staggered into the cabin. He actually wasted a second thinking the little kitchen table looked like a pretty good surface, but it was still covered with the remains of din-ner . . . and Finn's report.

Not wanting to think about any of that at the moment, he turned them toward the other doors leading from the main room.

"Left," she said, reading his mind.

"Bagel, stay," he said, groping for a piece of chicken from his salad as he passed by the table and tossing it in the gen-eral direction of the dog. "I hope you don't mind, but his ed-ucation is going to stop here."

She reached down behind her and opened her bedroom door.

Mac kicked it shut behind them.

"No," she said, kissing the side of his neck. "I don't mind at all."

With the door shut, it was fully dark, but his eyes were still more adjusted to dark than light, so he easily spotted her bed. Every aching step from the dock to right here, he'd thought of throwing her on the bed, following her down and going to it with the same abandon they'd started all this with.

Now that he was here, standing by her bed, the soft glow of moonlight filtering through the window just above the headboard, so seductive, so inviting, looking down into her face, turned up so willingly to his . . . he faltered.

It was completely ridiculous. Her thighs tightened around him, her fingers dug into the backs of his shoulders, and she continued raining hot, sweet kisses along his jaw and down the sensitive skin of his neck. His body clamored to get on with what it was all but howling for. Release, in the most primal fashion possible.

Only, now that he was standing here . . .

Kate's kisses slowed, then stopped, as she apparently caught on to his hesitation. "Donovan?"

He stilled. That name. Whispered so intimately. It should have jerked him the rest of the way out of this fantasy he'd foolishly indulged himself in. Instead, it did the exact opposite. Coming from her, only from her, it sounded . . . just exactly right. Which made no sense, none.

"What's wrong?"

"Nothing." *Everything.*

She unhooked her ankles from his back and, arms still wrapped around his neck, let her feet slip to the floor. "Something slowed you down. What is it?"

"I don't know," he said, never more honest. "I've wanted you forever. I want you right this second more than I've let myself want anything in a very long time. But—"

She tried to smile, smoothed her fingers along his cheek. "If you're worried I'll expect some kind of—"

"No, no, that's not it. I just—" He shook his head. Idiot! What in the hell was wrong with him? The words came, and he let them, figuring it was the only way to make sense of it. "Maybe I've wanted it too much, for too long. I mean, I never thought we would, never thought I'd see you again, but I don't want this to be some kind of retroactive—" He stopped again, shook his head again. "I don't know. I don't know what this is." He looked her in the eyes. "But, what I think I do know, what you should know, is that it won't just be a casual roll in the hay. Not for me."

And right there was the raw, stunning truth of it. Shocking, really, since he'd never come up against that particular problem before. And sure as hell hadn't expected to here, now.

"Maybe it's the past getting tangled up in this, I don't know," he said. "I just don't know." He pushed her hair from her face. "And I think I need to. Know, that is. Before we . . . before I can . . . or should . . ." He trailed off, feeling like the biggest fool on the planet. "I'm sorry. I'm making a mess of this. I know this isn't what you want to hear right now, but—"

"Shh. You don't know what I want," she said gently. "You couldn't, because I don't know either. I'm guilty of a little fantasizing myself. I've wanted you for a long time, too. And yes, I'm surprised my desire for you has only grown with distance and time. I don't know if it's the boy I still want, the memory of that, or the man you've become. To be honest, it's probably a little of both. I'm not sure what that says about me."

"It says you're just as caught up, as confused, as I am." Which was a major relief. And also that much more terrifying. And did nothing whatsoever to ease the immediate situation. If anything, it served only to intensify his need further. "We should figure things out before we—"

"Or maybe we should just not think everything to death. We're adults, we're unattached, we want each other. Maybe it can be that simple."

He drew his thumb across her bottom lip, making her body quake. A soft moan escaped her lips. "You really believe that?"

She closed her eyes and dropped her chin, resting her fore-head on his. "No. I don't know. I wish it could be, though." The silence grew as they stood there, holding on to each other. Finally, she laughed a little, and looked back up at him. "You should have taken me on the dock. Now it's complicated."

He smiled a little. "It's always been complicated. Nothing was going to change that."

"You're probably right." She kept her arms looped around his neck, kept her body meshed to his. And since that was right where he wanted her, he didn't do anything to change that.

"So, let me ask you this." She toyed with the collar of his jacket. "Are you proposing we just cease and desist? Because I'm thinking the attraction isn't going to stop just because we think it would be too complicated to act on it."

His mouth twitched. "So, you're saying we have to be slaves to the passion? That we can't rise above it, control ourselves, and behave?"

She nudged her hips against his, making the very rigid length of him jerk hard in response. "Doesn't feel much like you want to behave."

No. No, he didn't. At the moment, he wanted nothing more than to let loose his inner Neanderthal. But she didn't have to know that. More than she already did, anyway. "I didn't say it was what I wanted, just that maybe it was for the best."

"Best for who? Whom? Whatever."

"You. Me. I don't know. You've got a tough situation to sort out here, and I—my life isn't here anymore. And I don't want it to be."

"And you think dancing around this, and pretending we don't want to drag each other's clothes off is preferable to just giving in to it, enjoying ourselves, then going on with life as it happens? I'm a big girl, Mac. I can handle disappointment. If that's what happens. Who knows, we might go to bed once and find out it's not all that we thought it was cracked up to be."

So, he was Mac now. He should have been pleased. Why he wanted to hear her call him Donovan, in that breathy little voice, he had no clue, anyway. "Do you really think that will be the case? And if it is, then things will be that much more awkward, trying to help you sort things out here, dancing around each other."

"Like it wouldn't be a juggling act either way."

"At least the other way, there will be no regrets. No one gets—"

"Hurt? No regrets? Speak for yourself. I might have a few. Like not taking advantage of what might be my only opportunity to—"

"Have sex with your teenage crush?"

She didn't flinch. "Maybe. I'm human after all." She grabbed his belt loops and tugged him full up against her hips, moving on him when he surged against her. "But this is no teenage crush now. I'm very adult, as is the desire I have for you, who happens to have grown up into a very desirable, very adult man. Give us some credit for being able to take what we want, get what we need, and figure the rest out later."

He took her hands from his belt and held on to them. "Maybe you can. And maybe I could. I have. In the past. With other women. But . . . not with you, Kate." He stepped back, his body resisting the action with every beat of his heart, but he did it nonetheless. "Not with you."

Her eyes widened. "I can't believe you're really going to stick your head in the sand."

"At the moment, I'm going to stick some other part of me in a very cold shower."

She lifted her hands in disbelief, then let them drop to her sides. "You're really serious."

"I really am. I'm sorry." And he was. Sorrier than he'd ever been. But what he felt at the moment was relief, not fear that he'd just made a big mistake. Which told him it was the right thing to do. He stepped farther back, before he changed his mind.

"So . . . now what? We pretend that there's no screaming sexual tension between us and just go about our business?"

He smiled briefly. She was direct. He liked that about her. "We try. At least until we know more about what's really at stake here."

And he wasn't talking about the case. The idea that he was worried he was getting emotionally involved should have been the douse of cold reality her raging hormones needed.

Not so much, as it turned out.

"I already know all I need to know." She turned away and paced across the small room, then stopped abruptly, her back still to him. Even in the dim lighting, he watched as her shoulders slumped a little, and finally felt the twinge of the regret he'd hoped not to feel.

"I believe there is a cold shower with your name on it," she said at length, quietly, but with no overt recrimination in her voice either. Weary resignation was more like it.

He took a step toward her, then checked himself and walked to the door instead. He paused, looked back at her. Her face was still averted. "It's not for lack of want. But because we'll want too much. Or I will, anyway. And while you'd probably never disappoint me, I can guarantee I'd disappoint you."

Chapter 12

Kate woke to the sound of rain pattering on her roof . . . and somebody drilling. Groggy, she sat up and pushed her hair out of her face. Bagel raised his head and looked hopefully at her. "Not yet, buddy. Give me a minute."

What was that racket? Who the hell was drilling at—she squinted at her bedside clock—seven o'clock in the morning?

Then the fog cleared and she remembered. She flopped back onto her pillow and stared unseeing at the ceiling. In her mind's eye, she pictured him, walking toward her on the dock. Pulling her into his arms. Then later, catching her on the path, both of them laughing as he pinned her against the lodge wall. The feel of him, strong, hard, sure, moving between her legs. All but dragging each other into her bedroom . . .

She squeezed her eyes shut. She really didn't need to start what was sure to be a challenging day reliving that particular rejection.

Bagel whined.

"Yeah, yeah." She slid her legs off the bed and dragged herself upright. "I know how you feel." She wasn't mad at Donovan, not really. He hadn't been playing games. He'd been sincerely confused, trying to do what he thought was right. Odd that he thought he'd disappoint her in some way, when he seemed to have a stronger sense of himself and their unusual dynamic than she did. Maybe that was part of his problem, too.

She reached down and scratched Bagel behind the ears, sending him into a sigh of wriggling ecstasy. "See? I can make you happy." She heaved one last self-indulgent sigh and got up. He was probably right anyway. It probably was better, or at least smarter, for them to leave well enough alone. She talked a good game about them being consenting adults who could do what they wanted, when they wanted, but he might have had a teensy point there, about risking wanting more. Wanting too much.

What was important was getting her camp up and running. Her camp. And she wanted that more than anything. Better not to dilute one want with another. Especially one as potent as Donovan MacLeod.

He would do his job here and go back to Virginia, or on to his next Good Samaritan mission, and she would launch her camp and fulfill her dreams. They both would, it seemed. Just not with each other. She let out a short laugh. See? He was right. She was already thinking about a future apart, which meant that somewhere in her subconscious, she'd at least contemplated the idea of a future together. Which was completely impossible. Youth Camp Director meets Secret Mission Man. Yeah, like that was ever going to work.

She recalled what he'd said about this place, of his past never being any part of his future. So that was two strikes, in case anyone was counting.

She glanced back at her bed. If he were sprawled there right now, sheets draped over a body she'd felt pressed against her so intimately last night, and yet nowhere near as intimately as she wanted . . . yeah. She might find herself wanting a bit too much.

She slapped her thigh and scuffed into the bathroom. "Come on, Bagel. Let's brush my teeth and get your leash."

Trudging though the main room minutes later, feeling only slightly less subhuman, she did her best to ignore the remains of dinner that still littered the dining room table as she turned on the coffeemaker and grabbed Bagel's leash off the back of the chair by the door. She did manage to notice that Donovan had wasted little time before leaving last night. Finn's report was right where he'd left it. All neatly stacked and waiting for her on the kitchen counter. Great.

She dragged on her rain gear and mud boots. He was certainly making it clear it was all business now. "I get it, already," she muttered. She snapped on Bagel's leash. Not that there was any real reason out here for him not to run freely, but he liked to chase things, and he had zero sense of direction. She'd cut him loose, and within fifteen minutes she'd hear his mournful howl from somewhere on the property. Which inevitably led to her plunging into the woods to untangle him from something. She'd realized early on he was probably meant to be a city dog, so she treated him like one. Especially on wet, rainy, muddy mornings.

She stepped out onto the porch, and the drilling sounds got exponentially louder. They were coming from somewhere beyond the main lodge building. It was only drizzling now, so she flipped her hood up and purposely set off in the opposite direction with Bagel, refraining from giving in to the childish urge to stomp through the mud puddles. Still, she didn't exactly avoid them either. Her emotions were pretty muddied at the moment. Might as well have the boots to match.

She continued on down the outer boundary route, not even glancing in the direction of the lodge. She wasn't quite ready to deal with Donovan just yet. She needed to shake the cobwebs loose first. Getting rid of that image of him sprawled naked in her sheets was probably a good idea, too. The path looped in and out of the trees, meandering its way along the base of a ridge, eventually dumping out on the opposite side of the lake. There were no cabins over here, only another dock and a service shed where canoes and paddles were stored in the off season.

It wasn't until she passed the shed that the Day-Glo color

caught her eye. She turned back and read the message sprayed there, all loopy with drips running from every letter. RICH BITCH, GO HOME!

Same color, same amateur paint job. Same message.

She tucked her arms around herself, pulling Bagel in closer in the process. She should be used to them by now. Irritating, but mostly because of the expense involved in removing them. Now? Now it gave her the creeps. And suddenly made her feel way too far away from her cabin.

She shrugged off the feeling and forced her arms down to her sides. It was simply everything that had been going on for the past forty-eight hours making her so jumpy. She hadn't been over on this side of lake yet, so she had no idea how long it had been here. For all she knew, this could have been the first message sprayed. Though why put it on the far side of the lake, on the back side of the shed, where no one could really see it from any vantage point, save the close one she had right there, she had no idea. It made no sense. All the others had been painted where anyone entering the property or traversing any main path would easily see from a distance.

Then, as she stared at the message, she realized something. The running paint drips hadn't dried that way; they were still actively running down the side of the shed.

She froze, and her throat closed over. She instinctively tugged a resistant Bagel to her side. But rather than run—or call for help, not that Donovan would hear her over the sound of power tools—she stepped closer and touched the paint. Sure enough, her fingertip came back Day-Glo orange. The hairs on the back of her neck stood on end, and she had to forcibly keep from spinning around and looking for somebody watching her. It just felt as if there were eyes drilling holes in the back of her head. It was her imagination. Besides, maybe the spray was water based and the rain was making it run.

She shivered, and not entirely from the chilling rain. Somehow she doubted that was the case. Spray paint was meant to stay where it was put. She looked down at the ground, looking for any other clues, although what those would be, she wasn't clear on. Footprints maybe. As it was, with the rain, the mud, her two feet and Bagel's four, they'd already obliterated any footprints that might have been right there. She scanned the immediate area, but saw only mud puddles and fallen pine needles.

Then the sound of drilling stopped. And the sudden quiet, disturbed only by the soft sound of rain pattering on the tall trees overhead and plopping against the otherwise calm surface of the lake, sounded altogether too eerie and somehow sinister. Like those horror movies where the kids all went camping . . . and the lunatic always stalked them in weather just like this.

Surely no one had just been by the shed, or she'd have heard or seen something. Wouldn't she? The drilling sounds had echoed through the trees, bouncing around and distorting the usual forest noises, but certainly not enough to mask something like that.

Except, just how much noise was an interloper with a spray can and mud boots going to make?

Keeping Bagel close to her heels, she started moving along the path that bordered the lake edge, which was the most direct route back to camp and the relative safety of her cabin. Who was she kidding? It was the most direct route back to Donovan.

Now she actively scanned the campground across the lake, trying to locate him. Another month and the leaf canopy would be too heavy, the underbrush, too, and her view that far up the hill would be mostly blocked. Only the roof of the main lodge in the center and her own cabin farther up the ridge would be noticeable.

But it was early enough in the season that from back on the far dock, she'd have been able to look across the lake and more than likely see what Donovan was doing. Or at least hear exactly where he was doing it. She'd had a vague idea that maybe if she watched him from afar for a bit, she could steel herself against the effect he so effortlessly had on her. "Right," she muttered.

Yep. A little time spent standing in a chilly drizzle would surely have numbed the heated attraction right out of her. Instead, she was all but running toward him. She looked down at her fingertips, but the paint had dripped back off. It had to be the rain making the paint run.

Didn't it?

Then another thought occurred to her. If she could see Donovan through the sparse tree cover, so could anyone else. Had someone been watching him install his equipment? Had that same someone watched as she set out around that side of the lake and decided to leave her a message to find when she got there?

There was no will strong enough to shut down the little spurt of pure fear the very idea shot through her. Bagel hustled his stubby legs to keep up with her quickening gait.

The sudden sound of hammering made her heart skip a few beats. She paused just long enough to focus on the sound and follow it . . . adjusting her view upward as the ringing echo continued. And upward farther. Dear Lord, he was halfway up a forty-foot pine tree. Hanging on by . . . his wits, from the looks of it. She skimmed her gaze downward and noticed there was no ladder leaning up against the trunk, then shifted her gaze immediately back to him. *Is he crazy?*

She checked that question. Of course he was. All three of them had been daredevils, to a degree anyway, growing up. Rafe and Donovan had taken great pleasure in besting the rich boys at whatever ridiculous testosterone-measuring event they came up with. That was, when Donovan and Rafe weren't trying to best each other. Usually with Finn right there, devising the competitions. Finn being the most fearless of the three, they usually involved risking at least several limbs, if not life itself.

She'd watched them shimmy trees like young forest creatures. Rafe being the fastest, with Donovan a close second. But that was shimmying for the sake of seeing who could get the highest . . . then they slid back down. Clinging tenuously twenty feet above the ground while hammering stuff? That was idiocy. He was gripping the trunk with two legs and one arm, while he hammered something with his free hand. No one clinging to a tree that high up in the air should have a free hand.

Her pace increased as she drew close. It was harder to see him that high up now, too many trees in her line of vision. There continued to be alternating hammering and silence. Hammering. And silence. Every time she heard the hammer again, she realized she'd been holding her breath . . . and speeding up until she was all but dragging Bagel through the mud puddles. Of course, given that the dog's belly had the clearance of a vacuum cleaner, he wasn't going to arrive home clean no matter how slowly they walked.

She finally passed the dock they'd been on last night and started up the trail directly to the main lodge. She was less than twenty yards away when a grunt, followed by a string of curse words, rippled through the damp air, followed by the thud of a falling hammer.

Better than the thud of a falling man, she thought, arriving at the base of the tree as Donovan began gingerly scaling down its trunk. He pushed off about twelve feet up and landed in a wincing crouch, before slowly straightening.

"What in the hell do you think you're doing up there?" Kate demanded. "You could have killed yourself."

"Good morning to you, too." He lifted his hand and closely inspected his finger. "Just mangled it a little." He shot her a tight grin. "I'll live."

"Not if I catch you hanging off of pine trees again, you won't."

He looked down at Bagel. "She cares about me."

Bagel wagged his stub and went immediately to Donovan's side, sitting dutifully next to his foot and leaning his mud-encrusted tubby body up against his hero's equally mud-encrusted jeans. He wriggled in ecstasy when Donovan leaned down and scrubbed him behind the ears. "Now, that's a proper greeting."

"Men," she stated, glaring at both of them.

"And what would you do without us?"

She wisely chose to ignore the question. "What were you doing up there?" She framed her eyes and squinted up into the trees, but the falling rain made the angle impossible to maintain without getting water in her eyes. All she could make out was that some kind of metal bracket had been attached to the trunk.

"Installation."

She looked back at him. "Of?"

"Security system. It's wireless and solar powered."

"There isn't much solar today."

"Doesn't matter. It stores the energy over a long period of time."

"Like winter?"

He smiled. "It'll do the job."

She squinted back up again, but quickly gave up. "So what is that, some kind of sensor? Won't the wildlife trigger it?"

"It's a camera, not a sensor. Well, more a monitor than a camera. It doesn't film anything, just projects back to the command control center."

"The command control center," she repeated. "What, exactly, is a command control center? And where, might I ask, is it going to be located?"

"A command control center is just what it sounds like, a main console base that monitors the entire system. It will be located in your office in your cabin, and it's the size of a laptop."

"While that sounds very . . . *Mission Impossible,* I can't very well sit at a computer all day watching the campgrounds. And I don't have the money to hire—"

"Slow down. The central com is, in fact, similar to a small

notebook computer. Not only so it takes up less space, but it's portable. So you can take it with you to the lodge, or even down to the stables and the lake."

"Do you really think that's necessary? And how often would I need to look at it? Will it store images, or just beam them live? Because someone could sneak in and vanish and I'll be too busy overseeing construction or something to—"

"That's something to consider later on, yes. But right now, the only thing you're overseeing is finding out who is sabotaging your camp. And why Shelby isn't signing the papers to make your ownership official. Once we get that resolved, you'll be able to keep the system, and you can use it however you want, whenever you want. Right now, we'll keep track continuously, until we figure things out."

"We?"

"Unless you want to pull twenty-four-hour shifts."

Her eyes widened. "You mean one of us has to sit and watch the monitor all day long?"

"Unless you want the night shift."

She looked closely at him, but he didn't seem to be referencing last night. For that matter, he seemed to have forgotten it altogether. Which should have reassured her. For some reason, it just irritated her instead. After all, he might have been right that they needed to back off from getting physical with each other, but he could at least act like it was costing him a little.

"You wanted to be involved," he reminded her. "But don't worry, there is a backup alarm system."

"Alarms? Out here?"

"It triggers silently, inside. So we know and they don't."

"How will the alarm know to trigger for an intruder and not some forest animal. It could be going off every five minutes."

"It's set to mass and body temperature."

That set her back. "Oh."

He smiled. "Technology is cool, isn't it?"

"Yes," she said, somewhat absently, once again shaken by the seriousness with which he was tackling her problem. Which reminded her about what had sent her scrambling up here in the first place. "So, do you have any set up yet that could scan across the lake?" She glanced back that way, shivering all over again as visions of the running paint skipped through her mind, and that sensation she was being watched crawled down her spine.

His grin faded a notch, and he stepped closer and turned her to face him. "Kate, listen, I promise, that while this is state-of-the-art stuff, it's not as intimidating as it sounds."

"There's something I need to tell you. The reason I came up here."

"I thought it was to yell at me for playing in trees."

"That, too, but . . ."

His smile faded completely now. "What's up? What happened?"

"Someone spray painted the side of the boat shed across the lake. Same spray, same message as the others."

"How long has it been since you've been over—"

"I haven't been over there since I moved in. It's not high on my to-do list. So I have no idea how long ago it was done. Except—" She looked down at her fingertips to see if any remnants of the paint remained, but it was all gone. "Does spray paint usually run in the rain?"

Donovan shifted his gaze to one of the nearby trees that still had one of the GO HOME messages sprayed on it. Kate followed his gaze. The tree trunk was glistening wet. The message was intact. He looked back to her. "Not usually. Why?"

"The message on the shed . . . the paint was running. I thought maybe—"

Whatever she'd been about to say was cut off when Donovan took her by the arm and began moving them swiftly up the path to her cabin.

"Hey, wait a darn minute! You can't just bodily move me—"

"The hell I can't. Don't talk. Move. You can yell at me later."

"I can yell at you just fine right now." She tried to tug her arm free, but to no avail. Bagel barked and followed them up the path. "You're scaring the dog."

"At least he's smart enough to be scared." He glared at her over his shoulder. "Unlike his owner."

"Who said I wasn't scared? But I'm pretty sure if someone was still out there, he or she would have made their move when I was alone on the other side of the lake, don't you think?"

"We can argue about this in about five minutes."

She gave up, but pulled her arm free with one good tug. "I can imprison myself for no reason on my own just fine, thanks."

He tugged open the screen door on her porch and hustled her and the dog inside, closing the door behind them in short measure. "Bagel, sit," he commanded, and to her shock, though why he did it at this point, she had no idea, the dog plopped his muddy butt down right inside the door. "Got any rags? I'll clean him off while you go change."

"Change into?"

"Whatever won't track mud through your home." He looked pointedly down at her pant legs and boots.

She looked down to discover that Bagel wasn't the only one who'd adversely suffered from her march around the lake. "Right. Rag towels are around the side of the porch. If you think it's safe enough." She didn't wait for his retort, but toed out of her boots and tiptoed gingerly across the main room, not stopping until she was in her bathroom. She closed the door and locked it behind her. More for her peace of mind and to make a statement, than anything else.

When she came out again, clad in sweats and a Boston

University sweatshirt, Donovan was standing by the door punching numbers into a cell phone. A familiar-looking cell phone.

"Hey, what are you doing with my cell—"

"Catch," he said, then tossed it to her.

She stopped talking to focus on catching. Cradling her phone, she looked up in time to see his hand on the door. A toweled-off Bagel trotted over to him, not exactly clean, but not trekking muck through the cabin either. "Where are you going?"

"To check the boat shed."

"You won't find anything. By the time I realized what was happening, Bagel and I had pretty much mucked up the area. The rain did the rest. I'm sorry."

"Not a problem. I'm still going." He motioned to her phone. "If anything, or anyone, pops up that makes you the least bit nervous, press two on your speed dial."

"Why would I want to call my friend Amy in Boston?"

"I don't know. But if you dial two, you'll get me."

"You're not two on my speed dial."

He grinned and waved his sat phone at her. "I am now." He looked from her to Bagel. "Protect," he ordered.

She rolled her eyes. "You're kidding, right?"

"I wish I wasn't. Sorry, mate," he said to the dog, then looked back to her. "We work with what we've got. And don't underestimate him just because he's stubby."

"Right. How long will you be out there?"

"As long as it takes."

She folded her arms across her chest and clung to her cynical point of view. It was that or fling herself at him and beg him not to take one step outside the cabin until they were sure it was safe. "Why is it I feel like I'm suddenly in a Kathleen Turner-Michael Douglas movie?"

"You know, Kathleen never did it for me. Are you really a Michael Douglas fan?"

"Donovan," she said warningly.

His grin was a quick flash. "I shouldn't like it when you say it like that. But I do." The grin vanished, and he was all business again. "Don't go anywhere. I'm serious."

"I'll try and refrain from all my many outdoor activities." She scooped up Finn's report. "Besides, I have some reading to do. Be prepared to answer some questions when you get back from your *mission*," she told him, using air quotes on the last part.

He looked a bit pained at that part, but said nothing. Then, at the door, he turned. "Take this seriously, okay?"

She nodded. Then as he walked out the door, she blurted, "Be careful!"

He paused and smiled back at her. "And ruin all the fun?" Then he was gone.

"Men," she muttered for the second time that morning. Bagel whined. "You're included in that gross generalization, so watch it."

The dog padded over to her and sunk to the floor, propping his chin on her foot.

"And it's precisely knowing when to do stuff like that, that keeps us from giving up on you altogether." She reached down and patted his head. "Come on, let's get some food and then we'll see just how much trouble I'm really in." But instead of walking to the fridge, she went to stand by the window, where she could see Mac moving quickly straight down the ridge toward the lake. "For a guy with bum knees, he sure moves fast," she murmured. And again her mind went to the bed they might have shared last night, and other fast moves he was really good at making.

She swore under her breath and turned resolutely back to the kitchen. Men, indeed.

Chapter 13

Mac rubbed the paint off his fingers across the wood of the shed. Some of it had permanently adhered, enough to read the message, but most of it had mixed with the rain and moisture on the wood and was running off in Day-Glo orange rivulets.

Kate was right about the ground around the shed. She and the dog had obliterated any footprints that might have been remaining. Not that it would have told him a whole lot, but any additional information was better than the none he had at the moment. He turned slowly and scanned the surrounding area, looking for any kind of disturbance that would point to the direction the intruder had entered or exited by. A shame it wasn't a little later in the season, when the leafy underbrush would have made it almost impossible not to make some kind of lasting mark.

He hunched over as the rain started to come down harder and make rivulets of its own, right down the back of his neck, past the collar of his jacket and his sweatshirt. He slowly began a methodical search, sectioning the area off in pie-shaped quadrants. The rain wasn't doing him any favors, but if the vandal had moved close enough to the base of one of the pine trees, he'd have left a shoe impression that likely hadn't washed away yet.

He just had to find that random print. Then he could track

from there. With a track came a direction, and with a direction, he could locate where the intruder made his entrance to camp property and get a feel for how well they knew the area. He'd already tracked one entrance/exit point to the driveway. But from this vantage point, he doubted they'd double all the way around to that point. Way too far, and almost impossible to do with any stealth. Especially in broad daylight. Or, well, broad rainy daylight.

Whoever had done this, it was a pretty ballsy move. Mac hadn't made any attempt to disguise what he was doing this morning, and he'd been pretty noisy in making his presence and whereabouts known. Which, on the one hand, made it easier for the vandal as he knew Mac's whereabouts while he did his artistic deed. But one glance from Mac across the lake could have easily revealed his position.

He looked back at the running paint. Too much was murking up the puddles at the base of the shed to have been there for very long. Certainly not before daybreak. He glanced back across the lake and up the hill to Kate's cabin. Just thinking about her wandering around over here while the jackoff who did this was anywhere nearby made his eye twitch. *Ballsy and stupid*, he thought. *Because now you've really pissed me off.*

He continued his grid search methodically, albeit increasingly soggily. He should have grabbed some better rain gear, but he'd been too busy playing Douglas to her Turner. Now who was being stupid? Maybe if he got wet enough and cold enough, he'd remember to think with the head on his shoulders instead of the one between his legs. Well, more often, anyway. There had to be a law against anyone who could make baggy sweats and a faded sweatshirt look sexy as hell. That or he needed to get laid in the worst way.

Or both.

He went back to his search. His pocket hummed a second later. Adrenaline punched into his system as he quickly slipped his phone out, ducking his head down to keep the phone dry as he moved instantly toward her cabin. "What's wrong?" He knew he shouldn't have left her up there alone.

"Find anything?"

He stopped short. "Tell me you did not just call the Bat phone to ask me how my day was going?" He willed his heart to descend back out of his throat.

"Bat phone?"

"I'm lightening the mood."

"Yeah, I can tell. I'm sorry. You've been out there forever. And I—I wondered if you'd found something."

Or she was worried about him. He wasn't sure if he should like the idea of that so much. Usually, he preferred no one worry about him. It made what he did for a living much easier. "You read Finn's report."

There was silence, then, "Yes. Yes, I did."

Good. Maybe she'd stop waffling now. But whether he liked it or not, for her sake, he didn't need her worrying about him on top of the rest. "I'm trying to track the entrance/exit point. Stay put."

"Yes, sir, oh Defender of Gotham City."

He couldn't help it, he chuckled. "I'll be back when I'm done. Keep Robin in the house, will ya?"

"He's presently deep into some doggie dream, so I don't think this will be a big issue. Some guard dog you left me with."

"Hey, you adopted him. I didn't."

"He seems to have adopted you, and you put him in charge."

He looked up the ridge to the cabin and wished like hell he didn't feel what he was feeling. Like she fit him. Effortlessly. "I liked it better when you were bitchy," he lied. "It keeps you sharper."

"No problem. Just say something else to piss me off. Shouldn't be too hard."

"Very funny." He could feel her smile. And maybe that was why he'd done it. Except making her smile and distracting her from her problems might make him feel good, but that wasn't what was going to keep her safe. "Make a list of the questions you want to badger and annoy me with. And a hot lunch when I get in wouldn't be turned down, either."

"Bingo," was all she said, then clicked off.

He stared at the now dead phone. "So, would that be 'bingo, sure no problem, chief,' or 'bingo, bite me'?" He really shouldn't be smiling as he pocketed his phone. This was serious business. But he was.

At this rate, they were both doomed.

It took him another very wet twenty minutes to find the trail, what there was of it. But it was enough to track. Eventually it led him to one of several old dirt roads that had been cut through the mountains back in the fifties, to allow fire equipment access to the higher elevations. Kids with four-wheelers enjoyed off roading on the overgrown, rutted trails, and hikers occasionally used them as a short cut, but otherwise the fire roads were largely ignored. Or had been during his childhood. The condition of this one led him to believe that hadn't changed much. But whoever had parked their big-ass truck here had been away from it long enough for the rain to make turning around a bit of an adventure. Either that, or the driver had been in a hurry.

The tracks were relatively fresh, which tied in to the fresh paint. He wondered why Kate hadn't heard the engine, though between the rain and him drilling, he could understand it going undetected.

"Dammit." He didn't bother tracking farther. He knew where the cut-through road went, where it emptied out, and the driver had two choices. Drive straight into the camp, or across the mountain and down into the valley toward town.

He turned back to the lake and began the hike back to the cabin. Why would someone risk entry during daylight hours, with obvious sounds of inhabitants, just to spray paint another sign like all the rest? The risk didn't make sense.

He stopped by the cabin down the hill from hers and

grabbed his duffel. When he was back on the porch, he pulled off his boots after knocking as much mud off them as possible, then left them beside the muddy rags before rapping on the frame of the door and letting himself in. "Hi, honey, I'm home."

She looked up from the papers she was reading. Finn's file. "You look like something the cat and the dog dragged in."

"You have to be willing to get dirty if you want the job done right." He skirted the table and moved toward her bedroom.

"Where are you going?"

"Shower." He sniffed the air. "I don't smell any lunch. You know, us superheroes, after putting in a long couple of hours tracking bad guys, really go for a hot meal."

"So I hear."

"I'll be out in a few minutes."

"Oh, please, make yourself right at home."

It was on the tip of his tongue to ask her if she wanted to help him with the hard-to-reach places. She was cranky because of last night. Not that he could blame her. It wasn't a habit of his to take a woman all the way to the edge like that, then walk away. And it took considerable control now not to nudge her in that direction again. But then, he hadn't expected resisting her would be easy. He just wanted to see her smile was all.

And if she was naked in the shower with him at the time, well, he wouldn't say no.

He swore under his breath and closed her bathroom door behind him before he did something he'd live to regret. This was the right thing to do. He knew it, and he bet she knew it, even if she was pissed off at him. Tangling themselves up any further than they already had was just begging for trouble. He couldn't stay focused on the job if he was focused on getting her naked. And he would be. Hell, he already was. And the little tugs he was experiencing inside his chest whenever he looked at her were downright terrifying. He'd been back in her orbit for only a couple days. No way should she be having this effect on him. But there was no denying she was affecting the hell out of him. And it was more than sexual need fanning those flames.

He shucked out of his muddy clothes, carefully putting them in her sink, then climbed under the steamy spray. He closed his eyes and let the water beat on him while he tried to clear his head. Focus. They needed a game plan. He'd finish installing the security system tomorrow after the rain let up. Shimmying any more trees wasn't happening until things dried out a little. Which meant being stuck in the cabin with Kate.

No problem. He'd fix them both lunch, then answer her questions. Keep it business. He imagined she'd want to know exactly what it was he was doing security-wise, so he'd sketch it out. Walk her through the process, and how it was going to work. They also needed to come to an agreement on how they were going to proceed with the rest. He could handle security, the town, and Timberline if he had to, but she was going to have to handle her stepbrother.

So. That agenda should take them through dinnertime. And with daylight still at a premium, even if it stopped raining right that second, it would be too dark to do any more work outside tonight. Nothing was hooked up yet, so he planned to do a perimeter patrol. Maybe walk the interior paths as well. If for no other reason than if someone was watching from any point, they'd know he was out there, watching right back. He could walk the lake path, too. Just in case.

Anything to keep him out of this cabin for the rest of the night.

He'd moved his gear into the cabin just down the hill last night, but with this latest escalation in the vandalism, it would be best to stay closer. He wondered how long it would take him to convince Kate of that. Not to mention how he was going to last the night on her couch, knowing she was mere feet away. And, as of last night anyway, willing to share her nice warm bed with him. If not her nice warm self.

He groaned and reached for the soap.

"Hurt something?"

The soap went shooting out of his hand, and he almost lost his balance. "What the hell?"

A hand emerged between the shower curtain and the wall, and a mug was thrust at him. "Coffee. It's not a hot meal, but it's a start."

"Uh, thanks. And I mean that," he added quickly, before she dumped the scalding contents on some part of his naked body. "You can just set it there by the sink if you don't mind. And don't freak over the muddy clothes. I'll take care of it when I get out of here."

"Yes, you will. Exactly what were you planning on putting on when you got out?"

"I—" He'd been so caught up in trying not to do anything stupid, like drag her into the shower with him, he'd sort of forgotten about that part. "I left my duffel on the porch."

"How convenient."

He swallowed a sigh. "I don't suppose—"

He heard a thud as something soft and heavy hit the bathroom floor. "Don't mention it."

"Thanks." He frowned, still trying to figure out what she was doing in here. "I—uh, was kidding, before."

"About being a superhero? Good, because I was already really disappointed about last night as it was. If I thought I'd missed out on some kind of other hidden superpowers, I'd be really pissed off."

His lips twitched, and he fought a laugh. "I meant about lunch. I'll put something together when I get out."

"I'm making some soup. And there might be a sandwich or two in your future."

He heard the slap of her closing the toilet seat lid, then, "So, about Finn's report."

Wait. She wanted to do this . . . here? "I don't suppose we could wait until I'm done here?"

"You've had the upper hand since you walked in here. And you put me at a distinct disadvantage last night that I really didn't appreciate."

"Listen, you know that wasn't any kind of rejection of you. And I know you don't know me all that well now, but I don't do that. Ever. I just—I had no choice. I should have never let it go that far, and I take full responsibility for it. It's not like it's easy for me, either."

Silence.

He was tempted to tell her exactly what he'd been thinking since he'd stripped naked, but he doubted that would help either of them out. "Kate? Can we do this out there? Please?"

"I think it's Shelby," she said quietly, so he could barely hear her over the spray. "I didn't think it was him at first. Then I waffled. Then I tried to convince myself again it just couldn't be him. I've tried to think it through, figure out why he'd be doing this. I'm still not sure it all follows." There was a long pause, then, "But my gut tells me he's probably behind this. I don't have a clue how, but it would just be too typical of him."

Holding the curtain closed in front of his body, Mac poked his head out. "I'm sorry."

"Don't be. It's not like we have any love lost each other. I just didn't think he'd go to these lengths to screw me over. Do you think there's a chance he's not involved? That maybe the developer contacted him and he turned them down, so now they're going after me, knowing I'm the future owner?"

Mac just held her gaze. He hated seeing her look so defeated. "Not much of one, no. If it was just them behind this, they'd come straight to you and offer a buyout."

"Except I'm not the owner. So they went to Shelby."

"Looks that way."

"Even if he's in it with them, why the stupid graffiti threats?

If I back away from wanting this place and agree to renege on our inheritance deal, he stands to lose so much. Why would he risk that?"

"Maybe the development deal is bigger."

"Could that really be?"

"I don't know. Maybe he's trying to find a way to keep both, or to just buy you out altogether, and by sabotaging the place, he can get it from you for a lower price. You said he felt he deserved it all; maybe that's what he's angling for after all."

"So why not just tell me flat out he's not signing, that he wants a new deal?"

"Because he thinks you'll fight him and tie things up longer, and maybe he can't afford that either. So maybe he's trying to make you want to walk away. I don't know."

"Where does Ralston fit in, then?"

Mac pressed his forehead against the tile and sighed. "Let me finish up here, and we'll sit down and develop a plan of attack, okay?"

He looked up in time to see a surprising hint of a smile curve her mouth. "Oh, I'm fine right here." She crossed her legs and leaned back, her gaze dipping pointedly lower.

He realized he'd released his grip on the curtain just slightly while they'd been talking and quickly snatched it closed again. "Okay, you've had your little revenge."

"No, not really. It's not every day a girl gets rejected bedside. Her own bedside, for that matter."

Mac sighed. He was going to turn into a prune at this rate. "I explained about that."

"I know." She hooked her arms around her bent knee. "Go on. Don't let me bother you. After all, you won't let anything happen. And if this is the only way I can get your undivided attention, then . . ."

He'd show her his undivided attention. His grip tightened on the edge of the curtain. Did he deserve this little power play? Well, yeah. But if she thought ignoring the roar of chemistry between them was easy, she was sorely mistaken. For a whole second or two, he allowed himself the luxury of imagining her expression if he just reached out and yanked her into the shower with him. Fully clothed. Although that would be of limited concern, as he'd peel her wet clothes off, one delectable inch at a time.

He swallowed. Hard. And considered begging her to leave.

She rocked back and forth, smiling at him.

"You know," he warned. "You play with fire, you get burned."

"But that would mean you're hot. And you already proved you run cold where I'm concerned."

His gaze narrowed. "Are you testing me?"

She lifted a shoulder in a dismissive shrug. "Why would I do something like that?"

"Why, indeed."

"I just wanted the edge for once, that's all. I can't help it if you're in there naked, thinking whatever thoughts naked men think. I'm just sitting here, quite innocently, trying to determine the fate of my entire future. But sure, if you think I have ulterior motives—"

His hands were on her before he even realized his patience had snapped. And her eyes did widen in surprise when he bodily pulled her into the shower with him. She even squealed, much as he imagined she would. Only it was in delight . . . not protest.

"Naked men are so easy," she said, laughing as he yanked her up against him.

"Has that been your personal experience?" he said, more mad at himself for caving than at her for taunting him.

"I don't have that much experience."

He turned, pushed her up against the tiled wall with his body, and scraped his thumbs across the wet strands of hair that clung to her cheeks. "I find that really hard to believe."

Her eyelashes were wet and clumped together by the spray, which somehow managed to make her eyes sparkle all that much more brightly. Or maybe it was the impish edge to her smile that did it. "I said I don't have that much. But maybe what little I have is enough."

"Who are you?" he asked, his body raging to have her, his mind as muddled as ever.

The gleam faded a bit. "You know who I am."

"No," he said, studying her, trying to clearly see who she really was. "No, I don't. One minute you're all vulnerable and worried you'll lose your camp. The next you're all self-assured and seducing your way into my shower."

"Do I have to be all of one or the other? Can't I be both?"

He shook his head. "I've never claimed to understand women, though I have made an effort from time to time. But you . . ."

She reached up then, and undid what little defense he had left, flimsy though it already was, by tracing her fingertips over his face. His forehead, his cheeks, his lips. All the while staring steadily into his eyes. "I'm not supposed to be something you solve, Donovan, like some kind of puzzle. Or case file. Don't analyze me so much. Just go with your instincts."

"That's the problem," he said. "My instincts with you are all over the place."

She frowned a little, and her fingers paused in their journey of discovery. "What's so wrong about me?"

It wasn't the question that gave him pause. It was the immediate answer that came to his mind. *There's absolutely nothing wrong with you. That's the problem. You're perfect for me.* Or the fantasy of her was. Logic told him he didn't know her, that he was confusing the fantasy of his youth with the woman of his present. His heart told him he knew all he needed to know, only wanting to know more.

"There's nothing wrong with you. I just—"

"Don't want to get involved with a client? I'm not paying you. You're here by choice."

"You cloud my judgment already. Who's covering expenses is beside the point."

She smiled a little at that. "And ignoring this"—she nudged her hips against the rock-hard length of him—"is going to make things clearer?"

He groaned at the contact, and it took every scrap of will he had not to drill his hips into hers. He dropped his chin, swore under his breath. "I don't know what the hell to think anymore. You're driving me crazy."

She nudged his chin up until he met her gaze. "Good. I'd hate to be alone out here in crazy land."

He smiled a little at that. He couldn't help it. "You need me clear-headed and focused if you want my help in finding a way out of this."

"And here I was thinking I needed you naked, so maybe we could take the edge off all this . . . muddled thinking."

"So this"—he risked nudging himself between her thighs, catching his breath when she moaned a little, went a little more pliant against him—"is all about muddled thinking, is it?"

"Maybe only a little about muddled thinking," she managed on a short gasp as he pushed against her again. "Although I am feeling pretty muddled at the moment."

He nudged her head to one side, dropped his mouth to the spot below her ear. "Do you honestly think one time will clear things up?" He placed a hot, wet kiss on the side of her neck, then gently sunk his teeth into her earlobe, making her gasp, and his body jerk. "Or do you think it will only make me want you naked and underneath me as often as I can get you that way?"

"I—I don't know what to think." She sunk her fingers into his shoulders and tilted her head back on the tile, allowing him greater access to the sensitive underside of her chin. "I just don't think ignoring it is going to make it go away." She sighed when he began to drop kisses along the underside of her jaw.

"No, probably not. But it complicates things, Kate. I'm not good with . . . complications."

She was silent for a moment, then said, "Understood."

He paused and pressed his forehead against her cheek. His body was one big hard-on at the moment, but his heart . . . She'd always had a way of tangling that up without even trying. "Are you?"

"We have our own paths. Like I said before, we're adults. We're not kids anymore, with fantasy dreams and unrealistic expectations—" She paused, he waited. "I won't lie. I've always wanted you."

He lifted his head then, looked her directly in the eyes. "Kate—"

"But I'm not a kid. And I know what I'm asking for."

A lot of trouble, was all he could think. For them both.

"Maybe even that is more than I can give."

"Maybe. But I won't know that till I ask."

He'd denied her—and himself—once. He'd like to think he was strong enough to do the right thing every single time, no matter how difficult, no matter how challenging. But he already knew he was far from perfect. And he also knew he was about to be far from perfect with her.

"I've always wanted you, too," he told her, which made her eyes darken with need, her body soften in anticipation of him, and what was left of his resolve disintegrated. He wanted to see that look in her eyes again and again. He wanted to see it when he was inside of her, when he was making her climb the peak, when he was the one who pushed her over. He wanted to be the only one who saw that look, ever, and it was that fierce, ridiculous surge of possessiveness that almost gave him back the edge he so desperately needed.

"Then stop denying us both what we've always wanted. Not many people get the chance. I want mine. Don't you want yours?"

Put like that . . .

"Yeah," he said, his voice rough now, with need, with anticipation, and not a little apprehension. "Yeah, I want mine."

Chapter 14

She hadn't planned this. Not really. Yes, she'd come in with the intention of making him squirm just a little; he'd deserved that much. She'd wanted to let him know that she had her own mind in this. But maybe she'd been lying to herself. A tiny bit. Because, if she were being brutally honest, and now was the time for that really, then the rest was true, too. This was exactly where she wanted to be.

Maybe with a few less sodden clothes on, but still . . .

"Donovan—"

He paused in the string of devastatingly seductive kisses he was dropping along the line of her jaw and looked into her eyes.

"I mean Mac," she said, belatedly realizing the slip. God, leave it to her to screw up the second chance she didn't think she'd even have.

"No."

"But—"

He pressed a finger against her lips. "I mean it's okay."

"I shouldn't—"

He didn't move his finger away; in fact, he continued to press the pad of his finger against her lips as she spoke, then stopped her by pressing his fingertip inside her mouth. Her thighs trembled at the soft penetration. The contrast to the rock-hard length of him currently pressing between her thighs was a sweet paradox. He watched her eyes as he slid his finger along the surface of her tongue.

She watched him back as she closed her mouth around it, pulled it in, and sucked on it, reveling in the brief surprise, followed by the punch of desire she saw in eyes that were already almost swamped with it. It was heady, powerful stuff, knowing she moved him like this. She tried not to think about how ambivalent he'd been before about doing this with her. Logic and rational thought were not going to stop this from happening.

She sucked harder, then groaned deep in her throat when he slid another finger inside her mouth. She pushed up on her toes, allowing him to tuck himself farther between her legs, wanting nothing more than to make her soaking wet clothes magically disappear. He groaned now, too, and bucked against her.

She slipped his fingers free of her mouth and simultaneously pulled his head down to hers. She wanted something more immediate than his fingers inside of her. She kissed him hard, and he returned it with equal fervor. He tugged her hands from their grasp on his hair and pinned them on the tile wall beside her head, then slowly slid them upward, until her body bowed away from the wall, pressing the wet shirt covering her breasts up against the hard planes of his water-slicked chest.

He crossed her wrists, then slid his hands down her arms to the ragged neckband of her sweatshirt, and with excruciating slowness, he ripped it right down the middle, baring her to him one inch at a time. She thought she'd scream with need as he slowly peeled away the heavy wet cotton, wanting nothing more than to finally be free of the stupid thing so she could feel something equally wet but far warmer covering her skin.

His gaze flickered up to hers as he finished the last bit with a yank, then slowly, deliberately, dragged the shirt open, so it slid across nipples that were achingly tight and sensitive.

"My beautiful Kate. But then, I knew you would be."

"Nothing special," she managed, knowing it to be true. She'd been genetically blessed with silky blond hair, and a nice facial structure, she knew that, but her body was quite average. No matter what Donovan thought. Her waist was straight rather than narrow, and her shoulders a bit more broad than was strictly feminine. When you added breasts that had blossomed small and remained quite defiantly so, it all added up to—her thoughts scattered instantly as his warm lips closed around one of those aching tips.

She gasped and arched into him, the exquisite sensations spearing through her rendering her speechless as well as mindless.

"You taste pretty damn good, too."

She was focusing on trying to keep her knees locked and herself from sliding down the tile wall into a puddle at his feet as pleasure shot through her, from the tips of her breasts, like an arrow straight down between her thighs.

He left her sweatshirt hanging open, clinging to her sides, as he slowly began sliding his hands, and his body, downward. "I wonder where else you taste good."

"Oh, my God," she breathed, not at all certain she would survive that. But pretty damn sure she wanted to find out.

He slowly peeled down the heavy cotton sweats that molded to her thighs. He paused briefly when he got to the wisp of lace at her hipbone and glanced up. "Camp girl on the outside . . . all woman on the inside. I like that."

If he only knew. She'd dug through her drawer of undies, wanting to put something on that would make her feel sexy, bold, confident, even if she was the only one who knew. Okay, so maybe there'd been some latent fantasy that at some point he'd be overcome by lust, rip off her clothes, and see her in them. But she'd never actually expected it to happen. She'd certainly never expected this.

He hooked his fingers around the stretch of lace and tugged. Slowly. Excruciatingly slowly. She wanted to tip her head back, close her eyes, and just focus on feeling every sensation, every ripple of pleasure. But she couldn't take her eyes off him. She tried not to tremble so hard, but she couldn't seem to stop. The warm water sheeted across her naked torso, tapping her aching nipples, sliding across her skin, drenching his hair, dripping off his jaw as he continued baring her skin to his intently focused gaze.

Her thighs quivered in anticipation of his touch. Even with the clouds of steam hanging heavily in the air, she could feel his warm breath brush against her oh-so-sensitive skin. She wanted to sink her fingers into his hair, urge him closer, urge him to please put an end to the torturous wait. But he continued pushing her clothes and panties down her thighs, over her calves, slipping his palms up one leg to help dislodge her foot from the wet pile, one then the other.

And then she was naked to him, except for the torn sweatshirt. He slid his hands slowly back up the front of her shins, then around the backs of her knees, and slowly up the back of her thighs, nudging them apart, just slightly.

She sighed as, once again, his breath fanned across her inner thighs. And thought she'd scream if he didn't stop there and finally—"Oh!" Something that resembled part whimper, part moan, slipped from her mouth as he slowly drew his tongue along her most sensitive flesh.

She realized her arms were still crossed above her head when she lowered them, looking for something to brace herself on, trying to stand despite the exquisite bliss literally shuddering through her as he continued his dedicated mission. She slapped her palms to the tile and arched her back as he slid his fingers around the backs of her thighs . . . and upward, until he was inside of her. His tongue never stopping its delicious assault, until she was forced to bend over, brace her weight by gripping his shoulder with one hand, the back of his head with the other, as long moans, one after the other, poured out of her while she spiraled up and up . . . and finally over the peak.

She was shaking so hard, she wasn't sure how she remained upright as wave after wave continued to rock through her. He slid up her body, bracing her between himself and the wall, as he trailed his lips up over her torso, peeling the sweatshirt down her arms and off before pushing her hands up again, and linking his fingers through hers as he pressed them to the tile beside her head.

"That was . . ." She had no voice. The words were barely formed. Her thoughts weren't much more gelled than that either. She was still trying to come back to her senses. "I should be . . . you need . . ."

"Shh," he told her, then pulled her arms down around his neck and tipped her chin up, and kissed her.

She was pliant in his arms, thankful for his strength, his guidance, his support of her, as she was nothing but a languid pool of bliss at the moment. Any moment now she'd regroup, she'd be a more active partner, giving as well as taking . . . but at the moment, his kisses were almost as drugging as his tongue had been, and she was swimming again, floating away on waves of pleasure. Later . . . later she'd return the favor. He didn't seem all that insistent at the moment anyway. And this felt too damn good. Nothing had ever felt this good.

He was both gentle and urgent, making her feel both cosseted and desired at the same time. He tucked his hips against hers, still kissing her deeply, twining his tongue along hers as he slid his hands down and pulled her thighs up over his hips, pinning her to the wall. "Kate . . . ," he murmured against her lips. "I don't want to stop, but—"

"Then don't." She buried her fingers in his wet curls and tugged his mouth back to hers. "Not this time. You can't. You wouldn't."

"Protection," he said, his body tensing as she hooked her heels behind his thighs.

"I'm safe," she said. "It's okay."

He lifted his head, looked her in the eyes. "Are you sure?"

"Very."

His eyes were so very dark, she'd never seen him this intense, which was saying something. And it was all in want of her. A heady rush raced through her all over again.

"Kate—"

"I'm protected. And I'm safe. And I want you . . . deep inside me. Right now." She couldn't believe she was saying this to him. She wasn't one for such direct talk, but somehow with him, it was not only expected, it felt necessary. She wanted—no, needed—him to know she was a true partner for him. In every way. And this was only the beginning of how she wanted to show him.

That feeling, that need, was as thrilling as it was intimidating. But now was certainly not the time to worry about that. Right now, all she wanted to feel was—"Oh . . . oh . . ." And the rest was one long groan of intense satisfaction as he slid slowly, fully, and completely inside of her.

"Hold on to me," he commanded, the words more growl than anything.

She didn't hesitate to comply with this demand. She dug her fingers into his shoulders and locked her ankles more tightly behind him as he eased back from the wall, leaving her leaning back so he could angle her hips upward . . . and thrust. His broad palms covered her hips, guiding her down onto him. She arched, moaned, and when he began to move faster, she might have even screamed. She'd never been all that vocal during sex. With Donovan, she couldn't imagine being quiet.

This wasn't quiet, polite mating. This was basic, earthy, raw . . . primal.

She clung to him, both of them grunting as his thrusts grew deeper, faster. She wanted to slow things down, so she could remember every second, revel in every feeling, every sensation, but she couldn't even keep her eyes open to watch him. He was driving her up again, and she could only give herself over to it, to the powerful emotions bulleting through her.

This is just sex. Somewhere in the back of her mind, she reminded herself of that. Or tried to.

What she felt was an irrevocable bond being forged, a union like no other. Ridiculous. A feeling she'd be thankful she never shared with him, as she was certain when it was all over, she'd laugh at herself and her silly emotional reaction to what was just extraordinary sex.

And it was Donovan. Her fantasy finally come to life. So surely she was just tangling fantasy with the moment.

Though, God, it was one hell of a moment.

And then whatever thoughts she had scattered completely as he slowed, and she could feel his body coil, tense, pull back, all in preparation for what she knew was coming. It was enough to send her over, water pouring over her sweat-slickened torso, as she gasped for air and gave back equally with every thrust he made.

He was all but growling when he came, his fingers digging into her hips in a way that she knew would leave marks, marks she felt ridiculously proud to bear, as she felt like a marked woman now anyway. She gave herself over to him, reveled in his shuddering release, tightening around him to give themselves both every last breath of pleasure.

He was shaking as he slid from her body and let her legs drop from around his waist. He rolled them both so his back was against the tile, and he held her tightly against him as they both fought for breath. Her knees were woozy, her muscles pliant on the verge of uselessness.

It was long moments before she realized the shower had, at some point, grown cool. It actually felt good on her overheated skin, but she blindly reached down and pushed the lever off. Donovan made no move to leave, or to let her go. And she made no move either. The steam slowly dissipated as their heartbeats eased to a somewhat steadier rhythm. It was the only thing steady about her at the moment.

It felt good, she decided, being in his arms. Held so tightly, both cuddled and coddled. It wasn't like her to accept that from anyone, most especially in a moment like this. She'd fought so long and hard for independence, it had carried over to all aspects of her personal life, including intimacy. So why she so willingly accepted his protection, his surprising tenderness, she had no idea. She chalked it up to the moment . . . and to the past. To the fantasy. Because a lot of what had just happened couldn't be reality.

Her reality was simply never that good.

She must have withdrawn then, in some way, because he tightened his hold slightly, then slid his hand up to tip her chin up.

"Hey."

She smiled a little at that. Men. Such conversationalists. But it was the look in his eyes, a little stunned, but a lot tender, that kept her from teasing him. She felt much the same way and wondered if he saw that in her eyes. "Hey, yourself."

"That was . . ." He let the words trail off, but held her gaze, his own intensifying in ways that had her heart rate kicking up again.

"Yeah," she said softly. "It was."

He gathered her closer, settling her between his legs, so she was pressed against the full length of him, chest to chest, hip to hip. The soft places on her easing against all the hard planes of him. It felt remarkably fantastic . . . and far too perfect. She never wanted to leave . . . and she had to force herself to relax. She knew what was coming. He'd warned her this was what it was, nothing more. No matter how stunned and replete he looked.

He rested his chin on her head, and she took the easy way out, nuzzling his chest, keeping their gazes disconnected a little while longer. She didn't want to risk him seeing anything in her gaze, especially when she hadn't sorted it all out herself just yet.

When the silence spun out, and reality began to creep in,

he pressed a kiss to her hair and said, "So . . . about that lunch."

Thankful for the easy out, she nudged him in his ribs. "Men. Hungry or horny."

"At least we're easy to maintain."

"I don't know about that. I'm quite sure there are going to be parts of me that will be a little more vocal tomorrow when I get up." She shifted in his arms, felt the slight strain in her calves, and laughed lightly. "Or maybe sooner."

"I'll make you a deal," he said, pulling back the curtain and grabbing towels.

She was wrapped in one before she knew quite how she'd ended up on her bath mat, and he tied the other around his waist. "What would that be?" She snagged a smaller towel and began squeezing the water out of her hair. And carefully avoided any and all glances into the clearing glass of the mirror. She felt happily drowsy and satiated at the moment, thankful the mood between them was comfortable and easy. There was no guarantee that would last through the next ten minutes, much less the evening, or longer. She'd like to make the fantasy bubble she was in last as long as possible. Seeing what her hair and face looked like at the moment was almost a sure-fire way to abruptly burst it.

He whipped the towel out of her hands and nudged her around so her back was to him. He began kneading and squeezing the water out of her hair for her. She felt both pampered and sort of stupidly jealous. He was far too comfortable in this role, and she couldn't help but do the insecure woman thing and wonder who else he'd performed that intimate little task for.

Then he leaned down and kissed the spot where her neck curved into her shoulder, and suddenly she didn't give a rat's behind who else might have played the past role of Kate. At the moment, she was. And, for now, that was all that really mattered.

She sighed and leaned back into him, knowing her walls had crumbled so swiftly that there was sure to be a big, ugly reckoning coming her way later. She found she really couldn't make herself care much about that eventuality either. What was done was done. And pretty damn well if you asked her. No point in wasting the good parts.

"You finish putting together the soup and sandwiches," he said, lifting her hair and kissing her nape, sending a delicious tingling sensation skittering over her skin. "And I'll see what I can do to relax those mystery muscles later."

If only it were that simple. Playing house in the middle of the woods.

Her shoulders slumped a tiny bit as she tried hard to fight off the inevitable reality check. Would it kill anyone if the good parts lasted just a little bit longer? "Pretty tough to say no to that plan," she said, only to be turned around, her chin tipped up again as he peered into her eyes. Clearly she wasn't pulling off insouciance as well as she thought she was.

"Lunch, some talk, a little planning and strategizing session. Then a little fun." He kissed the tip of her nose. "Balance."

For some unknown reason, it was that last little kiss, so natural and so damn sweet, that undid her. Tears welled in her eyes, horrifying her, but there didn't seem to be any stopping them.

"I don't want to lose my camp." *And I don't want to lose you*. Which was where the tears had really sprung from. But he didn't have to know that. Could never know that. Not after she'd been the one to all but force him to take their relationship to a place he hadn't wanted it to go. For this very reason.

"So then we make sure you don't." He handed the towel back to her. "Hey, come on, now. Where's the woman who doesn't take crap and storms showers? Come on, let's get dressed and do something about it."

She took the towel and watched him as he picked up his

duffel bag and rooted through it for fresh jeans and a sweat-shirt. She dabbed at her eyes, wondering when she'd become such a blubbering idiot. Well, idiot in general.

That was easy. The moment she'd stopped taking care of herself and let herself lean on somebody. Maybe he'd had the right idea all along. Letting themselves want each other, giving in to that want, led to allowing themselves to depend on each other. To needing things that they shouldn't be needing . . . and wanting things they couldn't have.

She turned abruptly away and scrubbed her face, catching her reflection in the mirror as she did so. She was surprised to see that rather than look splotchy and defenseless, she looked quite . . . empowered and satisfied. God, she was so confused. With a roll of the eyes, she left the bathroom and escaped to the hopeful haven of her bedroom. She'd wring out her sopping wet clothes later. Right now, she needed a little privacy, a chance to regroup, to figure out what she wanted—no, what she *needed* to do next. She knew what she wanted.

She leaned back against her closed bedroom door and let out a long, satisfied sigh now that Donovan couldn't see her. *Yeah, what you want is a lot more of what you just got in the shower.* She squeezed her eyes shut. It only made the images in her mind stronger. The sensations, how full she'd felt when he'd been thrusting inside of her . . . made her thighs clench together as her aching muscles twitched right back to life.

She opened her eyes, and her gaze landed directly on her bed. How realistic was it to think they wouldn't end up there? Perhaps only a few short hours from now. She crossed her arms over her chest as her body responded quite happily to that little idea. So much for regrouping.

She jumped when a knock came at the door at her back.

"Your watch Bagel is looking rather pitiful. I'm going to run him outside. Spend a little guy time with him. I think he's jealous."

Yep. She was a goner. How was she supposed to shore up

her defenses, resume her steely-eyed distance from a guy who'd just taken her to heaven and back, then offered to bond with her dog?

"Okay," she said, knowing she sounded nothing like the no-nonsense woman she really needed to be if she had any hope in hell of surviving the next few weeks with him, and keep her heart intact. She should have never gone into the bathroom, should have never taunted him. She looked again at her bed.

"Stop overthinking this," came his voice through the closed door. "What's done is done. And pretty damn well if you ask me. We'll handle it, Kate."

Was he reading her mind now? She turned and rested her forehead on the door for a long moment, then went ahead and opened it. Just in time to see him close the front door behind himself and a very ecstatic Bagel. She didn't know her dog could do a full body wag quite like that.

"I know exactly how you feel," she murmured, then went back into her room and got dressed.

Chapter 15

"That smells heavenly," Mac said as he and Bagel came back into the cabin, all damp and chilled. "Food smells good, too."

And Kate looked way too damn good puttering around the kitchen. He'd been in lust before, had even come close to falling a few times in his life, but he'd never once had the urge to play house with anyone. Bedroom, yes. Shower, definitely. A hallway now and again. But, in the end, the need to get back to his own personal space always beckoned far more strongly than the desire to share space under one roof with someone.

Right now his space was a nice little bungalow tucked away in a shady corner of Dalton Downs, Finn's property in Virginia. That was home now, to Finn, Rafe, and himself, as well as Trinity. He loved his space there. It was quiet, redemptive, a perfect place to recharge between adventures. Which was pretty much how he thought of his new career. The occasional bomb explosion notwithstanding.

Kate wasn't even doing anything particularly impressive or adorable at the moment. She was heating up some soup and making coffee. Dressed in faded jeans now, along with a light green T-shirt and an oversized sweater that refused to stay on both shoulders at the same time. Her hair was pulled up, no makeup on her face, her cheeks a little flushed from the steam rising from the soup. Or perhaps a leftover from their time spent in the shower together . . .

The mere thought of which brought his body leaping to life as though it hadn't just gotten more satisfaction than it had in a very long time. He immediately bent down to use the rag towel he'd grabbed on the way in to towel off Bagel, before she looked up and caught him staring at her all moony-eyed or something. Because that was exactly how he felt.

It was just the shower talking. Or, more specifically, what they'd done in the shower. He'd get over it.

Right, his little voice said, *just as soon as you have her like, maybe, a hundred or so more times.*

If then.

She bent over then and pulled a baking pan out from inside the stove. "I made some corn bread muffins to go with the soup. I didn't have enough stuff to make decent sandwiches, sorry." She straightened and caught him staring anyway. She blew an errant strand of hair off her face and smiled at him. "They're box mix, so don't get too excited."

If only she had a clue how easily she excited him, she'd bolt herself in her bedroom and never come back out.

He finished up rubbing the dog dry, maybe spending a bit too long on the task, much to Bagel's delight. "It smells great. I appreciate it."

She ladled out the soup and popped the muffins into a basket and moved everything to the small kitchen table. The coffeepot was already there, sitting on a hot plate, with two mugs and a sugar bowl next to it.

"Cream?" she asked.

"Straight," he said, pulling out a chair. So, it was both comfortable between them and incredibly awkward. And he wasn't sure exactly why, except maybe now that they'd had a few minutes apart, time to think, cool off, sort things through a little, they weren't sure where things stood between them, or where they wanted them to stand. At least he wasn't, anyway. They both dug into the food, neither speaking for several centuries-long moments. "It looks like the rain is finally letting up, but it's still too wet to do any more installation today. I'm going to get a head start in the morning on finishing the system install. Then I figure we'll head into Ralston again and have a sit-down with Gilby about the vandalism, see what we can ferret out of him."

Kate sipped from her spoon, swallowed. "Exactly what is this system you're installing? I mean, I understand the whole command center, monitoring thing, but what exactly does it do?"

"Your property is too difficult a landscape to secure the boundary of in terms of a quick fix; the terrain and topography are too vast and varied, especially on the far side of the lake, which has been an entry point."

"So I can't keep them off my property?"

"Unless you electric fence it or patrol it, if they want to get in, they'll get in. A determined soul could find a way. But I can get coverage on the cabins, main buildings, your cabin, the service and barn areas, and the docks. Your main assets, essentially."

"So to keep tabs on it, I watch the monitor? How can I do that and run the camp? I can't afford to hire security personnel yet, but—"

"Right now, you're not running the camp, and it's now that you need to do this. If you want to have a camp."

She lowered her spoon. "Do you think the jerks who are spray painting stuff are actually dangerous?"

He lifted a shoulder. "I know it seems a rather innocuous form of intimidation, and I'm inclined to agree with that, except—"

"Except what?"

"Except we're still not sure who is behind it. And that determines what they're capable of."

Kate sighed. "Well, anyone who knows me would know that this wouldn't deter me from staying here."

"Does Shelby really know you?"

"I don't know that he'd go this route, but then maybe I don't know him, either."

Mac paused, thought about that. "You said you hashed out this contract agreement over months, so I'd assume he would have a pretty clear indication of how badly you want this place."

Kate nodded. "Yes, I believe he does. So . . . are you saying now that it follows that he wouldn't take this kind of tack to get me to walk away from our agreement? That he'd know better?"

"Could be."

She gave him a quelling look.

"What?" he asked, lifting his hands. "I've learned not to assume, to keep all paths open."

"What happened to all that gut instinct talk?"

He grinned, he couldn't help it. "Well, my instincts told me not to get too tangled up with you, and you can see where that landed me." He watched the color steal into her cheeks, but she didn't look away. "So, you're saying you only listen to them when they suit your purposes?"

"Or until someone ambushes me in the shower."

"I didn't ambush—"

Now it was his turn to give her the quelling look. The blush that flushed her skin was even more becoming this time around.

"Okay, so maybe I did. Just a little. But it wasn't my plan for us to end up . . . the way we ended up."

"But . . ."

She didn't bother pretending. Her grin was as bold as his was. "Okay, but I'm glad it did." She folded her arms on the table in front of her. "So, now what do we do?"

His eyebrows lifted a fraction. "Regarding which event?"

She laughed.

And his heart teetered dangerously inside his chest. At least that was what he attributed that sudden wobbly sensation to. "You're going to get us both in trouble, you know that."

"I thought I already had. You're the protect-and-defender, you're supposed to keep us on the straight and narrow, focused on the mission at hand." She lifted her shoulders and batted her eyelashes at him. "I'm just the helpless female in this scenario, remember?"

He snorted. "There is nothing remotely helpless about you."

"Thank you," she said. Then, in a more serious tone added, "Most of the time, I'm pretty fearless about going after what I want."

"I'll vouch for that," he said dryly, hoping to bring back that cocky smile.

Her lips curved ever-so-slightly. "But I'll admit that while I wasn't exactly ready to run up the white flag or call in reinforcements, the situation here was starting to rattle me a little." She held his gaze steadily. "I should have been more thankful for your timely intervention."

"You'd have done something about it, taken action, whether I'd shown up or not."

"Probably," she agreed. "But I don't think I'd have put it all together as quickly. And that might prove to be the difference in keeping this place." She was such a paradox. Here she was, admitting she needed him, that she was grateful for his help, the same woman who'd just about undone him in the shower . . . and yet there was still a wariness about her that had him wondering what it was going to take to win her over completely.

Which was insanity. Because winning her over was not the objective here. Solving her problem was the only goal that needed achieving, and when that was accomplished, he'd go home. And she'd stay here. So there was no point in winning anything. He'd tried to tell her that last night. He'd been trying to tell himself that since the moment he'd stepped onto her porch that first night.

And yet, he couldn't manage to find any regret for what had just happened between them. Sure, it wasn't going to end well. Shit happened in life, and some of it was no fun. But being with her was giving him something he'd never had or felt before. Sometimes when shit happened, it was good.

And sometimes, the good was so good, it was worth the bad that was sure to follow.

Mac finished his bowl and wiped his mouth with a napkin before crumpling it up and tossing it on the table. "So, here's the plan, then."

Kate pushed aside her half-eaten soup. "We have a plan?"

"The start of one. I'll finish up installation tomorrow, so we can start to keep tabs on our uninvited guest or guests. I know several points of entry now, so I'll keep an eye on those, specifically. When we get something—"

"When?"

He merely nodded. She smiled. "*When* we get something, we'll take it to Gilby, push him into taking action. We'll see what additional insight that might give us into the town mentality where you and your camp are concerned."

"But—"

He raised his hand. "Hold on. The other thing we have to do is narrow down the list of possibles."

"Possibles?"

"Possibly Shelby is involved, possibly Timberline is involved, possibly certain citizens of Ralston are involved. Other than Finn's report on Timberline's interest in the area, we can't prove anything about anyone through normal channels."

"So what do we do? Where do we start?"

"I start with trying to nab a vandal, and you start by tracking down your stepbrother."

"And say what? 'By the way, you don't happen to be in discussions with a resort developer to sell my camp out from under me, do you? And would you perhaps be responsible for turning an entire town against me? Oh, and about that vandalizing . . .' Whatever his involvement, if any, I doubt he's just going to come out and tell me, or he'd have confronted me directly about it already."

"So you question him about pulling a no-show, which he should be expecting anyway, and dig from there. He doesn't have to know what you are digging for. Steer the conversation however you have to, but you'll have the upper hand at least in this initial conversation, because he doesn't know you suspect what might be going on here."

"And he doesn't know about you."

Mac nodded. "As far as we know, anyway. And, if he is involved, that news will make it to him sooner rather than later."

"I'm not sure what I'll get from this, but regardless, we need to talk about the appointment and what he wants to do about rescheduling the contract signing."

"Bingo. That right there is a perfect example of what I mean by digging. Any reticence on his part to reschedule? You attack. You have a perfectly legitimate reason to do so without raising undue speculation that you're on to him in any way."

"Assuming there's anything to be on to in the first place."

"I still don't believe in coincidences."

She shot him a considering look. "No? What do you call finding that article about me, then?"

"Serendipity," he said instantly, then grinned. "Or karma."

"Karma, the bitch? Or karma—?"

"Just karma," he said, enjoying that combination of wary amusement he saw on her face. He liked that she fought her attraction to him, or at least questioned it. It meant she was taking this seriously. He didn't examine why that part was so important to him. "The rest will sort itself out," he went on. "Always does."

She looked as if she were going to say something to that, but instead, chose to stay focused on the matter at hand. "Of course, this whole plan hinges on the idea that I'm actually going to be able to track Shelby down."

"If you can't, then that's information to be considered, too. If he just doesn't show, and doesn't call to explain why, and then can't be found, that's telling. That isn't typical behavior, and the workday is half over already today and no contact has been made, no apology delivered."

Kate nodded. "True."

"And if you do track him down, any information you can glean from him, even if it's just gauging his mood, his tone, whether you think he's lying to you—or not—with anything he says regarding his sudden change of plans, any of those things can help steer us toward the right path."

She leaned back in her chair. "Okay." She paused, sighed, then seemed to pull herself up a little. "Okay," she repeated, with a bit more confidence and a little less weary resignation. "Do you want me to call him now?" She looked at the clock on the wall. "It's possible he's in his office—"

"Not yet."

"But, you're right, he's probably expecting me to try and contact him today after what happened."

"Don't do the expected. Not yet, anyway."

"The fact that I've waited this long is already not like me. So when do you want me to call? I'm confused."

"Which is the exact state we want him to be in. Doing the unexpected jars the framework. It did yours, right? When you don't behave as predicted, it forces the other players to adjust their planning. It ups the chances that something or someone might slip up, at least enough to give us another piece of the puzzle. Your reaction to his jarring the framework is the one thing you can control in this situation right now, so use what little leverage you have to your best advantage."

She nodded again, but her gaze was more intent on him, her thoughts seemingly not as inward now.

"What?" he asked, when she continued to regard him in silence.

"Nothing. I just . . ." She trailed off, lifted a shoulder.

"You're so focused in all this, clearly in your comfort zone, very confident and methodical. On the one hand, it reassures me, makes me feel like I can trust you."

"You can," he said automatically. "Always."

She nodded right away, and it was almost ridiculous how good that made him feel. "I know that, in ways that aren't necessarily rational or even proven." She held his gaze. "But I do know that."

"Good," he said, trying like hell to keep it business. Which was hard to do when his heart was celebrating what felt like an important milestone in their relationship. A relationship that didn't exist, because it had nowhere to go, he reminded himself.

"On the other hand," she went on, "it scares me. You so clearly see this as a bigger-than-life drama, and there is a part of me still resisting that, even though I know, or think, anyway, that you're probably right."

"That's perfectly normal. No one wants to believe that the things most dear to them are truly being threatened. What matters is that you're doing something about it anyway." He leaned his elbows on the table, would have reached for her if he could. "One way or the other, it's all going to get resolved now. The truth will out itself eventually."

"And then?" She sank down a little in her seat. It was the first time he'd seen her look truly vulnerable. "What if the truth is I'm going to lose this place no matter what I do?"

He wished he could outright guarantee her that wouldn't happen. That he'd win every battle, slay every foe for her. But he couldn't do that. She trusted him, and that meant telling her the truth, even when it was a truth she didn't want to hear. "Then we'll deal with that reality when or if it happens."

She held his gaze for a long moment, then nodded. "Thank you."

"For?"

"Being straight with me."

"Always," he said, again, automatically. Only this time the response didn't sit as well with him. He was absolutely being straight with her where her camp's future was concerned. And he'd tried to be up front with her on a personal level as well. He'd admitted he might not be able to keep their personal interaction from affecting him on a more serious level. He was only now really beginning to realize just how deeply it already had. Even before their little shower interlude. But telling her that would be confessing it to himself. And he wasn't ready to deal with the repercussions on either front.

"So, when do I call?" she said, mercifully pulling his thoughts back to business.

"Ideally, I'd like you to track him down when he's not in a business environment, not on his own turf, so to speak. Do you know his socializing habits well enough to know when he'd most likely be out to dinner, or with friends?"

"What makes you think he'd talk to me in that situation? It's doubtful he'd be able to talk freely."

"Exactly. Which gives you a chance to do most of the talking."

"You've lost me."

"He'll be thrown a little, being as he's not in a situation where he can talk freely. If he can think on his feet, he'll likely cover himself well, but on the chance that he can't, you keep pressing. It's possible he'll slip."

"And if he doesn't?"

"You inform him that he'll agree to meet when and where you say, or you'll park yourself in Louisa's offices—the very offices he wants legal control over—until he agrees to see you and discuss the situation with the contract."

"Sounds . . . convoluted. Why don't I just ask him outright?"

"It's kind of like a dance. If he's not involved, he'll just come right out and tell you whatever you want to know anyway. Case closed, you go sign papers, and we move on from there. But if he is involved, you have to play things just right if you want to maintain any leverage at all."

"I technically own Louisa's entire empire. That's not leverage enough?"

"Not if he wants that and your camp, too."

Her face lost a little color.

"Both of those things are imperative. One, that he's risking losing everything, all over this property, is rather telling. And you could set up camp anywhere, but you just made a deal to give him a fortune for this specific property. He's banking on that, too."

She blew out a long sigh, then pushed wayward strands of drying hair out of her face. "I'm really hating this. I'm not cut out for espionage. I just want my damn camp. My God, he can have freaking everything else." She looked over at him. "Why does this have to be so damn complicated?"

"Money. Best complicator in the world."

She nodded, looking more defeated than he'd like to see her. "He doesn't even want this place."

"I'm betting he might if Timberline wants to develop it into some top-notch resort. It's possible he'll want to retain ownership, much as Louisa did while it suited her. At the moment, it's not worth a whole lot, other than to the developer, but not enough to screw the deal he has with you, just to sell it off. But after it's developed? It's worth a whole lot more zeros then. It would be worth multiple millions, millions that would keep coming in if the place is managed properly."

"You think he wants to be, what, a partner? But partnerships take money."

"He owns the property."

She shook her head. "I just don't see it. Not the money part, that screams Shelby. But the maintaining ownership part. He and my mother both willingly let this place go to seed in order to focus on other business ventures. I'm frankly surprised they didn't sell it off a long time ago."

"They might have tried, you don't know. Probably let it go too far to hell to get any interest. Out here, who's going to want this place?" He smiled. "Besides a child psychologist looking to build a camp for kids, I mean?"

That did elicit a small smile from her. "I guess it would take something on the scale of a huge resort to make it worthwhile."

"And lo and behold, just when he thought he was dumping a white elephant to keep an empire, someone comes along wanting to turn his elephant into an empire in and of itself."

"And you think that was just coincidence?"

Mac gave her a dry look. "We can't prove who contacted who first, but what do you think?"

"Why would Shelby hunt for a developer now?"

"Remember what you said? About him being pissed off at having to give any of Louisa's holdings away? He thinks he's entitled to all of it. All. So maybe he's trying to find a way to keep it all and nudge you out."

Kate buried her head in her hands and dug her fingers into her hair. "I don't know, Donovan. It all sounds pretty far-fetched. Even for Shelby." Mac stilled momentarily, again affected by the way she said his name. All soft and vulnerable like that . . . made his body stir. And something inside his chest as well.

Just as he was thinking how badly he wanted to drag her across the table and into his lap, she straightened and pasted a brave smile on her face. "I guess we'll find out more when I talk to him later on. So . . . what do we do in the meantime?"

Mac's body leapt fully to life, and he knew he should probably fight the urge, but he was already grinning and pushing his chair back. "Now we put business aside for a few minutes."

A smile ghosted her lips, and a spark returned to her eyes. "I thought we just did that."

He circled the table and came to stand behind her.

She didn't tense or shift away when he put his hands on

her shoulders and bent low so his mouth was next to her ear. "Is there a rule that says we can't take another break?"

"Break? Is that what we're calling it?"

"I believe I bartered lunch in trade for help with a few tight muscles. Besides, it's too wet outside, so I can't put the gear up. Shelby needs to percolate for a few more hours." He glanced over at Bagel. "And the dog clearly needs his beauty sleep."

Kate glanced over at Bagel's prone body, ears akimbo and belly exposed to the world, as he snored softly. "If only life were so simple for all of us."

Mac pulled her up from her chair and turned her around to face him, trapping her between the table and his body. "It can be. For whole hours at a time, even."

She wiggled her eyebrows teasingly. "Whole hours, huh? Pretty cocky."

"What, you don't think I can back it up?" He braced his hands on the table on either side of her, pushing her back. "Don't think you can keep up?"

She giggled, and his heart sang, hearing that sound come from her again. In that moment he hated that life really wasn't simple, then shut the thought out completely. Here and now. That was what life was truly composed of. The here and now. And right here, right now, he had Kate in his arms again. He pushed dishes and mugs out of the way and kept pressing her back onto the table.

Besides, simple was for sissies.

Chapter 16

Kate knew the instant her back hit the table and his chest pressed against hers that she was never going to get tired of feeling his weight on top of her. She'd thought having him drive her literally up the wall in the shower had been pretty damn intense, but there was something even more primal in feeling him on top of her.

A spoon clattered to the floor as she gripped the front of his shirt and pulled him closer, praying the table wouldn't splinter beneath them.

His grin widened, and the spark that flared to life in his eyes almost undid her right then. "I like it when you get demanding."

"Do you?" she queried, pulling him close enough to nip his chin. The growl of approval sent little shock waves all through her body. He triggered responses in her she didn't even know she was capable of feeling. It was crazy how badly she wanted him again. She felt like she was in heat.

"You know," she said, nipping her way along his jaw, "I do have a perfectly good, very soft mattress, just in the other room."

He pushed against her, sending the napkins flying. "We'll get there." Leaving her prone, he raised up and tugged at the waistband of her sweats, pulling them down and off as he crouched between her legs, sliding her thighs over his shoulders. "Eventually."

If this was his idea of tight-muscle relaxation, she'd be willing to barter a hell of a lot more than regular meals. Too busy gasping at the sudden invasion of his warm breath and soft tongue between her legs to form a single, coherent thought, she instinctively grabbed at the edges of the table. Arching into him, heedless now of where the dishes and silverware ended up, she was unable to keep the gradually louder whimpers from slipping out. Whimpers turned to moans, loud moans, as he continued his devastating assault on her most sensitive spot. Bagel was barking somewhere in the background, but the house could have been burning down and she doubted she'd have been able to stop Donovan. She didn't want to stop him, stop this stunning intoxication of her senses, until every last delicious tremor shuddered through her.

Her hips thrashed wildly when she came, and she was pretty sure that rafter-rattling scream that accompanied it actually came from somewhere inside of her.

Blinded by her need for him and unable to focus on anything except the overwhelming need to have him buried deep inside of her as soon as humanly possible, to continue the assault on her deliciously sensitive nerve endings in the most intimate manner possible, she grabbed at his hair, his shoulders, tugging him back up.

She groaned with absolute satisfaction when he settled his weight on top of her, between her legs, where she so badly wanted him to stay. Forever. Somewhere in the process he'd shucked his clothes because all she felt was his deliciously warm skin brushing against hers as he pulled her legs around his hips and pinned her down to the table.

"Pure madness," he breathed into her ear as he buried his face against the side of her neck and sunk deeply into her with one thrust.

"Yes," she agreed, arching to meet him, to take him, seeking more when she didn't think more was possible.

He drove himself into her, no gentleness in him now. She scored his back with her nails as she grabbed for any purchase she could find, finally grabbing at the hair that lay against his neck, tightening her thighs against his increasingly deeper thrusts, taking every one of them with growling acceptance, wanting more with every bit he gave her.

"Kate," he panted, moving faster, and faster, turning her face to his and laying claim to her mouth as deeply and intimately as he was her body.

She took him there, too. Wanting to take him into every part of her with a desperation that made her almost frantic. Somewhere in the recesses of what was left of her mind, she knew it was a form of desperation, this need to take every last bit of him now, while she could, before the inevitable happened and she lost him.

Then there was that other part, buried even deeper inside her, but becoming incessantly harder to ignore. That part that said if he needed her badly enough, wanted more of her as desperately as she did of him, then maybe, just maybe, he'd find a way to give them both what they wanted. Now . . . and forever.

Madness, indeed.

His body coiled above hers and tore his mouth from hers. "Kate," he demanded hoarsely.

Her eyes flew open to find the dark, stormy depths of his own pinning her down as tightly and fully as his body was pinning hers.

"Donovan," she choked out.

And he came right then, his gaze locked to hers even as his body thundered into hers, shuddering mightily as he poured himself into her in ways more than simply physical. She was drowning, but not simply in his body. That gaze, that look . . .

Was she seeing what she wanted to see? Or . . .

"Come here," he said roughly, and pulled her up against

him, sliding his arms beneath her as he slid out of her. "Come on."

"Wait—"

But he didn't. Wincing as his knees protested, he pulled her up with him as he stood, ignoring her protests as he scooped her up against his chest. "Just let me," he told her, kicking a chair over accidentally as he staggered the two of them toward her bedroom. He banged the door shut behind them, blocking out Bagel's mournful howl. She'd make it up to the dog later. She had a lifetime with her dog. She had no idea how many more precious minutes of this she'd have with Donovan. Shamelessly, greedily, she wanted them all.

His legs gave out as they fell to the bed. He rolled to his side, dragging her with him. "Shower again later," he promised, tucking her against his side.

She rolled her body along the length of his, her legs tangling easily with his, her head coming to rest atop the beat of his heart as if she'd slept that way many a time. And despite the exhilaration of what she'd just experienced with him, the anxiety over where this would lead them, compounding the fears about what else lay in store for her in the next days or weeks . . . the sweet drowsiness of such complete satiation threatened to claim her swiftly. She felt him press a kiss on the top of her head and pressed one against his heart. His arm tightened around her, and she smiled . . . and let sleep take her.

The dream was odd. She remembered thinking when he was deep inside of her that the house could be burning down around them and it wouldn't have mattered. Figures she'd dream about the burning building and not the lovemaking. She was more stressed out than she thought. Snuggling closer, making a soft noise of pleasure when Donovan automatically tightened his hold on her and nestled her closer, even in his sleep, she pushed her sleep-muzzy brain to other, more pleasurable dreams. But the burning building just wouldn't leave her mind, so real it made her nose twitch in reaction to the acrid smoke and—

Just then Donovan came fully awake and was pushing her gently but firmly aside as he leapt from the bed.

She pushed her hair from her face and levered up on one arm, nose still twitching. Then her eyes widened, and she scrambled out of the bed behind him and stumbled to the window where he stood. "Oh, my God!"

Thick black smoke roiled into the air, but there were no flames shooting from the cabin situated just down the hill below hers.

"What the hell is going on?" Kate demanded, the adrenaline punch kicking the last vestiges of sleep from her muzzy brain, but making her almost nauseous at the sudden shift.

Mac reached for the nightstand where he'd set his phone. "Obviously, whoever was here earlier was paying closer attention than we thought. I'd swear it was amateur hour out there, but now I'm not so sure. Maybe they saw what I was doing up that tree and decided to strike before the surveillance went into effect."

"Is the rest of the equipment—"

"Going up in flames? Yes."

Kate's eyes widened as the full impact of the situation hit her, and as Donovan turned to punch numbers into his phone, she ran to open her bedroom door and all but tripped over a very grateful, clearly shaken Bagel. "Sorry, little man," she said, stepping over him as she went for her purse and the phone buried somewhere in it. "I'll call the fire department."

"Already done," Donovan said from the doorway behind her.

She turned to find him, a wiggling Bagel in his arms, standing naked in the open doorway to her bedroom. And even with her entire future literally threatening to go up in flames, her body responded, her brain flashed immediately on a few very specific stored visuals, and her heart tripped all over itself. "Now what?"

"You stay here. I'm going down to check out what's what."

"But—"

"It's been burning for a while, I don't think there's anything that can be done to save it now. But I want to make sure. The rain has made the exterior and surrounding trees wet enough to keep it from spreading to anything else."

"What if someone is still out there?"

Donovan crossed the room and plopped Bagel into her arms, then pulled on his clothes, which were strewn on the kitchen floor. "I won't be gone long."

"You didn't answer my question."

He pulled on the still damp raincoat he'd left by the door after walking Bagel earlier, then walked back over to her, leaned down, and soundly kissed her. "I know. Don't—do not—come outside. Not even on the porch. Fire trucks will take a long time to get here, and I want to make sure nothing else is going on."

"Donovan—"

His expression softened a little, and so did his tone. "Let me do my job," he said, and kissed her, this time more gently. "Please do as I ask, so I don't have to worry about you while I'm at it. Promise?"

When he looked at her like that, and asked rather than commanded, it was beyond her to debate him. It was scary in its own way, how grateful she was that he was there. "Yeah." She squeezed a still-wriggling and whimpering Bagel more tightly to her chest. "My trusty sidekick and I will be here waiting for your report."

He grinned. "I won't be long."

He turned to go, and she grabbed his arm, tugged him back, and kissed him soundly. "Be careful."

She'd expected a roll of the eyes, or some casual retort. So it surprised her when his expression faltered, almost as if she'd caught him off guard. "What?" she asked.

"Nothing. And I will." Then he was out the door and off

the porch before she could regroup enough to call him on what had obviously been a dodge.

She did as he asked and stayed away from the porch and the front door, which he'd closed behind him. But he hadn't said anything about her bedroom window. She went quickly into the room, dumped Bagel gently onto the tangled pile of bedsheets, and stepped to the edge of the window, careful to keep most of her body off to one side and out of plain sight.

Donovan was nowhere to be seen. Probably already on the backside of the cabin, she thought. It was early evening judging by the fading light, though the cloudy skies made it hard to tell. She glanced at her nightstand. Four o'clock. They'd been asleep for several hours. The acrid smell of smoke was stronger now after Donovan had opened and closed the front door. She rubbed at her nose and tried not to inhale any more deeply than she had to. God only knew what it was like out there. Hopefully, the damp air was stifling it somehow, though for all she knew, it might make it worse.

She leaned closer to the windowpane, almost pressing her cheek against it as she squinted in the rapidly growing gloom for any sight of Donovan. An uncontrollable shudder shot through her as she realized the intruder had been that close without their knowledge. With her and Donovan going at it like wild animals right in her kitchen, they could have been standing on the porch watching for all she knew.

She shuddered again and folded her arms against her chest, hugging herself, trying not to let the idea freak her out completely. Whoever it was, was likely long gone by now. They'd probably seen Donovan go inside her cabin after walking the dog and figured that was their chance. That they hadn't waited until dark, that they'd risked it in broad daylight, unnerved her more than a little. Of course, the rain and mist made it a bit more shrouded, but if either one of them had happened to look out her bedroom window while the perpetrator was setting the fire or going in or out of the cabin, they would have caught him dead to rights.

Maybe they'd thought Donovan was going to head back out and finish the installation of the cameras, so they had to strike when they had the first opportunity. It was the only thing that explained taking such a risk.

Though, she realized, as she thought about it, they'd been pretty bold with the boat shed earlier. Maybe this had been the plan all along. She kept running a visual scan over every part of the property she could see from her vantage point, but she'd yet to see Donovan. Her mind was spinning with all the ramifications. She tried not to think about the damage itself, all the incredibly expensive gear Donovan had just lost, or about how badly it was going to set back her timetable for getting the camp up and running, not to mention the money involved. At the moment, unless they could figure out who the hell was behind this, it wasn't going to matter.

She turned then, stared through the open door of her bedroom, directly at the table in the kitchen where her purse lay. And her cell phone.

Donovan might be out there chasing monsters, but there was another potential one out there that she had the power to fight.

He hadn't said when he wanted her to call Shelby, but as far as Kate was concerned, the cabin fire had just sped up any timeline Donovan might have had. She dug her phone out and immediately called Shelby's private line. She got his generic voice mail request on the first ring. "Call me," she said flatly, in a tone that brooked no argument, then clicked the phone shut. Shelby never answered calls directly. He liked the pretense that his calls needed to be screened for importance. Well, if he knew what was good for him and his beloved empire, he'd—the phone buzzed in her palm, startling her. She looked at the screen, then flipped it back open. "We need to talk."

"Don't harangue me about the meeting. I know you're all caught up in making plans for your little camp, but I'm running an entire corporate complex, and sometimes things come up."

"Which is why they make cell phones. Or, better yet, lawyers with banks of office phones. Why didn't you call me? Why leave me sitting there, steaming? Was it some kind of power play? What do you want now?" She was trying to keep Donovan's earlier guidelines in mind, but between the fire, her badly shaking hands, and the heavy cost of trying to keep that same shakiness out of her voice, she could only go on instinct. "What more could there be? We had an agreement."

"And we still do," Shelby assured her, in a tone that made it clear he was being sorely taxed by her intrusion into his oh-so-busy life. "We merely have to reschedule."

"This deal is worth everything that matters to you," she needlessly reminded him.

There was a pause. "What are you implying, Katherine? Is that some kind of veiled threat? Because we both know that I could keep you tied up in court for years and you'd never touch your inheritance."

"It would also keep you from taking over her empire and running it the way you want to." She raked her hands through her hair, stared through the window at the thick black smoke, temporarily losing track of the phone conversation as she sought out Donovan and still couldn't spot him. "We've been over this a million times."

"Precisely why we'll reschedule and dot all our *i*'s, cross our *t*'s."

She was silent for another long moment, trying to decide how to frame her next question to best get her stepbrother to tell her the truth.

There was an aggrieved sigh on the other end of the line. "Don't be punitive just because I didn't inform you of my inability to attend."

"And when were you going to get around to calling me to set this new meeting date up?"

"I may not be the lawful owner of all of our corporate holdings as yet, but I'm still the defacto head in the meantime. It's slightly more involved than setting up camp. Things come up that can't be put off. I really wish you'd grasp this fact."

"What things could possibly come up that are more important than signing the very documents that will make you the rightful king of all you survey?" Sensing the tension in the air and in her tone of voice, Bagel whimpered and pressed his full weight against her ankle.

There was a significant pause, then, "You're reading too much into what was a simple scheduling issue."

"Am I? There isn't anything else I should know about? Any last minute concerns you might be having?"

"My dear Katherine," he said, as unctuous and condescending as he'd ever been, "if I were, don't you think our lawyers would already be hashing them out?"

Not if you didn't want them to know about whatever deal you're working on the side. "Fine, then. When do we meet?"

That seemed to catch him off guard. "I—I'm at my club at the moment, hardly able to do any actual scheduling. Besides, Laurel handles that for me, you know that."

Kate decided to go for broke. "You're stalling. What's the real hold-up here, Shelby? What's the real reason you didn't you show up?"

He affected another weary sigh, but she wasn't buying it.

"Honestly, Katherine. The drama is unnecessary. I'll have Laurel call you first thing. My dinner has been delivered to my table, and I'd like to get back to it before it cools."

She tried to think like Donovan would. Shelby normally enjoyed holding court at his table, talking to people, working deals, and taking important phone calls, or at least giving every appearance of it, looking for all the world as if he were in demand in every possible way. And yet, he'd excused himself to call her back. A call he'd returned immediately. Had she pulled him out of his comfort zone, as Donovan had said she might? And if so, what did it mean? She blurted out the first question she thought of. "Who are you dining with?"

"Why on earth would that matter to you? Now, I really must go. We'll talk later in the week when the schedule has been adjusted." He clicked off before she had a chance to reply or say good-bye. Rude, and seemingly evasive, but typical.

She sneezed several times as the soot began to waft into the cabin through the stovepipe. She hurried to shut the front grate before it covered everything in the house. She almost tripped over Bagel, who was glued to her heels. "Careful there," she cautioned, adjusting the grate and checking the flue. She turned and looked down at her dog. "I don't know what to make of it, Bagel. For all I know, he was just being the insensitive asshole he can be, making sure everyone knew how important he was by having to reschedule something so vital." Or, he could have been sitting down to dine with executives from Timberline right then and there. She wished she'd been able to read him better. He was such a smug, patronizing asshole, it was hard to tell when he was being insincere.

Ignoring Donovan's orders, she walked to the front door and peeked through the window curtains covering the glass panes. If she didn't spot him in five minutes, she was heading out there and to hell with his damn rules. The dog whimpered again.

The rain had stopped, and the smoke was rising more directly upward through the trees now. She finally heard sirens in the distance, but close enough she decided it was safe to go outside. She wondered if Gilby was on the way, too. "It would be about damn time," she muttered, pulling on her mud-encrusted boots. "Stay here," she told Bagel, who was already at the door, all but vibrating to be let out. "You don't need to breathe that stuff." She grabbed a rag off the porch and dampened it, in case she needed it to cover her mouth, then grabbed a second one for Donovan, dampened it, too. She pushed out the screen door, sighing as Bagel started howling behind the cabin door, and started down toward the smoking cabin.

The sirens grew louder by the second. She could hear the powerful engines grinding up the steep incline of the camp road by the time she'd reached the cabin. Her heart tightened even further inside her chest as she surveyed the extent of the damage. Coughing, she lifted the rag to her face, careful to stay back as far as she could, yet still peer through the smoke to try and see just how badly the cabin had burned. Much of the exterior walls looked okay, but when she rounded the back, she saw the roof was half gone, and the windows had all blown out and were scorched. The rain had probably kept the exterior from going up, but from what she could tell, the inside was completely ravaged. Which meant the whole thing would have to come down and be rebuilt.

She didn't even try to mentally calculate what that was going to do to her start-up costs. At the moment, she was too busy getting mad. In fact, the longer she stared at the charred remains, the angrier she got.

"What the hell are you doing out here?"

Chapter 17

Kate spun around, rag still clamped to her face, to find Donovan standing several yards down the slope, soot streaked, and not very happy. The heightened emotions of the past few days, coupled with the rage building inside her at this latest violation of her property, all fused together in that moment to form one huge outburst of fury. "What the hell am I doing out here? I'm surveying the ruins of my goddamn cabin, that's what I'm doing. I'm trying to figure out who the hell wants to do something like this to me and what the hell I ever did to them to deserve it. That's what I'm doing out here. I'm trying to figure out who to hunt down and pin to the nearest tree until they tell me what in God's name this is all about." She threw her spare rag at him. "That's what I'm doing."

He caught it in one hand and was in front of her a heartbeat later. It wasn't until he'd pulled her into his arms that she realized there were tears on her cheeks. "I'm sorry," he said sincerely.

She pushed at him, not wanting his sympathy. At the moment, the anger felt good, energizing, as though she was finally coming out of a long daze and taking action. "I'm pissed, is what I am."

He let her move back a space, but kept his hands on her

arms. "That's good. Just don't let it make you do anything stupid."

"Thanks. I heard the sirens, so I knew it was only a matter of minutes before the place was swarming with people anyway."

"More people doesn't lower the chance of something else happening. In some cases, chaos is a good distraction."

"I wasn't going to stand in the cabin like some helpless idiot and watch." She slipped from his grasp and turned back to the cabin. "Did you find anything out? Do you have any idea how it was set, or what they used? Any evidence that you can track back?"

"Not yet, I can't get close enough. I don't have the right gear. The fire marshal will collect whatever evidence might be in there. I'm not equipped to do much more than look from a distance."

"I'm betting the marshal is also from Ralston. Maybe he's like the rest of them and not particularly interested in helping me figure out who is doing this."

"Maybe," Donovan agreed, which didn't make her feel better in the least, but was better than building false hope. "I plan on keeping a close eye while they take a look."

"Well, the cabin didn't just spontaneously combust—" She paused, looked at him, then down at his ankle, remembering the gun he'd had strapped there yesterday. "Did it?"

"No, I didn't have rounds of ammo stockpiled in there, or anything. The most combustible thing I had was a few cans of beer," he said, but with a dry smile.

"Sorry, I was trying to consider all possibilities," she said, "as someone I know is trying to teach me to do."

He nodded his approval. "There was no thunder or lightning either, so I think Gilby and the authorities will have to look at this as at least a possible arson, no matter how much they do or don't like you."

"What if they don't connect it to the vandalism? They

could just say the evidence is inconclusive if they wanted to. God, now I sound like a bigger conspiracy theorist than you do."

Donovan didn't respond to that. Instead, he said, "What I want to know is why torch the place now? Why the sudden surge in action and the escalation of damage and risk from graffiti this morning to this. If it hadn't been for the rain, this could have easily caught and taken out the whole camp."

"Do you think they knew it wouldn't do more than burn the one building?" She turned back to him. "Or do you think they were trying to burn down the whole place?"

"That they didn't start with your cabin at least indicates it's not you they intend to harm."

"But it was your cabin. If they've been watching me, then maybe someone saw you move your gear in there last night." She shuddered, remembering how she'd been nonchalantly wandering about the camp grounds last night, sitting like a big fat duck on the end of that dock. "They had to hear the drilling and hammering when they sprayed the shed. Maybe your gear was the target."

"I thought of that, too. It's definitely a possibility, but it seems a huge risk just to shut down the security setup. It can still be installed."

"Yes, but replacing the equipment slows things down."

Donovan didn't say anything to that and fell silent for a long moment as he appeared to mull things over.

"I agree with you. It just seems a lot to go from spraying words to setting a building on fire," she said.

"Unless they saw me putting up the cameras and realized that instead of spooking you, all the vandalism did was make you bring someone on board to try and stop them, or possibly catch them."

"I didn't exactly bring you on board."

"They don't know that."

"Whoever the hell 'they' are." She took a deep, calming breath, which only made her start coughing. She brought the rag back up to her face and looked at the smoking remains again. She tried to imagine what it had taken to make someone do this. "It still seems like a pretty sudden change in tactics to me. I just don't get it." Then she remembered the call she'd made. "I talked to Shelby."

Donovan's eyebrows lifted at the news, but before he could say anything, the trucks rolled in. "We'll talk about that later when we're alone."

Kate nodded in agreement as doors opened and firemen poured out in full gear, faces set, their attention focused on the smoking cabin. Donovan moved toward them with Kate right beside him. "Follow my lead here, okay?"

"Lead? What are you doing now?"

Kate didn't notice the police SUV that had pulled in behind the trucks until Gilby appeared from behind the second one. Despite the fact that she'd wanted his attention on the matter all along, instead of being relieved, his appearance just unnerved her all the more.

He was somewhere on the far side of sixty, with a military-style flattop that would probably be graying on the sides if not buzzed down to the skin. Of average height and slender, he walked with the swagger of a man sporting a far bigger frame. Even with the overcast skies and late hour of the afternoon, he wore his mirrored sunglasses. It was all Kate could do not to roll her eyes.

"What seems to be the situation here?" he asked. He directed the question at her, but not before giving Donovan a quick once-over. Gilby might appear like a self-important asshole, mostly because he probably was, but he'd been a fixture in Ralston for a very long time. Somehow Kate didn't think he missed much.

"Someone torched one of my cabins," Kate said flatly. She'd gone to him before and had more or less received a patronizing pat on the head. She wasn't going to pull any punches today. She was angry, and she wanted this to be taken seriously.

"Did you see someone set fire to the building?"

"No, sir. But—"

"Then let's not be hasty about pointing fingers and making accusations."

Donovan spoke. "The cabin has been empty and unused for several decades. There were no combustible materials stored inside, and although it has been raining, there have been no lightning strikes. The grounds here have been under an almost constant barrage of vandalism, which Ms. Sutherland has duly reported with your office. What would your professional assessment of the situation be?"

Gilby turned to face Donovan. "Are you questioning me, son?"

"I'm merely asking for your view on the situation. What else might we be dealing with here, if not arson?"

Gilby slid his glasses into his front pocket and hitched up his pants. But no amount of adjusting was going to put his stature on the same level as the very imposing Donovan MacLeod. As angry as she was, Kate had to stifle the urge to smile. Gilby might be able to "little lady" her, but she doubted he'd get around Donovan.

"And who might you be, son?"

Kate tensed, but Donovan seemed as relaxed as ever. "Donovan MacLeod."

If he remembered Donovan from the past, it didn't show on the sheriff's face. "And your relationship to Ms. Sutherland?"

"Concerned friend."

"I see."

Kate wondered what was going on behind those flat, brown eyes, but, to his credit, Gilby didn't give much away. "Well, Mr. MacLeod, there can be any number of other possibilities, including, but not restricted to, insurance fraud."

"Insurance fraud?" Kate spluttered. "But I'm not even the—"

"How long do you think it will take the fire marshal to assess the situation?" Donovan smoothly cut in.

Gilby clearly didn't like Donovan's unruffled demeanor. "Roger will be out here in due time. Now, I need to go talk with some of the fine young gentlemen here who have come to handle this situation. I'll talk with both of you when I'm done." He didn't wait for their response.

"Do you think he was trying to sound intimidating?" Kate asked.

"I think when Roger gets here we need to dog him like a shadow."

Kate turned away from the cabin and the firemen swarming around it with hoses and other equipment. "Why do you say that?"

"Just a precaution. If Gilby is intentionally turning a blind eye out here, then we need to figure out whether the fire marshal might be inclined to do the same."

"Do you think he really didn't recognize you?"

"Hard to say, it's been a lot of years."

But his tone made it clear that he didn't think Gilby missed much either. She swore under her breath. "God, I'm just so sick of this, all of it. I decide to resurrect some stupid property that no one has wanted in years, and all hell breaks loose."

Donovan went still.

"What?" Kate asked. "What did I say that I haven't already said a billion times?"

"Just making a possible connection."

"About?"

"The timing. Maybe there's something completely different going on here, something we didn't even consider." Donovan raked his hand through his hair, streaking more soot across his forehead and cheek. "Something we didn't even consider because we were distracted by Timberline's interest and Shelby's interference with the will. Maybe those things were coincidental after all."

"What? Wait a minute . . . what are you thinking?"

"I don't know yet. I need to—" He stopped and looked past her shoulder. "Gilby."

Kate smoothed her expression and folded her arms across her chest as she turned to face the sheriff, fully prepared to do battle if Gilby so much as attempted to pat her on the head about this latest run-in, much less accuse her of anything. *Insurance fraud, my ass.* "Have you heard from the fire marshal?" she asked, deciding a preemptive strike might be best. "What is the status of the fire now?" She looked past Gilby and saw that the firemen were already pulling in their gear. The fire had pretty much played out by their arrival, so other than the continued plumes of thick gray smoke rising from the burned shell, there wasn't much left to do, she supposed.

"Fire is out. Damage assessment, along with probable source and cause, will be determined after Roger has a chance to go through it. Until then, we're going to tape it off. That means no entry to you until we say so."

"So, you do consider it a crime scene, then." She phrased it more as fact than a question.

"We don't know what it is. But until we do, it's off limits. To everyone." He made a point to include Donovan in his line of vision, then after a moment, added, "You're Donny's boy. Didn't recognize you at first." Kate cut her gaze to Donovan, but there was no visible reaction to the statement.

"Been a long time," was all he said.

"That it has. Any particular reason you decided to come back now?"

He'd asked it casually enough, but Kate was pretty sure everyone standing there felt the undercurrent of tension. It was palpable. Like watching a potentially dangerous tennis match, she shifted her gaze from Gilby to Donovan.

"Just helping out an old friend."

"Helping, huh?" Gilby took a step back and shifted his gaze up into the trees. "That your handiwork up there, then?"

Donovan didn't bother to look up at the camera he'd installed earlier that day. "It's my field. New place like this, what with the recent vandalism, makes sense to secure it."

Gilby didn't react to the slight censure in his tone when he'd mentioned the vandalism. "Your daddy always was good with a piece of mechanical equipment. Guess some of that rubbed off, eh?"

Donovan simply raised a shoulder.

A smile curved Gilby's thin lips for the first time. It wasn't a pleasant sight. "Long as his other habits didn't rub off. One MacLeod spending every weekend in our drunk tank was enough. Seem to recall hauling you in there once myself."

If he was trying to get a rise out of Donovan, he was apparently going to have to work harder than that. Kate silently prayed he'd end this pointless pissing contest now.

"You won't have to worry about that," was all he said.

"Hope not. Saw plenty of your daddy." He gave Donovan a once-over that was less than polite. "Don't have much the same look. Voice is the same, though. That's what triggered it for me. Guess you take after your mama."

It was only because she was looking at him that Kate noticed the slight shift in Donovan's demeanor. Just a slight hardening of the jaw, but she doubted Gilby had missed it.

"I couldn't say. I never knew her. What's your estimate on getting a report back on this place? When is Roger due to arrive?"

Gilby's smile spread, apparently happy that he'd hit on a sensitive spot. Kate tensed, waiting for him to poke at it, but instead, he turned back to the cabin. "Few days, he's . . . out of town at the moment. Place'll probably be condemned, have to come down."

Kate sensed a different kind of awareness in Donovan and shot him a look behind Gilby's back, but he wasn't looking at her. His gaze went from drilling holes in the back of Gilby's head, to the burned cabin. Something Gilby had just said had sparked another reaction, but for the life of her, she couldn't figure out what. No way was the cabin reparable, so it was no surprise it would have to be torn down and rebuilt.

"I'll expect to hear from you and the marshal as soon as he

gets his report," Kate said, wanting nothing more than to expedite this little interlude so she could get Donovan alone and find out what was going through his head.

"Is there anything else you need from us, Sheriff?" Donovan asked, apparently of the same mind as Kate.

Gilby turned back to them and slipped an official police notebook from his chest pocket and flipped it open. "There are a few questions, yes. I'd like to get an official statement from both of you. We can do that here, or you can come down to Ralston with me."

Kate tried to mask her surprise. "Here is fine. What do you want to know?"

"I'll need to know what kind of insurance you have on this place, who your policy is with."

"You really think this is some kind of insurance scam?" Kate flung her arm out, trying to rail in her frustration and renewed fury. "You think I went around spraying my own trees with graffiti, too?"

"Stranger things happen every day, Miss Sutherland."

"Have you done any follow-up at all to my report on the vandalism?" she countered.

"Not much I can do. No other reported similar acts in the county." He dabbed his pencil on his tongue, made a few notes. "You haven't made any visual contact with intruders, have you?"

Kate was dying to lift up on her tiptoes and peek over the edge of the pad, but somehow managed to refrain. "No. No, I haven't. But they sprayed my shed across the lake just this morning, then surprise, surprise, no sooner does Donovan move his stuff in, than one of my cabins goes up in flames."

Gilby looked up sharply, and Kate could feel Donovan drilling her, but it was too late now. "You say Mr. MacLeod was residing in the burned cabin?"

"No, I said he moved in some gear bags. Nothing combustible, just cameras and surveillance equipment."

"Expensive equipment," Donovan put in. "Someone has

been keeping an eye on the property and possibly Miss Sutherland personally."

Gilby scribbled some more. "And you were residing where, specifically?"

"On camp property," he replied. "I haven't stayed in the same place twice since arriving here several days ago. But I've kept Miss Sutherland under equally close observation." Donovan held his gaze as if he was almost begging Gilby to go for the easy jibe.

Gilby stared him down, but didn't make any further notes or ask anything else, apparently not willing to be that predictable. He looked to Kate. "The insurance information, Miss Sutherland?"

Kate groaned inwardly. She should have kept her mouth shut, as Donovan would no doubt tell her later. She wasn't making them look good here. Now this. "I don't hold the insurance policy on the camp property. My stepbrother, Shelby, does." Not that the information wasn't public knowledge that Gilby could find out on his own, but she hated handing it to him.

Donovan mercifully stepped in. "Is there anything else?"

Gilby kept his gaze fixed on Kate. "So you don't stand to personally gain from any insurance claim that might be filed?"

"No," Kate said through gritted teeth.

"Why is the policy with your brother? You do own the place, do you not, Miss Sutherland?"

"The property is in the family," she replied.

Gilby eyed her, and she could feel Donovan's gaze on her as well. She didn't give any more information. Let Gilby work for it this once, she thought.

Just then one of the firemen came up behind the sheriff and cleared his throat. Gilby turned, and the young man said, "We're done here, sir. The marshal just radioed in. He's back early from his fishing trip, bad weather up north. He'll be here in the morning."

Kate sent Donovan a look and had to work at not rolling her eyes. Gilby had made it sound as if Roger was out of town on some urgent business. Fishing.

Gilby simply nodded, but rather than look back at them, looked past the fireman instead to where the others were just finishing securing the yellow-and-black tape that they'd strung around trees, enclosing the entire site with several yards to spare all the way around. "Thanks, Bud."

The young man stood there a moment longer, until Gilby, patience obviously strained, said, "Yes?"

"Uh, we need you to move your car, sir. Not enough room for the trucks to make the loop here. We'll need to back out."

Kate bit down hard on the urge to smile at the tiny patches of pink that bloomed in Gilby's cheeks. "Pack up your gear, son," he instructed him. "You can follow me out."

Leave it to Gilby to make it sound like it was his idea, Kate thought.

The sheriff faced them once again, flipping his pad shut. "I'll have further questions for both of you," he said. "Keep yourselves available."

Donovan and Kate both nodded, but neither commented.

It was clear from his tight expression that Gilby was not happy at having his little power play trumped by some low totem pole emergency worker. "Steer clear of the site. And leave the marshal to do his job tomorrow. I don't want to hear about any interference."

Kate spoke up then. "Trust me, Sheriff. I want to find out who is attacking my property more than anyone."

"Let's not jump to conclusions. Attack is a strong word, Ms. Sutherland."

"I've been vandalized and my property trespassed on repeatedly, as recently as this morning. And now this. I'll expect that you'll do your best to see if this time we can make some forward progress with this most recent surge in activity."

Gilby visibly bristled at her tone. "I've been doing my job for a very long time. Don't you worry. We'll get the answers." He eyed her, then Donovan. "Whatever they might be. Now, if you'll excuse me." With that he shoved his pad in his pocket and stalked off.

Chapter 18

Mac watched as Gilby walked over to where the firemen were loading the last piece of gear on their truck. The retardant they'd put down had subdued a lot of the smoke, so at least it was easier to breathe now. His lungs still burned from what he'd already inhaled.

"What the hell did he mean by that?" Kate asked, keeping her voice low so only he could hear her.

"Come on," Mac said, taking her elbow and turning her toward her cabin. "We need to talk, and we're not doing it here."

Kate stretched to keep up with his long-legged strides. "Was he just trying to intimidate, or do you think he's really going to try and pin this somehow on me?" Her eyes widened. "Is this how they're going to get me out of here now? Arrest me? Can they do that?"

"It's a small town, so the powers-that-be, whoever that is in this case, if it's not Gilby, are probably used to using intimidation to get what they want. The locals can't really do anything about it. Most aren't equipped to hire an expensive attorney, and it would have to be one from another area, who would have a hard time fighting the local magistrate anyway. And it's not like they could simply relocate."

"Well, the lawyer who is handling my estate dealings with Shelby could maybe—"

"You won't need to hire a lawyer." Mac climbed the stairs to Kate's porch and let them both in. He opened the door for a howling Bagel and let the dog wriggle in paroxysms of joy all over his soot-streaked legs, then outside to relieve himself, before parking all three of them on the porch.

"Why don't we go inside?"

"I'm filthy, for one, as is your dog now. I also want to keep an eye on our visitors until they roll out of here."

Kate nodded and took a seat on the wicker chair across from where Mac had perched on the wicker lounge that faced downhill. She dragged her chair around next to his so she could also watch the firemen pull out under the close supervision of Sheriff Gilby. "So, you don't think he's coming after me, then? What was all that, then? Force of habit?"

"Partly. Partly to make you think you were in danger, maybe see what you'd do. Distract you from worrying about what you should really be focusing on."

"He knows you're here putting up security. Do you think he'd try and target you now? I'm sorry, too, about that whole thing with your father. I—"

"Don't be. Doesn't matter. If anything, if he thinks I'm just Donny Mac's loser son trying to be something he's not, all the better for me." He stared down the hill, watching as the firemen climbed on their trucks and started up their heavy engines. "I don't think that's the case right now, but I don't think I'm his focus either. Just his excuse for expediting things."

"Meaning?"

"Did you happen to notice the change in his demeanor and tactics when you revealed that you aren't the technical owner of this place yet?"

"No, not really. I guess I should apologize for running off at the mouth, too. I knew better than to hand over information like that, but he was really pissing me off."

"It's okay. It was interesting to see his response. Ties in with my earlier suspicion."

Kate turned to him. "Yeah, about that. What do you think we missed?"

Mac watched as Gilby barked into his radio unit before climbing into his car and backing around so he could lead the way out. The fire trucks took a bit longer to pull the same maneuver, their big tires digging muddy trenches on either side of the narrow lane as they finally maneuvered themselves around.

He didn't respond to Kate's question until they disappeared over the crest and down the road leading to the camp exit. The rumble of the truck engines echoed through the deepening mist gathering in the trees now that the rain was over and evening was falling.

"You said you talked to Shelby," Mac said. "What did he say?"

"You're not going to tell me what you figured out?"

"I need to hear how the phone call went."

"Hard to say, really. He was . . . pretty much himself. Self-important bordering on rude."

"Did he say why he was a no-show?"

"He said something came up, but not what. I pressed, and he got kind of pissy, but nothing that struck any real chord." She lifted a shoulder. "Other than the fact that he left the room to take my call, I'm half inclined to believe it really was just one of his ridiculous power plays."

"Left the room? What do you mean?"

"Shelby loves for everyone to know how important he is, and he was at his private club when I called. But instead of telling me he was too busy to sign papers securing his entire future in front of whatever cronies he was dining with, he stepped out of the room to return my call." She shrugged again. "Not really noteworthy. Who knows who was sitting at the table with him." She lifted a shoulder. "He pissed me off as he usually does, but to be perfectly honest with you, I didn't really feel anything all that suspicious about it. If you hadn't been here digging this all up and trying to link it together, I know I would've been mad, but I wouldn't have suspected anything weird."

Mac nodded, but didn't say anything right away.

"So, does that help or hinder your new theory? You said maybe the Timberline thing and the will weren't connected?"

"Did you come to your conclusion about not doubting Shelby's reasoning before or after I said that?"

"Before, I guess." She paused, then nodded. "I mean, I hadn't analyzed it or anything, but that was my gut reaction at the time."

"How did you leave it with him?"

"That he didn't want to screw around on this, that I needed this to get done so I had the power to move forward."

"And?"

"And, that seemed to be it. His assistant will call with a time and we'll go from there. My gut feeling, to be honest, is that it will happen this time. I'm sorry if that screws up your theory, and it's not because I don't want you to be right. At this point, I just want to know the truth, whatever it is, I just . . ." She trailed off, lifted a shoulder.

Mac sat there for a moment, mulling over the new direction his thoughts were taking, then abruptly stood up and reached a hand out for her. She took it, and he pulled her up, then kept pulling until she bumped up against him. "What does your gut instinct tell you about this?"

"This, meaning us?"

"This meaning us."

She gazed into his eyes, and he spent a moment thinking he could get used to looking back. That maybe he already was. "I'm trying not to overanalyze it." A ghost of a smile curved her soot-streaked face. "We're doing enough of that about every other facet of my life at the moment. This part is working out okay, so I figured it was best to just leave it to go as it goes. Or try to."

He should shut up, should be happy she was okay with their current arrangement, not pushing for more, not further complicating an already complicated situation. So why he opened his mouth, he had no idea. "Just okay?"

She rolled her eyes, smiled dryly. "Men and their egos."

He snagged her hand, pressed it against his chest, kept his gaze on her. For the life of him he couldn't have said why it was suddenly so important to get a straight answer, but there it was. "I wasn't talking about the sex."

"What else is there?" She immediately looked contrite. "I'm sorry, that didn't come out right. Not at all. I guess what I meant was—"

He let her go, stepped back. "No offense. I know what you meant."

"I don't think you do, or you wouldn't be pissed off at me right now."

"I'm not pissed off at you. If I'm pissed off at anyone, it's my own idiotic self." Now it was his turn to heave a sigh, roll his shoulders. "It was an unfair question, one I wouldn't have appreciated, so I had no right. You're right. Let's not analyze, let's just enjoy what is. There's enough crap going on; it's nice to have some balance." He walked to the porch door.

"Where are you going?"

"To poke around the cabin. You don't think for one minute I'm going to rely on Gilby or Roger to give us the real story?"

"But, the yellow tape, Gilby's orders. It's a crime scene, Donovan."

"And I believe I know my way around one of those pretty well by now. Don't worry, I'm not going to do anything stupid." He pushed through the door. "At least not with the cabin," he added under his breath.

She was at the door behind him. "What are you looking for?"

"I'll know when or if I find it. Mostly I want to find out how it was started, see if what I find matches up with what

Roger finds. Don't worry, I'm not going to alter anything, just get a lay of the land with my own two eyes."

"Wait," she called out, when he was a dozen steps down the hill.

He paused, turned.

"You didn't tell me what you thought you'd figured out."

"Still not sure I have."

"You don't even want to share your theory?"

He smiled then. "It's all just theories yet, right?"

She nodded, leaned against the frame of the porch door. "Something's going on, though."

"That part is fact. Something is most definitely going on."

"Just because I question your theories doesn't mean I don't want to hear them, or don't necessarily believe them. I'm just trying to sort this out, same as you. I don't have the same training as you, and I don't think like you, so you'll have to be patient with me. I'm sure I'm frustrating the hell out of you."

His smile broadened. "You do a whole lot of things to me, Kate Sutherland. And I don't mind that we think different. Keeps my mind more open that way."

Her smile was wry. "Could have fooled me."

"I'm guessing that doesn't happen all that often." He turned back, started walking. "I won't be long. Go ahead and grab a shower first if you want."

"Might," she called back. "Might wait."

He didn't look back, but it took him all the way to the burned shell of the cabin to wipe the grin off his face. She was something, she was. The only thing frustrating about her was how quickly she'd gotten to him. He liked that she didn't back down from her own opinion on things, that she kept poking, kept asking, didn't just take things on faith, or because he said so. Sure, it was irritating at times, because he wanted to make sure she was being careful, that she was taking things seriously enough to make wise decisions.

He carefully avoided thinking about the piercing little jab he'd felt when she'd dismissed their—whatever the hell they were having—as nothing more than a convenient physical outlet. Hadn't he basically said the same thing? About enjoying some balance to the worry, the stress?

Except he hadn't been thinking about sex. Well, not just sex. It shouldn't irritate him that she had been. Would make things easier when they sewed this up, in fact, if she kept a level head. "One of us should," he muttered, then shut down that line of thought completely and did a quick walk around the circumference of the taped-off area. He studied the ground, the cabin, storing information, looking for clues, as well as the best place to breach security without leaving a trail. He didn't know the fire marshal, so he had no idea how thorough a man Roger was, but, as he ducked under the tape, he took no chances. If his most recent suspicion proved to have any weight behind it, it was imperative he knew what Roger would find, before Roger found it.

Or had a chance to alter it.

Chapter 19

It was full dark and had been for a short time. Kate had just about talked herself into heading back down to the burned cabin, when Donovan pushed in through the cabin door. "Hi, honey, I'm home."

Bagel barked and wagged vigorously as he danced around Donovan's ankles, and Kate tried very hard to remind herself that his greeting, like last time, was just a joke. Not something she was going to hear every day for, oh, the next fifty years. That she'd even thought about it was a major heads-up on how not casually she was handling all of this. She forced herself to glance at him with nothing more than a quick smile from the pot of chili she was stirring. "Hey, Superhero. How goes the stealth hunt?"

Her entire body hummed in anticipation when he crossed the room toward her. Not that she could really fault the reaction. He'd done some pretty amazing things to her body earlier; of course it was going to hum a little. Okay, a lot. But there were more important things to be thinking about than how long it was going to be before they discussed tonight's sleeping arrangements. Even if she'd spent more time than absolutely necessary on that very topic and very little on the actual important ones as she'd put dinner together.

She'd have to be disgusted with herself later, however, because he came up right behind her, not stopping until she could feel his breath fan the back of her neck, as if her personal space had a huge open sign hovering over it exclusively for him. Which, apparently, it did, as her immediate response was to lean back into him. Or try to.

He took a quick step back. "I'm disgustingly filthy and you smell incredible."

"That's just dinner."

He leaned in and brushed his lips just below her ear, inhaling deeply. "Nope. It's you."

She couldn't help it; she was impossibly charmed, even if he did smell as if he'd slept inside an old barbecue pit. Dipping her chin to hide her ridiculously big grin, she continued to stir the mix of beans and hamburger meat. "I thought you might be hungry."

"Mmm," he hummed. "Very."

Her body went from humming to outright singing, and it took considerable willpower to keep from tossing the spoon down and turning into his arms, maybe even pushing him down on the small kitchen table and having her way with him, smoke stench or no.

"You didn't wait for me," he said, still hovering, still sniffing.

"I did for a bit, but when it looked like you were going to be out there for a while, I thought it would be a good idea to put something together to eat, and I didn't want to do that all covered in soot and grime." She had every intention of asking him what he'd found in the cabin that had kept him down there so long, and then grill him on whatever his new theory was, until he told her everything, so it was as much of a surprise to her as anyone when she smiled over her shoulder at him and said, "Doesn't mean I can't scrub your back."

His eyes, ringed in grime and soot, flashed a bright silver that turned her insides to mush. "I don't suppose it does."

No law that said she couldn't ask questions in the shower, she told herself as he nudged her hips and shifted her around to face him. She lifted the spoon between them. "We're going to talk business at some point. Fair warning. I want to know what's going on."

He covered her hand and guided the spoon to his mouth, where he slowly licked the chili sauce off, while watching her with twinkling eyes. "Mmm hmm," he agreed.

Her knees went decidedly wobbly, and she knew she should be ashamed at how easily he could seduce her into putting everything important in her world on hold, but damn the man, he made it really hard to concentrate. And it wasn't like there was anything they could do to solve the mystery in the next fifteen minutes anyway. Or the next hour. Or two.

Or three.

"I'm serious, Donovan," she told him, the reprimand aimed more at herself than him. But if she'd been hoping to enlist some of his control in the matter, she was going to be sorely disappointed. Except disappointment wasn't really what she was feeling at all when his eyes went dark and he slid the spoon from her hands and placed it back on the holder on the stove, deftly popped the lid onto the pot, and turned the burner all the way down to simmer.

"What you do to me," he murmured as he backwalked her from the kitchen all the way to the bathroom, without ever once actually touching her, but staying so deep in her personal space, she felt intimately connected to him nonetheless.

But then, she always felt that way around him.

"Did you find anything suspicious on your prowl?" she asked him, hearing the thread of need in her voice, even as she tried valiantly to keep from going under his spell without a sign of struggle. He wouldn't be around long, and she was warring with the need to indulge herself mightily while she could, and preserve some sense of control to keep from coming to want too much. Certainly more than she was ever going to get to keep, as that was going to be precisely nothing.

"Depends on what you define as suspicious." He kicked the bathroom door shut behind them, keeping a very disappointed Bagel on the other side.

"Confirm your theory?" she asked, although the words weren't much more than a hushed whisper as he leaned past her to turn on the shower.

Maybe she just needed to jump him and keep on jumping him until they both burned their need for each other out of their systems. Apparently they hadn't come close to reaching that point yet. Not if the inferno of sexual tension currently raging between them in the small confines of her bathroom was any indication.

"I need to do a little more investigation," he said, keeping his eyes pinned on hers as he started to peel off his shirt. It wasn't until he started shimmying down his pants that the amused smile tautened the corners of his mouth. "You're not planning on getting in the shower completely dressed again, are you?"

She'd been so caught up in watching him, she'd forgotten that part. Stepping out of his pants, he pushed aside her own fumbling hands and lifted her shirt himself. "I guess not," she said, smiling herself, shamelessly enjoying how his hands felt as they brushed against her skin. "You wouldn't be seducing me in order to keep me from pestering you about your latest opinion on matters, would you?"

He tugged her sweatshirt over her head and tossed it behind him. "Would it work?"

She shook her head.

"Then I guess the answer is no." He stepped in closer and tugged at the waistband of her sweatpants. "Have I mentioned how much I like your easy access choice in clothing?"

"No, but I'm considering wearing just a T-shirt from now on. This is taking way too long."

He yanked her sweats down in one motion, which put him in a convenient crouch in front of her. She let out a gasp and balanced herself by gripping his shoulders when he took a wicked detour with his tongue. "We're so completely shameless," she gasped.

"Great, isn't it?"

"Yeah," she said, torn between a laugh at how freeing it was to be with him, and a soft moan on how deliciously good the things he was doing with his tongue made her feel. The soft moan won as he continued his very focused, tender assault on her most sensitive little bundle of nerve endings. "It's a little insane how great it is. Have I mentioned that your idea of foreplay is pretty damn incredible?" She groaned when he slid his tongue away from where she needed it most, up over her torso, gasped again when he captured one turgid nipple for a brief, succulent moment, then moved up to nip her chin. "You stopped," she said, perhaps pouting, just a little.

"I hate being predictable."

"Remind me to shut the hell up more often."

He simply continued to nip along the line of her jaw as she felt the rock-hard length of him brush between her thighs. The muscles there clenched repeatedly, and heedless of the shower running behind her, she gripped at his hips, wanting some part of him inside of her right that very second. Only to be disappointed again when he continued kissing and nipping along her neck as he turned her around. "Watch," he whispered against the side of her neck.

She opened her eyes to find herself staring into the rapidly steaming mirror over her sink. Her gaze locked on his as he pulled her hips back. Black soot streaked his face, his hair, and his hands, leaving marks on her skin where he touched her. Instead of turning her off, it made him look wildly primal, and her ache for him intensified.

The sound that slid from her was deep and guttural as he pushed fully into her. She was so ready for him, and pushed back onto him, but there was nothing hurried this time. His strokes were slow, controlled, and oh so deep, but the connection she felt with him as their gazes held with each thrust was as visceral as it got. She braced her hands on the sink as he leaned over her, nipping at her ear, while his hands slid up her torso, streaking her skin with black. He toyed with her nipples, wrenching groan after groan from her, but nothing matched the low shout of pleasure he wrung from her when he slid one hand between her thighs.

She crested quickly, almost violently, and he kept his fingers there, slick and clever, kept her quivering and shuddering, until he was shaking with the effort to stave off his own imminent climax. She pushed back against him, needing more of him somehow, and yet feeling so completely full of him, she wasn't sure what more there was to have.

His hands slid back to her hips, his fingers digging in tightly as he began pumping harder, faster. She met him thrust for thrust, her hands slipping on the porcelain of the sink as she fought to keep her grip. The mirror had fogged completely over at some point, but she didn't need to see him now. She felt him so thoroughly it was as though she was part of him, as he was part of her. His climax, when he finally let it overtake him, was almost mindless in the frenzied way he drove into her, body slapping against body, animal grunts—his and hers—filling the steamed air.

He collapsed over her, and they both fell over the sink. She braced their weight on the mirror, leaving handprints on the steamed glass, as he wrapped his arms around her waist and held her tightly to him, his body still shuddering in the aftermath.

It was hard to breathe in the thick air, the shower still pumping out more steam as their hearts raced and their bodies quivered. She had no idea how much time passed before he finally lifted her up and turned her around, saying nothing as he pulled her into his arms. He shifted, resting his weight against the sink as she leaned into him, oblivious now to the soot, the smoky smell, still trying to slow her pulse, breathe. He seemed to be doing the same as he stroked her hair, pressed his cheek against the top of her head, and just held her.

Hot and dirty sex, she thought. Literally, figuratively, any and every which way she wanted to look at it. It had felt like more, a lot more. It had felt like . . . She couldn't find the words. *Bathroom fun, sweaty and intense, but fun is all it is*, she told herself. That was all it was, all it could be. Then she felt him press a kiss to her hair, and her heart bloomed so swiftly it made her eyes burn. *So stupid, so silly*, she scolded herself. Mistaking sex for love. For anything other than what it was. Pleasure. Profound in this case, life altering even, but mere physical gratification nonetheless.

Yet there was so much more there for her, and no amount of silent scolding was going to change that. She knew then just how much she'd gambled, letting him in at all. It wasn't money, or success, or anything with an absolute value she'd risked. It was priceless. It was her heart. How had she been so foolish as to think it was something she could give away and not suffer for in the end?

And it was all she could do to not cling to him. She couldn't force herself to step away, climb in the shower, toss off a light laugh, make some pithy remark about the mind-blowing sex they so effortlessly managed to have, as casual lovers would.

He slid his fingers beneath her chin, nudging it up, and she resisted for a second, not wanting him to see what might be in her eyes at that moment. She felt unmasked, naked, and vulnerable in a way that had absolutely nothing to do with her physical state at the moment, and everything to do with her emotional one. Donovan missed nothing. Even if he was unprepared for what he might find, she doubted he'd miss that either.

Selfishly, she wasn't ready to let this go yet, to let him go. If she was going to risk it all like that, lay her heart out like that, shouldn't she get as much out of the devil's bargain as she could?

But then, she already knew there wasn't going to be any getting enough where Donovan was concerned. More now was only going to hurt more later. And yet the battle waged.

He nudged a little harder. "What's going on in there?" he said, his voice hardly more than a gravelly rasp.

Sighing softly, knowing she had no other choice, she let him nudge, let him tip her chin, until their gazes met. And realized she was the one who was going to find the unexpected. Stunned, she could only stare into his eyes. Eyes that weren't just filled with desire, or satisfied pleasure. In those silvery gray depths, she saw an easy, honest affection, so direct, so open, so . . . naked. Exposed. As exposed as she felt. He looked so far into her, with such blatant need, she felt touched so deeply she didn't know it existed within her.

Projecting? She forced herself to ask. *No,* came the swift answer. Even she couldn't imagine something that profound, that raw. "I—"

"Kate," he said at the same time.

"What?"

"You go," he said, again speaking over her. Their lips both twitched, but his arms banded more tightly around her. When she didn't speak, he said, "The shower is going to run cold. And we need to talk."

Her heart tightened inside her chest. She had no idea what she'd expected. Some silly declaration of love? So it was to be business, then, no matter what his eyes said. He was the pragmatic one, after all. He wouldn't let the fantasy of the moment, of what they might want it to be, cloud what could only be.

"I know," she said, and started to pull away.

He didn't let her budge. "I know it, too." He sighed heavily, then pressed his head to hers. "And yet I can't let you go," he said, the words hardly more than a rasp.

Her fingers dug into his back of their own volition, so clearly did her heart mirror that sentiment. Only she never wanted to let him go, well beyond any afterglow moment. But she'd bask in what she could. No point in pretending not to be shameless at this late stage. "Yeah," she managed, "I know the feeling."

"It's not the sex," he said as the moment spun out. "Though

I swear I could take you again, right now. I'm—insatiable, apparently, where you're concerned."

She tried to lift her head, intent on smiling, on saying something smart and clever. And ignore completely the thread of confusion she heard in his voice that so clearly mirrored her own.

Again, he held her in place, kept her face tucked next to his, their gazes, for once, not on each other. Maybe that was the only way he could say what he needed to say, she thought, the words necessary to make clear what this was, and what it wasn't, even if they both wanted it to be.

She told herself that the fact he'd wanted more at all, wanted anything near what she found herself yearning for, was gift enough. It told her she hadn't tossed her heart into the ring completely selfishly or foolishly. That would have to be enough.

"We've talked about not knowing each other, about time being a measuring stick for knowledge. The kind of knowledge you're supposed to have about someone in order to know for certain what your feelings are for them."

She stilled then, even as her heart began racing.

"It's supposed to be something built upon, slowly, over time, so you know, for sure, what it is, what it can be, and what it isn't or will never be." She lifted her head then, looked into his eyes, and her heart lifted to her throat at the stark vulnerability she saw there, the fear. "Donovan . . ."

"So explain this to me," he said, his voice almost gone now, the rasp was so deep. "Explain how I know it's you. How it's always been you." He paused, looking almost help-less. "How it will always be you."

Tears sprang to her eyes, and her attempts at scolding and coercing herself into being smart and responsible came to an abrupt and permanent end. "Because you just do," she said, her throat tight with the threat of those unshed tears.

"Maybe I can't get enough of you, sexually, because it's the fastest way to get as much of you as possible, on me, in me, in some permanent way. I don't know. But it's like the more I have, the hungrier I become. It's only been a matter of days, and yet I have no perspective left where you're concerned. There's nothing rational about this, Kate, and I don't know what to—"

She covered his mouth with her fingers. "Not everything is rational, Donovan. Not everything has to be."

He pulled the pad of one of her fingers between his lips, gently pressed his teeth down, making her shudder in instantly renewed need. But it was more than her erogenous zones in play. Her heart was all the way out there, and it was both exhilarating and terrifying to think his might be, too. What did it mean? What would it change?

She didn't want to think about any of that. She just wanted to be right where she was, in that particular moment, exulting in the intensity of the connection they seemed to be sharing. Knowing she wasn't in it alone made giving in to it unbearably seductive. She pressed her finger against his tongue and felt his body jerk against hers.

"Come on," he murmured around her finger, not letting it go. He stuck his hand under the spray, then tugged them both carefully into the tub. The water wasn't scalding, but it was still hot enough. There was enough steam in the room to keep them both comfortable under the spray.

There was no further conversation. As if by silent agreement, Kate reached for the body soap and sponge and took her sweet time lathering his entire body. Finally it was her turn to enjoy exploring. She missed nothing, and he was growing hard again, and bracing his weight against the wall by the time she was done. Then he tugged her directly under the spray with him so the water cascaded over them both, rinsing the foamy soap off as he pulled her into his arms and kissed her. Slow, and deep, she fell completely into it, feeling him growing harder, nudging between her thighs. At this rate, they'd have to be wheeled out in chairs by morning.

The thought made her giggle, which had Donovan positioning her under the spray so it doused her, making her splutter, and they both laughed. A second later he'd captured her mouth again, this time in a soul-searing kiss, the water pounding down over both of them. Her laughter faded as she wove her arms around his neck and returned his kiss with everything she was feeling.

He reached behind them and shut the water off, but recaptured her mouth before she could say anything. He pulled her closer, took the kiss even deeper, until she shivered involuntarily. They both groaned a little in regret as he let her go and reached for the towels on the near wall rack.

She said nothing as he slung a towel around his hips, then wrapped her in the other towel and began gently drying her off. She was still quietly stunned by what they'd just done. Not the lovemaking, not the continued extended foreplay they seemed incapable of avoiding every time they were in reach of each other. But that last kiss . . . That joining had been more intimate than anything they'd shared up to that point. So gentle, so poignant, with so much poured into it, words that couldn't be said, emotions that had no other avenue of expression.

She wondered what was going through his mind as he, too, remained silent as he finished up and grabbed her robe from the hook on the back of the door. He held it open for her, and their eyes met for the first time since stepping out of the tub. His were dark silver now, filled with open desire, penetrating intensity . . . and maybe a little of that stunned shellshock she was feeling, too.

She slipped her arms in, and he tugged her back against him, helping her knot the belt in the front, his chin pressing into her shoulder. He turned his head slightly, caught her earlobe for a quick nip. "We need to talk."

Her heart wobbled, dipped, but held on with valiant effort. She wasn't ready for this part. Couldn't they just play house for a bit longer? Couldn't they just pretend this wasn't going to have to end sooner rather than later?

She knew the answer to that. And she had the charred remains of a cabin a hundred yards downhill as a glaring reminder, in case she wanted to try and forget.

"I know."

He opened the door and immediately squatted to give the very relieved Bagel a good belly scratch. Watching them, Kate thought how ridiculously easy it would be to fall head over heels in love with this man. When he glanced up just then, his lips quirked in a bit of a smile, her heart squeezed, and she knew she was already well on her way.

"Eat and then walk, or walk then eat?" he asked.

She looked at Bagel, writhing in ecstasy, and thought, *That makes two of us. He's gifted like that.* "Eat first. I need to feed him, too. Give my hair a chance to dry a little before heading out."

He straightened. "I can walk him."

Kate started to gather up their clothes from the bathroom floor, but left them lay. Hers were on top of his, and they'd all need washed now. "It's okay," she said, walking into the bedroom. "We'll both go. Talk while we walk?" She rooted around in her closet as Donovan put his duffel on the bed and pulled out clean clothes. Good thing he'd grabbed that from his cabin when he had.

"I'm sorry. About losing all your stuff, all that equipment. I didn't say that before, but I truly am."

"It's okay. Stuff is replaceable."

She nodded, then watched in unabashed pleasure as he pulled on jeans and a plain white T-shirt, a combination Kate found incredibly appealing in the most basic of ways, especially with the little bit of stubble on his cheeks now, and the freshly washed hair. Then she laughed when he pulled on one of the new sweatshirts he'd bought on their mall run. "How did I miss you buying that one?"

He looked down at the red *S* emblazoned on his chest and grinned back at her. "What were you expecting? Care Bears?"

She walked over to him, reveling a little in the proprietary buzz she got from knowing she was welcome in his personal space, and, in fact, encouraged to spend as much time there as she wanted. She wanted.

"Well, you are kind of snuggly."

He looked so instantly offended by that remark that she burst out laughing.

"*Cuddly?*"

"I said snuggly."

"Same thing. I just took you up against your sink like—"

"I know," she said, shivering in remembered delight. "But that doesn't mean you can't also be—"

"Snuggly."

She slipped her arms around his waist and tugged him up against her. He grudgingly put his arms around her. "You're very cute all the time, but you're especially cute when you pout."

"I never pout."

"If I said I still expected you to sleep in one of the other cabins—"

"Do you?"

The look on his face was so startlingly vulnerable, though he swiftly masked it, she immediately felt bad for teasing him. She wasn't used to thinking of him as remotely vulnerable, not in any immediate way. The idea that he was, with her, disconcerted her, even as it moved her. She lifted up and kissed him softly, full on the lips. "No, of course not." She smiled into his eyes. "But see? You do pout."

Understanding dawned, and the most devilish twinkle sparked to life in those silvery depths. "You are so going to pay for that."

"What? I think it's sexy."

"First you think I'm snuggly; now pouting is sexy?"

She lifted a shoulder in a half shrug. "Just saying. But, you know, if you think I should pay . . . exactly what kind of retribution did you have in mind?"

A half second later she was on her back, on her bed, a

squeal of surprised delight whooshing out of her as Donovan's weight pressed down on top of her. "You want the detailed list?"

She wiggled her eyebrows. "I'm a big believer in showing, not telling."

"Really?"

Bagel chose that moment to let out a particularly mournful howl from outside the bedroom door, which made them both laugh. The dog followed that up with a very pathetic sigh, then collapsed in a thumping heap and snuffled along the crack at the bottom of the door.

"I think we've neglected the children about as long as we can," Donovan said, still chuckling.

It was an off-the-cuff comment, a joke they'd already made before, so there was absolutely no reason to feel a twinge somewhere deep inside of her. Children. Donovan's children.

"What?" he asked, the laughter fading from his voice.

She had no idea what he'd seen on her face. He was far too observant at times. She blinked, smiled. "Are you kidding? Bagel's never had it so good," she said, but the pause had been too telling, and the quip fell a little flat.

He held her gaze for the longest moment, but rather than push, he simply leaned down and kissed her soundly. "Neither have I," he said, then climbed off the bed.

She watched him stroll out of the bedroom, slapping his thigh so Bagel followed him to the front door. *Why couldn't it be this easy?* she wondered.

"You coming?" he called, crouching to put on Bagel's harness and leash.

Kate slid off the bed, reveling in the very thought that they'd be back in it, together, tonight. And, at the same time, dreading the talk they had to have first. "Well, until the dog howled, I thought I had a pretty good shot at it. I guess I shouldn't be greedy."

Donovan grinned over at her as she slid on a jacket and

stepped on the porch to shove her feet into her muddy boots. "I don't know," he said. "Day's not over yet."

She smiled, but turned just enough as she buttoned up to keep him from seeing whatever might be showing in her eyes now. Because she wanted a lot more than a day. Or a night.

Chapter 20

Mac held the leash in one hand and tucked his free hand in Kate's. "Chilly," he said, shivering a bit, and tugging her closer as they went the opposite way around the loop from the burned cabin.

"I thought you wanted to show me something," she said, looking surprised at his chosen path.

"No, I wanted to tell you something."

He felt her tense beside him, and it tugged at his heart. She did that a lot, that heart-tugging thing, mostly without even trying. He didn't want to add to her worries, especially when he had a pretty good idea what she was worrying about at the moment had nothing to do with the damage to her property. This part was supposed to be about pleasure and simply enjoying each other. The balance to the bad stuff, as he'd told her earlier. As he'd told himself a hundred times. And that was just in the last ten minutes.

Only now that the moment had arrived, he suddenly didn't know what to say. *I think I've solved your case, and, well, it's been a blast, hope we can get together again sometime?*

Or, *The idea of having to leave you is scaring me senseless. I'm not used to needing anyone, but, I need you.*

Flip was out. And brutal honesty . . . well, he wasn't quite ready for that one himself. So, when she remained silent rather than badger him with questions, he took that cue and remained silent, too, and they just walked.

Surprisingly, rather than become more tense or awkward, their steps gradually slowed, they relaxed their hold on each other's hand, strolling at a leisurely pace as Bagel sniffed out every rock and pinecone, and the moon flitted between breaks in the clouds.

Mac absently rubbed his thumb along the side of her hand and wrist, pausing by the next tree as Bagel finally decided that this was the exalted place this evening to do his business.

The mistake was lifting his amused gaze from the dog, to Kate. The moon chose that moment to blink through the night clouds, illuminating her face. She wasn't smiling, or frowning. She looked . . . contemplative. Normally such a look would make him want to run for the hills, and there was a twinge of that, although for entirely different reasons than usual, but more than that, he really wanted to know what she was thinking.

"Come here," he murmured, tugged her hand next to his hip, turning his body into hers.

"What?" she said, but let him pull her right up against him. He loved how easily they did that, framed each other. So effortless, so damn good. "What's going on in there?" he asked, pressing his forehead to hers.

"Mmm," she hummed, kissing his chin, then rubbing her cheek on his stubble. "As little as possible." She sighed a little then, and the smile that had begun to curve his lips tripped up some. "I just want to feel," she said. "Touch, taste, sound, smell . . ." She tipped her head back and looked up between the tall stalks of the trees at the sky above, but the moon was swallowed up again, leaving her upturned face in deep shadow. "But I guess I'm not going to get to do that, am I?" She sighed and looked back at him. "So . . . what did you find?"

"I'd rather talk about the touching and tasting part."

She smiled a little. "Me, too. But the stubborn realist in me apparently won't let go. So, spill. What's the theory? What did you find?"

He held her gaze for a long minute, then sighed a little himself. She was right, no matter how badly either of them would like to think otherwise. "Well, the good news is, I don't think your stepbrother has anything to do with this."

Her eyes widened. "Why do you think that?"

"I started thinking about the cabin and why they'd torch that particular one. Yes, I moved surveillance gear in there, but it's in direct view of your cabin, and, like you had mentioned, it just seemed too big a jump in terms of the previous level of vandalizing. I initially thought maybe spray painting the shed was a diversion, to pull you away from your side of the lake, but then, it was only by chance you walked over there. From your side of the lake, you'd have never seen it."

"So, why spray it at all, then? Oh. Wait, you're saying someone really has been spying on me. Us. They sprayed the shed because they were already there, watching, and saw me walking around the lake. Maybe they thought I'd call you over to see it so we'd both be all the way around the lake."

He nodded. "So it was a diversion after all, just not how I originally thought of it. I think they were already planning to get into my cabin. It was just a matter of waiting for us to leave. But we weren't leaving, and then they saw me putting up surveillance stuff and—"

"But wait, that means they were already there when they figured out the surveillance part. So, they were planning on burning that particular cabin before knowing about your gear being in there?"

"I think so. Then you said something earlier, when Gilby was here, about how it wasn't until you decided to do something to a piece of land nobody wanted, that all hell broke loose, and that was when it all fell together for me."

"Well, put it together for me. I'm still not getting it."

"I mentioned Shelby's no-show and the whole developer angle might have actually been a coincidence after all."

"Yes, but you said yourself it was one too many things all related to the same event."

"I did, and it's distracted me, tying that all together, making it work. But then we just couldn't find a truly plausible reason for the vandalism, for the graffiti. It didn't fit with the players we had involved."

Kate made a hand motion. "So, bottom line it for me."

He smiled a little, liking how her brain latched on to things and ran full steam ahead, just like his did. "Okay. I think the people of Ralston, or specifically those who are behind the vandalism, and now the fire, have been using the Winnimocca property. And I think they have for some time now. As you said, no one has been here in a decade, and there didn't seem to be any chance of that changing."

"Until I suddenly show up." She looked past Mac's shoulder, at the campgrounds, despite the darkness. "So . . . what in the hell have they been doing here? What are they using it for?"

"I don't know. But I think there must have been something in my cabin, something they needed to get back or, failing that, destroy. And when they couldn't make you go away with vandalizing and limited scare tactics, they realized they needed to get out here and take care of it once and for all. It might not have even been my surveillance gear at all, but just the fact that I moved in to that cabin, that made them panic."

"So why not come in when I'm away, like they do with the graffiti?"

"Maybe they have been. And maybe you've been here when they sprayed the graffiti. I know they've been watching your cabin. I've found evidence of it that first morning I was here."

She shuddered. "So, you're saying whoever it is might have been watching me all along? Or, that whatever it was they needed to get back took more than one trip to get out of here?"

"Maybe it's not so simple as all that, or maybe we're once

again overthinking it. We're talking about the fine citizens of Ralston here, hard to say what it is that would make some of them panic like this. As for access, directly bringing a vehicle in here would be risky as the road in and out is very long and they could easily pass you coming or going. They have snuck in from other, more remote parts, places through which it would be difficult to haul things out. And it might just be a matter of difficult timing. You've been here a few weeks. How often have you been away from here?"

"Not often. Only a handful of times."

"And no real routine to the pattern of coming and going."

She shook her head.

"So that makes it pretty damn hard, unless someone is stationed here watching, to know when the coast is clear, especially if it needs to be a concerted effort in removing . . . whatever had to be removed."

"What do you think it is? Drugs? Or something else illegal, I'm guessing. You think they were storing something in your cabin?"

"I think so. That it's in direct line of sight of your cabin might also explain why it's been hard for them to get into it without being seen. How closely have you inspected all the buildings since your return?"

"The lodge, my cabin, some of the bigger ones that needed the least amount of work, I've gone through, but not with a fine tooth comb or anything. I am planning to do things in phases. I mean, I needed a general idea of what needed to be done, but I focused on the big jobs first. The barns, the lodge, my residence. I've been in or around most of the buildings, your cabin included, and I certainly didn't see anything that looked suspicious."

Mac listened to her, his mind still spinning, still puzzle solving. "Maybe it isn't anything big, then. Maybe they weren't all that worried when you didn't immediately do anything, or find anything, and they chose to try and scare you off instead. But then I show up in town with you yesterday, and suddenly things start to escalate, and they get sloppy."

She seemed to think about that, take it in. "Okay. So . . . what do you think it might be? And who do you think it might be?"

"I don't know. But I've been thinking about your reception in town, or the lack thereof, and it makes me think it's more than one or two people involved. And I'm betting that they're not low on the food chain, if you know what I mean."

"Why would you say that?" "

"They have to be risking something potentially pretty damaging to risk discovery like they did today."

"Well, if someone is dealing drugs, or whatever, that'd be pretty damaging no matter who they are. And would they really risk being seen here if that's the case?"

"Probably not, but that doesn't mean they didn't pay someone else to do their dirty work. In fact, I think that degree of separation is highly likely."

"Do you have any suspicions on who is involved? Up the food chain, I mean?"

Mac debated on spelling everything out before he had more proof, but she was good at analyzing details, looking at both sides of things, and he realized it might help him to talk it through with her. Besides, she should know what the possibilities were. "Gilby already knew I was installing security devices. He might not miss much, but I don't think he just happened to notice when he stepped out of his cruiser while there was a cabin fire still in progress. And he couldn't have known about the equipment, because—"

"Finn flew it in on the sly. I begin to realize why you go to those lengths now."

Mac just nodded. "So, that means someone had to tell him about it, about what I was doing, and where I was installing it."

Kate's eyes widened. "You think Gilby is part of this? But

he's been a cop forever and a sheriff almost as long. Would he really risk—"

"Stop and think about the number of people with far bigger power in the world who have shown some exceedingly bad behavior. Sometimes with power comes a false sense of security, of entitlement. I can imagine Gilby being possessed of more than one or two of those characteristics."

Kate simply shook her head. "Wow. I guess you're right, but it's still a lot to take in. We certainly have to consider it, though. I just—well, good luck taking him down without some pretty damning proof."

"That's what I was searching for today, in the remains of the cabin. Anything that might tell me what's been going on in that cabin for the past ten years."

"Whatever it was, it has to be enough to make them want to commit arson, to risk destroying it all."

"And you heard Gilby today, saying he thought it would have to be completely razed. I'm sure that is exactly what they were hoping for."

She shook her head again. "It all makes a kind of twisted sense when you put it like that, but still . . . I just wish we knew who 'they' were. Do you think the marshal might be in on it, too?"

"Hard to say who's involved, but if Gilby is, it could be anybody. I'm thinking he and the sheriff are probably, at the very least, fishing buddies, or something close to it. So it's possible. Hell, a town the size of Ralston, anything is possible. Enough that I wanted to make sure I had first crack at searching the place. I was limited in my ability to search, but I plan to be a complete pest to Roger tomorrow when he shows up, and stay as much in his back pocket as I can."

Bagel finished up his business and tugged on the leash, so Mac took Kate's hand again, and they continued down the path.

"So, what do you think they've been doing out here?

Drugs? Guns? Stolen stuff? I mean, in Ralston? Gilby is a pompous ass, but I don't know that I see him as some kind of, what, warlord? I totally don't get that."

"And you think because I was a New York City cop, that I'm the jaded one?" Mac chuckled.

Kate bumped her shoulder against his. "Very funny. But what else could they be hiding up here that would make them go to such lengths to scare me off?"

"Well, the lengths haven't been all that great until today. It could be anything, but it might be something that's important to them but that we might not even consider. Did you happen to notice Gilby's face today when you let it slip that you don't own the property? And why do you think he was out here personally overseeing what would be, in any other case, a routine fire run?"

"It is suspicious. I guess." They walked on in silence for a few steps; then she said, "Did you find anything today in the cabin remains that backed up your new theory?"

"How the fire was set could be deemed suspicious. I was interested mostly in where it originated. The starting point would be set to cause maximum damage, or to make sure the spot of origin specifically burned, or both."

Kate slowed. "And?"

"And I still think I'm on to something."

"How do you know what to look for? You were a cop, not a fireman."

"I've learned a few things since starting to work with Finn."

"Oh, really?"

He smiled. "Oh, really."

She didn't pursue that line of questioning, but he could tell from her contemplative expression that it was only going to be a matter of time. That was fine with him. He liked it that she was curious about him, that she'd want to know more. Oddly, he'd never once felt compelled to share the day-to-day parts of his life with anyone. In fact, while he'd been on the force, he'd been thankful there was no one waiting at home that he'd have to find a way around talking to. He'd never want to put someone he cared about through some of the gruesome or depressing realities of his job. Only now did he realize that when it was a true partnership, not only did she deserve to hear the truth of his life—after all, anything less was a sign of a lack of respect—but that, also, there might actually be some comfort in being able to share the lows as well as the highs. He'd never once looked at it that way. Now that seemed incredibly limiting to him. And kind of . . . lonely.

Of course, other than the occasional warehouse bomb, his life these days didn't involve the sorts of things he'd feel compelled to protect those he loved from knowing about. But that didn't mean his assignments weren't interesting. He'd actually enjoy sharing some of his Trinity exploits with her, seeing her reaction, hearing her take on some of the things they'd done, the people they'd helped.

Just as he wanted to know more about what it was, exactly, she did with the kids she was so determined to help. And if she'd ever thought about having any of her own someday.

Whoa. He had no idea where that had come from.

"Earth to Donovan," she said, a half smile teasing the corners of her mouth.

"I'm sorry, what?"

"I asked you why the cause of the fire seemed suspicious?" She bumped shoulders again, and they paused as Bagel went off the path, investigating as far as his leash would allow him. "Where did your mind just go anyway?"

It was enough that he wanted to share stories with her he'd never shared with anyone other than those who'd been involved at the time. No way was he telling her about that last little mental detour. "Just that you might be surprised by some of the things we've done." It was more truth than he'd intended to share.

"You'll have to tell me about them."

His eyes had adjusted enough to the dark that he saw the little shadow that crossed her face after she said it. They were so comfortable with each other, it was hard to imagine that in a short period of time, very short if his suspicions proved correct, they would be out of each other's lives. Possibly for good.

"But for now, I'll be happy with the story of what you found in the cabin that makes you think it was set to destroy rather than distract or deter me from staying."

"There wasn't much left to look at, and I was limited in what I could do and stay consistent with the firemen's movements, but the point of origin appeared to be oddly placed. Center of the main floor. Not the corner, where it would climb walls, consume the ceiling, burn faster. And opposite the fireplace, flue is melted, but the lever is still closed. I need to look around a bit, check out some of the other cabins, see what else I can find."

"You think they used more than that one? Should we be worried about more fires?"

We. He had to admit he liked how she thought of them as a team, so naturally, like that. "I don't know." He saw the slight slump to her shoulders, squeezed her hand. "I wish I could be more reassuring."

"What—what about my cabin?"

"I think they've done enough damage for one day. I'll go through the other cabins in the morning, then wait for the marshal, go through that ordeal, then we'll see what's what from that point. Possibly go into town, speak to Gilby again, depending on what we learn."

"Okay. Sounds like a plan." She squeezed his hand back, but there was clear trepidation in her voice.

"We're close, Kate." Close to finding out who was doing

this. Which meant close to him leaving. He turned his mind back to the matter at hand. "Tell me, are all the cabins built on the same blueprint? I mean, the ones of that particular size?"

She shrugged. "Some are. I haven't been in all of them. Some of them aren't safe to go into. I need inspectors to help me go through them, but, as of yet, I can't get any help that way. I've spent most of my time up here researching funding and loans. Besides, you'd probably know more about that than I would, growing up here."

He shook his head. "Never went in them."

She sent him a surprised look. "What do you mean?"

"I mean, in the summer, they were filled with paying guests, and in the off season, I had other things to do." Namely staying anywhere but Winnimocca whenever he had the chance. It was the main reason he'd played sports in school. Anything to keep him from going home each day until he absolutely had to.

"But, even with Raphael and Finn here? I mean, I guess I thought you'd been in and out of their cabins every summer while they were here."

He shook his head. "We hung out, but never in the cabins." Cabins filled with a half dozen other campers, none of whom would have welcomed the local trailer trash into their midst. Not that he, Rafe, and Finn couldn't have held their own against them, he just had no motivation to do so. He'd had nothing to prove to those boys.

She didn't ask, but from her quiet expression, he figured she didn't need to. Anyone who'd spent five seconds in the camp back then had known he wasn't one of them.

"Even the girls' cabins?" she asked.

That surprised a laugh out of him. "No, not even the girls' cabins." He'd had plenty of other places all scoped out when that was his mission. Staking his claim on them had been, in some ways, enough of a middle finger to the world at large, and the rich boys in particular. That they'd come to him willingly made it all the sweeter. He'd always treated the girls with respect, even as he was divesting them of their panties. It wasn't something he was particularly proud of now. But he wasn't going to beat himself up over it almost twenty years later either.

"But the way the girls talked, it sounded like—"

"I never went in their cabins."

"Hunh," was all she said, making him continue to grin into the darkness.

She sounded almost a little . . . jealous. Or maybe possessive was the right word. It was silly, really, that he sort of liked that reaction from her, especially over something that happened so long ago as to be completely irrelevant. Still, he held her hand a little more snugly in his.

"So," she said, at length, "now what do we do?"

"Now we finish walking the dog, and, seeing as my place is a bit charred at the moment, you could invite me back to your place, we spend the night in your bed together, then we get up and find whatever we need to prove my theory."

"Where do we start?"

He stopped and turned toward her so she naturally stepped into the shelter of his body. She looked momentarily surprised, but she didn't move away. Yeah, he could definitely get used to that.

"What?" she asked.

"You wanted to know where I was going to start, and I seem to recall you saying something earlier about showing not telling. So I was going to show you."

"I meant where do we start to look for proof."

"Oh." He stepped back. "Okay." He went to turn, then smiled as she immediately tugged him back. "What?" he asked, parroting her.

"This . . . showing. I do believe in that. Strongly."

He leaned down, almost brushing his mouth across hers. "Strongly?"

"Mmm hmm. Very."

"Deeply?" He pressed a very soft kiss to the corner of her mouth.

She moaned a little. "Repeatedly." She lifted up on her toes. "Please."

He wrapped his arms around her. "You know," he began, dropping little kisses along her jaw, "I'm thinking the finding-proof thing can wait until morning. Late morning."

"Late morning," she agreed, sighing and letting her head drop back to afford him greater access.

"Ask me to come home with you, Kate," he murmured against her neck.

She tightened her hold on him. "Let's go home, Donovan."

His hold on her tightened almost convulsively. Home. A home with Kate. It sounded so good. It made him want to never search for proof, never find the answers, never conclude his only real reason for being here. It made him want things he couldn't have. Want them so badly he ached for it.

"Yeah," he said, his voice almost gruff. "Let's go home."

If he thought he could have managed it without his knee buckling, or getting them both tangled in the dog leash, he'd have swept her into his arms and carried her all the way back to the cabin, straight to bed. He'd never been a romantic before, but she made him want to make grand gestures, made him want to literally sweep her off her feet.

And maybe a part of him wanted to do whatever it took to keep them in this moment, this heady, almost euphoric, need-filled, anticipatory moment where nothing mattered but their want for each other. And all other talking would cease, talking that might lead to solutions, to him finishing the job and leaving, or worse, to him revealing how badly he wanted to stay.

As it happened, he didn't have to worry about that. Kate turned and tucked herself against his side, her arm snaking around his waist as she reached out and took the leash, gently tugging Bagel away from his rooting about. And they walked back to the cabin in comfortable, easy silence. If you didn't count the screaming sexual tension that always percolated between them. He slipped his arm around her shoulders and kept her close, their hips bumping as they strolled. Not racing, but not exactly indulging Bagel in any further explorations either.

The air was almost still now, and the smell of the burnt cabin lingered heavily. But the promise of tomorrow, of what they might find, and where that would lead, was something easily pushed away. For now. For now, he just wanted to focus on this moment, this walk, this woman. And Kate stayed in that moment with him, maybe, hopefully, wanting the same for herself.

When they got back to the cabin, they slipped out of their coats and boots. Then Mac unhooked Bagel from his leash, and Kate simply slipped her hand in his and took him to bed. It was different from the other times, gentler, more thoughtful, and yet familiar. Not just in the raging need he always had for her, but . . . it was Kate. She should feel new to him, a stranger, and yet he knew her, knew her in a way that went beyond carnal knowledge to some other place that defied rational thought or logic. He was utterly himself with her, in a way he'd never been with anyone else. No walls, no guarded moments, no worrying about where it might lead. It had already led.

Yes, she was known to him, in that soul-deep way where like recognized like, mate recognized mate. It should have terrified him, right down to his core. And, he supposed, if he let it, it would. But she was Kate. And she was his. And there was nothing terrifying in that; there was only joy. Life wasn't fair. He knew that better than anyone, both from personal endurance and intimate observation. There was never a promise of time, and anyone who thought otherwise was a fool.

He liked to think he was no fool.

Even if he could stay in this cabin forever, there were no guarantees on what he and Kate might have, or for how long. Plans could be made, but life, or fate, often had something else in mind. His time, their time, was now. He'd take the now, and worry about the later, later.

He brushed her hands aside and undressed her. If she had any inkling of what was going on in his mind, her expression didn't reveal it. Instead, she seemed much in the same place as he was, unhurried, enjoying the moment, wanting to, for once, not go at each other like starved animals. She tugged his shirt off, slowly slid off his pants. He pulled her close, liking how her bare skin felt pressed up against his own, suddenly in no hurry to toss her onto the bed.

He kissed along the side of her jaw, down along her neck, across her collarbone. She sighed, tipped her head back, and moaned softly as he indulged in a slow exploration that trailed around her breasts, with brief stops to pay particular attention to her nipples, before slipping lower. But when he reached her hipbone, she tugged him back up and began an exploration of her own.

"My turn," she said softly, making him wish he had something to hold on to as she made his knees weaken with her own lingering trail of kisses. When she reached his hip, he tugged her down on the bed, but she pushed him onto his back and went right back to exploring. "Just let me," she said, shooting him a quick smile, then returning to her mission at hand. Or at mouth, as the case may be.

He was going to object, going to pull her up on top of him, slide inside of her, and make love to her as slowly, as sweetly, as he was capable of, but then he was groaning, and arching off the bed as she took him into the delightfully warm and soft interior of her mouth. Her hands pushed at his chest, kept him in place, as she slid her leg over his, making her intentions clear. And far be it from him to not give her what she wanted. Especially when—

"Sweet Jesus," he said, followed by a long, slow growl as she began moving her mouth and hand on him. "Kate, that's—" But there were no words. So he groped for a pillow, pulled it under his head, and watched, and felt, and pumped, as she brought him screamingly close to the edge.

And she would have taken him over, but not this time, not tonight. He nudged her away, grinning when she pouted up at him. "Come here," he murmured, helping her slide her weight over him, then slowly easing her down onto him. Their sighs of pleasure matched. "You're so damn perfect for me." He didn't think he'd said that out loud, until she agreed.

Her hair fell forward as he brought her mouth to his. "Roll me over, Donovan," she whispered. "I want to feel your weight on me."

It caught at his heart, every time she said it. The way she said it. He was Donovan only to her. And it felt so damn good to know that. He shifted them both to their sides, paused there for a moment, kissed her, then moved the rest of the way, sinking deeply into her as she lifted up and wrapped her legs around his hips.

And he held her gaze, in between long, slow kisses, moving inside of her, feeling her match his steady rhythm as easily as if they'd done this for centuries. He finally slid his arm beneath her, tilted her hips up that extra bit, so he could sink a tiny bit deeper, reach that spot he already knew was there, the one that made her gasp and tighten around him almost convulsively. The one he knew would take them both over the edge. But he held her there, for that one moment out of time, and looked into her eyes. "Kate . . ."

And her eyes grew glassy then, at that one hoarsely uttered whisper. And it didn't scare him so much as hurt him. Because she was his, dammit, and he'd never do anything to hurt her, and the look in her eyes spoke of much the same, even as they both knew the reality of what they were doing to each other. And where it would leave them.

"With me," he said, pushing the rest of the way in.

"Always," he thought her heard her whisper, as she took him there, and they both went over.

Chapter 21

"I'll be fucked."

Kate stretched, smiled. "Highly possible. Probable even." She blinked her eyes open and found Donovan standing by the bedroom window. Bare-ass naked. Her eyesight was a bit blurred from sleep, but, even blurry, he was the best thing she'd ever seen.

"Sorry," he said, "I didn't know you were awake."

"What's going on? Uh oh." She pushed up on her elbows and shoved her hair out of her face. "Did something else happen?"

He turned, and the hard set of his jaw instantly softened. "Actually, nothing is going to be happening for a while."

She sat all the way up, only to have him flatten her right back to the bed. She'd never get tired of that. She smiled into his sleepy face and bumped her hips up. "Really? All tuckered out, are you? Because I thought—"

He rolled to his back and pulled her, squealing, on top of him. "I think we achieved that somewhere around three this morning. I can't remember ever being this worn out." He wrapped his hand around the back of her neck and tugged her mouth to his. "And yet, strangely energized, all at the same time."

She laughed against his lips, kissed him back. "Funny, I seem to be having the same predicament."

He started to shift up on the bed so she could straddle him, but she pushed his hands away, still laughing. "If we're going for some kind of marathon record, I need sustenance first."

His grin was as wicked as it was wide. "I thought last night when you had your mouth full of—"

"Men," she retorted, but snickered. "That was more like a dessert topping. I need real sustenance if I'm going to keep up with you."

"A dessert topping? Did you just call my—"

She rolled off of him. "You have a problem with that? I happen to really love my dessert toppings."

And with that she found herself on her back again, a grinning Donovan in her face. "I've been reduced to a sex condiment and you think I should be flattered, do you?"

"Trust me, nothing about you is reduced."

He laughed, then winced as he shifted his weight.

"You okay?"

"Cop knees."

She rolled him to his back, gently this time. "Sounds serious. Perhaps I should investigate." She slid down along his body.

"I thought you were starving?" He groaned a little as she slipped between his legs. "And, last I looked, that wasn't my knee."

"Hunger first, injury later. Besides, this will take your mind off of the pain, for a little while anyway."

"True." He let his head drop back against the bed. "Very true."

"So," she said conversationally as she teased him with a string of kisses along the velvety smooth length of him. "What were you looking at outside?"

"My eyes are rolling back in my head and you want to chat?"

She kissed the tip, making his hips buck, smiling at how easily they'd come to know each other's bodies so well. "I was just curious." And she didn't want the fire marshal rolling in and interrupting anything either. "Why won't anything happen today? Anything else, I mean." She looked up at him, wiggling her eyebrows.

But his head was back, his eyes shut. He was all hers.

She wished.

"Freak snowstorm last night," he murmured absently, his hips moving with the rhythm of her hand. "About a foot, if that's not all drifting."

Kate stopped what she was doing and sat up. "It snowed?"

Donovan opened his eyes. "A lot. Which means no one from Ralston is coming here. And we're not going anywhere. Now, about that pain management program you were beginning there—"

But she'd already scrambled off the bed. It said enormous things about the nature of their relationship that she didn't even think to cover herself up. Not that he hadn't seen her naked, but morning light was not always flattering. And yet she knew it wouldn't matter in the slightest with him.

Why can't I just keep him?

Then she looked out the window at the winter wonderland blanketing the camp property for as far as she could see, and she couldn't help but grin. Snow day. Looked like she was going to get her wish. For a little while longer, anyway. Normally, she'd be upset at yet another delay in getting things up and running for her camp, but she could hardly fight Mother Nature now, could she?

"It's still snowing," she said, squinting at the tiny flakes spitting from the leaden sky.

"Yep."

He didn't sound all that upset by the prospect either. She turned to find him still spread eagle on the bed, in all his quite estimable glory, hands propped behind his head, shit-eating grin plastered all over his face. Well, at least it appeared they were on the same page, anyway.

Lucky her.

She sent a silent thank-you to Mother Nature and strolled

back toward the bed. "So, then, the agenda for today would be—"

At that moment, Bagel pitched a very loud, very long, very mournful howl from the other room.

"What, does he have radar or something?" Kate said, crossing the room to the bedroom door instead. Peeking out, she found her dog sitting by the front door, looking quite plaintive. "It's cold out there," she informed him. "And the snow is deeper than you are." This did not seem to make much, if any, of an impression on him. She supposed when nature of a different sort called, it called.

She jumped a little when she felt Donovan's warm skin brush against hers as he came up behind her. He nibbled his way along her shoulder, and had her knees wobbly by the time he reached the side of her neck.

"Wrestle you for who takes Wondermutt out."

"I'm not sure we have that long." But her body was already in absolute agreement on his voting method. It took enormous willpower not to turn into his arms, push him right back to the bed.

"Well, then the problem takes care of itself."

"Ew," she said, laughing. "Not in my cabin, which means I guess we're going to have to figure out what to do about it at some point."

"It's not that hard."

She bumped her hips back against his. "I beg to differ."

He chuckled, and the warm sound sent tingles through her that reached places even the feel of his naked body could not. Which was saying something.

He nipped the edge of her ear. "Quite the voracious animal, you are."

She looked over her shoulder. "I'm just trying to keep up."

He grinned, not looking the least bit abashed. She liked that about him. Even more, she liked that about them.

Bagel continued to whimper and look longingly at the front door.

"Yeah, yeah, we're coming," Donovan told him.

"We?"

"Sure. It'll be good for us. A little fresh air."

"A lot of snow."

"Come on." He tugged her back into the room, leaving the bedroom door open, and began scrounging for his clothes. "We'll just shovel a path to the nearest tree, make a nice clearing around the base of it for him, and voilà. Porta-potty."

When she didn't say anything for a few seconds, he looked up from pulling on his jeans. "What's wrong?"

"Well, I hadn't exactly gotten around to buying a snow shovel. I wasn't going to need to one for a while, or so I thought."

"That's okay, any shovel will do."

"I'm sure there are shovels around here somewhere."

Donovan paused, his shirt bunched in his hands. "Somewhere?"

"Down in the service sheds. And the stables." Which were hundreds of yards away, through very deep snow. She smiled. "Hey, you wanted the snow adventure." She looked around the room. "I don't even have proper boots. Just my regular work boots and they're crusted with mud and smell like burnt cabin. I haven't had the rest of my stuff shipped out here yet."

Donovan pulled on his shirt and walked up to her and slipped his arms around her waist. "How about you make some breakfast and I'll see that the dog gets his business done? Deal?"

She hated sticking him with the cold, wet, doggy detail, but the offer was simply too good to pass up. Her stomach chose that moment to send up a particularly distinct grumble.

Donovan smiled. "I'll take that as a yes."

"I owe you," she said, never so sincere.

"Make mine scrambled eggs, and if there is hot coffee, we're even." He kissed her soundly on the mouth, groaned a little, and pushed her back against the wall to take the kiss a little deeper, before finally wrenching himself away. "Probably good it's cold out there," he said, then went to get his coat and boots on.

"I can't imagine why," she said, a bit breathless. She was still leaning against the door to her bedroom when he and Bagel took off out into the snow.

She smiled when she heard Bagel's barks of joy. "Men," she said, shaking her head and heading to the kitchen.

A half hour later, she was just getting muffins out of the oven when the door opened and a soggy, snow-encrusted dog came trotting in. She looked up, but a soggy, snow-encrusted Donovan didn't follow.

"He needs a rubdown, but you're out of rag towels on the porch. I—I'll be back in a few minutes. Don't hold breakfast."

Kate plopped the muffin pan on the stove and hurried to the front door. It was so blinding white, it took a moment for her eyes to adjust, but they did, in time for her to see Donovan wading through knee-deep snow, heading down the driveway to the road. "Wait! Where are you going?" She stepped on the porch and shouted the same question again, only louder. It wasn't snowing hard, but the wind made it difficult for sound to carry.

He turned. "I just need to check on something. Go ahead and eat. I'll warm mine up. Save me some coffee."

She could hardly understand him, but then he turned back, head down against the elements, and kept on trudging. It was either race out there after him, or wait for him to get back and grill him then. She looked down at Bagel, who was sitting, still soggy but looking quite contented with himself, next to her feet. "What is it with you guys and the call of the wild, anyway?"

She looked once again to the trail Donovan was leaving in the snow and debated with herself for all of two seconds. "I can wait." But she didn't head right back in. She watched him to see what direction he took. She thought maybe he was going to see what, if any, further damage the heavy snow had done to the cabin-slash-crime scene, but instead, he turned and headed down the path leading to the next set of cabins. He was quickly gone from sight.

She looked down at Bagel again. "What's going on?"

All she got was a tail thump and a short whine.

She sighed and stepped back inside the cabin, closing the door against the howl of the wind. After feeding Bagel, she went back to preparing breakfast, but decided to hold off scrambling the eggs until Donovan came back. She popped the muffins into a basket, keeping one out for herself, then covered the rest with a towel. Then, after slipping her coat on and jamming her feet into her fuzzy slippers, she went out on the porch again and nursed her cup of coffee while picking at her muffin. She squinted through the screen and the steady fall of tiny snowflakes, looking for any sign of Donovan's return. By the time she drained her mug, she knew standing around was not going to be an option.

"So much for a fun snow day." He'd said they'd go looking for evidence this morning, but with the storm, Roger wasn't likely to show, so surely he could have had breakfast first. And they were supposed to look together, although she hadn't exactly shown a lot of excitement for going out in the snow, so she couldn't really get mad at him for taking off without her. But still. She was getting tired of being left behind to wait.

She brightened when she remembered stashing a pair of tall rubber barn boots in the far corner of the porch after a day spent investigating the stables a few weeks back. She dug them out, then went back inside to put on another layer of socks and another pair of sweats, before heading out.

She kept to the trail Donovan had made through the snow, which was already getting blown in, wincing as the deep snow tipped into the sides of the wide rubber boot tops and slid down to soak her feet. She stopped and pulled one pair of sweats up and out, then tugged the elastic band down over the boots. Now her hands were numb, but at least her feet wouldn't get any wetter. She continued down to the road toward the lower cabins closer to the lake. "What on earth are you doing down here?" she murmured.

She got to the first cabin, and even with the wind and drifting, she could still see where he'd been around the outside, and inside as well, it appeared, as the snow on the front stoop was disturbed where the door had been dragged open. But there were more tracks leading down to the next cabin, so she just kept on going. It wasn't until she passed the third cabin that she realized that even with the drifting and fresh snowfall, the snow looked a lot more churned up down here than it had when she'd first left the cabin. She stopped for a second and looked back, then at the cabin in front of her. Donovan's self-made trail leading down the driveway had been pretty narrow, but down here . . .

Of course, the snow was deeper this far down the hillside, but not that much.

Had Donovan and Bagel come this far once already? And then she had another thought. Or had someone else been through the snow down here first?

Her heart, already thumping pretty good from slogging through knee-deep snow, picked up an extra beat. She opened her mouth to call out, then thought better of it. Whoever had been here, if someone had, had come recently, to make those kinds of snow tracks. What if they were still out here? What if they found Donovan, or her, out here stalking about? Then what?

She glanced wildly around for a moment, trying to see where Donovan might be. There were more tracks heading past this cabin, but were they just his? She couldn't tell at this point. She waded through the snow up to the cabin in front of her, wanting to know what they might have been looking for, not that they apparently found it, seeing as they'd continued on, but she wanted to look anyway. Maybe he was just spending more time investigating these and that was why the snow looked more churned up.

A peek inside the door showed nothing out of the ordinary. Bare bunk beds were shoved against the far wall, along with a few heavy wooden dressers and two huge oak footlockers, the same type of furniture she'd discovered in the other cabins she'd looked into. She hadn't gotten around to inspecting the furnishings up close as yet, mostly because she imagined the years of mold, heat, and dampness would mean replacing most of it.

She went to duck back out, then stopped, and ducked her head back inside. Her boots had left wet marks on the floorboards, but that wasn't what caught her attention. She couldn't put her finger on it, but something wasn't right. It didn't come to her until she looked back down at her damp bootprints.

"No dust," she murmured. She hadn't gone into every cabin yet, and none of the ones down here by the lake, but she had done a cursory examination of a few of the larger, more viable ones up the hill, closer to the main lodge. One thing she remembered most from her exploration was the sneezing attacks she'd gotten from the dust.

This cabin was musty and smelled a bit moldy, but was otherwise as neat as a pin. "That's odd."

"That's what I thought."

Kate stifled a scream and spun around with her hand clamped to her chest. "You really need to stop doing that."

"You really need to stay inside where it's warm so only one of us has frostbite to cure later."

"You never came back, and I got curious. I wanted to know what was going on. It's my camp," she said, knowing she sounded ridiculously defensive, especially since he was the one out here willingly sacrificing to help her out. "I'm sorry," she said before he could mention the same to her. "I guess I just don't do well with the helpless female role. I'm not the sitting around, eating muffins while the big strong guy does all the work, type. It just doesn't sit well with me."

"Understood," he said. "It's your numb toes. But next time—"

She kissed him to shut him up, then smiled when it worked. Before he could go back to lecture mode, she stepped into the cabin. Donovan knocked his boots against the doorframe, then stepped in behind her.

She took a slow scan of the room. "So, I'm guessing someone has been playing Goldilocks and the Three Bears in my cabins?"

"A more accurate assessment than you could imagine."

She shot him a questioning look. "So you think people were living in them? Or sleeping here, or whatever? Because if they were just using it for storing contraband of some kind, why bother cleaning, right?"

"Uh, I don't think they've been storing anything here. Not in the way you mean, anyway."

Kate raised an eyebrow. "Meaning?"

Donovan moved past her and pointed to the wall. "See these?"

She had to move closer. There were a series of small holes drilled, but no hardware in them any longer.

"And here?" He pointed to the headboard and baseboard of one of the bunks.

Kate leaned closer and saw they'd been drilled at the corners of the headboard and footboard, only these holes still had eyehooks in them. She looked at Donovan. "I have no idea what these mean."

To demonstrate, Donovan smiled and flopped down on one of the bunks. He put his arms over his head and spread his legs.

"Oh," Kate said. Then her eyes popped wide when he wiggled his eyebrows, then pumped his hips. *"Oh!"*

He sat up. "It looks like someone in town has set up a little . . . business out here. Of the kinky variety."

She walked over to the wall, looked at the series of holes, which were just above head level for her, and decided she didn't need all the details. She turned back to face him. "So instead of a camp for special needs kids, I have—"

"The best little whorehouse in Winnimocca."

"Oh, my God." She looked back at the holes in the wall, then at the beds, trying not to imagine . . . anything. She wasn't as successful as she'd hoped. "How did you figure that out? I mean, from a couple of holes in the wall, I'd have never put that together."

"Actually, I didn't find those first." He stood up and pulled an envelope out of his inside pocket. "I found these."

"Which don't belong to you."

Kate whirled around, but Donovan was already halfway across the room, placing himself between her and their newly arrived guest.

"And you would be?" Donovan asked.

"Stan Harris," Kate supplied, still frozen to the spot in shock. "Ralston Chamber of Commerce."

"Ah, Stan," Donovan said. "Sorry, I didn't recognize you without the makeup and . . . the heels, I think it was?"

Stan stepped into the cabin in a swirl of snowflakes, leaving the door open behind him. He stuck out his hand. "I'll take those."

Donovan tossed it to him, flustering him briefly as he tried to react quickly enough to catch them.

"Donovan!" Kate shouted, surprised that he'd so easily acquiesced, then realized the ploy the instant Donovan closed the gap and drove Stan into the cabin wall with one well-placed, fullback-sized shoulder.

Stan wheezed air at the heavy contact, but he managed to still be clutching the manila envelope as Donovan pinned him in place.

"You have a little explaining to do," Donovan said, the calm of his tone at severe odds with the menacing look on his face.

Kate stepped a little closer, keeping her eyes on Stan's hands, making sure he was holding only the envelope and nothing else. Like a weapon.

"I—I don't owe you any kind of explanation. You don't belong here."

"I belong wherever the hell I say I do. You, on the other hand, are trespassing."

Stan's lip curled slightly. "You have no place telling me what I can and can't do, much less passing any judgment, what with your drunk father and slut of a moth—"

Donovan's hand closed over Stan's throat, cutting off whatever else he'd been about to say. "Careful." He leaned in. "Now, when I remove my hand, the only words coming out of your mouth are going to be the ones explaining how and why you and some other fine residents of Ralston came to use this property for your own twisted little jollies."

"Go to—" Stan gagged as the pressure was increased, before Donovan relaxed his grip. But Stan doggedly continued. "I don't have to answer to you or anyone," he rasped. "What we do and where is our own business." His gaze strayed from Donovan, past his shoulder to Kate. "She isn't the owner of this property, so you have no legal right to hold me here or question me."

"I'm considering a citizen's arrest."

"On what grounds? Trespassing? I highly doubt Gilby is going to be interested in prosecuting that." He stretched his neck. "However, he might be motivated to arrest you for assault. Besides, you don't have proof that anything that might have allegedly gone on here wasn't done between consenting adults. Now, let me go."

"Let me ask you something," Donovan said, not moving so much as an inch, his face still up close and personal with Stan's. "The women in those pictures with you and a number of the other fine examples of Ralston citizenry, you know, the pictures you came racing out here in the snowstorm from hell to recover?"

"It wasn't supposed to storm like this," he muttered, but Donovan kept talking.

"Looking at the women—and thank goodness they all look like they're of age there, Stanley—but, you know, and this might be a wild guess on my part, but I'm thinking they don't look like English is their first language, or their second for that matter. I haven't spent much time in Ralston on this return trip, but, you know, I don't recall a sudden influx of Russian women in town. Hard to imagine they all just happened to show up to party with some of Ralston's kinkiest for a few drinks and some fun with leather."

Stan swallowed, and Kate noticed his knuckles whiten on the death grip he had on the envelope. "Like I said, you can't prove any different."

Donovan stared him down for a second, then finally backed away, the release so sudden, Stan sagged a little against the wall before recovering his balance.

"So that was what the graffiti was all about?" Kate blurted out. "Your sorry attempts to scare me off so you could continue having your perverted little sex parties?"

Stan's gaze darted to her again. "You're not wanted here, Ms. Sutherland. Why don't you take the hint and set up your precious little camp elsewhere. Your mother wasn't the most popular person in Ralston when she packed up and left here without so much as a warning or an 'I'm sorry.' We relied on the economic boost we got from the camp."

"So you'd think you'd be happy to see the return of that potential business revenue."

"Not from you."

"It was ten years ago," Kate said, truly surprised at the level of animosity in his voice, but not bothering to apologize for her mother. In this case, she had no doubt Stan was telling the truth, or close enough to it. It sounded just like something Louisa would have done.

Stan pushed away from the wall, but heeded Donovan's silent warning when he again stepped forward between the two. He moved closer to the door instead. "Ten very long, economically depressed years. We'd rather have Timberline come in here and change the whole town into some giant tourist trap than have the likes of any Sutherland connected with Ralston in any way again."

"So, you must have really enjoyed setting up your little sex shop here for a number of reasons," Donovan interjected. "A little source of revenue for the town, assuming you charged for the pleasure—and I use that term really loosely here—of an invitation to one of your little leather and chain parties. But, even better, a middle finger of sorts to the oh-so-fine Sutherland clan every time you cracked that whip. Just imagine Louisa Sutherland rolling in her grave if she knew what depraved acts were taking place on the grounds of her once high-and-mighty camp."

Donovan stepped closer. "But, let me ask you, though, did the Russian women get that part? And how much were you paying them, anyway, because from the looks of those pictures—and Stan, digital would be a real improvement over Polaroids, get with the new millennium—but, to be honest, they don't look like they're having near as much fun as you guys. So, what was in it for them?"

Stan darted his gaze from Donovan to Kate and back. "You have no proof any money changed hands."

"I don't have to. I'm sure the full-scale investigation into the arson perpetrated on Ms. Sutherland's cabin will lead to some interesting discoveries. Especially when I point Roger in the right direction." Donovan nodded toward the envelope. "That is, unless Roger is the guy in the full mask and chains getup. Doesn't look too comfortable to me, having your balls all knotted up like that, but who am I to say? Anyway," he went on, quite conversationally, "we can take this to the state level then, no problem. I have a few connections."

"It won't matter. You have no standing in this matter. And

neither does she. It's not her cabin. None of this belongs to her at all."

"Is that why you didn't even bother trying to hide your tracks this morning?" Kate asked, both furious and repulsed by the revelations. "Once you found out my name wasn't on the deed, you knew you could just tromp in here and—" She stopped, broke off, looked at Donovan. "Wait, the only person he could have heard that from would be—"

"Me."

Sheriff Gilby stepped into the open doorway, decked out in a heavy parka and fur-lined, state-issued uniform hat. But all Kate saw was the very big service revolver in his hand.

"I'll take that," he said, sticking his free hand toward Stan, who immediately handed over the envelope, looking almost sick with relief.

"It won't matter what you do here and now, Gilby," Donovan said. "Copies of those pictures are already being processed, and state officials are being alerted as we speak."

"I've been watching you all morning," Gilby said. "You haven't been back to the cabin since making your ill-advised little stroll down here. If it were me, I'd have still been up there in that nice warm bed of hers, bumping—" He broke off when Donovan took a menacing step forward, but he recovered quickly and leveled his gun at Donovan's chest.

"Donovan," Kate whispered in warning, as fear for his safety drove an icy spear of terror down her spine. All she could think of was that Gilby could shoot them both, bury them or toss them in the lake, and no one would ever be the wiser. Who would even care? She wondered how long it would take Shelby to notice if she disappeared. Of course, Donovan had Finn and Rafe. They knew where he was. At least one of them had family, so to speak.

She darted a glance to Donovan. Was he telling the truth about making contact with someone or was it a big bluff?

"You haven't done squat with that alleged evidence you

think you found," Gilby continued, "so the empty threats are just that."

Donovan nodded toward the gun. "How're you going to explain something happening to me or Kate? Bizarre hunting accident with a service revolver? I'll admit, I'm a bit surprised you didn't clean up after yourselves a little better already, so I'm not exactly feeling a lot of faith in your preplanning abilities here."

"Shut up, MacLeod."

Don't give him any ideas, Kate thought, wanting to muzzle Donovan as she saw the tic in Gilby's jaw and the way his tightened grip on the gun was making it waver. Goading the sheriff wasn't going to be as easy as goading Stan.

"I'm simply here to escort you trespassers off private property," Gilby said. "Seeing as I found you assaulting Mr. Harris here, and don't seem to be cooperating, I feel it necessary to use lethal force. As for the rest, I will officially state here and now that I have no idea what the rest of this nonsense is about and I don't care to know." He took a step back and waved his gun. "Now, if you'll follow me, I have a plow truck waiting to escort you to the county line. What you do from there I could give a good goddamn about, as long as you never come back here."

"Wait a minute," Kate said, ignoring Donovan's warning glare as she shouldered past him. Or tried to. He kept her corralled at his side with a firm grip to her upper arm. "I am here with the full permission of my brother, Shelby Sutherland. You have no call to escort me, or my guest, anywhere."

Besides, the last thing she was going to do was march through deep snow at gunpoint, to a supposed plow truck. Likely story. Unless the plow was just there to dig their graves. She could only hope Donovan was of the same mind and was presently working on an alternative plan, because stalling for time with this lame trespassing argument was all she had at the moment. And she doubted it was going to get them very far.

"Well, now, I can't manage to track down the owner of this property to alert him to the fire that has taken place, or find out what the truth is about his alleged guests, who, for all I know, set the fire themselves," Gilby said. "So, until I do, you'll have to vacate."

"Giving you time to clean up the rest of your mess here, Sheriff? Convenient," Donovan said, smiling briefly.

Kate, on the other hand, felt like throwing up. Perhaps Donovan was taking her cue too well. More provoking was probably not in their best combined interests.

"It was a bad day for you when Kate waltzed in unannounced and set up shop here, wasn't it?" he went on. "Did you really think you'd scare her off with a few cans of spray paint? Or were you just trying to distract her long enough to get into the cabins here and clean up whatever evidence you'd left lying around? I know why the fire was set, by the way. Your little hidey-hole wasn't completely destroyed, despite setting the fire right on top of it." He glanced at Stan. "Your work? Because, really, not all that great."

Gilby just smiled, and the malevolence she saw there made Kate's skin crawl.

"Good," he said. "Now I can arrest you on trespassing on a crime scene, MacLeod, as well as assault. Either way, your little return home visit is officially over. So which will it be? County line? Or county jail? Maybe I'll put you in your daddy's cell for old-time's sake. Always said trash doesn't fall far from the trailer. Looks like I was right."

Other than a slight flex in the grip he still had on her arm, Kate didn't sense the slightest change in Donovan's demeanor. She, on the other hand, wanted to rip Gilby's head off with her bare hands and shove it up us his leather-studded ass.

"Kate?" Donovan asked calmly. "Why don't you go give Shelby a call and we'll clear this property manner up. Then the sheriff and I can take care of this other misunderstanding."

Gilby moved more squarely in front of the door. "Nice try,

MacLeod. She doesn't leave, unless it's handcuffed in the back of my state cruiser, or in that plow truck."

Kate wasn't sure if she imagined the unholy gleam that lit Gilby's eyes at the mention of the use of handcuffs and her in the same sentence, but her throat tightened as did her hold on Donovan's arm.

Donovan merely handed Kate his satellite phone. "No need. She can use this."

Even as Gilby jabbed his revolver at them at the sudden appearance of Donovan's phone, Kate quickly fumbled with it, turning it on and quickly dialing, praying, for once, that her stepbrother was where he was supposed to be.

"I don't give a rat's ass who she says she's calling, could be anyone," Gilby informed Donovan. "That doesn't resolve the crime scene issue."

"It was a mere guess on my part," Donovan said easily. "And given that I found that envelope you're clutching in a similar space in the next cabin over, a pretty good one. You'd have to prove I trespassed. And with this storm . . ." He trailed off, shrugged. "Good luck with that." Then he nodded at the packet in Gilby's hands. "You have what you came for. You've got nothing on me, and now I've got nothing on you. I say we call it even. Unless you want to tell me about that leather hood you were sporting in that picture where the three girls are—" He broke off, cocked his head, and gave Gilby a visual once-over. "That was you, wasn't it? I guess I could ask around town."

Kate tried to mask her disappointment when Shelby's answering machine came on. She debated trying to brazen it out and pretend he was on the line, but if Gilby demanded to speak to him—then suddenly Gilby was waving his gun at Stan, and she forgot all about the call to Shelby.

"Stan, take these and hike out of here."

"But—"

"Don't question me, dammit."

Stan took the envelope back and scurried out of the cabin without looking back.

"Masterful control. Let me guess, he was the one bent over the chair with the plug up his—"

"You'll wipe that smug-ass grin off your face if you know what's good for you, MacLeod. You're in no position to bargain anything with me at the moment."

"And you being the one who would know about positions and all."

Gilby brought his other hand up to steady his gun, and Kate tugged on Donovan's arm, thinking the snow plow option might be the better bet. She was just wondering how fast she could run in knee-deep snow when Donovan slid the phone from Kate's hands. "Just so you know, it was no bluff. About alerting the authorities, I mean. This phone has a digital camera and satellite linkup, so I'm connected to the Internet and e-mail all the time." He smiled. "I tried to tell Stan about modern technology, but maybe you should consider upgrading, too."

For the first time, Gilby didn't look so fierce.

"I didn't get them all, but enough to get the point across. Especially the ones showing the women's faces clearly. I wasn't kidding about the connections either. You'll remember Finn Dalton from back in the good old camp days? Well, seems he inherited all of Daddy's money. Trust me when I say it's substantial. And with that comes a lot of power. With a lot of the right people." Donovan pocketed the phone. "And a few really, really wrong ones." He smiled. "So why don't you follow Stan out to that plow truck. You might want to get back to Ralston and talk to a few folks before word hits the papers. Even for a small town like yours, I imagine this will make at least a few news cycles."

Gilby stood there, throat working, for a few very long, nerve-shattering moments. "This isn't over yet," he said at length. "You don't get to come back to my town, son of some drunk asshole, and make these kinds of accusations. I will see you tarred and feathered every step of the way." He looked at Kate. "And I'll do my best to take her down with you, even if I just have to make shit up. By the time the papers figure out what's real and what's not—"

Donovan took two steps forward, but Kate dragged him back.

"Have a nice afternoon, Sheriff," Donovan bit off.

"Fuck you, MacLeod." But Gilby turned and stalked out of the cabin.

Chapter 22

Mac walked to the edge of the open cabin door.

"Is he really leaving?" Kate asked.

"Appears to be." He continued watching the two as they hiked through the snow, toward the main road, where, he assumed, there really was a plow truck waiting.

"What—what exactly was in the envelope?" Kate asked.

Donovan turned to find her standing in the middle of the cabin, her arms wrapped around her middle. He immediately went to her and pulled her into his arms. "Just the pictures, but a lot of them, and pretty damning to the folks in them. Come here." She was shivering, and he wasn't sure if it was due to the cold, or the aftermath of the adrenaline rush that came with having a gun pointed at you.

"Do you get used to that?" she asked. "Being a cop, I mean."

"Used to what? The gun?"

"That, the verbal maneuvering, all of it. You—you never even seemed nervous. I was scared to death the entire time." She shivered. "Still am, actually."

Donovan tucked her closer against him, rubbing his hands up and down her back. "I don't know if you get used to it, but you do learn to manage it. You learn to step outside of the immediate threat to you and work with your instincts on how to play a certain situation." He kissed her hair and hugged her more closely. "Harder to do when someone you care about is in it with you, though. I'm sorry, Kate."

"No, no, you were . . ." She couldn't finish, just slid her arms around his waist and held on tightly. "Did you think he was really going to give up so easily?"

"I think he's basically a small-town cop who is used to wielding the power he has without ever having to really back it up. I doubt he's ever really had his authority challenged and would prefer not to go there and find out what he's really made of if he doesn't have to. I don't think he has instincts because he hasn't had to develop them. And it's clear from the amateurish way they handled this whole mess that none of them is exactly a brain trust. I just had to find him a way out that suited his need to keep his chest puffed out and that stick up his ass."

Kate's teeth began chattering. "So is this all really over? Really?"

He tipped her chin up and kissed her until her body stopped tremoring, guessing the reaction had far more to do with the aftermath of the moment than the cold. "We have to decide what to do with the evidence, but—"

"So, you did take copies of the pictures?"

Donovan kissed his way along her cheek, then pressed a last one against her temple. "I kept some of the originals. Sent some digital copies to Finn for backup. If nothing happens in a few days' time, Gilby could think that I'm bluffing. But I could make sure he's so substantially worried about it that he leaves you alone, or becomes your best friend in helping you set things up here." He tipped her face up. "What do you want to do?"

"Well, I know I don't want the town to help me because I'm blackmailing them into it." She shuddered again, but this time it seemed to be in revulsion. "Hell, I feel like I won the battle but lost the war. How will I ever go into town again and look at . . . anyone? God, what a mess." She looked up at him. "Do we need to take legal steps? Were they . . . hurting those women?"

"I don't think so, no. I imagine they were in it for profit, but who knows if they're here legally. I'm guessing they're imports from north of the Canadian border. It wouldn't take much, though, to get those responsible for starting this whole thing to step down from their respective jobs, without bringing the media or the law into it."

Mac felt her slump a little in his arms, but her hold on him remained tight. He tried mightily to think only of her and her future in this particular moment, knowing the threat was over, but that the reality for her here was not pleasant.

"No matter what I do . . . it's just not going to all go away, though, is it? I mean, we can get Gilby to retire and Stan to find somewhere else to play dress up." She shuddered again, then looked at him. "But the town in general doesn't want me here because of Louisa."

"You could prove them wrong, win them over. It might take a while and some creative thinking, but—"

"I just cringe at the idea that they're small-minded like Stan, that they'd ever take out their hostility on me, on the kids in my camp, or their families, who will probably use some of the facilities and shopping in town during their stay." She groaned. "God, what a mess. And that's if I can get the damn camp built. There's no guarantee I'll get anyone to work for me still and—"

"I imagine there are enough folks worried about those pictures that they'll do anything you want as long as their secrets remain secret. Stan could see to that, or Gilby."

She shook her head. "No, that's just not in me, to do that. If I have to go farther away to hire, it's going to cost me a substantial amount more but maybe—"

Donovan tipped her head back and silenced the rest with a kiss. He hadn't meant for it to be more than a single, reassuring, thank-God-you're-okay affirmation kiss, but it didn't end right away. The kiss gentled then, and went from an affirmation of survival to an affirmation of . . . something else.

And when he finally lifted his head, he framed her face with his hands, and the words in his heart, the ones that had been there for some time now, just came tumbling out. "Don't stay here."

Her eyes widened. "What did you say?"

"I know it's going to sound crazy, but . . . don't stay here."

"I—I don't have much choice."

"Sure you do. You always have choices."

"But my camp—"

He kissed her again, softly, an entreaty to her to listen to him, to really listen. He hadn't meant to just blurt it all out; hell, he wasn't sure he'd ever meant to say anything. She was tired, confused, sick to her stomach, and overwhelmed. The last thing she needed was him adding to the pile of reality she was presently dealing with. At least not until they'd had more than five minutes to regroup. But he'd started the ball rolling now . . .

When he lifted his head, he looked directly into her eyes. "I know you're confused as hell right now, and I have no business putting pressure on you of any kind, but . . . I have another solution for you, if you're interested in listening."

"What other solution is there?"

He stroked his fingers across her cheek. "How much does it really mean to you to stay here? On this specific property?"

"What choice do I have?"

"I think you have a few options."

"Such as?"

Mac took her hand and tugged her over to sit on the edge of one of the beds. She shuddered a little, and he rethought the idea. "Yeah, let's get out of here, head back to the cabin, then we can talk the whole thing over."

"I'm going to have to burn those or something," she said, all but racing him to the door. She shuddered again. "I'm glad you didn't show me the pictures; the mental images I have are already bad enough."

He tugged her out onto the porch, but swung her back into his arms. Smiling, he said, "Why don't I give you some new mental images to replace those old ones?"

"That's the best offer I've had all day."

So far, he thought, praying she'd listen to what he had to say. It should shock him how certain he was about what he was about to offer her, but he had learned to trust his instincts, and when they were right, it was the easiest thing to do in the world. His were right this time. He didn't doubt that for a second. His only concern was that she wouldn't see it the same way.

"Hop up," he said, offering her his back.

"There is no way I'm getting on your back and allowing you to cart me through all that snow, up that steep hill. Your knees might never be the same."

So he did what he had to do. He scooped her over his shoulder. "Okay. So we'll do it the hard way, then."

She squealed and smacked at his back. "Put me down right this instant. You're going to hurt yourself."

"I'm a grown man," he said, stepping off the porch. "Something you know quite personally. Now, if you're really interested in helping my knees out, stop kicking."

She did, but he still heard her huff. It made him smile.

She let him go about twenty yards, before saying, "Really, you don't need this macho display to impress me."

"Oh, I'm not trying to impress you. I'm trying to preserve your strength. Besides, you had some really intriguing pain management methods that I haven't forgotten. Now I figure I can milk them for all their worth. No, ah, pun intended."

She swatted at his backside, and he laughed.

"Honestly, men."

"It's the sexy boots you're wearing, I can't help myself."

"Those are barn boots. For mucking out stalls. Still want to carry me over your shoulder?"

He slid his hand over the back of her thigh and slowly moved it upward.

She started squirming. "Okay, okay."

He got to the top of the trail, the cabin in sight, and let her slide off his shoulder until her feet hit the ground, then tugged her close. Yes, he did love how she always fit right up into him, without ever stiffening up or pulling away. Like she wanted to be as up close and personal at all times with him like he did with her. He silently prayed that was true, because now that he'd made his decision on what he wanted, he was going to be hell on wheels doing whatever he could to get it.

He tucked his hand under the hair on her neck and tilted her head back, so her mouth was just beneath his. "I'm always going to want my hands on you, no matter what. You have a problem with that?"

"I—uh, no." Her gaze connected with his. "No," she said, more quietly.

He hoped it was the only context in which he heard that word today. He kissed her with unhurried tenderness. If he had his way, there would be many more kisses between them. "Let's go inside," he murmured against her lips. "We need to talk. About a lot of things."

"I know," she said, and he wished right then he had a peephole into her thoughts.

He honestly had no idea how she was going to react to his suggestions, to his offer. She could be just as gung ho as he was when she wanted something. He just had to find out how gung ho she was about having her camp here at Winnimocca, on her family property.

They held hands the rest of the way, his knees screaming from his impulsive trek up the mountainside, but no way was he going to let her see that. So it amused him, and touched him, when the first thing she did after paying attention to a wriggling Bagel was head right to the freezer and make him a few ice packs. "Go put on something dry and comfortable."

"You want to help me with that?"

"We're talking, remember?"

He changed into sweats, his knees complaining just enough that he didn't try and change her mind.

"Here," she said when he came back out, her tone brooking no argument, not that she was going to get one from him. She poured two cups of what was probably very strong coffee at this point and grabbed a bottle of pain reliever out of the kitchen cupboard. "Come with me."

She led him over to the small living room couch, where she patted one end, and sat at the other. "Put your feet in my lap. Then you can balance the ice bags better.

It wasn't exactly the position he wanted to be in when asking her to change her entire life so he could very selfishly keep her in his, but now was not the time to buck her either.

Once they were settled in, she fussed with the ice bags, and he couldn't help but groan a little in relief when he took a sip of hot anything while she started rubbing his feet. "Okay, that seals it. You're sticking with me."

She smiled. "You're so easy like that."

He lowered his mug and held her gaze. "It is remarkably easy where you're involved. Almost scary."

Her hands stilled for a moment. Then she nodded. "I know," she said quietly.

The moment expanded, and he teetered on the brink of not wanting to move forward and risk everything, and having to so he could have everything he never knew he so badly wanted. "Kate—"

"So what are we—" They both spoke at the same time, smiled. "You go."

Moment of truth time. "I want you to hear me out, then think about it, before you answer."

"I will."

He took a breath, and debated on the best way to approach it. Logic seemed the best course. "The way things are here in Winnimocca and Ralston don't exactly make for a prime setup for what you want to do here. I know this is family property, and you have your heart set on building something good here, but—"

"Donovan," she interrupted.

He paused, looked at her, waited.

"What are you asking me? Just ask me."

And so he did. Holding her gaze, he said, "Come back to Virginia with me. Build your camp there. Give us a chance to . . . be."

The hope that immediately sprang to life in her eyes lit a fire inside him he'd never quite felt before. Which was why the trepidation that immediately followed scared the living hell out of him.

"I know it hasn't been very long with us, and I'm very aware that I'm not asking for any small thing. I also thought, if you were really wanting to make a go of it here, I could talk to Finn and see if there is a way for me to set up some kind of base of operations up here. It's not really conducive to how we do things, but—"

"You'd do that?"

He set his mug down, then leaned up and reached for her, sending ice bags sliding to the floor as he pulled her full length down on top of him. "I think I'd do anything," he told her, brushing her hair from her face. "I just want to look in those eyes and have a chance to taste you again. And again. I want to make you laugh, and make me smile more, and I want to know you'll always step into my arms like you do whenever I need you there."

"I know the feeling. I want that, too."

His heart rate tripled. "Then we'll find a way. I'll talk to Finn."

"What was your plan?" she asked. "If I came to Virginia, I mean, what was your plan? I don't have any income other than this property, and it's not even mine yet. I won't keep my original inheritance and do like Finn did; I won't go back on my agreement with Shelby. Even if he is being an ass at the moment, the papers will get signed."

"I know, and I want you to do that. But something Stan said, about Timberline, got me to thinking. What if, after all the *t*'s were crossed the *i*'s dotted, what if you contacted Timberline yourself? Shelby doesn't care what happens to the property, does he?"

"You mean find out if Timberline really is interested in developing this land and sell it to them?"

"Exactly. Or you could sell it back to Shelby and he can do whatever he wants with it."

Her eyes were alive now, and he could see the wheels turning. His heart was racing, but he tried hard not to get too far ahead of himself.

"And, by chance, did you have a certain someplace in mind for me to be looking?" she asked, the smallest of smiles beginning to curve her lips.

"Well, there is a lot of farm and horse country out in the Virginia countryside. In fact, I know a guy who owns a big huge chunk of it, complete with stables that aren't being used, that you might be able to work a deal with."

Her eyes widened. "Finn? But—"

"And if it doesn't matter, you should go with the developers in this case. Timberline won't care about the fire or the state of the property as is; they'll just come in and tear it all down anyway. The added bonus is that it puts a final end to Gilby and Stan's little sideshow events, and despite Stan's tourist trap comments, I can't imagine they'll turn down the economic possibilities a resort of that size would bring to the town. No history, no Sutherland stigma."

"What do we do about that part? About Gilby and Stan and the rest?"

We. He'd always been an "I" kind of guy, but he was beginning to think "we" was one of the best words in the universe. His hold on her tightened a little. "We can always clue Timberline in to the situation, if you think full disclosure is necessary."

"That's not it. I doubt a large corporation like that is going to care about what the sheriff in some tiny little town was doing, especially as it's done here for now and not a public spectacle unless we make it one. I guess I should just be happy it's over, in a sense, but if he was really doing here what you think he was, I don't think Gilby should just get off without any retribution. I mean, if Timberline bites, he wins all the way around. It just doesn't seem right."

Mac tucked her hair behind her ear. "Well, I do know of this company who can make it their business, once all is said and done and you're comfortably set up somewhere else entirely, to ensure he never even thinks about setting up shop again."

Kate's expression softened, and she leaned in and kissed him. "That would be great, wonderful, in fact, but I can't ask you to involve yourself here any longer, it's—"

"I can put Rafe on it. We can hire it out. We can do a number of things. But we can make it happen. Just not until you're safely out and away from here."

"I—" She broke off and shook her head. "It's a lot to even consider. I've been working so long and hard to make this happen, and I—"

"Don't overwhelm yourself with it. Just think about it and know there is more than one solution to this. Even if it doesn't involve me, you can still leave here if you want. Regardless, I'll do whatever I can to help you with—"

She cut him off this time, with a hard, fast kiss. Which led to another, longer, slower kiss that didn't end until his hips were moving and she was moaning softly. She finally lifted her head, and had to clear her throat not once, but twice, just to form words. "I want to explore my options, especially the ones that involve keeping you close enough for a lot more of this. I want you now, tomorrow, and for as long and as often as possible." She touched his face, his lips, brushed her hand through his hair, all while looking directly into his eyes. "You're right, it hasn't been long, but I already can't imagine a day without you in it."

His grin was so instantaneous, and so wide, he thought he might have pulled something. "Thank you, God."

"Are you sure you want this, Donovan?"

Just hearing his name, seeing the need and desire for him so laid bare before him. His heart tripped that final step. He kissed her. "More sure than anything in my life." He framed her face. "It's you, Kate. It's always been you, and always will be."

She smiled then, eyes shining, and he saw there exactly what he needed to see. "Funny how we think alike when it matters the most."

"Yeah," he said, kissing her again. "Funny."

"About the rest—"

"We have time, Kate. Plenty of time. And, God, doesn't that sound wonderful?"

Bagel chose that moment to snuffle his way along the edge of the couch, making them both laugh. "You do know," Kate said, "I'm a package deal. Love me, love my Bagel."

"I wouldn't have it any other way." He scratched the dog behind his ears, making him groan in glee, then turned his attentions back to Kate. His Kate. He was pretty sure he was the luckiest man alive. "We'll figure it all out, you, me, and Wondermutt, here."

"Together."

"Always." He slid his hands down her back. "Now, enough talking about big life changes. I have a more immediate problem."

She wiggled her eyebrows, and her hips. "Do you now?"

"Yes . . . about that therapy you were mentioning . . ."

"Ah, so you just want me for my . . . therapeutic benefits," she teased. "Hmm, maybe I need to rethink this whole thing."

He tucked his legs around hers and pulled her hips snug against him. "You should know that I believe very strongly in taking good care of my therapist."

"Strongly?"

"Very. Deeply in fact. Repeatedly. And often."

"Well, in that case, I think we need to start you on a long-term program, with routine maintenance."

"Long term?"

She smiled. "Very."

"I'm yours."

"Good." She kissed him. "It's about damn time."

Epilogue

"Nice legs. Sweet gait. Impressive." Mac leaned against the fence and looked out over the paddock and the landscape beyond. He loved springtime in Virginia, the colors, the return of life to the trees and the greening of all the pastures and hillsides. It was like rebirth. The annual chance to start fresh, to feel hopeful about the possibilities. And he'd never felt so hopeful as he did this year.

"Yeah, but I'm not sure she's not too spirited for the job." Rafe balanced his elbows on the top rung, careful not to get any marks on his brushed suede bomber jacket.

Mac cut a look at his partner and the direction of his gaze, before looking back at the woman presently exercising the sturdy roan in the training ring. "Are we talking about the horse? Or the woman?"

Rafe continued observing the activity inside the ring. "Both. If Kate is going to put those kids up on that horse, then she'd better be damn sure it's not going to spook. And her new trainer . . . I don't know about her either."

"First, do you honestly think she'd put her kids anywhere near a horse she wasn't a hundred percent on? And secondly . . . since when did you know shit about horses or how to train them?" Mac grinned at his partner. "Oh, yeah, since maybe you started wandering down to the barns all the damn time. Don't think we haven't noticed."

"Who's we? And I don't see how you or Kate notice any damn thing. Too busy mooning and rubbing all over each other all the damn time. It's been a year. You'd think you'd have gotten the itch scratched by now."

"Jealous?"

Rafe shook his head, then smiled. "About the regular sex, maybe. You can keep the rest of it, though."

Mac just smiled. Keep it he would, with great pleasure.

He watched the woman Kate had just hired to work and exercise the horses she used in her therapy sessions with the kids. The horse was a new arrival, too, but he trusted Kate knew what she was doing there. He didn't know much about Elena Caulfield. Yet. He made a mental note to have a quick chat with Finn later. Kate would have checked her out, of course, but though she was a smart businesswoman and amazingly lionesslike when it came to watching over her kids, she was a softie, too. And Rafe was already picking up on the same things Mac had sensed himself after chatting with the new hire a few days ago. Something wasn't all it seemed there. So he'd look into it. After all, he was pretty lionlike himself these days.

"So, you going to see if you can get yourself some of that regular . . . exercise?" Mac said, watching Rafe watching Elena. "Not sure Elena there is quite your type, though."

"What makes you think I'd be interested in her? And what about her isn't my type?"

Mac adopted a casually interested tone, not sure if he pulled it off or not. "She spends a lot of time mucking out stalls. You?" He reached out and plucked a piece of straw off Rafe's elbow. "Let's just say, I don't see you as the roll-in-the-hay type."

"I earned my high-thread-count sheets, bro. I make no apologies for wanting to sleep in comfort or dress in style."

"Nor should you. I was just saying, is all."

"Yeah. Just saying. You'd be right, too. She's not my type."

The leggy brunette looked over at them just then. Mac

nodded to her, she nodded back. Rafe, on the other hand, chose that moment to wander off. As if he hadn't noticed.

"Catch you later," he said to Mac, then took off toward the main house and the Trinity offices. "Got some case files to go over."

"Sure. I'll be up in a while."

"Right. Say hi to the little woman for me."

Mac smiled. Maybe he wouldn't need to talk to Finn after all. Rafe was already on the case. How long his friend fought that fact remained to be seen.

Mac pushed away from the rails and wandered in the general direction of the small outbuilding he'd constructed next to his and Kate's bungalow. She'd be in her office right about now. Hair pulled up in a messy knot, Bagel asleep at her feet. Probably dressed in something soft . . . and easily removed.

He snagged the picnic basket he'd packed earlier from the shed at the end of the barns, smiling when he saw someone had stuck a clean blanket in with the basket. So maybe she'd come to expect their Wednesday outings as much as he'd enjoyed planning them these past few weeks, now that the sun was out and warming the countryside. Maybe she'd decided they just might need a better cushion than his jacket . . . or her sundress.

He did like the way his Kate thought.

Smiling, he hefted the blanket and struck off toward home.

Please turn the page for an exciting preview of
Shannon McKenna's next book,
EDGE OF MIDNIGHT.
Available this month from Brava.

"You're going down the drain, and we're sick of sitting around with our thumbs up our asses, watching it happen," Davy went on.

Going down the drain. Goosebumps prickled up Sean's back.

"Funny you should say that," he said. "It gives me the shivers. Kev said the exact same words to me last night."

Connor sucked in a sharp breath. "I *hate* it when you do that."

His tone jolted Sean out of his reverie. "Huh? What have I done?"

"Talked about Kev as if he were alive," Davy said heavily. "Please, please don't do that. It makes us really nervous."

There was a long, unhappy silence. Sean took a deep breath.

"Listen, guys. I know Kev is dead." He kept his voice steely calm. "I'm not hearing little voices. I don't think anybody's out to get me. I have no intentions of driving off a cliff. Everybody relax. OK?"

"So you had one of those dreams last night?" Connor demanded.

Sean winced. He'd confessed the Kev dreams to Connor some years back, and he'd regretted it bitterly. Connor had gotten freaked out, had dragged Davy into it, yada yada. Very bad scene.

But the dreams had been driving him bugfuck. Always Kev, insisting he wasn't crazy, that he hadn't really killed himself. That Liv was still in danger. And that Sean was a no balls, dick brained chump if he fell for this lame ass cover-up. *Study my sketchbook,* he exhorted. *The proof is right there. Open your eyes. Dumb ass.*

But they had studied that sketchbook, goddamnit. They'd picked it apart, analyzed it from every direction. They'd come up with fuck-all.

Because there was nothing to come up with. Kev had been sick, like Dad. The bad guys, the cover-up, the danger for Liv—all paranoid delusions. That was the painful conclusion that Con and Davy had finally come to. The note in Kev's sketchbook looked way too much like Dad's mad ravings during his last years. Sean didn't remember Dad's paranoia as clearly as his older brothers did, but he did remember it.

Still, it had taken him longer to accept their verdict. Maybe he never really had accepted it. His brothers worried that he was as nutso paranoid as his twin. Maybe he was. Who knew? Didn't matter.

He couldn't make the dreams stop. He couldn't make himself believe something by sheer brute force. It was impossible to swallow, that his twin had offed himself, never asking for help. At least not til he sent Liv running with the sketchbook. And by then, it had been too late.

"I have dreams about Kev, now and then," he said quietly. "It's no big deal anymore. I'm used to them. Don't worry about it."

The five of them maintained a heavy silence for the time it took to get to Sean's condo. Images rolled around behind his closed eyes; writhing bodies, flashing lights, naked girls passed out in bed. Con's predator, lurking like a troll under a bridge, eating geeks for breakfast.

And then the real kicker. The one he never got away from. Liv staring at him, gray eyes huge with shock and hurt. Fifteen years ago today. The day that all the truly bad shit came down.

She'd come to the lock-up, rattled from her encounter with Kev. Tearful, because her folks were trying to bully her onto a plane for Boston. He'd been chilling in the drunk tank while Bart and Amelia Endicott tried to figure out how to keep him away from their daughter.

They needn't have bothered. Fate had done their work for them.

The policeman hadn't let her take Kev's sketchbook in, but she'd torn Kev's note out and stuck it in her bra. It was written in one of Dad's codes. He could read those codes as easily as he read English.

> *Midnight Project is trying to kill me. They saw Liv.*
> *Will kill her if they find her.*
> *Make her leave town today or she's meat.*
> *Do the hard thing.*
> *Proof on the tapes in EFPV. HC behind count*
> * birds B63.*

He'd believed every goddamn word, at least the ones he'd understood. Why shouldn't he have? Christ, he'd grown up in Eamon McCloud's household. The man had believed enemies were stalking him every minute of his life. Up to the bitter end. Sean had never known a time that they weren't on alert for Dad's baddies. And besides, Kev had never led him wrong. Kev had never lied in his life. Kev was brilliant, brave, steady as a rock. Sean's anchor.

Do the hard thing. It was a catch phrase of their father's. A man did what had to be done, even if it hurt. Liv was in danger. She had to leave. If he told her this, she would resist, argue, and if she got killed, it would be his fault. For being soft. For not doing the hard thing.

So he'd done it. It was as simple as pulling the trigger of a gun.

He stuck the note in his pocket. Made his eyes go flat and cold.

"Baby? You know what? It's not going to work out between us," he said. "Just leave, okay? Go to Boston. I don't want to see you anymore."

She'd been bewildered. He'd repeated himself, stone cold. Yep, she heard him right. Nope, he didn't want her anymore. Bye.

She floundered, confused. "But—I thought you wanted—"

"To nail you? Yeah. I had three hundred bucks riding on it. I like to keep things casual, though. You're way too intense. You'll have to get some college boy to pop your cherry, 'cause it ain't gonna be me, babe."

She stared at him, slack-jawed. "Three hundred . . . ?"

"The construction crew. We had a pool going. I've been giving them a blow by blow. So to speak." He laughed, a short, ugly sound. "But things are going too fucking slow. I'm bored with it."

"B-b-bored?" she whispered.

He leaned forward, eyes boring into hers. "I. Do. Not. Love. You. Get it? I do not want a spoiled princess, cramping my style. Daddy and Mommy want to send you back East? Good. Get lost. Go."

He waited. She was frozen solid. He took a deep breath, gathered his energy, flung the words at her like a grenade. "*Fuck*, Liv. *Go!*"

It had worked. She'd gone. She'd left for Boston, that very night.

He'd paid the price ever since.

You won't want to miss
THE NORTHERN DEVIL
by Diane Whiteside.
Also available this month from Brava.

"I must remarry quickly," Rachel announced.

Marriage to someone else? Well, he'd always known it would happen one day. But it seemed more wrenching now that he'd carried her and known the softness of her in his arms, and the sweet smell of her in his lungs.

"There is no time for a protracted struggle against Collins, here in Omaha. It is vital that he be immediately cut off from all revenues, especially as my trustee."

Lucas immediately came fully alert, recognizing her sharpened tone. "Why is it so urgent?"

"He means to trap William Donovan at the Bluebird Mine and kill him."

"*Murder* Donovan? Why, that bast—toadstool!"

She nodded agreement. "But if he's no longer my trustee—"

His mind was racing, considering the implications. "Then he can't give orders to the men at the Bluebird Mine in your name."

Her pacing brought her less than a foot from him. She stopped with a small gasp and pivoted, swishing her train out of his way. Did she glance too long at him over her shoulder? But if so, she wasn't behaving like a woman who knew how to flirt.

"Yes. Elias bought the mine several years ago from an old

friend, who needed to raise cash. He also sold an interest to Donovan, as part of a bigger deal."

"So Humphreys, the mine's manager, has always answered to Boston."

She sank down onto the settee by the coffee tray. "Exactly. I'll need to personally tell him that I've remarried so he won't help Collins in any way."

Every protective instinct in Lucas revolted. "No! You won't go anywhere near the Bluebird, not if there's about to be a murder attempt."

She raised a haughty eyebrow. Ah, that was more like the woman he was acquainted with—who enjoyed challenging his mind, not his loins.

He relaxed, ready for a pleasant round of debate.

"Mr. Grainger, it's critical that an innocent man's life be saved. That's far more important than any polite folderol about not sending women into danger. I'm certain that once Mr. Humphreys understands I've remarried, he won't assist Mr. Collins, and all will be well."

A Nevada mine supervisor would fall into line like a sheep when she crooked her finger? Appalled at her optimism, Lucas opened his mouth to roar objections but she was still talking.

"No, what I need your help for is to find another husband. Immediately—before Mr. Collins can take legal steps to regain my custody."

Lucas frowned. Rachel Davis and another man—in her wedding bed? Someone certain to be honorable, polite, and respectful even in the bedroom.

He growled, deep in his throat, and began to stride up and down the carpet.

Like hell, anyone else was climbing into her bed if she was willing to accept a marriage of convenience!

But marry her himself?

He swallowed hard.

She was right; the best way to protect Donovan's life, given

Collins's malice, was for her to marry. He owed Donovan a blood debt that his life alone would not repay—but his honor would. Marrying Rachel would even the scales.

Did his old vow never to marry carry any weight against saving Donovan's life?

He grimaced and spun on his heel. No.

But Rachel was his friend. She wasn't looking for love, just protection and companionship. They could build a solid union together on that basis.

But in marrying her, there'd be the necessity of siring children. For the first time in his life, he'd have to hope that his seed would set fruit. Fruit that could grow to become a little child, vibrant and alive, beautiful, intelligent, happy to see him. A true family, in other words, and his oldest dream.

He began to smile.

And finally, here's an excerpt of Karen Kelley's
DOUBLE DATING WITH THE DEAD,
which Brava will publish next month.

"Boo," a woman said in a very dry, sultry voice from behind him.

He whirled around. For a split second he thought the place might actually be haunted. But if he was looking at a ghost, he hoped she didn't vanish anytime soon because she looked pretty damned sweet as she stood in the open doorway.

No, not sweet. Nothing about her looked sweet. She was earth, wind and fire all rolled up into one magnificent woman. The combination was sexy as hell.

Slowly his gaze traveled over her. Past long black hair that draped over one shoulder to kiss a breast. She was like nothing he'd ever seen with her loose white shirt, bangles at her wrists and a multi-colored full skirt.

Selena James looked even better in color than she had in black and white.

He wondered if she knew that with the sunlight streaming in behind her, the skirt she wore was practically transparent. He didn't think he wanted to tell her. He rather enjoyed the view.

"Did I scare you?" she asked in a mocking voice, one eyebrow lifting sardonically. She swept into the room and shadows blocked the view of her legs.

A shame because he could've looked at Selena James's legs a lot longer.

"I don't scare so easily." He casually leaned against the balustrade and crossed his arms in front of him.

"But then, you've never stayed in a haunted hotel," she said.

"I can't stay in a place that's haunted since there are no such things as ghosts."

As she stepped closer, he could see her eyes weren't different colors after all. No, it was worse than that. They were a deep, haunting violet.

Her features were pure, patrician, and she was tall. Maybe five-eight. For some reason he'd pictured her much shorter.

When she breezed past him, he caught the scent of her perfume. It wrapped around him, begging him to follow her wherever she might lead. She was definitely a temptation, but one he'd resist.

She faced him and his heart skipped a beat. She was alluring and sexy. Probably the reason she had so many followers who faithfully read her column. She was like a spider, weaving her web for the unsuspecting fly. But he knew her game and wouldn't be drawn in. No, Miss James had finally met her match.

Definitely tempting, though.

Man, he'd been spending way too many hours closeted away in front of his computer while he finished his last deadline, then been consumed with promotion for his current release. Dating hadn't been a top priority.

Maybe two weeks alone with Selena was just the time off he needed.

Selena watched Trent and the changing emotions on his face that finally settled into speculation.

Would she or wouldn't she?

She'd seen that interested look before in men's eyes. Trent wasn't bad himself—even better in person then he had been on television. His shoulders were wider up close and his eyes more green, the color of finely cut emeralds.

The kind of eyes, and the kind of smile, that could talk her right out of her clothes and have her naked on a bed before she realized how she'd gotten there.

Oh, yes, he was a clean-shaven devil in an expensive suit and if she wasn't mistaken, wearing designer cologne.

But she wasn't stupid, and she wouldn't fall for his charm. He'd figure that out soon enough.

Trent was a skeptic. Her enemy. He'd made jokes about her column. She could very well lose her job if she didn't change his opinion about the supernatural by the end of their stay.

Lust could not enter the equation.

She faced him once again, tilting her chin and looking up at him. He was very tall, too. "You said some pretty ugly things about me on television. Do you always take potshots at people you've never met?"

"Nothing personal."

Was he serious? The bangles on her wrists jangled when she planted her hands on her hips. "Nothing personal? You're joking, right?"

She gritted her teeth. She would *not* stoop to losing her temper. But she'd love to wipe that sardonic smirk right off his face!

His smile turned downward and it was like a thundercloud hovered over him. Well, she was the lightning bolt that would strike him down.

"I go after all cheats, not just you," he said.

"Now I'm a cheat?" *I won't lose my temper*, she told herself.

"You're bilking the public when you feed them a line of crap about ghosts being everywhere and that you can talk to them."

"And how do you know they aren't?"

He swung his arm wide. "Do you see any?" He looked toward the second floor. "If there are any ghosts here, show yourselves," he yelled.

Silence.

He looked at her. "See, no ghosts."

If there were any in the old hotel, he'd probably pissed them off. One thing she hated more than a skeptic was a pissed off ghost. They could get really nasty when they were riled.

"I wouldn't do that if I were you," she warned.